SWITCHBOARD
SOLDIERS

SWITCHBOARD SOLDIERS

A Novel of the Heroic Women
Who Served in the U.S. Army Signal Corps
During World War I

JENNIFER CHIAVERINI

WILLIAM MORROW
An Imprint of HarperCollinsPublishers

SWITCHBOARD SOLDIERS. Copyright © 2022 by Jennifer Chiaverini. All rights reserved. Printed in the United States of America. No part of this book may be used or reproduced in any manner whatsoever without written permission except in the case of brief quotations embodied in critical articles and reviews. For information, address HarperCollins Publishers, 195 Broadway, New York, NY 10007.

HarperCollins books may be purchased for educational, business, or sales promotional use. For information, please email the Special Markets Department at SPsales@harpercollins.com.

A hardcover edition of this book was published in 2022 by William Morrow, an imprint of HarperCollins Publishers.

FIRST WILLIAM MORROW PAPERBACK EDITION PUBLISHED IN 2023

Designed by Elina Cohen
Title page art illustration courtesy of Shutterstock / Daniela Iga

Library of Congress Cataloging-in-Publication Data

Names: Chiaverini, Jennifer, author.
Title: Switchboard soldiers : a novel / Jennifer Chiaverini.
Description: First edition. | New York, NY : William Morrow, [2022] | Includes bibliographical references.
Identifiers: LCCN 2021036940 | ISBN 9780063080690 (hardcover) | ISBN 9780063080713 (ebook)
Subjects: LCSH: World War, 1914-1918—Participation, Female—Fiction. | United States. Army. Signal Corps—Fiction. | LCGFT: Historical fiction. | War fiction. | Novels.
Classification: LCC PS3553.H473 S95 2022 | DDC 813/.54—dc23
LC record available at https://lccn.loc.gov/2021036940

ISBN 978-0-06-308070-6 (paperback)

23 24 25 26 27 LBC 5 4 3 2 1

TO MARTY, NICK, AND MICHAEL,
WITH LOVE AND GRATITUDE

YOUNG WOMEN OF AMERICA
ATTENTION!

Here's your opportunity to serve your country in France with General Pershing's Expeditionary Force—a chance to do as much to help win the war as the men in khaki who go "over the top."

Uncle Sam wants to have his telephone system in France operated by the most efficient operators in the world and that means by American young women. The Signal Corps have asked the telephone companies in the United States to secure these "switchboard soldiers" for them.

Just because you are or have been a telephone operator, don't think that you therefore can easily secure a position in this expeditionary operating force. The first and fixed requirement is an ability to speak and read both French and English fluently and be able to understand readily French spoken over a telephone line. The American telephone system in France not only links General Pershing's headquarters with various points of military importance, but it also connects directly with the French Government telephone system, and so unless your French is very, very good, do not consider yourself a qualified applicant . . .

Therefore, if you can handle the French language as well as you do the English and are dependable, resourceful, and able, if necessary, to "go it on your own" as the soldiers say when the tide of battle compels prompt, individual action to meet a serious situation—then by all means apply. Nearly a hundred young women have already been selected and judging from them this unit will meet all those requirements and be one of the most democratic and truly representative American forces sent abroad . . .

In every respect these young women will be soldiers coming under military restrictions at all times. The pay will be $60 a month for operators, $72 for supervisors, and $125 for chief operators, in addition to which allowances will be made for rations and quarters when these things are not provided by the Army.

The Signal Corps authorities point out that this operating force is not going on a pleasure trip or "joy ride" and that no evening dresses need be taken and that social opportunities are not at all included in the program. It will be a war task of the nature and size that always appeals strongly to American womanhood and for handling it, the Signal Corps seek level-headed young women who are resourceful, able to exercise good judgment in emergencies and willing to work hard and even endure hardships if necessary . . .

Information as to how application may be made can be obtained by calling upon the manager of your local telephone company, or application blanks, etc., can be obtained from the Chief Signal Officer of the Army, Room 826, Mills Building Annex, Washington, D.C., who makes the appointments to this work.

—*Bell Telephone News,* February 1918

AUGUST 4, 1914

Cincinnati

MARIE

Marie glowed with pride and anticipation as her mother took her customary place in front of the gleaming grand piano in the gracious parlor of their Mount Auburn home. From the far side of the room, Marie glimpsed only the faintest traces of silver in her mother's honey-gold hair, which she wore in an elegant knot on the back of her head, a few stray wisps curling around her lovely face. A fresh breeze through the open window stirred the lacy ruffle on the bodice of Maman's rose silk poplin gown, carrying birdsong and a faint scent of wisteria from the garden, offering a momentary respite from the heat and humidity of the late summer afternoon. Maman could make her parlor seem as grand as a stage and a concert hall as intimate as a room in her own home. In everything, she was effortlessly graceful, poised, and stunningly beautiful, a manner her eldest daughter strove to emulate but could not yet master. She often feared she never would.

Her father sat before the piano, his long, supple fingers poised above the keys, the sunlight picking up the auburn highlights in his chestnut brown hair, only slightly darker than Marie's own. Awaiting his cue, he gazed at his wife with the admiration everyone there shared and the warm, enduring affection that was his and hers alone. A trickle of perspiration wended its way down Marie's back beneath her ivory muslin dress—invisibly, she hoped—but like everyone else in the room, she held perfectly still, riveted by Maman's presence as she prepared to let her voice take flight. Squeezed between her two younger sisters on a small sofa behind their guests' chairs, Marie waited, breathless, for the first exquisite notes. When little Aimée mewed a complaint and squirmed about for a better view, Marie clasped her hand to settle her down. She took Sylvie's hand too, although at fifteen Sylvie knew how to behave properly at a concert, even a casual one among friends such as this. In reply, Sylvie squeezed her hand and flashed a quick smile. As often as they heard their mother sing, they never tired of it.

Nor did any of their parents' friends who had gathered there for their weekly musicale, most of them colleagues from the Conservatory of Music, longtime friends from the city opera company, or new acquaintances from the Cincinnati Symphony Orchestra. Their Tuesday afternoon gatherings had become a favorite summertime tradition ever since the Miossec family had come to America two years before so Marie's father, a renowned pianist, composer, and music historian, could accept a professorship at the conservatory. The provost had sweetened the deal by offering Maman a position on the voice faculty. Papa liked to claim that the provost had really wanted the magnificent diva Josephine Miossec, and had recruited him only to acquire his otherwise unobtainable wife. Whenever he said such things, Maman would gaze heavenward, shake her head, and murmur demurrals, but the warmth in the sidelong smile she gave her husband told the three sisters that he had charmed her once again.

Marie longed for a love like theirs someday, and she knew Sylvie did, too. They often confessed their hopes and dreams to each other, but only late at night after Aimée had fallen asleep. Although Aimée was a darling, she was too young to understand, and she might accidentally blurt out an embarrassing secret in front of their parents or, worse yet, their neighbors or classmates.

Sylvie alone knew how much Marie wanted to be like their mother, to travel the world as she had done at the height of her career, enchanting audiences in the glorious concert halls of Europe, performing iconic roles in the world's most hallowed opera houses, garnering rave reviews on both sides of the Atlantic, inspiring the greatest composers of the era to create songs perfectly suited for the unique timbre of her own voice. Ever loyal, Sylvie never cautioned Marie to set her sights a little lower, never admitted aloud what Marie had begun to suspect as she completed her first year at the Cincinnati Conservatory of Music—that she indeed had a lovely voice, but fervent hope and diligent study could take her only so far. If she persisted, she would surely become better than she was now as a mere girl of nineteen, but would that be enough? Or would all that she desired forever remain just beyond the touch of her fingertips?

When Sylvie squeezed her hand again, Marie glanced up to find her sister studying her, a question in her eyes. Marie managed a small smile and deliberately turned her gaze toward their mother, who just then broke the expectant hush with the first splendid notes of a Schubert *Lied*, one of three on the program. Within moments Marie's nagging doubts subsided, swept away on a river of music. All around her, she sensed a sudden easing of tension she had not been conscious of until it was gone, like a breath held too long, finally released.

She savored the moment, knowing the tension would surely return when the music ceased.

All summer long the dreadful news from Europe had troubled their family, ever since that fateful June day when Archduke Franz Ferdinand, the heir presumptive to the throne of Austria-Hungary, had been assassinated in Sarajevo by a Serbian nationalist. Long-simmering disagreements between rivals had boiled over as friendly nations strengthened their alliances and locked arms against enemies. Marie's beloved France was an ally of Russia, which in turn had an alliance with Serbia; thus in the steadily worsening conflict, her homeland was opposed to Austria-Hungary and its longtime ally, Germany. A few weeks after the archduke's assassination, Austria had attacked Serbia for harboring terrorists. In response, Russia had moved troops to the border it shared with Germany to discourage Kaiser Wilhelm II from strengthening his ally's position. Diplomats from many nations had worked frantically to restore calm ever since, but it seemed to Marie that their voices were drowned out by the accusations of treachery and threats of greater military force flying back and forth above their heads.

Only three days before, on August 1, Germany had declared war on Russia. The next day, Germany had sent troops into Luxembourg and had demanded unimpeded passage across Belgium, the neutral country standing between the kaiser's armies and France. Then—had it really been only the previous afternoon?—Germany had declared war on France. Within hours France had declared war on Germany in return, crushing the peacemakers' last hopes for a diplomatic solution.

Now France was preparing to move troops into Alsace-Lorraine, provinces lost to Germany in the treaty that had ended the Franco-Prussian War more than forty years before. When Marie's father was a young boy, his parents and aunts and uncles had abandoned their homes and businesses in the annexed territory and had resettled in Nancy, preferring to remain proudly French rather than have their nationality legally and forcibly changed to German. Now German troops were massing on the border of Belgium, and politicians in Great Britain, a nation committed to Belgium's neutrality and to peace in Europe, had set aside their own partisan disagreements to unite in opposition to German aggression. It had seemed to Marie that this boded well for France, but when she thought of her beloved family and friends back home, her heart ached with worry. She could only imagine how frightened they must be, waiting in dread for the first distant sounds of artillery and cannon.

For days, Marie's parents had been tense, their words brief and quiet, their smiles rare and quickly fading. Marie had assumed they would cancel the musicale, but earlier that day her mother had asked her daughters to help her tidy up and prepare as always, and later she had withdrawn to her bedroom to warm up her voice while she dressed and fixed her hair. "We need the solace of music and good company today more than ever," Marie had overheard her tell Papa moments before the doorbell rang, heralding the first arrivals.

Their friends must have agreed with Maman, for nearly three dozen guests crowded into the parlor that day, one of the best turnouts of the summer. If their smiles were a bit strained, if their laughter was somewhat forced, they all seemed to share an unspoken agreement not to spoil the gathering with dark speculation about events beyond their control unfolding thousands of miles away.

Their determination to gather despite their worries was rewarded with Josephine Miossec's beautiful soprano.

Her friends and family listened, spellbound, until she finished her third *Lied*, with a final note so pure and resonant it seemed to linger in the air until it was only a memory. A warm crash of applause followed. Maman bowed graciously, and Papa too rose to take a self-deprecating bow, but he waved his friends to silence when he decided they had gone on too long, evoking fond laughter. Then he summoned his friend and fellow professor, a gifted cellist, to take the stage, and soon, with Papa as accompanist, the rich, mellow notes of Saint-Saëns filled the room.

A guitar duet followed, and then a piano, flute, and violin trio, and so passed an hour and then some, until Maman brought the concert to an end by inviting everyone outside for refreshments. Recognizing their cue, Marie and her sisters bounded up from the sofa and hastened to the kitchen to help their mother. In deference to the heat, they served iced lemonade, chilled wine, and cold beer alongside a tempting assortment of light sandwiches, delicate pastries, and fresh fruits and cheeses.

Well practiced in their roles, the Miossec sisters circulated with trays, collected empty glasses, and kept an eye on their mother in case she beckoned them over to receive new instructions. Someone turned on the Victrola, and the lively notes of an Irving Berlin tune wafted outside through the kitchen windows, a bright counterpoint to the thrum of cicadas and the distant, intermittent clang of the streetcar. Amid the laughter and conversation, the friendly teasing and academic gossip and ardent discussion of all things musical, Marie occasionally caught a wisp of anxious speculation about the strife overseas. Each time she quickly moved along with her tray of sweets and savories, unwilling to dispel the illusion that all was well, if only there and if only for now.

Even so, when she returned to the kitchen to reload her tray, she stopped to listen when she heard her father's voice, urgent and serious, just outside the open window. A name caught her attention—Bertha Baur, the president of the conservatory. "All we know is that she's vacationing in Germany," Marie's father was saying. "She sent a letter from Berlin, but that was weeks ago."

"Last I heard, she was in Munich," another man said. "She was planning to spend the entire summer in Germany. With things the way they are, who knows if she'll be able to return in time for the fall semester?"

"The Germans won't detain her, will they?" a woman asked. Marie recognized her voice—the flutist.

"They might not need to," one of the guitarists said darkly. "All they have to do is make the ocean crossing too dangerous."

"Has anyone heard from Louis Victor Saar?" asked the cellist.

At the sound of her music theory professor's name, Marie drew closer to the window. At the end of spring semester, he had mentioned plans to visit his native Holland in June and spend the rest of the summer performing and lecturing in Bavaria.

"We had a letter from him in July," said Marie's father. "He was in Munich at the time. He said nothing about any political or military developments."

"Perhaps the Germans are censoring the mail," said the guitarist. "That would explain why we've heard so little from all of our colleagues abroad. Surely they couldn't *all* be too busy to write."

"I can't imagine any of our friends will be forbidden to leave Germany even if war comes," said Marie's father. "Except, perhaps, Kunwald and his wife. I admit I'm concerned for them."

The others murmured agreement.

Marie had met Dr. Ernst Kunwald, the Austrian conductor who had left the Berlin Philharmonic two years before to lead the Cincinnati Symphony Orchestra. A few months ago, he had also taken charge of the Cincinnati May Festival, where he had conducted the American premiere of Gustav Mahler's Symphony No. 3. In his two years in the Queen City, he had impressed audiences with his flashing blue eyes, commanding presence, and striking discernment for repertoire. Rumor had it that he was corresponding regularly with his countryman Richard Strauss in an effort to secure the American premiere of his as-yet-unfinished new tone poem, already years in the composing.

"But Kunwald isn't in Germany, is he?" asked the flutist. "At the end of the symphony season, he told us he was returning to his home in Vienna for the summer. Austria hasn't declared war on anyone."

"Yes, but considering Austria's traditional alliance with Germany, that may only be a matter of time," Marie's father said. "Kunwald retired as a lieutenant in the reserve army of the Austrian Empire. He may be called back into service."

"Surely not," the flutist exclaimed, and everyone chimed in an opinion.

Marie had heard enough. She finished replenishing her tray with hors d'oeuvres and carried it outside, past her father and his companions, whose voices had become low and urgent.

"Marie," her mother called from the far end of the garden, smiling and beckoning.

Setting the tray down on the nearest table, Marie hurried over, tousling Aimée's hair in passing. Her mother was conversing with a dark-haired, mustachioed man in his midforties. He carried a cigar in his left hand, and a gold watch chain crossed his ample midsection and disappeared into the waistcoat pocket of his light gray suit.

"*Ma petite*," said Maman, reaching out to clasp Marie's hand and drawing her near. "Allow me to present Dr. Stephen Brooks. Stephen, this is my eldest daughter, Marie."

Dr. Brooks inclined his head in a slight bow and extended his hand. "Delighted to meet you, mademoiselle."

"It's my pleasure, sir," said Marie, shaking his hand.

"Dr. Brooks will be joining the conservatory faculty as a visiting professor this fall," her mother said. "The last time he came to Cincinnati was for the May Festival."

"As I told your mother, I was quite impressed with the conservatory chamber choir's performance," Dr. Brooks said. "Imagine my surprise to learn that Josephine Miossec's eldest daughter was one of the sopranos."

"Oh." Marie felt heat rise in her cheeks as her mother and Dr. Brooks beamed at her. "She mentioned that?"

"And why not?" said her mother. "It was a wonderful performance, and it's a mother's prerogative to boast."

"Of course it is," said Dr. Brooks, chuckling. "I understand only the very best students are selected for this ensemble."

Marie offered a small shrug and a smile. "It's true the audition was very competitive."

"*Ma petite* is too modest," her mother protested. "She was the only first-year student to make the cut."

"Indeed?" Dr. Brooks's dark eyebrows rose as he puffed on his cigar. "Most impressive, Miss Miossec. I look forward to hearing you as a soloist. Perhaps at next week's musicale?"

"Oh, I—" Marie fumbled about for an excuse. "Well, I would, but—" Just then the telephone rang inside the house, faint but unmistakable. "If you'll excuse me—"

"No, stay, *ma petite*. Your father will answer it." Her mother nodded toward the house, and, sure enough, Marie glimpsed her father entering through the back door, ruining her excuse and quashing her hopes for a quick escape. Fortunately, her mother changed the subject, so Marie managed to avoid committing to sing the following week, or explaining why she would not. How could she confess to a probable future conservatory teacher that she was not good enough yet to sing in such company, at least not the way she wanted to? She didn't want her parents' colleagues to indulge her as a precocious child. She wanted them to respect her, if not as an equal, then at least as an aspiring artist in her own right.

Lost in her own thoughts, it took her a moment to realize that her mother and Dr. Brooks had stopped speaking, and that their attention had shifted somewhere behind her. Turning, Marie observed other guests drawing closer to the rear windows, where her father stood just inside, candlestick phone raised to his mouth with his left hand, the speaker raised to his right ear with the other. He was repeating the conversation for the benefit of their guests, but Marie was too far away to grasp more than the most urgent phrases: Great Britain had issued an ultimatum to Berlin. The Germans must cease military activity along the Belgian border or provoke war with Britain as well. Belgium's King Albert had made a formal appeal for help to France and Britain as guarantors of its neutrality by international treaty.

"*Mon dieu*," Maman murmured.

Heart thudding, Marie felt her mother's hand close around her own, and together they joined those gathered around the windows.

"Germany has declared war on France and Belgium," her father repeated, pausing to listen between sentences. "This is their third war declaration this week, having already declared war on Russia and invaded Luxembourg. German troops have moved into Belgium at three points, violating their neutrality policy. It is reported that there are already one million French men near the frontier line, but France is at an even greater risk with Germany's invasion of Luxembourg and Belgium, right on their border. France has very limited defenses along the Belgian border, making it vulnerable to attack on that front." A long pause as he listened. "You can't be serious." Another pause. "Yes, I hear you. I can't believe it, but I hear it. Thanks, Paul." He hung up, shaking his head and frowning.

"What is it, *mon cher*?" Marie's mother prompted.

"Wilson has officially proclaimed that the United States will remain neutral in the conflict, 'impartial in thought as well as in action.'"

"What exactly is that supposed to mean?" asked the cellist.

"Your guess is as good as mine," Marie's father replied grimly. He stepped away from the window to return the phone to its usual table.

Marie caught a few muffled oaths in several languages as the guests murmured in consternation and anger and worry. Her father reappeared in the doorway, arms folded over his chest, his expression bleak as he sought out Maman's gaze in the crowd.

Suddenly it seemed that everyone had been seized by the urgent need to return home. For many of them, Marie knew, for her own family, their true homes were thousands of miles across the sea, in the line of fire or somewhere near it. Two of Maman's friends lingered to help tidy up, but she soon sent them on their way, with tight smiles and embraces and mutual assurances that everything would be all right, somehow.

As soon as the family was alone, Aimée burst into sobs. "What will happen to *Grand-mère* and *Grand-père*?" she asked tremulously, tears slipping down her cheeks. "Our family, my friends. Our home. My school."

Papa swept her up in his arms. "Our friends and family are very clever and careful," he declared, kissing her cheek as she snuggled her face against his shoulder. "They'll keep themselves safe, whatever comes. Who knows? Maybe those Germans will decide to stay right where they are. It's a long walk across Belgium in this summer heat. Why should they leave their homes and *biergartens* just to annoy their neighbors?"

His words and gentle tone soothed Aimée, but Marie and Sylvie understood perfectly the look he gave their mother over their younger sister's head, apprehensive and full of warning. They knew, though Aimée apparently had not figured it out, that soldiers would go wherever their generals commanded, regardless of their own preferences.

"How can America remain neutral?" Marie overheard her mother lament to her father later that night as Marie and Sylvie helped Aimée prepare for bed. "They cherish freedom and democracy and justice, or so they say. This German aggression is an outrage. How can the United States stand by and do nothing when their closest international friends are forced into a war of self-defense?"

"The Americans don't want any part of a conflict in Europe," Papa replied. "They think it's none of their concern."

"That's an astonishingly provincial attitude for this day and age!"

"A vast ocean separates our continents. A certain provinciality should be expected, even in this century." Papa sighed. "Try not to worry. That same ocean protects the girls, and you and I."

"Try not to worry?" Maman's lovely voice was choked with tears. "How can I not worry? We may be safe, for now, but everyone else we love, everything else we hold most dear—oh, Stephane, I—"

"Hush, my love. The girls are not yet asleep."

Their voices descended into whispers, and Marie heard no more.

1

APRIL 1917

New York City

GRACE

She would tell her parents that night, Grace resolved as she waited on the platform for the early train to Manhattan. After supper, when her parents and siblings were pleasantly sated and content thanks to Mother's delicious Sunday roast and potatoes, she would announce her intention to move out of her childhood bedroom and into an apartment in the city.

It was an eminently reasonable plan. Grace just had to help her family see it.

Three friends from work had invited her to move in with them months ago, and her answer was long overdue. The girls' fourth roommate was getting married in June, and they unanimously agreed that Grace was the ideal choice to fill the vacancy. A few weeks earlier, Grace had toured their lovely two-bedroom flat in Chelsea, a charming brownstone in a safe neighborhood only minutes via streetcar from the American Telephone and Telegraph Company headquarters. There were ample windows to let in the sunshine, a private bath, an efficient galley kitchen, and a spacious front room for entertaining and relaxing. It was absolutely perfect, and if not for her parents' firmly held belief that girls should not leave the family home until they married, Grace would have signed the lease on the spot. She couldn't have, of course, not only because she loved and respected her parents too much to go behind their backs, but also because the law required a man to sign as her guarantor.

Grace shifted the straps of her bag to her elbow and drew back the sleeve of her sage green broadcloth coat to check her wristwatch. Though her train was not due for another five minutes, she glanced down the tracks anyway, hoping to catch a glimpse of it. She didn't usually work on Sundays, and she had misjudged the time and arrived at the station earlier than necessary. One of her prospective roommates had asked for the day off, and although Grace had been promoted to instructor, she still liked to keep her switchboard skills fresh, so she had offered to cover the shift. Sunday afternoons were usually quite busy, especially on the long-distance board, as families scattered across the country reunited over the phone lines between church services and Sunday dinner.

Grace's commute would be much shorter from Chelsea—which was exactly the sort of pragmatic reason most likely to win over her parents. Thanks to her recent promotion, Grace could well afford the rent. Her parents had encouraged her to live in the dormitory when she was at Barnard College; she would remind them how she had thrived among the other bright, ambitious girls, and sharing an apartment would be much the same experience. Her prospective roommates were as responsible and levelheaded as Grace herself, each of them a capable telephone operator with more than a year's experience. That ought to be character reference enough, since everyone knew that AT&T set exceptionally high standards for their female employees' deportment.

Grace had been well prepared to meet those standards, since her family's own expectations exceeded them. Like all the Banker children, Grace had been brought up to be eminently responsible, a good daughter and citizen, trustworthy, honest, and industrious. She had graduated from college with honors with a double major in history and French. She had a job she loved, with excellent prospects for advancement. But the bottom line was that Grace was twenty-four years old—twenty-four and a half, to be precise. It was high time she set out on her own. Hadn't her father often declared how proud he was of her independent spirit? Surely he and her mother understood that she was a smart, capable, modern young woman who could look after herself and did not require a father's or a husband's benevolent protection to mind her own affairs. And she wasn't even asking to be *entirely* on her own, for she would be living among trusted friends, nice girls from good families who were familiar with the city and would show her the ropes. Perhaps if her parents met them, and saw for themselves—

Grace sighed and shook her head to clear it. At Barnard she had participated in Debate Club and had performed in theatricals; surely she could construct a better argument than the one she was currently rehearsing in her head. The problem wasn't finding the right words to prove how sensible her plan was, but doing so without hurting anyone's feelings. Her parents would be dismayed to learn that she was anything less than perfectly happy at home. They would also be bewildered, because her elder sister still lived with the family even though she was gainfully employed as a schoolteacher. Why should Grace not do the same?

Grace would explain, as kindly as she could, that she adored her family and she would always love their home. Nevertheless, the time had come for her to leave the nest, as her younger brother Eugene was planning to do soon. But of course, sons were expected to leave home one day; that was a young man's trajectory from birth. Not so daughters, at least not without a ring on her finger and a white tulle veil on her head. For folks of her parents' generation, a properly brought-up young woman was expected to move from her father's home to her husband's with nary a stop in between, with the possible exception of an interim stint at college, which remained a rare privilege for the best and brightest.

Grace tucked her hands into her coat pockets, considering her options and wishing she had begun preparing her parents for her eventual flight months ago. The throaty whistle of the approaching train interrupted her reverie. She'd find the right words to persuade them, she told herself as the train halted at the platform and she climbed aboard. Once they got over their initial shock, they would admit that her plan made a lot of sense. Besides, she would only be a train ride away, and there was always the telephone for conversations that couldn't wait until her next visit.

She settled into a seat near a window, loosened her scarf, and unfastened the top two buttons of her coat. It was chilly for mid-April, and the cinereous clouds threatened rain, but there was still enough sunlight to read by comfortably. Yet the news was anything but comforting, as she discovered when she took the paper from her bag and scanned the headlines. Thus it had been since war had broken out in Europe, increasingly so after a German U-boat sank the RMS *Lusitania* two years before. More than one thousand souls, including many American citizens, had been lost in the cold waters off the southern coast of Ireland. In response to international outrage, Germany had insisted that they'd had every right to treat the unarmed ocean liner as a military vessel, since in addition to the great many civilian passengers aboard, the ship had also carried munitions, in defiance of the German blockade of Great Britain. But although the German government had not admitted wrongdoing, their navy had left passenger liners alone after that, focusing their attacks on vessels that were verifiably British. For nearly two years the dangerous tension at sea had persisted, finally shattering only two months before, when Germany announced its intention to resume unrestricted submarine warfare. In a speech before a joint session of Congress in early February, President Wilson had declared that although the United States did not desire a hostile conflict with Germany, if the Germans sank any American ships, they would soon find themselves at war. With diplomatic relations between the two nations severed, each day brought new reports from Washington and Europe that seemed, to Grace at least, that her country was moving steadily and inexorably toward war.

Her heart cinched at the very thought. Her brother, Eugene, was the ideal age for a soldier, brave and smart and fit, full to the brim with honor and love of country. All the Banker children had been raised with a strong sense of patriotism and duty, for their ancestors had come to America before the Revolution and America had been very good to them. If their country went to war, Grace knew her brother would set down his clerk's pen and take up arms, but what could she and her sisters do?

Grace folded the newspaper on her lap and gazed out the window. The hourlong route from Passaic to Manhattan wasn't particularly scenic, but familiarity lent it charm. Even so, her thoughts were so far away that she could have been traveling with the blinds drawn, so little attention she paid to the passing landscape.

If it came to war, Grace supposed the women of her family would redouble their efforts to support the relief efforts already under way. From the moment descriptions of the devastated villages and desperate refugees had reached American shores, women's clubs throughout the country had organized fund-raisers for widows and orphans in France, Britain, and Belgium. Ladies' magazines offered pages of advice on how to grow a proper kitchen garden and to preserve the fruit, vegetables, and herbs. Still other women's groups were preparing for America's entry into the war by doing everything they could to prevent it. A few of Grace's college chums had joined the Women's Peace Party, which held vast parades, rallies, and conventions to promote their staunchly antiwar platform. "As women, we must have a unique commitment to peace," a friend had explained as she appealed to Grace to join the cause. "As mothers, and as future mothers, we have a vested interest in making sure our sons are not slaughtered on a battlefield. As citizens of a democracy, we must advocate for our more vulnerable sisters. We all know that women and children are always and invariably the most devastated by war."

Grace could not disagree, but other friends involved in war preparedness efforts made valid points too, and she found it impossible to side wholeheartedly with one group against the other. Even the suffrage movement, united in its desire for the vote, was split on the question of whether the United States should enter the war. And the more that politicians and businessmen insisted that it was in the country's best interest to stay out of the conflict—in inverse proportion, it seemed, to how desperately their friends overseas needed them—the more dubious Grace became.

A light drizzle had begun by the time the train pulled into the station, so Grace adjusted her hat, disembarked, and sought shelter beneath a market's awning while she waited to catch the streetcar to lower Manhattan. She got off at the closest stop to 195 Broadway and walked briskly from there, chin nestled in her collar, hands tucked into her pockets for warmth. She would cut her commute time by two-thirds if she moved to Chelsea, she reflected as she crossed Fulton at the corner and hurried toward the entrance to the twenty-nine-story Telephone and Telegraph Building. It was scarcely a year old, with an impressive neoclassical façade of white Vermont granite accentuated by layers of Greek columns of gray granite. Atop the stepped roof of the Fulton Street wing stood *Genius of Electricity*, an enormous gilded bronze statue of a winged male figure poised upon a globe, encircled by cables, with two lightning bolts clutched in his upraised left fist. The statue's original title had been *Genius of Telegraphy*, but the president of AT&T had renamed it after the corporation spun off Western Union to forestall antitrust allegations. Like most of her coworkers, Grace much preferred the more playful nickname the figure had acquired, *Golden Boy*.

Entering through the Fulton Street bay, Grace loosened her scarf and began slipping out of her coat as she crossed the vast lobby, her low-heeled boots clicking on the gray marble floors, which gleamed in the warm light cast by the bronze-and-alabaster chandeliers suspended from the forty-foot ceiling, coffered in a grid of green-and-gold-embellished beams and supported by Doric columns of white marble.

No customers and only a few tourists wandered the lobby so early on a Sunday morning, guidebooks in hand, gazes upturned in admiration, so Grace was able to make her way unimpeded down a discreet hallway reserved for employees. She exchanged brief friendly greetings with the equally preoccupied coworkers she passed on her way to the telephone operators' lounge, where she hung up her coat and hat, left her bag in her cubbyhole, and paused to examine herself in the mirror, adjusting the bow at the throat of her blouse and running a hand through her dark brown bob to fluff the locks flattened by her hat.

"Good morning, Grace," a voice sang out. "Have you spoken to your parents yet?"

Grace turned and discovered one of her would-be roommates rising from the sofa in the corner, her white blouse and long, navy blue skirt nearly identical to Grace's own, her glossy black hair arranged in a perfect Gibson Girl coif.

"Good morning, Lily." When her friend regarded her expectantly, Grace added, "No, I haven't broken the news to them quite yet, but I intend to this evening."

Lily planted a hand on one hip and regarded her skeptically. "Intend to, or will?"

"I will," Grace replied emphatically. "I have it all planned out, more or less. After work, and after supper—"

"Oh, I see," teased Lily. "So that's why you're giving up your day off to fill in for Molly at the board. To avoid your parents."

"I'm not avoiding anyone," Grace protested, laughing. "I'm not procrastinating—at least, I won't anymore, not after tonight."

"Whatever you say, Miss Banker." Smiling, Lily beckoned her closer and gestured to a few pamphlets spread out on the coffee table. "Say, remember when you came to see the apartment, and we were chatting about how we girls could do our bit besides knitting and gardening and saving pennies for war orphans?"

"Sure, I remember." Grace joined her at the table and picked up one of the pamphlets. "'The National Service School,'" she read aloud. "I think Caroline in the steno pool went to one of their camps last month."

If memory served, it was about a year ago that the Women's Section of the Navy League had established the National Service School, a series of two-week camps where young women were taught military calisthenics, cooking for the infirm, and how to change hospital bed-linens and make bandages and surgical dressings. Far more intriguing to Grace and her friends were the classes in operating the wireless and the telegraph. And yet Grace had been too skeptical to enroll, not only because the majority of the WSNL was known to be ultraconservative and antisuffrage, but because she knew AT&T could not spare an instructor like herself for two weeks, even if she were inclined to spend her valuable vacation time on such a dubious endeavor. From what she had heard, a working girl like Caroline was an exception among the participants, who tended to be well-meaning young socialites with indulgent parents, time on their hands, and no need to earn a living.

With a dubious sigh, Grace tossed the pamphlet on top of the others. "Are you thinking about signing up?"

Lily shrugged and bent to pick up the pamphlet Grace had let fall. "I don't know." Studying the one in her hand, frowning thoughtfully, she glanced at the others and picked up one with an appealing sketch of a pretty young woman smiling demurely, eyes downcast, as she wound white cloth into a bandage roll. "I like the thought of serving my country."

Grace glanced at her watch and edged toward the door. "If you really want to serve your country, enlist in the Naval Reserve."

Lily's nose wrinkled in displeasure. "Be a yeomanette and work in an office, filing papers and typing?"

"To free up a sailor for duty at sea, sure."

"It doesn't sound very glamorous."

"I don't think glamour is the point." Amused, Grace paused in the doorway. "See you at the exchange. Don't be late for your shift or I'll have to write you up."

"You wouldn't."

"I might." Grace tossed a grin over her shoulder in parting. "Dare me."

"Pushing paper in a navy office would be duller than what I'm doing now," Lily called after her. "I want adventure, excitement. Who joins the navy to be bored to death?"

"It's about service, not adventure," Grace called back, hurrying on her way.

She arrived at the exchange with minutes to spare, her pulse quickening at the familiar, delightful clicking of plugs and murmur of voices. Tall rows of switchboards filled the room, arranged back to back with aisles in between for the operators to sit, each at her station. As she found her place, Grace exchanged greetings with friends, sometimes no more than a nod or a smile if the operator was engaged in a call. Taking a seat, she put on her headset, adjusted the mouthpiece, scanned the rows upon rows of tiny lightbulbs and numbered jacks and keys to be sure all was in order, and awaited her first call of the morning.

It didn't take long. Grace had barely settled back in her chair when a bulb lit up, signaling an incoming call. Swiftly she took a flexible black cord in hand, located the corresponding jack from among the many arranged in rows at the bottom of the switchboard, and plugged it firmly into place.

"Number, please?" she inquired, her voice clear and professionally cordial. Telephone operators were emphatically instructed to be "the girl with the smile in her voice," and whatever did not come naturally must be attained through practice and polish.

"Yeah, operator, I need BA 5-7121 right away, please," a man said.

"Yes, sir," she replied. This was an easy one, a call within his own network. Grace quickly plugged the other end of the cord into the other party's jack and pulled the peg that rang his telephone's bell. When the receiver picked up, Grace lingered on the line for a few moments to make sure that they were connected, but then another tiny bulb lit up and she was obliged to move on.

This time the caller wanted to reach someone outside his own network, so Grace had to stretch a bit and plug the cord into a jack in front of the operator on her right. They often had to reach across and in front of one another, extending a cord from here all the way over there, and on very busy days it became quite a feat of acrobatics as they all tried to connect their calls swiftly, efficiently, and accurately without getting in one another's way and creating an awful snarl. Every so often, they had to check on completed calls to see if the parties were still conversing; if the callers were finished, the operator unplugged the cords to free up the jack. Woe to the operator who pulled the plug when the parties were merely pausing to gather their thoughts. A long-distance call was an even more elaborate production, involving multiple operators establishing a relay between different exchanges in one or more cities between caller and recipient, a process that could take hours.

Most customers were friendly and kind, but unfortunately, others were curt or impatient, upset or uncertain or downright rude. Sometimes a caller supplied an incorrect number and castigated the poor operator who, through no fault of her own, could not reach the person they sought. Sometimes the recipient would not pick up, and a caller would take out their annoyance on the operator. Sometimes a cheeky fellow would become intrigued by a lovely voice and would abandon his original call in favor of chatting up the operator, who, much to his frustration, was absolutely forbidden to tell him her name. Through it all, the operator was expected to remain unflustered, courteous, and helpful, never taking offense, never losing her temper, and absolutely never bursting into tears. As an instructor, Grace often observed novices on the lines, and sometimes when the operator's replies indicated that call was going awry, Grace would stand behind the girl's chair, rest a comforting hand on her shoulder, and murmur encouragement or phrases the girl could parrot into the mouthpiece. Only very rarely was she obliged to take over the headset and firmly but with unimpeachable courtesy set a caller straight. Grace had heard rumors of certain nononsense supervisors who handled offensive customers by yanking the plug from the board and declaring that the old so-and-so could call back after he cooled down, but she had never witnessed any such unprofessional displays from her colleagues, nor could she imagine ever losing her temper in such spectacularly disastrous fashion.

Undoubtedly, theirs was a fast-paced, demanding job that required a lot of energy, nimbleness, and steady nerves, and it was common knowledge that women were much better suited for it than men. At least, that was what telephone company executives told the press whenever a new exchange was constructed and they needed to recruit new operators. Women were more diplomatic, more willing to soothe irate customers rather than engage them in argument, more agile at the boards, better able to juggle many simultaneous tasks, and more willing to endure the low pay, fast pace, long hours, and stressful conditions, all with a "smile in her voice."

Grace appreciated the praise, but she winced at the inadvertent condescension. No one should have to put up with an angry tirade from a customer, not even if they had been brought up to be nice and ignore it. If the work was exhausting and stressful, management should improve conditions, not seek out employees who had fewer career options and dared not complain. But those were minor quibbles compared to the great many things Grace adored about her job. It was work she was intellectually and temperamentally suited for, especially since she had been promoted to instructor, and as far as she was concerned, the faster and busier the pace, the more she relished the challenge.

Even so, after a few hours, she was glad to remove her headset and return to the operators' lounge for her lunch break. She had brought a sandwich and an apple from home, and some darling girl had put on a fresh pot of coffee. It was fun to sit and chat with her chums, and even to accept their friendly teasing about whether she was still up to the real work of the switchboard after idling away in the Instructor Department since her promotion. "I haven't dropped a call all morning," she retorted, feigning indignation. "The Detroit exchange is still in Ohio, right?" Her friends burst out laughing, and were still chuckling as they hurried back to the boards.

The afternoon passed as swiftly as the morning, and by the time her shift ended, Grace was pleasantly fatigued, filled with a sense of accomplishment for a job well done.

"Talk to your parents," Lily reminded her back in the lounge as she put on her hat, checked her reflection in the mirror, and adjusted the angle of the brim.

"I will." Grace pulled on her coat and wrapped her scarf loosely about her neck. "Promise."

"Tonight?"

"Tonight," Grace echoed agreeably, slipping her arm through the straps of her bag. "Or maybe tomorrow morning after breakfast, or maybe Tuesday—"

"Grace," Lily protested.

"I'm only joking," Grace quickly assured her, laughing. "I'll talk to them tonight, and with any luck I'll have good news the next time I see you."

Lily regarded her for a moment, dubious, but then she grinned. "All right. Fingers crossed they say yes."

"Fingers crossed," Grace replied, holding up hers.

They clocked out and left together, and when they stepped outside onto the corner of Broadway and Fulton, they were pleased to discover that the rain had passed and the sun was shining in a clear blue sky. "A good omen," Lily declared, and Grace agreed. Above the city smells, she thought she caught the fragrance of gardenias in bloom, and her heart was light as a sudden breeze swept her bobbed locks away from her face. She and Lily walked up Broadway together for a few blocks before parting ways, Lily for the charming apartment in Chelsea, Grace for the streetcar and the train back to Passaic.

Once aboard the train, she settled back into her seat and silently rehearsed her case, arranging and rearranging her most salient points. What would she do if her mother objected, if her father refused to sign the papers? Frowning thoughtfully, Grace gazed out the window as the train crossed the bridge over the Hackensack River. She figured she had two options: She would either regroup and return with a stronger argument, or she would learn to live with the disappointment. Either way, she would be fine. She could hardly fuss and lament about being obliged to remain in her comfortable home with her loving family when so many other girls her age were suffering in Europe, homeless, hungry, and bereft.

She sighed, tired of rehearsing her case. Her mother would have dinner nearly ready by the time she reached home, but there would still be time to freshen up, change into a comfortable housedress and sweater, and help her youngest sister set the table. After supper the family would gather in the front room to while away the hours until bedtime. Grace would offer to help Marjorie with her homework. Her father would bring in the evening paper and settle down in his favorite armchair to read, sharing the most interesting bits aloud. Helen and their mother would take their usual seats near the brightest lamp and murmur quietly over their sewing or knitting. Eugene would sprawl out on the floor and play chess against himself—his most worthy opponent, or so he often said, feigning a smug air of superiority that never failed to provoke laughter and eye rolls. And so another ordinary Sunday evening would pass in peace and contentment.

As much as she longed to spread her wings, it would be difficult to leave all that behind.

A strange new ambivalence took hold of her as the train pulled into the station at Passaic. She hoped it would pass, a momentary case of cold feet, but the feeling only intensified as she walked home, crossed the threshold, and called out a greeting that was cheerfully echoed back to her.

The evening unfolded exactly as she had predicted it would. She was tempted to put off her private chat with her parents until the next day, but she had promised Lily that tonight was the night, and she owed it to her friends to either accept their invitation or decline so they could find someone else before the rent came due.

Grace steeled herself. "Mother, Dad—" She paused to clear her throat as everyone glanced up at her—everyone except her father, whose gaze remained fixed on the newspaper. "After you put Marjorie to bed, could I speak with you? Alone?"

"I can put myself to bed, thank you very much," said Marjorie indignantly, glancing up from the piece of yarn she was dangling in front of Patches, their calico cat. "Anyway, I'm not tired."

"Of course, Grace, dear," replied her mother. "Is something wrong?"

"No, not wrong, but I do have something I'd like to discuss with you both."

"Is it about a fellow?" Eugene yawned lazily and put the white king in check. "If so, please talk quietly so I won't accidentally overhear."

Grace nudged him with her toe. "It's not about a fellow."

"That's a relief. So what is it?"

"It's none of your business, little brother." Grace turned back to her mother, only to find that her gaze had shifted, and that both she and Helen were studying their father. He had folded the paper on his lap and was frowning at the floor, hands on his knees, his expression fixed in a grimace.

"Dad?" Helen asked. "Is something wrong?"

At the note of worry in her voice, Eugene propped himself up on his elbows and peered up at him. "Dad?"

"It's—well, it seems that tomorrow—" Their father paused, steeling himself with a deep breath. "It says here that tomorrow President Wilson is going to address a joint session of Congress and request a declaration of war against Germany. He has said that neutrality is no longer feasible or desirable where the peace of the world is involved."

"Heaven help us," their mother gasped.

"That's it, then," said Eugene, sitting up and rubbing his hand across his jaw. "We're in it now."

"Congress might refuse," said Helen, her voice trembling. "Then America won't go to war. We couldn't. Isn't that so, Dad?"

Their father, lost in thought, said nothing.

Grace felt her heart thudding in her chest, and she heard the answer in her father's silence. Congress would not refuse. Eugene was right. After years of stalling, the United States was going to war.

2

AUGUST 1917

Los Angeles

VALERIE

Something roughly shook her awake, too vigorous and loud to be ignored. "Valerie, get up."

Reluctantly she stirred, blinded and dazed by the sunlight streaming through the window. "Earthquake?" she asked through a yawn over that incessant ringing, less worried than she ought to be, if she had guessed right.

"No." Hilde gave her one last good shake and released her shoulder. "You slept through your alarm again. You're going to wake up the whole house."

Groggily, Valerie sat up in bed and noted that indeed, her alarm clock was ringing shrilly on the nightstand. Just beyond it, Hilde's twin bed was already neatly made, with crisp hospital corners and plumped pillows. Propping herself up on her elbows, Valerie raised her voice to be heard over the alarm. "Why didn't you just turn it off instead of waking me up to scold me?"

Her sister planted her arms on her hips and frowned down at her, exasperated. She looked as if she had been up since dawn, with the sleeves of her floral cotton dress rolled up to the elbow, a spotless white apron tied around her waist, and her long, light brown hair neatly braided and coiled atop her head. "Because it's your clock and your responsibility, and if I *had* let you sleep through the alarm, you'd complain about how I'd made you late for work."

Fair point. Flinging back the corner of her light candlewick coverlet, Valerie swung her legs over the side of the bed, stretched her arms wide, and inhaled deeply, savoring the fragrance of bougainvillea and its birdsong accompaniment drifting through the window. Only then, mindful of her sister's rising impatience, did she reach out and smack the alarm clock, silencing it. "That's better," she said, smiling brightly up at her sister. Hilde rolled her eyes and left the bedroom, shutting the door behind her with a soft click.

Released from the weight of her sister's critical gaze, Valerie bounded out of bed and hurried to wash and dress. As she brushed out her long, golden curls and deftly swept them up into a chignon, it occurred to her that, compared to Hilde's, her bed looked like it had been tumbled by the Santa Ana winds. Unfortunately, she decided as she slipped a last hairpin in place, she couldn't spare the time to tidy it up.

She hurried downstairs, cheerfully greeting one of their new boarders when they passed on the landing, suppressing a grin when he blushed and stammered out a reply, all shyness and admiration. At the foot of the stairs, she turned and nearly collided with her younger brother, who was pulling on his suitcoat as he raced from the kitchen, a piece of buttered toast in his mouth. "Henri," she gasped, startled into laughter. "Where are you going in such a hurry?"

"I'll explain later," he said, tugging his gray tweed cap over his blond curls as he downed the last bit of his hasty breakfast. He was slender and graceful, as Valerie was, as their father had been, and she had not yet become accustomed to looking up to meet his dark blue eyes. "Got to go."

"Henri, what in the world—"

But he had already raced out the door, unintentionally slamming it behind himself in his haste. Bemused, she watched the closed door for a moment before shaking her head and continuing on her way.

She found her mother and sister bustling back and forth between the dining room and the kitchen, tidying up after serving the boarders their breakfast. Her mother brightened as she entered, while Hilde merely pursed her lips and shook her head. "Good morning, Mama," Valerie said, reaching over her mother's head to take down a mug from the cupboard, pausing on her way to the coffee pot to give her a peck on the cheek.

"Good morning, dear," her mother replied warmly, patting her cheek, the gesture and the accent harkening back to her Belgian homeland—*their* homeland, actually, although Valerie barely remembered living there. Most of her memories of the old country were inspired by family photographs.

"You missed breakfast," said Hilde, setting an armful of dirty dishes on the counter.

"That's fine," said Valerie, pouring herself a cup of coffee. "I'm not very hungry."

"You should eat something," her mother protested, wiping her hands on her apron. "We have plenty of brioche left over, and that strawberry jam I made last week. I could fix you a plate."

"Don't bother, Mama. You have enough to do, and I don't have time." Valerie spied an orange on the counter, plucked earlier that morning from their own backyard grove. She picked it up, tossed it from one hand to the other, and eyed it appraisingly. "Perfect."

She moved to the far end of the counter to keep out of the way, spread out a napkin, and deftly peeled and sectioned the sun-warmed fruit. With one eye on the clock, she spared a moment to delight in the sweet, sharp fragrance, savoring the juice as she alternated between hasty bites of orange and sips of black coffee. Her mother and sister chatted as they went about their work, finishing each other's sentences as they charted the course of their day.

"Where was Henri going in such a rush this morning?" Valerie interrupted, inclining her head toward the front room. "We barely avoided a smash-up at the foot of the stairs."

"He didn't say," her mother replied, "but I saw him pass by the window, and he seemed to be heading toward the university."

"He probably went to pick up his schedule for the fall semester," said Hilde.

"Yes, they'd be ready by now." What a strange, small detail to remember, and how annoying that it pained her. "Did he take a check for his tuition?"

Her mother shook her head, and her sister arched her eyebrows at her. "Who would have written it?" Hilde asked. "The last time I touched the checkbook without your permission, you nearly bit my head off."

"That's only because you forgot to record the amount paid and threw off the balance." Valerie carried her orange peels to the trash bin and left her coffee cup in the sink. "I wish he'd told me he was going to campus. He could have taken the payment to the bursar today and saved himself a trip."

"It doesn't matter." Their mother wet a dishcloth beneath the tap and began wiping down the counters. "He can do it tomorrow."

"Tomorrow's Saturday," said Valerie, thinking aloud. "The bursar's office will be closed, and the bill is due Monday."

"He can take it Monday, then," said Hilde, impatient. "Honestly, how you can remember such minutiae but neglect to turn off your own alarm clock when it's ringing within arm's reach, I'll never understand."

"I have a talent for small but consequential details." Apparently her sister was in quite a mood, but it was a beautiful morning and Valerie refused to be drawn into an argument. "It's been fun, girls, but I'd better go or I'll be late for work."

"Don't forget your lunch," her mother said, gesturing toward a small brown paper bag on the hall table beside her purse. "I put in some of those dried apricots you like."

"Thanks, Mama." Valerie gave her a quick hug. "Don't keep supper waiting for me. After my shift, I'm going out for a bite to eat with some of the girls."

"A bite to eat," Hilde scoffed, attacking the floor with her broom. "More like going to a club on the beach to drink gin and dance with strange men."

"That's where you're wrong. My friend Cora always calls dibs on the strange men, which leaves the merely ordinary fellows for the rest of us." Tucking her lunch into her purse, Valerie hesitated in the doorway and studied her sister. She was always so busy, and so rarely content. "Do you . . . want to join us?"

Pausing, Hilde straightened and regarded her for a moment before shaking her head and resuming sweeping. "I can't. I have to turn in early. I have a busy day tomorrow."

"Busy? With what?"

"The laundry, for one." Hilde's gaze was fixed determinedly on the crumbs falling in line before the dustpan. "It's a lot of work stripping the beds every Saturday, washing all those sheets and pillowcases and blankets, making the beds up again before our lodgers turn in for the night—"

"You don't have to get up at the crack of dawn for that. The lodgers will still be asleep. And later I could help, it would make the work go faster—"

"No." Hilde planted the broom firmly and squared her shoulders. "That's not what we agreed. Your contribution to the household is your wages, and the bookkeeping and bill paying, since you have a knack for it and won't trust anyone else to do it. Mama and I run the boarding-house."

"I'm happy to pitch in with the laundry every once in a while if it means you get a night on the town."

"Listen to your sister, Hilde," their mother cajoled. "You girls are entitled to a bit of fun."

"Saturday is her one day off," Hilde reminded their mother, then fixed her gaze on Valerie. "Thanks, but I'm not interested in gin and dancing. That sort of thing is for girls your age."

"Oh, please. You're not that much older than I am." Valerie was tempted to snatch the broom and swat her sister on the bottom with it. "You used to love the beach, and dancing, and men, and you can have a lemonade if you prefer it to gin—"

"You're going to be late for work," Hilde interrupted, stooping to brush the crumbs and debris into the dustpan.

Valerie sighed and looked to their mother, who offered only a silent, helpless shrug in reply. "I'll be off, then," she said, strangely disappointed. Hilde didn't even know Valerie's friends from work and probably wouldn't have fit in with the lighthearted group of younger women, so it was perhaps just as well that she had declined. Still, for a moment Valerie had imagined her sister laughing and smiling again, maybe even accepting a dance with a handsome fellow. Hilde was four years older than Valerie, but even at that, she was not yet twenty-five. She wouldn't be stuck on the shelf if she hadn't put herself there, and she could climb down anytime if she wanted to.

Valerie would have lingered to argue the point, but it would have been a waste of words.

The argument had delayed her just long enough to make getting to work on time a challenge. She nearly had to sprint the last block or she would have missed the downtown trolley, no small feat in a long skirt despite the relatively low heel of her half-boots. A handsome fellow smiled a greeting as she climbed aboard, but the scene in the kitchen had left her in no mood for witty banter, so she pretended not to see him. She settled into a seat near the front, breathless, thankful she had worn her corded batiste waist beneath her light blue poplin suit and ecru blouse instead of a boned corset. Clasping her purse on her lap, she took in the view of sun-dappled desert fan palms, eucalyptus, live oaks, and flowering bushes between the low-slung buildings of bleached wood and stucco, but the bright, busy, familiar scene did little to improve her mood.

She tucked a loose strand of hair behind her ear, quashing a tiny pang of guilt before it could ruin her morning. She supposed she could do more to help around the boardinghouse, but after putting in a full day at the switchboard, housekeeping chores were not exactly high on her list of relaxing pastimes. Besides, their current division of labor had been her sister's idea. They had decided more than a year ago that one of them had to go out into the world to earn wages while the other assisted their mother with the boardinghouse, and as the eldest, Hilde had claimed the privilege of first choice. How lucky it was that Valerie had found a job she enjoyed, especially after her original ambitions had been crushed so abruptly.

Father's death had changed everything, for all of them.

Valerie was only six when her parents broke the news that they would be leaving their home in Brussels and sailing for America so that her father, a gifted artist and photographer, could seek his fortune in New York City. There he had soon discovered motion pictures, a newfangled amusement swiftly rising in popularity. Within a few years, he had mastered the emerging technology so well, and had impressed the right people so much, that he had been offered the opportunity of a lifetime, making movies with stars like Douglas Fairbanks and Mary Pickford. The new job obliged him to move to the other side of the country, but after crossing an ocean, what were a few thousand miles more?

Southern California quickly proved to be a paradise of sunshine and ocean breezes and limitless possibilities, and not only for their father. Their mother made many friends among the wives of her husband's colleagues and the women who worked as costumers and designers on the sets. The children enrolled in school, but while Valerie and Henri had quickly picked up English back in New York and thrived in their new classrooms, Hilde struggled. When she earned her diploma two years later, she declared her education complete. She claimed to be content to help their mother keep house and look after her siblings, but it was obvious that her greatest happiness and hope for the future came from courting a young man she had met at church, Edgar, a second-generation Californian and a rising young executive with the Southern Pacific Railroad.

Two years later, Hilde and Edgar were tentatively discussing marriage when German tanks thundered across the border into the DeSmedts' homeland. Deeply apprehensive for their family and friends, their mother and father tried in vain to reach them by telegram and through the Belgian embassy. The family agonized over reports of the German army's relentless march across their once peaceful land, the artillery bombardment of the fortifications at Liège, the siege and fall of defensive fortresses along the Meuse River, and the occupation of

Antwerp and Brussels. One and a half million desperate refugees fled ahead of the Germans' inexorable drive through the heart of Belgium and into France. The DeSmedts' fear turned to horror as word came of the *Schrecklichkeit*, the policy of terror the Germans implemented in their conquered nation: the brutal suppression of Belgian resistance, the massacre of 674 civilians in Dinant, the retaliatory burning of medieval Louvain, the incarceration of hostages, executions, more massacres of civilians, the seemingly endless burning of whole towns and villages—

The atrocities soon became known as the Rape of Belgium, a phrase that sent icy shivers down Valerie's spine. As they frantically sought news of their loved ones, the family's only consolation in that long season of anguish was that they were safe in California, thousands of miles out of harm's way. They waited for President Wilson to announce that the United States would join the Allies in pushing the aggressors out of France and Belgium, but their hopes turned to ashes when the White House offered nothing but declarations of neutrality, hollow promises that satisfied many of their neighbors but broke the DeSmedts' hearts.

Together with sympathetic friends and fellow expatriates from Belgium and France, the DeSmedt women raised funds for refugees and supported Red Cross campaigns to provide food, essential goods, and medical care to the suffering. Though women had the vote in California and Hilde and their parents were of age, they were not naturalized citizens, so they were powerless to help elect officials who rejected Wilson's policy of neutrality. Instead they did what they could to raise money and awareness, and in time their horror faded to a constant, dull ache. Life went on, though to Valerie it seemed more fragile than before.

Ten months after Germany invaded Belgium, Valerie graduated from high school, and that autumn, she entered college. She had always loved math, and the University of Southern California accepted girls into their program, so her parents encouraged her to follow her heart. For one thrilling, illuminating, wonderful year, Valerie reveled in learning, commuting to campus in the morning, attending classes and lectures and labs throughout the day, and returning home with books and assignments she pored over from the time the supper dishes were cleared away until she could scarcely keep her eyes open and her mother ordered her to bed.

Henri, who was exactly one year and one month younger than Valerie, hung on every word of her tales of campus life, and he resolved to follow her to USC the next fall. Like her he was mathematically inclined, but he preferred all things mechanical to numbers and theorems on a page. He mused aloud about studying physics or engineering, but it was no secret to his family that his true passion was photography and filmography. He had toddled after his father on photography shoots from the time he could walk, and had experimented with his father's old camera as soon as he was old enough to be trusted not to break it. On his own, he had transformed his bedroom closet into a darkroom, and whenever he was not in school, he could be found shadowing his father on movie sets, observing everything, asking questions, carrying equipment and fetching coffee for the crew in exchange for impromptu lessons and advice. No one would have been surprised if he had asked to apprentice with his father instead of going on to college, but soon after he received his diploma, Valerie's mother confided that she and Papa were relieved that Henri had decided to attend the university. "He can always pursue filmography after he graduates, if he wants to," her mother said, "but with a college degree, he'll be far more likely to find a good, steady job with a reliable paycheck. Even as popular as movies are becoming, that kind of security is in short supply in the motion picture business."

Since it was Henri's choice, Valerie was inclined to agree. As for herself, she had no idea what career opportunities might exist for a girl with a degree in mathematics, but she was confident that she would figure it out when the time came. In the meantime, she was learning loads and earning top marks in her classes and having a wonderful time. Despite the war across the sea, and the rising discord in their adopted country between preparedness advocates and isolationists, Valerie had every reason to hope that her future, and her family's, remained full of promise.

Then tragedy shattered the illusion that they had ever truly been safe and protected.

Valerie's father was filming on a set in the Santa Monica Mountains when he complained of a tingling in his left arm and collapsed. Later, his grieving family would be told that he had not survived the winding, precarious drive to the nearest hospital. He had always meant to buy life insurance, but he had not expected to die of a heart attack in his midforties, and he had left behind only a very small savings, as Valerie discovered when her mother asked her to review her father's ledgers. Edgar offered to pay some outstanding debts, but while their mother was touched by his generosity, she and Hilde agreed that it would be inappropriate to accept money from a suitor, even if they euphemistically called it a loan. Hilde tried to find work, but her accent and limited literacy in English left her with few options other than domestic service or tutoring in French and German, neither of which could support the family.

Decisions had to be made quickly. Their mother invested some of the precious savings into refurbishing the house so she could take in lodgers, dividing the attic into two small bedrooms for the children, fitting a narrow bed into the sewing room for herself. Valerie and Henri posted signs on the USC campus offering room and board, plus French and German lessons, if desired, for an additional fee. By early August, the bedrooms and the converted living room had been leased to several students and a visiting professor.

Her mother's second decision dealt Valerie a heavier blow, and demanded a far greater sacrifice than giving up her bedroom for the cramped attic with its sloped ceiling that made it impossible to stand up straight anywhere but in the center.

She knew something was up one afternoon in mid-August when her mother invited her outside for a chat, and she found Hilde already waiting for them on the bench in the shade of the orange and lemon trees. "What's going on?" she asked, immediately wary, trying and failing to keep her voice light.

Her mother gestured for her to sit, but Valerie didn't budge, so, with a sigh, her mother took the seat next to Hilde. "You've kept the books since your father passed"—her mother paused to take a shaky breath—"so you know the dire state of our finances."

Valerie nodded, shifted her weight from one foot to the other, folded her arms, and waited, dreading the words to come.

"We can only afford one college tuition," Hilde said. "You must have realized this already."

A knot tightened in Valerie's throat. "It did occur to me," she managed to say.

"We hoped—*I* hoped—you would be willing to give up your education for Henri's sake." Her mother's eyes implored her to understand. "I know it's not fair, after you've worked so hard and done so well, but Henri is a young man."

"He'll have to support himself and a family someday," Hilde broke in. "He needs a college education more than you do."

"You do understand, don't you, dear?" Her mother regarded her steadily, but she clenched and unclenched her hands in her lap, loathing what she had to say as much as Valerie dreaded hearing it. "For Henri, a degree may mean the difference between success and failure, but for you—well, it's not the same. You'll quit work when you marry. Your husband will support you and your children."

Valerie resisted the urge to point out that her father's unexpected inability to support them was what had brought them to that unhappy moment. Nothing she said would make any difference. She knew they could barely afford one college tuition; two was out of the question. How could she deny her little brother his opportunity when, truth be told, employers were hardly clamoring for girl mathematicians? Whatever job *she* was likely to be offered, she could probably get it with a high school diploma and a letter of recommendation. Henri, on the other hand, would never become an engineer or a physicist without years of study and a college degree.

Besides, it was her mother's money to spend, and clearly she had already decided how to spend it. The only real decision Valerie faced was whether to accept her disappointment with selfless grace, or to concede bitterly and make an unfair, unhappy situation absolutely miserable for everyone.

"Of course I'll do it," she said. "You're right. It really is the best way forward for all of us."

She waited a week just in case a windfall of cash miraculously rained down from the skies, but when that failed to happen, she withdrew from USC. First, though, she insisted that no one tell Henri until the check for his first semester's tuition cleared and there was no turning back. Sure enough, once Henri found out that Valerie intended to sacrifice her education for his, he was stung by the injustice, and angered that he had been left entirely out of the decision. When he argued that they could probably convince the bursar to transfer the payment from his account to hers, Valerie just laughed, tousled his blond curls, and teased, "We could do that, or you could just say thank you, and promise me that I'll always be your favorite sister. I've earned it."

"Thank you, Valerie," he said, solemn and abashed. Her took her hands and held her gaze, his dark blue eyes so much like their father's. "I promise I'll make you proud of me."

"Of course you will." She hugged him, blinking away tears before he noticed them. "I already am."

So Henri went off to college, and Valerie set out to find work. Thanks to a tip from a neighbor for whom she had often babysat and run errands, she soon landed an interview with the Pacific Telephone and Telegraph Company. She knew her credentials were impressive, she had always been a good talker, and she knew how to dress for a part, so she was not entirely surprised when she was offered a job on the spot. "You're the very ideal of the girl with a smile in her voice," the supervising operator enthused, reaching across the desk to shake her hand vigorously. Two days later, Valerie was learning how to work the switchboard at one of the busiest telephone exchanges in Los Angeles, the new company headquarters on South Hill Street.

Soon thereafter, just as the DeSmedts were getting back on their feet, Edgar was offered a wonderful promotion that would require him to move to the Southern Pacific Railroad headquarters in San Francisco. He asked Hilde to accompany him as his wife.

Valerie was thrilled for her sister—and utterly stunned when Hilde refused him. "But you love Edgar," Valerie protested, as their mother tearfully begged Hilde to reconsider.

"I'm needed here," Hilde replied, looking dazed but resolute. "Mama can't run the boardinghouse without me."

"I can look after Mama," said Valerie. "Who cares about the boardinghouse? You'll marry Edgar, we'll sell this place, and we'll buy something smaller and more affordable. Don't sacrifice your future happiness on our account."

"*You* did."

"That's different. I traded one career for another. I didn't give up the man I love!"

But Hilde had made up her mind, and nothing Valerie and their mother said would dissuade her. Heartbroken, Edgar moved to San Francisco, and although at first he wrote to Hilde often, Valerie had no idea whether her sister ever responded. Eventually the letters stopped coming.

It was such a foolish waste of love, and although Valerie would never hurt her sister by saying so, she remained convinced that the sacrifice had been entirely unnecessary. Valerie's plan to economize would have been enough to keep them afloat until Henri graduated and began bringing in a salary. And if Hilde was nobly giving up what she held most dear because Valerie had and it was only fair that they suffered equally—well, that was utter nonsense. Valerie was hardly suffering. Sometimes she wondered what career in mathematics she might have pursued if things had gone differently, but whenever such idle musings crept into her head, she swept them aside. After a year with Pacific Telephone and Telegraph, she could honestly say that she loved her job, and she felt only the occasional pang of regret that she had not earned her college degree. What other work would have been as exciting as being a telephone operator, where the pace never let up, every second counted, and there was absolutely no room for error? And where would she have found coworkers and friends as lively, fun, and smart as the girls with whom she shared the switchboards? Some of them were immigrants, like herself, or the daughters of immigrants; others were Golden State born and bred; but they were all independent young women full of ambition and hope and grit, and Valerie fit right in.

Her spirits were much improved by the time she got off the trolley and walked the last block and a half to the six-story Italianate structure of concrete and steel that housed the Pac-Tel exchange. She greeted a few acquaintances who had happened to arrive at the same time, and together they crossed the lobby and left their purses and hats in the operators' lounge, which was tucked away on the first floor behind the administrative offices. Then, with minutes to spare, they all darted off to their stations at the switchboards, which filled the second, third, and fourth floors. Above that, the two highest floors were entirely devoted to electrical equipment.

The hours passed swiftly, sped along by continuous waves of calls. Valerie had not a moment to spare chatting with friends or discussing their plans for after work, not that she would have allowed her attention to stray from the lights and switches, leaving a hapless caller ringing in vain. Not when Mrs. Johnson was on duty as supervising operator, anyway. Unlike Mrs. Clark, who had been charmed by the "smile in her voice," Mrs. Johnson interpreted Valerie's sunny attitude and cheerful grin as signs of a frivolous mind. Valerie's blonde curls, blue eyes, and fondness for pretty frocks probably contributed to her prejudice. If Mrs. Johnson knew how much Valerie adored the elegant perfection of a good geometric proof and passed the time waiting in lines silently going through the Fibonacci sequence, she would probably have fainted from sheer astonishment. Valerie honestly didn't give a fig what her sourpuss boss thought of her, except where her performance at the switchboard was concerned. Not even Mrs. Johnson could find fault with her there.

Valerie's break, halfway through her shift, was the first chance she had to catch up with Cora and the other girls. They collected their lunches from the lounge and settled themselves on a small patch of lawn alongside the building to eat and chat while basking in the sunshine. After they had thoroughly analyzed every detail of a dinner party Mabel had attended at the home of her most recent beau, the conversation turned to the worrisome possibility that he might enlist, and from there, to all the other young men they knew who had answered President Wilson's call to arms. Not nearly enough young men had, apparently, for in May, Congress had passed a new Selective Service Act. While any man between the ages of eighteen and forty could volunteer to serve, all male citizens between the ages of twenty-one and thirty, inclusive, were required to register for the draft. The War Department had learned hard lessons from the Civil War, and this time around it was no longer permitted to purchase an exemption or hire a substitute to fight in one's place. Men working in certain occupations essential to the war effort were exempt from the draft, but university students were not, nor were only sons of widowed mothers, as many families had hoped. Valerie would have been desperately worried for Henri except that at nineteen, he was safe from the draft, even though he had become a naturalized citizen after their father passed. She only hoped the war would end in a decisive victory for the Allies well before his twenty-first birthday.

"Men have all the adventures," lamented Irene, absently wrapping a strand of her thick auburn hair around her finger and releasing the curl in a spiral spring. "I wish we girls could do our bit for our country."

"We can and we do," Cora replied, tucking a strand of her crimped black bob behind one ear. "Red Cross nurses are already Over There setting up hospitals."

"I could never be a nurse." Irene shuddered. "The sight of blood makes me ill."

"You're too young, anyway," said Mabel. "My sister applied. She's a registered nurse, but they turned her down. They only want mature women twenty-five years of age or older, sensible matrons who won't distract the soldiers from their duties."

Irene pulled a face. "Did they bother to ask the soldiers what *they* want?"

"There are girls serving with the Salvation Army, the YWCA, and the YMCA," said Valerie, finishing the last bite of the strawberry jam and farmer's cheese sandwich her mother had made for her. "Can you serve coffee and doughnuts? Set up a cozy reading room? Play endless games of checkers? Look pretty in a khaki suit?"

Irene nodded, thoughtful. "I could do all that."

"You don't need to go Over There to do your bit," said Mabel. "You don't even need to find a new line of work. Mrs. Johnson told me they're looking for telephone girls to work the switchboards at the army training camps they've built for all the new recruits in the Midwest and on the East Coast."

"Is that so?" said Cora.

Mabel nodded. "Word is, they've trained soldiers to do the work, but they just aren't as good at it as we are."

The operators laughed, delighted. "Oh, the poor fellows," said Cora. "Maybe they just need more practice."

"They probably resent being assigned to do women's work," said Valerie, selecting the plumpest, reddest dried apricot from among those her mother had packed. "Maybe they figure that if they perform badly enough, they'll be reassigned."

"Oh, that's rich," said Mabel. "Would they rather scrub latrines or peel potatoes?"

"I'm sure our boys are doing the best they can," said Irene stoutly. "They can't help it if we girls are just, well, better!"

The friends dissolved into laughter again.

"As bad as the telephone service may be at the army training camps, I hear it's even worse Over There," said Mabel. "When General Pershing arrived in France in June, he was absolutely horrified by the outdated equipment. They're practically working with antiques, even in Paris, and the French operators are dreadful. They don't care about keeping a smile in their voices, and they don't understand the meaning of the word *efficiency*. If you don't engage them in pleasant chitchat before you ask them to connect you, they'll berate you and pull the plug."

"They wouldn't dare," said Cora, wide-eyed. "Would they? It's wartime. A dropped call could cost lives."

Mabel shrugged. "I'm just telling you what I heard. French phone service is the worst." She glanced at Valerie. "No offense."

"None taken. I'm Belgian." Valerie gathered up the remains of her lunch, got to her feet, and brushed crumbs and bits of grass from her skirt. "Are we still on for dinner after work? We could take the Red Line to Venice Beach and find a nice café."

"I'm in," Mabel declared, and the others quickly assented, except for Irene, who had to work an early shift the next day and needed her beauty sleep. Mindful of the time, they hurried back to the operators' lounge, took turns inspecting themselves in the small mirror above the sink, and returned to the switchboards.

The afternoon seemed to pass more slowly than the morning had, now that tantalizing plans awaited her at the end of her shift, but when Valerie connected her last call and relinquished her station to another girl, she found Mrs. Johnson waiting for her in the hallway outside the room.

As her friends threw Valerie curious glances in passing, Mrs. Johnson handed her a folded piece of paper. "I'll remind you that operators are not supposed to receive personal calls during their shifts," she said primly. "I took a message. I won't write you up this time, because it does seem to be an emergency."

Valerie's heart plummeted. "Thank you," she murmured, unfolding the paper as she continued toward the lounge. Mrs. Johnson had taken down only a few vague phrases, but the meaning was clear: Hilde needed her at home right away.

Her sister was well enough to place a call, Valerie thought, quickening her pace. That meant the emergency was with their mother, or Henri, or both. Heart pounding, she burst into the lounge, snatched up her hat and purse, breathlessly made excuses to her friends, and hurried off to catch the southbound trolley. The wait seemed interminable, the ride even more so, but eventually she reached her stop and her own block and finally her own front door. Darting inside, she startled two of their lodgers playing chess in the front room. She looked around wildly for her family and raced off to the kitchen. There she found her mother seated at the table wiping away tears; Hilde in a chair pulled up close, her arm around their mother's shoulders; and Henri pacing, hands thrust in his pockets, his expression mutinous and abashed.

"What's going on?" Valerie exclaimed, letting her purse slide from her shoulder to the floor, overwhelmed with relief that they were all alive and apparently unharmed.

Her mother looked up at her through her tears, bereft, and shook her head.

"Henri has enlisted," said Hilde grimly.

For a moment Valerie couldn't breathe. "What?"

"This morning he didn't go to campus to pick up his schedule," her sister said, her eyes bleak, her voice trembling. "He went to a recruiter's office. He's joined the American Expeditionary Forces."

"But—" Valerie closed her eyes, pressed a hand to her heart, and steeled herself. Only then did she look to her brother. "But why? You're safe from the draft. Classes start next week. You didn't have to do this."

"I'm old enough to volunteer. I want to do my bit," he said, his gaze entreating. "It's our country being blown to bits by the Hun, our people being driven from their homes—hungry, desperate, dying. I'm an American now, but I'm Belgian too, and that makes this fight mine as much as anyone's." He paused, clenching his jaw. Valerie realized then that he had expected a much different reaction to his exciting news—surprise, yes, but then joyful embraces and praise for his patriotic courage. "I—I thought you would be proud of me."

Their mother sobbed and pressed her handkerchief to her mouth.

"We *are* proud of you," Valerie forced herself to say. She crossed the room to embrace her brother. "Of course we are. You just caught us by surprise, that's all."

He pulled away so he could study her face. "Really?"

She pressed her lips together, forced a smile, and nodded, not trusting herself to speak.

He grinned, relieved, and hugged her so hard her heels lifted off the floor. She closed her eyes and held him close, fighting back tears, wanting to scold him, to shake him, to make him undo what he had done, as if he could, as if he would not consider it a crushing betrayal if she asked.

3

NOVEMBER 1917

Cincinnati

MARIE

Either Dr. Kunwald had forgotten their appointment, he had met with some unfortunate calamity, or, unbeknownst to her, Marie's audition was actually in progress at that very moment. Perhaps rather than being forty minutes late, the conductor was secretly observing her from the wings, judging her poise and adaptability when confronted with the unexpected. But such trickery seemed highly improbable from the dignified, punctilious maestro, a consummate professional and a good friend of her parents.

Where was he, then?

Marie might have assumed that she had put the wrong date on her calendar, except that the choir director had arrived on time. Mr. Nichols sat alone, second row center of the renowned Emery Theater, leafing through a folder of sheet music and sparing an occasional glance for his watch, his thinning blond hair and wire-rimmed spectacles making him seem older than his forty-odd years. The accompanist had also shown up as expected, and was seated at the piano behind Marie and a bit off to stage right. He seemed to be around her own age, a conservatory student perhaps, and his dark locks tumbled over his forehead as he quietly ran through passages of Marie's songs, keeping his fingers limber. As for herself, she had arrived early, had warmed up backstage, and had performed all the little rituals that helped calm her nerves before an important concert. And now she sat onstage in the folding chair Mr. Nichols had brought out for her when Dr. Kunwald was merely fifteen minutes late, trying not to fidget or frown or become tearfully despondent as the minutes ticked by.

Surely he was on his way. Any moment now Dr. Kunwald would stride down the aisle, apologize profusely, and beg her to sing for him. When she finished, his profound embarrassment for keeping her waiting would compel him to immediately invite her to join the symphony chorus. She'd rather be accepted on the merits of her talent alone, but after a discouraging summer audition season, she'd take the spot however she could get it.

She shifted in the uncomfortable chair, and when Mr. Nichols caught her eye, she smiled, hoping she looked more at ease than she felt, even as her elegant blue silk taffeta concert gown with the low neckline and the ruffled train wrinkled beneath her, as her nerves frayed and her vocal cords became incrementally less supple. Her dark brown hair, arranged in a Psyche knot and adorned with pearls and satin ribbon the color of her gown, seemed a weighty extravagance now. If her audition didn't begin soon, she would be late for work, even if the streetcar made the run from Over-the-Rhine to Hartwell in record time. If Dr. Kunwald didn't show up at all, it would break her heart.

"I'm terribly sorry, Miss Miossec," Mr. Nichols called up to her, looking pained. "Dr. Kunwald is ordinarily very punctual. He must have been unavoidably detained, for I know he intended to be here. Would you care to warm up again?"

"Yes, I think I should." She rose, smoothed her dress, and took her place at center stage. To the accompanist she added, "The Vaccai, please, page four."

She had almost finished the second of two exercises when a door at the back of the house opened and Dr. Kunwald entered, still in his coat and carrying a briefcase. She continued to sing as he briskly approached the stage, but she noted that his mouth was fixed in a hard line and his hackles were raised, giving every impression of a man greatly inconvenienced.

Her heart sank, but when her voice faltered, Dr. Kunwald threw her a tight smile and waved her on. "Please continue, my dear. I'll be ready for you in a moment." He set down his briefcase in the aisle and shrugged off his coat. Taking a handkerchief from a pocket, he scrubbed his hands vigorously, first one and then the other. Marie glimpsed dark stains on his fingertips.

"What's the matter, Kunwald?" Mr. Nichols asked him, brow furrowing.

"What's the matter?" Dr. Kunwald shook his head, exasperated. "This morning, I was enjoying some coffee and strudel at a café near the conservatory when a pair of city police officers demanded that I accompany them to headquarters. There, I and two other gentlemen seized at the café were obliged to register as unnaturalized aliens." He folded his handkerchief, tucked it into his pocket, and held up his right hand, grimacing. "They fingerprinted me, and took *Polizeifoto*"—he gestured, grasping for the English word—"mug shots, as if I were a common hoodlum."

"Good heavens," Mr. Nichols exclaimed. "But you're Austrian. We aren't at war with Austria."

"Perhaps in their ignorance, they failed to discern the difference. More likely, they did not care. I speak German, after all, and before I came to Ohio, I lived for many years in Germany."

"Even so, we're a nation of laws," Mr. Nichols said, indignant. "Surely some probable cause must be required. You didn't inadvertently violate the Sedition Act, did you?"

"Certainly not. I know better than to criticize the president or complain about the draft among strangers. Although I suppose someone could have reported me for remarks they overheard when I thought I was speaking among sympathetic friends." Catching himself, he eyed Marie and the accompanist, and gave them each a curt nod. Turning back to the choir director, he added, "Perhaps they recognized me. My

Austrian heritage is no secret. Or perhaps they saw the Goethe text I was perusing, all those suspicious umlauts and ligatures." Muttering under his breath in German, he settled into the aisle seat and regarded Marie expectantly. "Well. On to business. My apologies for the delay, Miss Miossec. I trust you're warmed up and ready to delight us." He looked to Mr. Nichols. "If you care to take things from here?"

With that, her audition began. When prompted by the choral director, she first sang "Ici-bas!" by Gabriel Fauré, followed by Schubert's "Nacht und Träume." The Emery Theater was famed for its magnificent acoustics, considered second only to New York's Carnegie Hall. Marie made the most of it, thrilling to the way her voice carried from the stage, remembering her mother's most recent appearance there and the thunderous crash of applause and cries for an encore that had filled the hall afterward. Marie's small audience was far more reserved, smiling slightly and thanking her at the conclusion of each piece, but otherwise revealing nothing. Next Mr. Nichols asked her to perform a series of scales, and then he took over at the piano to test her tonal memory. Lastly, Dr. Kunwald gave her two pages from the middle of a score to sight-sing; although the title was missing, she quickly recognized the "Alleluia" from Mozart's *Exsultate, jubilate.* Although she had never sung the piece before, her mother occasionally had, and the familiarity, though slight, was enough to settle her nerves and allow her voice to soar.

When she finished, she clasped her hands demurely behind her back and awaited their judgment.

"Are you still at the conservatory, Miss Miossec?" Dr. Kunwald asked.

"I graduated in May."

Both men nodded. They conferred quietly for a moment, their voices too low for her to discern more than a few simple words. "Thank you, Miss Miossec," Mr. Nichols eventually said. "We'll let you know soon."

It was over. Marie inhaled deeply, bowed and thanked them, and thanked the accompanist as well. By the time she gathered up her sheet music, the two older men were so engrossed in conversation that it seemed they had quite forgotten her.

"Good luck," the accompanist told her in an undertone. "You were brilliant."

"Thank you," she replied, heartened, but she had no time to bask in the compliment. Gathering up her train, she hurried backstage, seized the handle of the satchel she had hidden behind the curtain, and hurried off to the dressing room to change into something more suitable for work.

She would surely be late, she lamented silently as she closed the dressing room door behind her with her foot. Out of the lovely and expensive gown, which she carefully folded in tissue paper to protect the delicate fabric from snags. She had worn the gown, a generous graduation gift from her parents, only once before, at her senior recital at the Music Hall. She had worn less glamorous dresses to the various auditions she'd had in the interim, but since each had ended in rejection, that morning she had decided to wear the blue silk for good luck. Removing her work clothes from the satchel, she tucked the gown carefully inside with her music folder and quickly slipped into her light gray suit and white blouse, trading her graceful heels for a pair of high-buttoned boots. She removed the pearls and hair ribbons from her coiffure, but since she could not spare the time to arrange her hair into a simpler style, she otherwise left it in place. A lock came free as she was pulling on her coat, dangling inconveniently in front of her left eye, but she tucked it behind her ear, tugged on her coat and hat, snatched up her satchel, and hurried off to catch the streetcar.

A cool gust of wind took her breath away as she climbed aboard, holding on to her hat with one hand, hauling her satchel with the other. She struggled to keep on her feet as the streetcar started up while she was still making her way down the aisle. She sank into the first empty seat, the satchel half on her lap, and muffled a rueful laugh. She'd had worse auditions. If not for Dr. Kunwald's foul mood and the disconcerting delay, she would have been fairly optimistic about her chances. Still, she couldn't quite silence the nagging doubts that she wasn't as talented and well trained as she had once believed, and that the only reason anyone offered her auditions anymore was as a favor to her much-admired parents.

Whatever happened, she could take heart in knowing that she had done her best under less than ideal circumstances. From the sound of it, Dr. Kunwald's morning had gone far worse than hers, and he had every right to be angry and indignant.

President Wilson's most recent proclamation against "enemy aliens" was scarcely a week old, but already Marie had observed its troubling consequences. Her family was unaffected, as they hailed from an allied nation, but German immigrant men who did not report voluntarily were being rounded up from their homes and workplaces and brought in to register, as Dr. Kunwald had. Germans were no longer permitted to become American citizens, and they were subject to a myriad of new restrictions forbidding them to enter the District of Columbia, or to ride in an airplane, or to travel upon the water except on a public ferry, and so many other prohibitions that Marie could hardly remember them all. It astounded her that millions of people with German ancestry who had been living peacefully in the United States for years had, almost overnight, become suspected spies and saboteurs.

Lost in thought, she only gradually became aware of the man in the seat behind her, who had been speaking increasingly loudly as the streetcar headed north. "Hey, girlie," he suddenly barked, his voice shattering her reverie. "I'm talking to you."

She glanced over her shoulder, and for the briefest of moments she was relieved to discover that he was not addressing her, but had turned around in his seat to berate the woman sitting behind him. "Hey," he snapped, as the woman, a blonde perhaps a few years older than Marie, regarded him warily. "Don't you sprecken zee English?"

Color rose in the woman's cheeks. "I speak English fine," she replied steadily, with no trace of a foreign accent Marie could discern, "but I try to avoid conversations with rude strangers."

"Baloney," he scoffed. "Where are you from?"

Marie silently urged her not to respond, but the woman said, "Price Hill."

"No, where are you *really* from?" He reached over the seatback and snatched a newspaper from her lap. "Why are you reading this Hun rag if you're a red, white, and blue American?"

Indignant, Marie glanced to the front of the streetcar, hoping the conductor would intervene, but he had probably heard nothing over the clatter of the rails and the passing traffic. The woman reached for her newspaper, but the man held it out of reach, first to one side and then the other. Nearby a few passengers observed the scene, smirking, but most studiously peered out the windows or stared at their own newspapers, feigning ignorance.

Marie felt a flame of anger kindle in her chest. Without thinking, she snatched up her satchel, made her way down the aisle, and slipped into the seat next to the blonde. "Hello," she said brightly, as if she were greeting an old friend. Before the man could react, she grabbed the newspaper from his hand. "Are you finished with this? Thank you so much." She returned it to the woman. "I believe this belongs to you."

"Thank you," the woman replied, dumbfounded.

"My pleasure." Marie glanced at the masthead and read the title in blackletter type—*Tägliches Cincinnatier Volksblatt*, a popular local newspaper. "May I ask what you were reading before you were so rudely interrupted?"

The woman hesitated, then turned a few pages and gestured to a column. "This."

Marie was not perfectly fluent in German, but she knew quite a lot. "Marriage announcements?"

The woman nodded.

"Hey," the man broke in, annoyed.

Marie ignored him. "Anyone you know?" she asked her companion.

"This bride is my cousin," she said, indicating a paragraph above the fold. "I promised my aunt I would pick up an extra copy for her scrapbook."

"Hey," the man snapped. "I'm talking to—"

"Yes?" Marie inquired, smiling up at him. "May I help you?"

"You can help me by burning that Hun rag." He planted his beefy hands on the back of his seat and glowered down at them. "This is America. We only want American newspapers here."

"I don't understand." Feigning confusion, Marie pointed at the world *Cincinnatier* in the title. "This is printed just over the river in Covington. It *is* an American newspaper."

"You got a smart mouth, don't you? Your friend is a Hun. You read Hun papers. That makes you a Hun too."

"My passport says otherwise, but how can I argue with such unassailable logic?" Marie offered a helpless, girlish shrug. "Sir, you are as clever as you are charming."

Her companion pressed a gloved hand to her mouth to conceal a smile, but the man, frowning suspiciously at Marie, appeared not to notice. "Thank you," he eventually said, uncertain.

"Don't mention it," said Marie. "Ever. Really."

"This is my stop," the woman murmured.

Marie stood up to let her pass, but on second thought, she disembarked with her, in case the man decided to follow.

"Thank you," the woman said as they stood on the sidewalk watching the streetcar pull away. "You're very kind."

"I never could tolerate a bully." Marie extended her hand. "I'm Marie."

"Ursula." The woman shook her hand. "You're French."

"Yes."

Ursula hesitated. "I should tell you . . . I lied, back there."

"Oh?"

"I was born in Bremen. My parents brought me to America as a child. I am German."

Marie puffed a breath and shrugged. "What of it? Of course you didn't feel safe telling that horrible man the truth."

"I wanted you to know, though." Ursula studied her. "I hope you don't regret defending me."

"Not at all." Marie drew back her sleeve and glanced at her watch. "But now I really must go. Take care. *Auf wiedersehen*."

Ursula smiled. "*Au revoir*."

Marie turned to go, but something compelled her to pause and glance over her shoulder as Ursula crossed the street and continued down the block, some need to reassure herself that all would be well. How swiftly and insidiously the fear and hatred of war had begun to transform her adopted city. She hardly dared imagine how much worse the paranoia and mistrust might become until it was all over.

Anyone who believed that an ocean could protect the United States from the grim terrors of war was a fool. They would probably escape the worst of it, but its cold fingers would clutch at them even here. It was already happening.

Marie had disembarked two blocks short of her usual stop, and she quickened her pace to make up time. She was already five minutes late, and depending upon who was on duty as supervising operator, she might receive a written reprimand in her file. It would be an unfortunate blemish on a previously flawless record. Although she had worked for Cincinnati Telephone and Telegraph barely five months, she had moved from trainee to operator ahead of schedule, so well had she impressed her superiors with her dulcet tones, impeccable manners, quintessential "smile in her voice," and remarkable ability to decipher callers' accents, no matter how thick or obscure, an asset in a city with such a large and diverse immigrant population. Marie credited her musical training as well as her French heritage for that talent, which she had never considered a remarkable gift until her American-born acquaintances marveled at it.

Her parents had not wanted her to take a job after graduation. Her mother in particular had urged her to focus on her music as an independent scholar while continuing to audition for choirs and opera companies. Even that was a significant revision of Marie's original plan, which was to graduate from the conservatory, accompany her mother on an extensive tour of the United Kingdom, Scandinavia, and Europe, audition for dozens of opera companies along the way, and accept the most promising offer. The war had shattered that dream. Cincinnati had no permanent opera company, nor did any other city in the American Midwest. She had not passed the audition for a traveling company based in

Chicago, and her impressive pedigree had earned her a cordial letter in reply to her inquiry to the Metropolitan Opera in New York, but no invitation to audition. After a few weeks, discouraged but not entirely without hope, Marie resolved to find work so she could contribute to the household expenses while searching out new possibilities.

"Your job is music," her mother protested. "You'll strain your voice talking on the phone all day." Unlike so many other, less fortunate girls, Marie did not need to earn a living. Her parents would be happy to provide for her as they always had; it was their duty and their delight, for they wanted only her happiness. But Marie could not bear to be a burden, however beloved, and she was determined to earn her keep. The telephone operator position became available at the perfect time, and since the girls were permitted to swap shifts, she could arrange her schedule around her auditions—which, truth be told, were becoming increasingly few and far between.

She was a full quarter hour late by the time she arrived at the Valley Exchange in Hartwell, one of the newer buildings, constructed a few years before to accommodate increased telephone service in the growing northern neighborhoods. Swiftly, but without drawing undo attention, Marie passed the administrative offices, left her things in the operators' lounge, and hurried off to punch her time card—only to discover that it was not in the slot where she had left it. A quick search confirmed that a thoughtful friend had punched it for her, a minute before she had been due at the switchboard. If Marie could reach her station unnoticed, her supervisor would be none the wiser.

For the first time all day, luck was on her side. "You are an angel," she murmured to her friend Ethel as she took her place in the next seat over, donned her headset, and adjusted the mouthpiece.

"You would have done the same for me," said Ethel, pulling the plug on a finished call and doing a double take at the sight of Marie's elegant coiffure. "My goodness, look at you. And all for an ordinary afternoon shift. You French girls sure have style."

"I must do my part to keep up our international reputation," Marie replied, responding to a blinking light by swiftly inserting a plug in the proper jack. "Number, please."

A half hour passed before she and Ethel were able to talk again. "I was right about the phone service Over There," Ethel said in an undertone. "Didn't I say weeks ago that something was in the works with the army?"

"In the works?" Marie echoed, puzzled. Every operator knew that when General Pershing had arrived in France back in June, he had been dismayed by the state of telephone service there—the outdated equipment, the failing switchboards, the scarcity of intact wires and poles, and the limited number of skilled operators. Apparently the army had tried to train soldiers, former telegraph operators, to run the switchboards, but the men were said to be slow, inefficient, and inaccurate, frustrating the officers who expected the same swift, flawless service they enjoyed back in the States. But that was old news, hardly worth the eager sparkle in Ethel's eyes. "Do you mean our Reserve Signal Corps boys sailing for France?"

"No, not that. The poster. Didn't you see the poster hanging in the lounge?"

Marie shook her head. "I was in such a hurry that I only had time to—" A light blinked; she snatched up a cable and inserted the plug. "Number, please."

After that, the calls came in so steadily that there was never a lull long enough for Marie to ask Ethel to explain. What was Ethel referring to if not the work of the Reserve Signal Corps? As far back as January, even before the United States had joined the war, executives at the highest levels of American Telephone and Telegraph, their parent company, had forged a partnership with the U.S. Army to organize their skilled technical workers into reserve battalions that would be prepared to go to war as soon as they were needed. Their foresight proved invaluable, for General Pershing had no sooner discovered the antiquated state of the telephone system he was obliged to lease from the French than he realized he must construct an entirely new system using superior American technology, a wire network running hundreds of miles throughout France, connecting headquarters to essential outposts and bases. Earlier that fall, two American Expeditionary Forces battalions had begun construction, raising poles to hang lines in some locations, resorting to tree branches or fenceposts where poles were impractical or unavailable, or running wires through dedicated trenches closer to the front. It was extremely hazardous work, leaving linemen dangerously exposed to sniper fire while working atop the poles and trees, or requiring them to crawl out into no-man's-land to repair lines cut by the enemy.

It was not until she and Ethel left the switchboards for their dinner break that Marie was able to ask her friend what she was talking about. "The army needs us," Ethel said earnestly, linking her arm through Marie's as they set out for the operators' lounge. "Or rather, they need you, because as much as I'd love to apply, I lack one essential qualification."

"Qualification for what?" Marie asked.

In reply, Ethel led Marie to a small, plain poster hanging near the door to the cloakroom, understated black type on white paper, with no illustration.

"'Army Wants Women to Serve as Switchboard Soldiers,'" Marie read the headline aloud. Astonished, she paused and turned to Ethel, who grinned and gestured for her to continue reading.

The U.S. Army was urgently recruiting qualified women telephone operators fluent in French to serve in the Signal Corps as part of the American Expeditionary Forces in France. For this essential overseas war work, the Signal Corps sought levelheaded young women who were resourceful, were able to exercise good judgment in emergencies, and were willing to work hard and endure hazardous conditions if necessary. Applicants who passed the initial screening would be required to undergo extensive training and to pass examinations in French and telephone operations to qualify as Signal Corps telephone operators. These "switchboard soldiers" would enjoy the same status and privileges as nurses, would be required to wear standard uniforms as specified by the War College, and in every respect would be considered as soldiers, coming under military restrictions at all times.

"Doesn't it sound exciting?" Ethel sighed, wistful. "Unfortunately I don't qualify."

Marie's gaze was fixed on the poster. "Because you don't exercise good judgment?"

Ethel nudged her. "No, silly. Because I don't speak French. But you do."

"Yes, I do." Marie read the poster over again more carefully, noting the requirements, the application procedures, the pay, the warnings, the appeals to pride and patriotism. She had the exact skills they urgently needed. She was precisely what they were looking for—and it was the first time throughout the long, disappointing months of auditions she had been able to say that.

Her heart ached whenever she thought of the terror and suffering the Germans were inflicting upon her beloved France. The war was already beginning to change her adopted city into a grimmer, crueler version of itself, as fear, suspicion, and anger turned neighbors against one another.

Now fate had presented her with the means to make a difference, to help the Allies win the war, to speed the end of the horrific violence and destruction, to restore peace to the world.

How could she ignore the call?

4

December 1917–January 1918

Passaic, New Jersey, and New York City

GRACE

A few days after the United States declared war on Germany, Grace's brother enlisted, just as she had expected. Soon thereafter when Eugene was required to report for duty, her parents' proud smiles trembled as they all saw him off at the train station, so eager to do his bit, to fight for democracy. A week later, he wrote to tell them that he had been mustered into the 77th Field Artillery Regiment and was training at Fort Ethan Allen in Vermont. The days were long and the work fatiguing, but he had made several good chums among the men in his battery, who were all hale, hearty, and eager to liberate Belgium and France. The barracks were more comfortable than he had expected and the food worse, so he would be grateful for any homemade treats they could send.

In early fall, the 77th was moved to Camp Green, near Charlotte, North Carolina, where it was attached to the 4th Division of the regular army. French and British officers who had served in the trenches had been brought in to train the recruits for what they would face Over There. Eugene still had no idea when his regiment might ship out. Some officers said it could be weeks, others said months, and most grumbled that they shouldn't be so hasty to depart. "I agree we have a lot to learn before we could be considered battle ready," Eugene wrote. "There is more mathematics and physics involved in the operation of our heavy guns than one might have expected. And my but they are loud! Our ears ring for hours afterward."

Back home, the family was heartened by Eugene's buoyant tone, but for Grace, his words evoked harrowing images of muddy trenches, shell craters, gas clouds, and barbed wire strung across desolate landscapes. She had always looked out for her younger brother, the two middle children joining forces so that neither would feel overlooked, but now she was powerless to help him, and she could hardly bear it.

Nor could she bear to leave her parents to move in with friends when it was obvious, despite their forced good cheer, that they missed their only son terribly, and the house felt far emptier without him in it. It was just as well, for the Chelsea apartment no longer had a vacancy. Kathleen, the girl whose place Grace had been invited to take, had married in June as planned, but her new husband had enlisted and had been ordered to report for training a week after the wedding. The newlyweds decided it would be more frugal, not to mention less lonely for the bride, if they waited until he returned from Over There to move into a home of their own. Grace's friends apologized when they rescinded their invitation, but she assured them that she didn't feel slighted. With her new husband thousands of miles away for the duration of the war, Kathleen would need the reassuring company of good friends to make it through. Grace had her parents, her sisters, and her work.

One silver lining of remaining at home was that her commute from Passaic to Manhattan gave her ample time to read the papers. She followed the news of the war assiduously, from preparations at home to battles abroad. Eugene's regiment was only one of many quartered at army bases throughout the country, where soldiers trained for frontline combat or mastered important technical skills they would need at support bases closer to the rear. The U.S. Army had not yet confronted the enemy on the battlefield, but divisions of the American Expeditionary Forces had been dispatched to Great Britain and France, where they were building the infrastructure General Pershing needed to launch a successful ground assault. As for the U.S. Navy, destroyers and other escort vessels had been relocated to the British Isles, with some ships joining the British Royal Navy in the blockade of the German *Hochseeflotte* in the North Sea. The U.S. Navy had achieved its first victory at sea in mid-October, when the destroyer USS *Cassin* engaged a German U-boat off the coast of Ireland, attacking it with depth charges and forcing it to retreat. A month later, two American destroyers escorting an eastbound convoy sank their first German submarine, then fished thirty-nine survivors from the frigid waters and declared them prisoners of war.

Civilians had their role to play in the war too—less exciting, to be sure, but important all the same. Unlike their British counterparts, Americans were not subjected to government food rationing measures, but housewives were urged to cultivate gardens, to preserve the harvest, to serve less meat so there would be more for soldiers and sailors, to offer smaller portions at mealtimes, and to let nothing go to waste. Men who could not serve in the military were encouraged to purchase Liberty Bonds, mostly through advertisements that often cast thinly veiled aspersions upon the manhood of anyone who failed to open his wallet. When so many men resigned their jobs to serve Over There that it became difficult to find workers, women replaced them in offices, in factories, and on farms, wherever employers were willing to hire them. Many men were exempt from the draft because their occupations were crucial to the war effort, and Grace took pride in knowing that her work was similarly essential. Even so, she wished she could do more to directly contribute to a swift and decisive victory for the Allies.

One Sunday in early December, she was passing a quiet afternoon reading the newspaper when a headline above a single column caught her eye: "War Work Calls Women." Two subtitles followed, first "Taking the Places of Men in Many Different Lines," and then "Hundreds in the Navy Department—As Street Car Conductors in New York—Mail Carriers in Chicago—Sawmill Hands in South." The first paragraph of the article proper described the War Department's urgent call for graduate nurses to serve with the armed forces, but Grace had scarcely begun to read when a glimpse of a familiar phrase farther down the column riveted her attention.

ARMY CALLS TELEPHONE GIRLS.

The government has also called for 150 girl telephone operators, able to speak both French and English, for immediate service in France.

The operators, enlisted for the duration of the war, will be given the allowance of quarters and rations accorded nurses, in addition to their pay, and also will wear the same uniform.

Young women, physically fit, with command of the French and English language, desirous of obtaining these positions, should apply by mail to Chief Signal Corps Operator General Squier, Room 826, Mills Building Annex, 17th Street and Pennsylvania Avenue NW, Washington, D.C.

Grace stared at the page, thunderstruck. She could not imagine a more perfect way to do her bit for her country. She was an experienced telephone operator, with such exceptional skills that she had been promoted to teach others. Although she was not a native speaker of French, she was fluent, thanks to her college studies.

It was no secret in the telephone business that General Pershing had been extremely dissatisfied with the telephone service Over There so far—not with the brave Signal Corps soldiers who risked their lives every day constructing the network and maintaining the lines, but with those assigned to connect the calls. If the leader of the American Expeditionary Forces could not communicate with his counterparts among the Allies, or with his own generals at other bases, or with his officers in the field, he could not swiftly direct the troops, countermand earlier orders, warn of enemy maneuvers, or receive intelligence that would allow him to alter plans of attack to suit rapidly changing conditions. Grace realized that circumstances must be far worse than anyone had let on, or the army would not be recruiting women. Time and again, women had proven themselves superior to men at the switchboard, but the recalcitrant army would enlist them only as a last resort.

Grace's immediate thought was that she ought to apply. Her country needed her, and she wanted to go. But how would her parents feel about sending a second child Over There, especially a daughter?

She waited a day to see if her interest would fade after that initial burst of enthusiasm, but it only grew stronger. The more she mulled it over, the more certain she became that as someone possessing the rare pairing of skills the Signal Corps required, she was obliged to respond.

When she finally showed her parents the article two days later, they were first stunned, and then distressed. Anxiously they brought up one objection after another—hardships she would surely face, dangers she had perhaps not considered. Grace listened willingly and patiently, knowing that they protested out of love, and that their only concern was for her safety. Eventually they ran out of reasonable objections, their voices trailed off, and she was able to make her case. She reminded her parents of their country's urgent need, of her own intrinsic sense of duty, and of the tremendous amount of good she could do supporting the soldiers and speeding the end of the war. "Directly or indirectly, I may even be able to help our Eugene," she said.

"Maybe." Her father cleared his throat roughly, removed his glasses, and wiped them with a handkerchief, all the while avoiding her gaze. "Or maybe you'll connect the call that will deliver the order that sends him over the top to his death. How would you bear it?"

She felt a heavy pressure on her chest, and for a moment she could not speak. Then she realized that his eyes were glistening with unshed tears, and she understood that he had dealt her this unkind blow in one last, anguished attempt to keep her safe at home.

"Eugene chose to fight, just as I choose to serve in the Signal Corps," Grace said, keeping her voice steady. "He wouldn't condemn me for following orders, if it's for the greater good."

Tears slipped down her mother's face as she turned a resigned, beseeching gaze upon her husband. "William, she's a good girl. She's capable of making her own decisions. If she were a man, you wouldn't hesitate to let her go."

"If I were a man," said Grace, laughing shakily, "they wouldn't want me, not for the switchboards."

Her father tried to smile, but he managed only a pained grimace. But later that evening, he agreed as her legal guardian to write a letter granting permission for her to enlist.

The next morning, Grace wrote to General George Squier, chief officer of the Signal Corps, to apply for the position. "I should like to join for one year with the privilege of reenlisting," she noted. "If that is not possible, I will enlist for the period of the war. I understand both French and English and have a thorough knowledge of telephony." Adding her father's note to the envelope, she sent off her letter, wishing she could hand-deliver it to be sure it did not go astray.

Then she waited.

A month passed. The war churned on. Snows fell, Christmas came and went, and a new year began. Grace went to work, helped around the house, sent cheerful letters to Eugene, raised funds to support war widows and orphans, and vigilantly kept watch over the mailbox. Not a word came in reply to her letter.

In the first week of January, Grace arrived at work to discover an unusual amount of activity around the freight elevators. Rope cordons had been set up to prevent employees from getting in the way as burly laborers hauled what looked to be dismantled switchboards of various types into a vacant room on the floor above those where Grace worked. Curious, she asked around and was startled to learn that AT&T employees in the Reserve Signal Corps were setting up a facility to train and test potential army telephone operators who had passed the initial screening. The first group of candidates would report by the middle of the month.

Grace's heart sank. Apparently other applicants had already been invited into the next round of the evaluation process, while she had still not heard a thing. It pained her to imagine that those brave, lucky girls would be preparing for overseas duty in her own workplace, while she went about her ordinary tasks. Perhaps she would even be assigned to train them.

In that case, she would have to keep her chin up, set aside her envy, and teach them as best she could. Everything—soldiers' lives, victory for the Allies—depended upon the Signal Corps girls arriving in France prepared to perform their roles flawlessly.

On January 7, a month after she sent her first letter, Grace wrote to General Squier again, increasingly worried that she had been overlooked, but unwilling to give up hope. "If my application has not been accepted for the present, would I be eligible for a second unit if such should be formed?" she asked. "I would appreciate any further information in regard to this matter as my plans for the future must be governed accordingly."

She posted her letter and braced herself for another interminable, anxious wait, but a few days later, a thick envelope bearing the return address of the Mills Building Annex appeared in her mailbox. Pulse quickening, she opened the envelope and discovered a form requesting more information about her educational background, employment experience, and medical history. She was also asked to arrange for a supervisor to provide a reference, and to send a formal photograph or "a snapshot of a good likeness."

Swiftly she gathered the required documents. There was no time to have a formal studio portrait made, but the previous autumn, her sister Helen had taken a photo of her for the Barnard College newsletter. Grace promptly ordered another print, hoping it would suffice. She was standing on the lawn behind their home clad in a long-skirted cornflower blue satin suit with a white collar, no hat, but with her chestnut hair arranged in a tidy bun. Her hands were clasped demurely behind her back, and her expression was calm and steady as she gazed directly into the camera.

"I would hire you," Marjorie said helpfully, peering closely at the photo, which Grace had placed on the dining room table with the other papers—her application, her résumé, a transcript from Barnard College, an affidavit from her physician, and a brief but favorable recommendation from Louise Barbour, the chief instructor at AT&T.

"Miss Banker has been a member of the Instructor Department for the American Telephone and Telegraph Company for the past two years," Miss Barbour had written. "I should be sorry to lose her services." As she handed Grace the note, she had confessed that she was thinking about applying too.

Grace usually had weekends off, so she was not present on Saturday, January 12, when the first group of Signal Corps telephone operator candidates reported to the Telephone and Telegraph Building for training. Grace knew that applicants from other regions had been assigned to training centers in Chicago, San Francisco, Philadelphia, Jersey City, Atlantic City, and Lancaster, Pennsylvania. How she wished she were among them! Throughout the day, she caught herself brooding over her application, wondering where she had come up short. Could she have been rejected because in her first letter she had offered to serve one year, with the possibility of reenlisting? In the same sentence, she had told them that if this option was not possible, she would serve for the duration of the war, but perhaps that small, misleading suggestion that she was not wholeheartedly committed to service was enough to knock her out of the running.

"You might still hear something," Helen said, surprising her with a cup of hot cocoa later that evening as she sat by the fireplace, stroking Patches, a book abandoned on the sofa beside her. "At least they haven't written to reject you."

"True enough," Grace replied, resolving henceforth not to mope so obviously. She had heard that thousands of applications had come in from around the country for those first 150 spots; perhaps the chief signal officer's staff was still sorting through them, and hers had not yet come to the top of the pile. She had read in a company newsletter that the army had begun its recruitment campaign in French-speaking regions of Louisiana, and even in Canada, since there were no restrictions placed upon the women's nationality. Perhaps telephone operators from those regions were given priority, and Grace simply had to be patient and wait her turn. As Helen suggested, until she received an official rejection, she might as well think positively.

When she reported for her shift Monday morning, Grace thought she detected a new sense of purposeful excitement in the operators' lounge and along the switchboards, but perhaps she was only imagining it. Except for Miss Barbour, none of her friends at AT&T headquarters spoke French, so none of them had applied to join the new women's Signal Corps unit; it was perfectly understandable why they did not pounce on every new detail about the newcomers as avidly as she did. Grace didn't glimpse any unfamiliar faces in the hallways, but then again, her duties never took her upstairs to the rooms where the recruits were training. Yet even though she had not been chosen to join them, whenever she remembered how extraordinary it was that the U.S. Army was recruiting women soldiers, she felt a thrill of pride on behalf of women everywhere.

Later, back at home, she and Marjorie were setting the table for supper when the doorbell rang. Helen answered, and she soon joined her sisters in the dining room, carrying the distinctive yellow envelope of a telegram.

Their mother appeared in the kitchen doorway. "Good heavens," she murmured, her face ashen. "Is it about Eugene?"

"I don't think so," Helen quickly replied. "It's addressed to Grace."

Their mother heaved a sigh of relief, and Grace too breathed easier. A telegram from the army regarding Eugene would have been sent to her parents. Taking the envelope from her sister, she withdrew a thin slip of paper. "Pursuant to authority of Secretary of War Baker dated April 7, 1917," she read aloud, "you will proceed to New York City to interview for the position of Telephone Operator on January 15, 1918, reporting upon arrival to Mr. R. F. Estabrook, American Telephone & Telegraph Co., 195 Broadway. The travel directed is necessary in the Military Service. You should apply to nearest quartermaster for transportation. Signed Squier, Chief Signal Officer." She glanced up, stunned. "I have an interview."

Marjorie cheered, Helen applauded, and their mother pressed a hand to her heart, astonishment and worry in her eyes.

"That's tomorrow," Grace murmured, reading the telegram over more carefully. "'Apply to nearest quartermaster for transportation.' I suppose I'll just take the train, as always."

"I suppose so," said her mother, still nonplussed. "Do you know this Mr. Estabrook?"

"We haven't formally met. He's in the Traffic Department with AT&T, one of the top men. He's based in New York, but he works all over the country." Grace took a deep, steadying breath. "I have an interview."

"You said that already," Marjorie teased, and Grace had to laugh.

The next morning, she took the early train into Manhattan so she would arrive at work well before her scheduled shift. Drawing Miss Barbour aside, she quietly explained why she would not be able to report to the switchboard right away. "I'll cover for you," Miss Barbour said, smiling. "Good luck."

Grace thanked her and hurried off to Mr. Estabrook's office. His secretary took her name, offered her a chair, disappeared behind a closed door for a few moments, and returned to escort her inside.

Mr. Estabrook, a slight, bespectacled man with a cleft chin and a receding hairline, rose and regarded her with keen interest as she entered. "Miss Banker," he said cordially, gesturing to a chair in front of his mahogany desk. "Thank you for joining us this morning."

"Thank you, sir." As she seated herself, her gaze went to the military officer standing beside Mr. Estabrook, his arms folded, his faint grin giving him a casual air despite his crisp uniform. He was a captain, if she read his insignia correctly, and he looked to be younger than Mr. Estabrook, perhaps no more than thirty.

"Allow me to introduce Captain Ernest Wessen, U.S. Army Signal Corps," Mr. Estabrook said. "He'll be conducting your interview."

Grace folded her hands in her lap and regarded Captain Wessen expectantly. "I'm happy to answer any questions you might have, sir," she said.

"Thank you, Miss Banker," he replied, inclining his head. And with that, he began.

The first questions were easy enough, simply verifying details from her application. When he asked her to describe a situation in which she had endured physical hardship, she told him about camping trips and hiking excursions she had enjoyed with college chums. He posed hypothetical situations involving conflicts in the workplace and asked her to explain how she would have resolved them—a test, she assumed, of her judgment and leadership skills.

From time to time, Captain Wessen referred to her application, but then he glanced at another small folder of papers she did not recognize. "Your brother, Eugene Armstrong Banker, is serving with Battery C of the Seventy-Seventh Field Artillery, is he not?"

"Yes, sir," Grace replied, hoping this was not a test of her ability to play dumb when asked to divulge military information.

"I imagine he's told you what it's like, roughing it at a military cantonment."

"He's shared some interesting stories. Amusing ones, too." Grace hesitated. "He wouldn't want to upset our parents by complaining about hardships. I'm sure it's been more challenging than he's let on. I know it will be even rougher Over There, and that I too would be expected to endure very difficult, even dangerous conditions. I accept that."

"I'm glad you realize this won't be a sightseeing excursion of the great capitals of Europe," he said wryly. "But knowing the danger, why do you want to join the Signal Corps? Your brother has to go to France to serve his country. You don't. Why risk it?"

"My brother didn't necessarily *have* to go to France," Grace pointed out. "He volunteered. As for me, I believe women have a duty to serve their country as much as men do."

"That's commendable, but you're already an essential worker right here, in this very building. Why go Over There when you can remain a telephone operator here, support the war effort admirably, and still enjoy all the comforts of home?"

Grace considered her words carefully. "I applied to join the Signal Corps because I strongly believe that if I am selected, I'll be able to serve my country to better advantage than I'm doing at present." She shifted her gaze, directing her reply to both men. "Although my current position is one of great responsibility, I'm sure there are more qualified candidates for that role than for the one I'm seeking. It would be unpatriotic of me not to volunteer."

Captain Wessen smiled and, turning to Mr. Estabrook, said, "I've heard all I need to hear. I'm satisfied."

"I knew you would be." Mr. Estabrook rose and reached across the desk to offer Grace his hand. "Congratulations, Miss Banker. Your application is approved."

Quickly she stood and shook his hand. "Thank you, Mr. Estabrook."

"This is just the beginning," Captain Wessen warned her, smiling, as he shook her hand in turn. "The training program begins with practice on a large private exchange, but we trust you won't have any difficulty with that. Next you'll move to one of the bases and work on a cantonment telephone exchange, so you can become familiar with military terms. You should expect daily drills and instruction in military procedures and the duties of the Signal Corps in particular. Keep in mind that you've only cleared the first hurdle. All recruits will undergo additional training and evaluation before the final selections are made."

"I understand, sir," said Grace, unable to keep from smiling broadly despite his solemn words.

"We'll begin with the army oath of allegiance, if you're prepared to take it."

"I am, sir," said Grace, without a moment's hesitation.

Repeating the words the captain recited, she raised her right hand and swore to support and defend the Constitution of the United States against all enemies, foreign and domestic. The significance of her vow settled upon her shoulders not as a burden, but as a mantle of honor.

But as Captain Wessen had warned her, her oath was only the first step. She still must earn her place in the Signal Corps before she could become a true switchboard soldier.

5

DECEMBER 1917–FEBRUARY 1918

San Francisco

VALERIE

Soon after Henri reported to the mustering station at Fort McArthur in coastal San Pedro, he wrote to say that he had been placed in the 91st Infantry, a division comprised of recruits from California and other western states. His enthusiasm and pride were unmistakable as he described the barracks, his bunkmates, and the vigorous physical training that left him sore and exhausted but already noticeably fitter and stronger. "The chow isn't even remotely as tasty as home cooking, but I've put on ten pounds of muscle since you last saw me," he said. "You'd barely recognize me."

"I'd like to test that theory," said Valerie, pausing as she read the letter aloud to her mother and sister. "He's only twenty miles away. We could take the streetcar and spy on him through the fence. I assume there would be a fence around a military base."

"Don't even say the word 'spy' in the same sentence as 'military base,'" Hilde warned, glancing over her shoulder as if she expected to find a suspicious neighbor lurking outside the window.

Their mother shook her head, wistful. "As much as I'd love to see our boy, we could never embarrass him in front of his friends like that."

"You're both right," said Valerie, muffling a sigh. Her sense of humor was too often lost on her family.

She continued to read the letter aloud, her voice catching in her throat when she learned that in a matter of weeks, Henri expected to be sent to Camp Lewis near Tacoma, Washington, for more advanced training in drill, marksmanship, and combat readiness. As long as her brother remained in Southern California, Valerie could almost imagine that he was not really preparing for war, but news of the impending transfer rudely dispelled that notion. Although geographically speaking he would be no closer to the battlefields of France, a move eleven hundred miles due north would metaphorically send him halfway Over There.

Only a few days later, Henri sent another letter announcing a change of plans. The army had learned of his skill with photography and motion pictures, and had reassigned him to the Photographic Section of the Signal Corps. "By the time you receive this," he wrote, "I'll be on my way to New York, where I'll report to the army's new school for land photography at Columbia University. Wish I'd been able to see you all once more before I set out, but I'll forward my new address as soon as I know it."

Valerie was so disconcerted that she could barely stammer out his closing words of affection and reassurance. Henri could have been halfway across the country by then, speeding away from them on an eastbound train, and she had not even known that he had left California. They had hoped that he would be granted a day's leave so the family could spend Christmas together at home, but that would never happen now.

"This is good news, isn't it?" asked her mother, looking from Valerie to Hilde and back. "He'll be taking photographs, not fighting in the trenches. How much better for a young man like Henri to wield a camera instead of a gun! Surely this will be far less dangerous."

Valerie and Hilde exchanged a look. "It certainly sounds safer," said Hilde guardedly. "I imagine he'll enjoy his duties much more, too."

"Wouldn't it be thrilling if Henri were assigned to General Pershing's entourage?" said Valerie. "Imagine traveling around France, taking photos of the general while he tours cultural sites and meets with all those presidents and dignitaries."

When her mother brightened, Valerie could forgive herself the small deception. Many men from Pacific Telephone and Telegraph had enlisted in the Signal Corps, and the company's monthly magazine often reprinted letters from the soldiers alongside stories about the essential duties they performed and dangers they faced. Henri would not be a lineman, of course, advancing with the infantry to lay the wires connecting their forward positions to headquarters, but she knew that every division had a photography unit attached to it, comprised of a photographer, a motion picture operator, and several assistants. Although her brother was eager to see action, Valerie could only hope that he would be assigned to develop images in a darkroom far to the rear.

In the weeks that followed, Valerie discovered another reason to be glad she had allowed her mother to believe that serving in the Signal Corps was hardly dangerous at all.

On a cool, rainy day in late December, Valerie and a few friends gathered for lunch around a table for six in the operators' lounge. They were chatting about holiday plans when Irene darted over. "Have you seen this?" she asked, placing the most recent edition of *Pacific Telephone Magazine* on the table and creasing the spine so it lay open. "This is how we can do our bit. It suits us perfectly and it doesn't say a word about an age requirement."

Valerie couldn't read the page from her seat on the opposite side of the table, but she watched with increasing curiosity as the girls with a better vantage studied the article. "No age requirement, but you have to be fluent in French," said Mabel, tapping her finger on a line near the top. "That leaves me out, and I bet most of you girls too."

"I studied French in high school," said Irene, beaming. "I was president of the French Club in my senior year."

"Who needs French speakers?" asked Valerie. "And for what?"

Mabel pushed the magazine halfway across the table, Valerie brought it the rest of the way, and the girls seated on either side drew closer so they could read together. Valerie heard soft gasps of delight as they learned that the U.S. Army Signal Corps was recruiting French-speaking women telephone operators for immediate service in France.

"Girls in the army?" someone reading over her shoulder said, incredulous, but Valerie paid no attention. A strange pricking tickled the back of her neck, not a symptom of fear, but of uncanny recognition. The skills the job required so perfectly matched her own that she could almost imagine it had been designed especially for her.

"I'll need that back," said Irene, reaching across the table for the magazine. "I'm going to apply."

"So am I," said Cora, seated at Valerie's left.

"You don't speak French," said a girl on the other side of the table.

"Yes, she does," said Valerie. "Her accent is a bit odd, but—"

"It is not," Cora retorted, giving her a playful shove. To the others, she added, "My mother is French Canadian. We spent every summer at my grandparents' farm in Quebec when I was growing up."

Valerie searched her pockets for a pencil and a scrap of paper, and, finding none, borrowed a pencil from Mabel, tore off a clean square of the brown paper her mother had used to wrap her sandwich, and copied down the instructions for how to apply. Cora followed suit, but with a fine pen and a notepad she carried in her purse. Two more girls took down the details before the magazine found its way back to Irene.

"May the best girl win," said Mabel, glancing around the table, amused.

"We aren't competitors," Irene protested. "We all want the same thing—for the most qualified and best operators to go to France to help the Allies."

"Sure, that's what we all want," said Valerie, glancing at the clock and gathering up her lunch things. "As long as one of those operators is me."

As soon as she arrived home after her shift, she wrote to request an application, describing her qualifications in brief but pertinent detail. A few days later, a slender envelope arrived from Pac-Tel headquarters, bearing an application form and additional instructions. In the days that followed, Valerie gathered the requested documents, saving the most difficult part for last. As an unmarried woman under thirty, she was required to obtain a parent's or guardian's signature. She would have asked Hilde, and kept everything secret from her mother until she had been accepted into the program, but she knew Hilde wouldn't cooperate.

At first her mother seemed perplexed. "You want to join the army?"

"The Signal Corps," said Valerie, adding, "The same group Henri is in."

Her mother straightened in her chair, her expression suddenly alight with hope. "You'll be with him?"

Valerie was tempted to respond with a hearty affirmative—her mother would be far more willing to sign the form in that case—but Hilde was standing in the doorway, arms folded, frowning a warning. "I think that's unlikely," Valerie said instead. "I would be at the switchboard all day, and he'll likely be off taking photos or running a motion picture camera."

She handed her mother the form and a pen, which she accepted without looking at them, her eyes searching Valerie's face. "But you would be safe?"

Valerie didn't need her sister's sharp look to know to choose her words with care. "I'd take every precaution, but if I'm accepted, I'll be going to France in wartime. That's inherently dangerous, and yet—" She paused, but then the words tumbled out. "I'll be safer than our family and friends in Belgium are right now. Ordinary people all over Belgium and France are resisting the German occupation. If I can do anything—*anything*—to help them, I think I should. I think I must."

Her mother regarded her in silence for a moment, tears filling her eyes. She blinked them away, sighed softly, and signed the form.

Valerie sent off her application the next morning. Two days later, she received a telegram inviting her to an interview at Pac-Tel headquarters the following Monday. While chatting with her friends on her lunch break, she learned that Cora and Irene had received the same request, and they decided to meet at a convenient streetcar station and ride downtown together.

When the day arrived, Valerie was glad to have friends along for moral support. As they rode to the nearest stop and walked the short block to headquarters, they stoked one another's courage, straightened a friend's collar here, tucked away a stray curl there. From the lobby, a clerk escorted them to a room where four other young women as polished and professional as themselves waited, looking over prepared notes or paging idly through back issues of the company magazine. As they found seats together and settled in, Valerie surreptitiously observed the other candidates as she and her friends chatted in hushed voices. A secretary summoned two young women into an adjacent office, one about twenty minutes after the other, but neither returned to the waiting room. They must be leaving via another exit, Valerie realized, perhaps so they wouldn't share information with other applicants. In whispers, she told her friends what she had observed, and they arranged to meet up after their interviews at a fountain just outside the main entrance. Only moments later, Cora was called into the office, and then a girl who had arrived before them, and then Valerie.

The office was small, the furnishings spare but modern, with papers neatly stacked and no knickknacks or photos cluttering up the desks and bookshelves. Two men waited expectantly, the first wearing a charcoal gray suit and seated behind the desk, the other in a military uniform and sitting in one of a matching pair of upholstered chairs in front. They rose when she entered, introduced themselves as Mr. Connors and Lieutenant Ryan, and offered her the chair beside the lieutenant's.

They began with the usual perfunctory questions about her experience as a telephone operator, and then queried her about her nationality—when she had come to the United States and why, whether she felt like a true American. They seemed satisfied with her answers, and not the least bit troubled by the angry tremor in her voice when she spoke of how eager she was to help the Allies drive the Germans out of her homeland.

Then the lieutenant withdrew from her file several papers that she quickly recognized as her transcripts. "You graduated from high school here in California, and then went on to study for one year at USC, correct?" he asked.

"Yes, that's correct. I majored in mathematics."

His eyebrows rose. "*Vous n'avez pas étudié le français?*"

"*Non, je me suis spécialisé en mathématiques.*" She thought for a moment, and in the interest of accuracy, added, "*J'ai étudié des autre sujets aussi, mais pas le français.*"

"*Mais pourquoi pas?*"

Valerie regarded him quizzically. Had he not been listening? "*Je suis Belge,*" she reminded him. "*J'ai su déjà parler français. Je le parle toujours avec ma famille, à chez nous.*"

He nodded. "I see."

How awkward she felt, lamely struggling to justify her course selections for a degree she had been unable to complete. "My schedule was so full of math and general education requirements that I couldn't have fit in any French classes."

He smiled slightly. "Nor did it occur to you."

"Well, actually, no, it didn't."

Mr. Connors stepped in then with a few questions about her general hardiness and physical fitness, and then, before she quite realized the interview was over, the men rose, thanked her for coming, shook her hand, said they would be in touch, and showed her to the door—a different door than the one she had entered through, leading directly outside to a stone walkway.

Dumbfounded and somewhat deflated, Valerie followed the path around to the front of the building and found Cora sitting on a bench near the fountain. "How did it go for you?" Valerie asked, taking a seat beside her.

"I think it went well, except—" Cora winced. "I might have forgotten myself a bit when the officer asked why I wanted to go Over There."

"Really. How so?"

"I might have said something about wanting to slap the kaiser, and since the army wouldn't let me carry a rifle, I'd fight the Germans with the telephone."

Valerie stifled a laugh as an image sprang into her thoughts, her usually poised coworker swatting a baffled, battle-scarred Jerry with a black candlestick receiver. "No doubt they appreciated your enthusiasm," she said. "I'm sure you made a great impression, unlike myself."

"Oh, dear. What happened?"

Before Valerie could explain, Irene approached them along the stone path, tears in her eyes, shoulders slumped dejectedly. "What a disaster," she lamented. "I answered every question perfectly until they blindsided me with that test. I failed it miserably."

"Test?" Cora echoed. "What test?"

"You know, the part where the officer started talking to you in French to catch you off guard and see if you could understand him and reply in French."

Cora peered at her, bemused. "You mean, the *conversation*?"

Valerie smacked her forehead with the heel of her hand. "A test! Of course it was a test."

"You didn't know?" said Cora. "Does that mean you passed or failed?"

"Oh, I'm sure I passed," said Valerie airily. "I might have sounded like a ninny, but at least I was a ninny in French." She caught herself, noting Irene's mournful frown. "That was probably only a small part of the evaluation."

"Minuscule, I'm sure," Cora chimed in. "No one is faster or more accurate than you on the switchboards, Irene. That must count for something."

Irene managed a wan smile. "We'll see."

On January 19, Valerie's mother and sister were out grocery shopping when Valerie returned home from a half-day Saturday shift, so it was one of their lodgers who told her about the telegram awaiting her on the kitchen table. Her heart thudded as she opened the yellow envelope.

"Under authority of Secretary of War, dated April Seventh 1917, you will proceed to San Francisco, Calif., reporting upon arrival to L. S. Hamm, Pacific Telephone and Telegraph Co., 835 Howard Street, for temporary duty," the telegram read. "You will apply to the nearest quartermaster or recruiting officer for transportation. The travel directed is necessary in the military service. Transportation allowances to be accorded you same as prescribed for Army nurses in Army regulations. While on temporary duty at San Francisco, Calif. you will be allowed a per diem allowance of four dollars for first thirty days."

She sank into a chair. She was in—or if not quite in, one step closer.

Over supper that evening, when just the three of them were in the kitchen after the boarders were served in the dining room, Valerie broke the news to her mother and sister. "It's possible that I won't pass the tests and they'll send me straight home," she added, hoping to soften the blow.

"Don't be ridiculous," her mother admonished. "You've never failed an exam in your life. They'd be fools not to accept you."

"She's right," Hilde said, shrugging as she buttered her bread. "As far as French-speaking girl telephone operators willing to serve in the army go, you're probably among the best."

"Thanks," Valerie replied dryly.

Cora received a similar telegram, but Irene did not. When they consoled her, she brushed off her disappointment in favor of congratulating them. "You earned your places, I didn't," she said. "In a few years, I'll be old enough to volunteer with the YMCA. I might see you Over There after all."

Valerie and Cora were pleased when they learned the quartermaster had booked them on the same train to San Francisco, Southern Pacific No. 75, the *Lark*, which left Los Angeles daily at 7:40 in the evening and arrived in San Francisco at 9:30 the next morning. Valerie met her friend on the platform, where they both turned their luggage over to the porter.

"I wasn't sure if I should pack for a few weeks in Northern California or several years in France, so I settled for somewhere in the middle," said Cora, a bit breathless from excitement as they climbed aboard and found their adjacent berths in the same sleeper car.

"The advertisements said that Signal Corps girls would be required to wear uniforms," Valerie replied, "so I packed only for San Francisco. I assume they'll issue us our uniforms before we sail."

Valerie didn't mention how she had originally packed a second suitcase for France, but when she had carried the two bags downstairs that morning, her mother, watching from below, had suddenly become distraught, struck by the realization that Valerie might be gone a very long time. Guilt-stricken, Valerie had made a self-deprecating joke about how she always overpacked, left the first bag on the landing, and returned the second to her room. She could always ask Hilde to ship it to her later.

After stowing their belongings, Valerie and Cora enjoyed a light meal in the dining car just for the novelty of it, then returned to the sleeper car and settled into their berths. Although the train rattled and jolted throughout the night, Valerie slept surprisingly well and woke refreshed. She washed and dressed, and cajoled a sluggish Cora out of her berth so she could do the same. They had time for a quick breakfast of scrambled eggs, buttered toast, and coffee before the *Lark* pulled into the Third and Townsend Depot. When they disembarked and met up with their escort, they discovered that several other applicants had joined them along the way. Still more were already waiting in the meeting room at Pac-Tel headquarters in a northeastern part of the city. There they were introduced to Mr. L. S. Hamm, a tall, sandy-haired man with a midwestern accent and a steady manner, who explained what their rather alarmingly rigorous program for training and testing would subject them to in the weeks to come. Valerie had barely absorbed all that when a thin, smiling, bespectacled matron with her gray hair in a loose bun took the stage and informed them about their housing arrangements; they would be sharing rooms at the nearby YWCA, where they would also take their meals, enjoy social activities, and prepare for their examinations in any of several common rooms.

Exhausted from the long day of travel, Valerie and Cora, who were delighted to find themselves paired up as roommates, made an early night of it. The bedchamber was small but tidy, with two twin beds, a small nightstand between them with a lamp on top, a wardrobe, and a single wooden ladderback chair in the corner. The shared bath down the hall was spacious and clean, and on the opposite end of the hallway, a tall window offered a view of the San Francisco Bay if the observer craned her head just right. At breakfast the next the morning, Valerie overheard several girls murmur surprise that the rooms were so small and spartan. She could well imagine what some of her fellow recruits would think of the attic room she and Hilde shared back home. "Wait until we move into army barracks," she murmured to Cora, recalling Henri's comically woeful descriptions.

But as she soon learned, most of the girls were great fun, lively and smart and uncomplaining, eager to serve the country Over There, and apprehensive in varying degrees about their upcoming examinations. Everyone dreaded the thought of being sent home in disgrace, and so each plunged into their training with an energy and commitment that would have struck terror in the heart of the kaiser had he known about it. Each morning began with calisthenics and drill, followed by hours of intensive instruction on various switchboards, from PBX systems to hand-crank magneto boards to ordinary battery exchanges. They attended classes in French dictation and translation, military terminology, the history and duties of the Signal Corps, and the structure of the military chain of command. Signal Corps officers lectured them on the importance of communication in modern warfare, while women surgeons delivered presentations on personal hygiene. There were interviews and medical exams, and sometimes Valerie was so exhausted by the end of the day that she would have happily dropped into bed immediately after supper if she didn't need to stay awake to study the geography of France or memorize the French versions of English telephone terms.

Thankfully, she and the other girls got along well and always found time for a bit of fun in the evenings and on weekends. Valerie adored living in the YWCA among so many other bright, cheerful young women—sharing meals, studying in groups, commiserating over the misadventures of a tough day, laughing their way through homesickness, talking for hours, sharing photographs of beaus and family. Early on, Valerie and Cora befriended two beautiful and charming sisters, Louise and Raymonde LeBreton, whose family had immigrated to San Francisco from Nantes, France, not five years before. The sisters knew the city backwards and forwards, and they were always ready to recommend a favorite diner with tasty and filling but affordable lunches, a café with such delicious coffee and sweets whose very aroma would make a girl swoon, the parks with the loveliest views of the bay and the Golden Gate Bridge, and the best sightseeing in the city.

Valerie and Cora agreed that it was wonderful to have such friendly, proficient tour guides, but sometimes the sisters seemed more innocent and impulsive than one might expect, even of young women only twenty-one and nineteen. Once, when Valerie and Louise, the elder of the pair, were alone in the sisters' room quizzing each other on military jargon, Louise mentioned that her sister had read about the army's need for telephone operators from an article in the *Daily Cal*, the student newspaper for the University of California at Berkeley, where they had been enrolled in a special program for immigrants mastering English.

Something in Louise's inflection piqued Valerie's curiosity. "Just how old are you and your sister, anyway?" she asked.

Louise shrugged, nonchalant. "I'm twenty-one and Raymonde is nineteen."

"No, really," said Valerie, studying her. "The truth this time. I won't be twenty-one until June, and I know I'm older than you."

Louise hesitated. "Promise you won't tell anyone?"

"Cross my heart."

"I'm nineteen and my sister is seventeen," Louise blurted in an undertone, glancing over her shoulder to make sure no one was passing the open doorway. "We lied about our ages. We knew they'd never let us in otherwise, and that wouldn't be fair. Our telephone operator skills are just as good as those of any twenty-three-year-old here."

"And better than most," Valerie admitted. Louise, especially, was enviably swift and agile at the switchboard.

As if divulging one secret had primed a pump, Louise confessed a torrent of others, filling in gaps and correcting half-truths in what she had shared before. When she had mentioned that her family had immigrated to the United States from Nantes, she had left out the part in which a year before that, her father, an engineer, had died of yellow fever in Panama, where he had been part of the French crew attempting to build a canal. Her widowed mother had decided to bring her four daughters—there were two others younger than Louise and Raymonde—to California, which she had heard was the land of plenty, and where she now ran a boardinghouse for students at Cal Berkeley. "Raymonde and I help our maman with the housekeeping, but"—Louise puffed her cheeks and gazed heavenward—"the work was so tedious and degrading, I could not bear it. Maman agreed that I could find a job outside the home instead." And so she had. Until she reported for duty with the Signal Corps, Louise had divided her time between college classes, her work as a telephone operator, and a second, part-time job as a secretary for the French consulate.

Struck by the similarities between their experiences, Valerie could not help but be impressed by Louise's ambition and diligence. Of course she would not expose her young friend's insignificant falsehood about her age. How could she deprive the Signal Corps of such a recruit?

She cautioned Louise to keep the inaccuracies on her application to herself in the future, for like any group of girls working and living together, a few indulged in sharing stories that were not necessarily theirs to tell. Valerie learned—not from her own observations or from the woman herself, but from the girls who lived across the hall—that another recruit from San Francisco, Inez Crittenden, was a divorcée. The tall, serious, thirty-year-old brunette's scandalous secret made the LeBreton sisters' deceptions seem dull in comparison, not that it remained a secret for long. Aloof, ambitious, and singularly focused on her work, Inez was not inclined to make friends, which encouraged the other girls to gossip about her. Valerie knew she shouldn't join in, but once, when she wondered aloud whether Inez had become a telephone operator to support herself after the divorce, the LeBreton sisters eagerly supplied the answer, and then some.

"She's been a telephone operator since she was fourteen," said Louise, glancing over her shoulder to make sure Inez wasn't in earshot. "Her parents divorced, and she had to leave school and go to work to support her mother and siblings."

"Apparently divorce runs in the family," Raymonde interjected, eyebrows arched.

"She wanted to get ahead, and that meant continuing her education, so she scrimped and saved and managed to pay for a private tutor," Louise continued. "That's how she learned French."

"Through the years, she worked her way up to management, until she left the telephone company to take a job as the executive secretary to the Armsby brothers." Raymonde paused to allow Valerie a moment to be impressed, but when Valerie merely shook her head and shrugged, Raymonde prompted, "James and George Armsby, of the California Packing Corporation? 'From the Land of Sunshine Fruits'?"

"Oh, right," said Valerie, nodding, recognizing the slogan. "That sounds like a prestigious job. It must have been hard to give it up when she married."

"I don't know about that," said Louise. "The Crittendens are a wealthy San Francisco society family, and Inez was marrying up. She likely thought she'd be well looked after all the rest of her days."

"Little did she know," said Raymonde.

"It was in all the papers when she sued Nathaniel Crittenden for divorce on charges of abandonment last June," said Louise. "She's been living with her mother ever since."

"She hasn't been divorced very long, then." Valerie could only imagine what had led to those particular charges against Inez's husband. No wonder Inez had enlisted in the Signal Corps. She could leave heartbreak and scandal behind, and when she returned from Over There, her service to her country might be enough to erase the stigma of divorce and let her begin anew.

As pleased as Valerie was to have her own curiosity about Inez satisfied, she spread the gossip no further. In their classes on army protocol, the telephone operators had been warned of the danger of divulging military secrets through careless chatter. Shouldn't that same principle of prudent silence apply to their fellow recruits' personal lives as well?

After three weeks of intensive training, the candidates were assigned to busy telephone exchanges in towns all around the bay so their skills could be evaluated in the field. Valerie and the LeBreton sisters would be reporting to Richmond, just a rough ferry ride across the San Francisco Bay from the Market Street terminal. Cora and a few other girls were told to continue their studies in San Francisco.

"The problem is my French, I just know it," Cora fretted as she and Valerie prepared for bed the evening before the new stage of training would begin. "I understand what I hear, but I have to translate in my head before I can respond. And when our instructors test me, I get nervous and forget all those French technical terms."

"You'll learn," Valerie assured her. "Just stick to it. You've made so much progress over the past few weeks."

"Not quite enough progress." Cora hesitated. "Listen, Valerie. Some of the girls have been talking about leaving the YWCA and moving in with local French families."

Valerie's heart sank a little. "That sounds like a good idea. Nothing helps you gain fluency faster than immersing yourself in the language."

"I think I should try it too. I'm really sorry. You've been the best roommate—"

"It's fine. Don't worry about me." When Valerie spotted tears gathering in her friend's eyes, she bounded up from her bed and hugged her. "Just learn your French, and maybe we can be bunkmates again Over There."

In the meantime, Valerie would miss Cora, the only friend who had been with her from the beginning of her adventure.

After a week at the Richmond exchange, Valerie was ordered to report to the medical office at Pac-Tel headquarters for another physical, the most thorough by far, even though she assured the doctor that her health had not changed since the previous week. Later that afternoon, an instructor escorted her and about a dozen other recruits to the third floor of headquarters and told them to line up single file in the hallway outside a closed door. Offering no explanation, the instructor led the first girl into the room and shut the door behind them. After a brief interval, the instructor reappeared, shut the door, and stood with her back to it, eyes forward. About twenty minutes later, someone on the other side knocked on the door. The instructor led a second girl inside, only to return again less than a minute later. The first recruit did not reappear.

Raymonde, who preceded Valerie in line, murmured over her shoulder, "Well, that's disturbing."

"There must be another exit," Valerie replied. It reminded her of her interview in Los Angeles, and she wondered what was going on. They had been given no instructions except to wait quietly—a rule Valerie and Raymonde had almost broken—and to enter the room when invited. As time passed, the long, silent wait on their feet grew wearisome, the uncertainty intimidating—which, Valerie surmised, was precisely the desired effect.

Valerie wanted to wish Raymonde good luck before she entered the room, but with the instructor standing right there, she didn't dare. Instead she gave herself a silent, reassuring pep talk as the minutes ticked by. Eventually the knock came, and the instructor led Valerie inside.

She found herself in a small, dimly lit office, with a door on the opposite wall. In the center of the room stood a desk with a chair pulled out before it and a telephone on top.

"Please be seated," the instructor said. By the time Valerie took her place in the chair, the instructor was gone, the door firmly shut.

The phone rang.

Instinctively Valerie glanced over her shoulder, but of course no one stood helpfully by to advise her. Obviously she was meant to answer the phone, and so she did. "Hello?"

"Hello," a man said, his voice gruff, his accent American. "This is the adjutant, Tenth Division, located at Pont St. Vincent, in France. The commanding officer, General Jones, wants to talk to Colonel La Roux of the Eighteenth Brigade, Fifth French Army Corps, located at Vouxiers. General Jones understands no French, and Colonel La Roux understands no English. It will be necessary for you to translate General Jones's message into French, and Colonel La Roux's reply into English. Ready?"

"Ready," said Valerie, pulse quickening.

She had barely gotten the word out before the same man said, "Hello, this is General Jones now speaking." In clipped, rapid English, he described American troop movements along the Meuse River and inquired about French entrenchments along the Aisne. When he finished, Valerie translated the message as best she recalled it for Colonel La Roux, who was the same man but speaking French. In turn, Colonel Roux recited a message in French for General Jones, which Valerie translated into English. She wished she had been permitted to take notes, but she had not been given paper and pencil, and the whole conversation darted back and forth so swiftly that she might not have been able to keep up anyway.

The call ended, and after the man on the other end disconnected, Valerie hung up. The door on the far wall opened, and another instructor leaned into the room. "Could you please give that door a knock?" he said, nodding to the one through which she had entered. "After that, come with me, as quickly as you can."

Valerie swiftly complied, scooting out of the examination room before the next recruit was brought in. "Well done," the second instructor said, gesturing for her to accompany him down the corridor. "That's all for today. You're dismissed, but don't stray too far from quarters over the next few days."

"Yes, sir," she replied, wondering what was going on.

Back at their YWCA quarters, the other recruits were equally curious. Cora and her cohort had not been included in the unannounced examination, which she gloomily declared boded very ill for them.

"Until you're sent home, you're still in the running," Valerie reminded her, but Cora only managed a wan shrug in reply.

Two days later, a messenger arrived with letters for several recruits, which had been sent to them from the War Department in care of Mr. C. B. Allsop at Pac-Tel headquarters. Valerie received one, as did the LeBreton sisters, Inez Crittenden, and five others who had translated on the line with General Jones and Colonel La Roux.

Cora did not receive a letter, but her eyes shone with excitement as she asked Valerie to read hers aloud. "Pursuant to authority of Secretary of War dated April 7, 1917," said Valerie, a trifle breathless, "you will proceed to New York City reporting upon arrival to Mr. R. F. Estabrook, American Telephone & Telegraph Co., 195 Broadway, for final training and preparation for service as a Telephone Operator with the United States Signal Corps. The travel directed is necessary in the Military Service. Transportation allowances same as accorded army nurses. You should apply to nearest quartermaster for transportation. Signed Squier, Chief Signal Officer."

"You're in," Cora exclaimed, seizing her arms and jumping up and down. "You did it! You're in!"

Similar cries were going up all around them. Joy and relief swept over Valerie, and she smiled and jumped up and down with Cora until they were both laughing so hard they had to stop to catch their breath. "I only wish," Valerie gasped, "that you—"

"Don't say it," said Cora, and though she smiled, Valerie saw tears in her eyes. "I'll meet you Over There. Save a place at the switchboard for me."

"I will," Valerie promised, taking her hands and squeezing them tightly to show just how strongly she meant it.

The next day, Valerie, the LeBreton sisters, Inez, and the five other qualified recruits swore the military oath of allegiance before an army colonel and their proud instructors in the lobby of the Pac-Tel headquarters. From there, they and their luggage, one bag and a suitcase each, were transported across the bay to the Oakland Pier, where they boarded the *Overland Limited* for Chicago.

From Chicago they would continue on to New York City, and soon thereafter, to France.

6

FEBRUARY 1918

Chicago and New York City

MARIE

Millicent fastened her suitcase shut, hefted it off the bed, and set it down with a thud by the door to the boardinghouse room she and Marie shared. "You'd better hurry or you're going to miss lunch—or, worse yet, the train to New York."

"One last sentence," Marie promised, finishing her letter to her parents and hastily scrawling her signature. The War Department's summons to report to New York had come so suddenly that she had not had time to write home any sooner. She only hoped her family would receive the news that she had been officially sworn in to the Signal Corps with fewer tears and better grace than they had weeks ago, when she had been accepted into the second round of the selection process and ordered to report for temporary duty in Chicago.

In December, when she had told her parents she wanted to apply, they had been reluctant to give her their blessing, even though they shared her desire to save their beloved France from the horrors of war—horrors they too would have experienced had they not come to America years before. "As immigrants, we have a special obligation to prove our loyalty to the country that has given us a safe haven," Marie had pleaded, for without her father's signature, she could not apply. "Since I have no brothers, the duty falls to me."

"But your music," her mother protested. "You'll be gone during the most important stage of your career."

Marie had suppressed a sigh. What career? She had not had a single audition since she had sung for Dr. Kunwald and Mr. Nichols at the Emery Theater, and she had yet to hear back from them. "I'll keep my voice limber," she promised. "I'll practice as often as I can. But let's not get ahead of ourselves. The Signal Corps might not choose me. I'm sure most of the applicants will be far more experienced than I am."

"You'll be chosen," her father said, resigned. "They'll consider themselves very fortunate to have you, and they'll be right."

A week later, Marie had received a telegram summoning her to an interview at Cincinnati Bell headquarters downtown. She had become so accustomed to auditions that she had not felt even the slightest fluttering of nerves as the phone company executive and the army officer asked her about her experience as a telephone operator, her loyalty to the United States, and whether she had been surprised by the outbreak of hostilities.

"Surprised that Germany and France went to war?" Marie asked, puzzled by the question. "I suppose I can't say that I was. My grandmother lived through the War of 1870, and she often told us children, 'We have lost Alsace and Lorraine, but we will get them back.' I did not, however, expect the war to break out when and how it did, nor did I expect the United States to enter the war once President Wilson declared neutrality."

The two men exchanged a significant look. "Did you agree with the president at the time?" the officer asked.

"No," she said without hesitation, meeting their eyes steadily. Let them accuse her of violating the Sedition Act if they wanted; she had promised to answer their questions truthfully, and she was a woman of her word. "I understand why he wanted the United States to remain neutral, but I believe that was a very costly mistake. I'm thankful he changed his mind."

"You wanted the United States to come to France's rescue?" the telephone executive asked, a faint smile curling his lips beneath his neatly trimmed mustache.

Marie allowed a small smile as well. "Just as France came to the rescue of those brave colonials fighting to wrest their liberty and independence from the grasp of King George the Third."

The army officer made a noise in his throat as if he were trying to conceal a laugh with a cough. "You sound as if you have a personal grievance with the Germans," he said, composing himself.

She had acknowledged that she did, and when he asked her to elaborate, she had fought to keep her emotions in check as, quickly and sparingly, she described the friends and family known to have been killed, the others from whom they had heard nothing for years, her cousins fighting in the trenches, the beloved places devastated by German artillery, the unbearable insult to French sovereignty.

"There are other ways a girl can support the war effort without joining the Signal Corps," the telephone executive pointed out. "You can buy Liberty Bonds, conserve food, roll bandages for the Red Cross—all without risking your life."

His lazy dismissal of her skills and how badly General Pershing needed them sparked her anger. She bolted up from her chair and slapped her palms flat on the desk. "You still cannot understand why I need to go to France, after everything I've told you about what the Germans have done to my homeland and the people I love? I tell you this, I would enlist to go to France a thousand times, even if I knew that the first day I set foot on French soil would be my last!"

Startled, the men regarded her in silence for a moment. "If you were a man," the officer eventually said, "I'd give you a gun."

She lifted her chin, inhaled deeply, and sank gracefully back into her chair. She thought, but did not dare to say aloud, that if she were a man, she would already have a gun, for she would have enlisted months ago.

Marie had been certain that her outburst had doomed her application, but soon thereafter, a telegram had arrived from the War Department ordering her to report to the Chicago Telephone Company school for advanced training and evaluation. Later that same day, she received a letter from the Cincinnati Symphony Orchestra inviting her to join the chorus.

She had laughed aloud, pained by the irony. "If this letter had come two weeks ago," she told her parents, shaking her head, "I might never have applied to the Signal Corps."

"I'm sure their decision was delayed because of Dr. Kunwald's resignation," her father said. "You shouldn't misinterpret it as a lack of interest."

"Not at all." That had been the least of her worries as far as the conductor's sudden departure had been concerned. In late November, the Cincinnati Symphony Orchestra had traveled to Pittsburgh for a performance at the Syria Mosque. Mere hours before the concert was to begin, the director of public safety had revoked their permit, insisting that he never would have approved it had he known the conductor was a citizen of Austria and a reserve officer in the Austrian army. Dr. Kunwald was able to prove that he'd had no connection to the Austrian military since 1910, but his Austrian citizenship had been justification enough to withhold the permit. When a substitute conductor could not be found, the concert had been canceled, the tickets refunded, the musicians angered and humiliated.

Soon after the orchestra returned to Cincinnati, Dr. Kunwald had offered his resignation to the board of directors. "My fate is in their hands," he told Marie's parents afterward. "I don't want the orchestra to suffer because I am Austrian. What happened in Pittsburgh could happen elsewhere. What's more, I've heard rumors that many longtime subscribers are not renewing their season tickets because they don't believe their orchestra should be conducted by a citizen of the Central Powers. And yet, if the board stands by me and refuses to accept my resignation, I will gladly and gratefully stay on."

His circumstances had become even more precarious after the United States declared war on Austria on December 7. The next day, he had been arrested by the U.S. Marshals Service, accused of violating the Sedition Act by making remarks against the U.S. government and

President Wilson. In the absence of any evidence of wrongdoing, he had been released the following day, but the arrest was the final blow. A few days later, the orchestra's board of directors accepted his resignation.

Marie knew her parents wanted her to reject the summons from the Signal Corps and join the orchestra chorus, but how could she have passed up the opportunity to serve the Allies and strike a blow for France?

As she had made her tearful goodbyes with her parents and sisters, her mother pressed a brass key into her palm. "I hope you will not go so far east that you can visit Papa's family in Nancy," she said. "I would rather have you safe in Bordeaux, near my relations. However, if you're assigned to Paris, would you look in on our apartment? Perhaps the army would permit you to stay there rather than whatever dreadful barracks they have in mind."

"I don't think they would," Marie said, pocketing the key, "but of course I'll stop by, if I can."

"We never meant to stay away from France so long, but this war—" Her mother gestured, graceful and impatient. "How could we have taken you girls back into such danger and hardship? And yet here you are, going nonetheless—"

"I'll be all right, Maman," Marie said, embracing her and kissing her on both cheeks. "The sooner the Allies win, the sooner we can go home. Now do you understand why I have to do my bit?"

Soon thereafter, Marie's father had escorted her to the train station, and after another heartfelt farewell and more promises to write, Marie boarded the *Daylight Express* for Chicago via Indianapolis and Logansport. Upon her arrival, she had reported to the Chicago Telephone School, where she had barely set down her suitcase before her training had begun. After weeks of military instruction, practice on a variety of switchboards from antique to modern, a stint at the switchboard of a military cantonment, and multiple examinations, she had been selected as one of eight telephone operators from the Midwest who would travel to New York in preparation for service overseas.

If, as her roommate reminded her, she didn't miss the train.

As Millicent stood in the doorway, already dressed for the outdoors and playfully tapping her wristwatch, Marie sealed and stamped the letter, swept a scarf around her neck, and slipped into her coat, hat, and gloves. Suitcase in hand, she followed Millicent downstairs two flights to the boardinghouse lobby, where their fellow Signal Corps telephone girls waited—all of them bright, smiling young women, chatting excitedly as they awaited their chaperone's departure instructions. The landlady agreed to post Marie's letter for her, and no sooner had Marie entrusted the envelope to her than the lead instructor clapped her hands for attention. "Leave your bags on the carts outside," she said, raising her voice to be heard over the few whispered conversations that had not quite finished. "They'll be transported to the station for you, while we meet the San Francisco contingent at the Hotel LaSalle for lunch. Girls, if you would, please."

Beckoning with both hands, she led them outside and down the block, where they all squeezed aboard a streetcar that carried them to the Loop, and to the famed Hotel LaSalle, a luxurious twenty-two-story Beaux-Arts building on the corner of LaSalle and Madison. The San Francisco girls were waiting for them in the lobby, which was opulently furnished with marble floors, desks, and statuary, as well as elegant green-and-gold carpets and draperies. The West Coast recruits had arrived earlier that morning and had come to the Hotel LaSalle to rest and freshen up before continuing the journey east.

One of the older girls in their contingent, Inez Crittenden, had been appointed their chaperone; she evidently had supervisory experience and seemed very comfortable in command. She took charge of both groups, instructing them to follow her to the Dutch Room, the least formal of the hotel's dining rooms. Before they were shown to their tables, Inez admonished them to mingle the two groups so they could get to know one another better. She had barely finished speaking when Millicent slipped her arm through Marie's. "Let's stick together so we aren't the odd ones out," she murmured, then indicated a pretty blonde who was chatting with an older, shorter, stouter brunette with large, shy brown eyes. "They look all right. Let's invite them to join us."

Millicent steered Marie through the crowd of milling girls to the pair she had selected, smiling broadly as she introduced herself and then Marie. The pretty blonde—Valerie, a Belgian from Los Angeles—cheerfully accepted the invitation, and her companion nodded. After they seated themselves, two younger girls—beautiful, lissome, and so alike in appearance that Marie immediately knew they must be sisters—claimed the two remaining seats at their table.

The two sisters were French, which Marie had also guessed, and as they enjoyed a delicious lunch of tomato soup, filet of sole, dilled potatoes, and bread and butter, she and Millicent learned all about their companions, who already knew one another well from their weeks of training together. The brunette was Berthe Hunt, one of the oldest recruits at thirty-three, a graduate of Berkeley and a first-generation Californian born of French immigrants. Marie was surprised to hear that Berthe had been a public school teacher, and had never worked on a switchboard until she had reported to Pacific Telephone headquarters for training. "It was no snap, I'll tell you that," said Berthe, pulling a face, revealing a glimpse of the high spirits concealed behind her tranquil demeanor. "It was easier to teach seventh grade."

Marie was even more surprised to learn that Berthe was married. Marie knew of no other recruits who were, and only one—Inez—who had been. Berthe's husband, Reuben, had served as the head physician of the U.S. battleship *McArthur* for many years, but when they married he had left the navy for a job as the resident physician at a Northern California resort. When the United States declared war on Germany, he had rejoined the navy, and was at that moment serving as a medical officer aboard the USS *Moccasin*.

The elder of the two sisters gasped aloud. "Your husband is an officer?" she whispered, leaning forward to be heard, eyes darting to their chaperone, two tables distant. "Wives of officers are ineligible to serve in the Signal Corps."

Valerie gave her a sidelong look. "You're a fine one to lecture anyone about regulations, Louise."

"I'm not lecturing." Louise's cheeks flushed pink. "Nor am I going to tell Inez. What do I care? More power to you, Berthe, if you can get away with it."

Marie glanced at Berthe and read the sudden uneasiness she was trying very hard to conceal. "Perhaps that rule only applies to *army* officers," Marie said, tossing off a shrug. "Perhaps since her husband is in the navy, Berthe is exempt."

"Or maybe they made an exception for her because her French is perfect and she's very good at her job," Millicent chimed in. With a friendly grin for Berthe, she added, "I assume that's true."

Berthe nodded her thanks, but her expression was solemn. "I wouldn't have applied if I thought I might let anyone down Over There."

"Of course not," said Valerie. "And you wouldn't have made it this far if you weren't qualified. None of us would have. So take heart. We're comrades now. We'll look out for one another, come what may."

As everyone murmured assent, Berthe offered Valerie, Marie, and Millicent a small, grateful smile. Although she had not confessed to it, not exactly, Marie was certain that Berthe had applied to the Signal Corps in order to be on the same side of the world as her husband, on the slim chance that they might be able to reunite while on leave. Marie could hardly fault her for wanting to be near the man she loved, even if it meant going to war.

After lunch, Inez called them to order by standing and clapping her hands twice, sharply, then instructed them to assemble in the lobby for their departure to the LaSalle Street Station, a ten-minute walk four blocks down Clark Street. Marie fell in step beside Millicent near the back of the group, behind Berthe and Valerie and just ahead of the LeBreton sisters. An icy wind gusted down the corridor between the tall buildings lining the street, teasing the end of Marie's scarf until it streamed behind her like the tail of a kite. But none of them minded the cold, or the wind, or the inch of snow that dusted the sidewalk. They all understood that their adventure was about to become quite a bit more adventurous, and even the most reserved among them could hardly contain her excitement.

They looked so much like a group of carefree college girls setting off on a holiday that they attracted quite a few sidelong glances and double takes as they approached the train station. Just inside the main entrance, a group of khaki-clad soldiers halted in mid-conversation, their trunks and duffel bags piled at their feet, to stare as they passed.

"Say, ladies," a tall, red-haired fellow called out, grinning. "Where are you all headed off to? Wish I was going there."

"You might be," one of the girls near the front teased back. "We're going to France."

"France?" said the redhead, incredulous. "The one in Europe?"

The girls laughed, delighted. "Is there any other?" inquired Valerie archly.

"There's a Paris in Texas," another soldier countered, leading the others closer, "and a Bayonne in Jersey."

"We're going to France," said Raymonde primly. "*La République française.*"

Another soldier who stood near the back of the group—tall, dark-haired, and dark-eyed—studied them, curious. "You do know that France isn't safe for tourists these days, right?"

"Oh, yes," said Marie, perhaps more sharply than the question deserved. "Just this morning, we read in the papers that there was a—what was it, girls? Oh, yes. A war." She locked her gaze on the soldier's in a challenge, and felt her cheeks growing warm when he didn't look away.

"We're going to France for the same reason you are," said Louise, "to fight for freedom and democracy."

"We're in the Signal Corps," said Raymonde, lifting her chin proudly. "General Pershing himself requested our presence."

The soldiers regarded them with new respect, even the dark-haired one in the back, whose eyes kept finding Marie's even when she tried to avoid them. "You're hello girls," a sturdy blond soldier exclaimed. "My sister's a hello girl back home in Milwaukee."

The redhead looked delighted. "You mean we're going to have American hello girls connecting our calls Over There?"

"Your commanding officers will, at any rate," said Inez, appearing out of nowhere with their tickets in her hand. "Come along, girls. Show some decorum. You haven't been properly introduced to these . . . gentlemen."

As she herded the recruits toward the platform, Valerie blew the soldiers a kiss. "Take care Over There," she said. "Keep your heads down and come home safe."

The soldiers grinned. "For you, we will," one of them called.

"'Bye, boys," Louise sang, smiling and waving over her shoulder.

Marie glanced back too, and she felt a strange fluttering in her chest when she found the dark-haired soldier still watching her, his expression curious, as if he thought he recognized her but couldn't remember where or when they had met.

C'est rien. It didn't matter. She would never see him again.

They walked down the famed red carpet and boarded the *20th Century Limited*, and when they made their way to their sleeper cars, they were pleased to find their luggage waiting for them. Marie took an upper berth, above Millicent and across from Valerie, with Berthe below her. The corridor rang with chatter and laughter, which swelled into cheers when the whistle blew and the powerful locomotive chugged away from the station, steadily building up speed. Someone suggested that they find the lounge and relax before supper, and everyone chimed in agreement except for Inez, who wanted to rest, and Berthe, who needed to finish a letter to her husband.

They had the lounge car almost entirely to themselves, except for a middle-aged couple with a very active young son, and two dowagers who looked on indulgently as the young women admired the walnut paneling and comfortable leather chairs.

"All we need is a piano and this would be quite a lively place," Millicent remarked. Brightening, she seized Marie's arm. "Sing for us, won't you?" The Chicago girls promptly seconded her plea, drowning out Marie's demurrals. "She has the most beautiful voice," Millicent told the California contingent. "Our boardinghouse had a piano, and if we asked nicely, one of us would play—okay, *I* would play—and she would give us a concert worthy of Carnegie Hall. She's a famous opera singer back home."

"I wouldn't say famous," Marie broke in. Nor would she necessarily claim to be an opera singer. Shouldn't one have to be a member of an opera company, or at least perform opera arias in concert fairly regularly, to call oneself an opera singer? If so, she was an *aspiring* opera singer, no more.

"Someday you will be," Millicent declared. "You're about to launch your first European tour! Won't you please give us a few songs, so we can tell our grandchildren that we were there when you were first starting out?"

At that, Marie began laughing too much to sing, but she soon agreed, gesturing for her companions to settle down while she caught her breath. She would have preferred to perform with an accompanist, but her friendly audience probably wouldn't mind. Reading the room as she warmed up her voice, she decided they would prefer popular tunes, so she began with "Send Me Away with a Smile," and followed that up with "Love Will Find a Way."

As she bowed to their enthusiastic applause, Millicent called out, "Sing that one from the opera, you know, where you're supposed to be a young boy? Let's give these girls some culture."

Everyone laughed, and the nearest girl gave Millicent a playful shove. "We're plenty cultured," she protested, feigning indignation.

"Are you sure you want that song?" Marie asked, hiding a pang of worry. She knew the one Millicent meant, but although the aria was in Italian, the composer was Austrian, a fact that anyone who recognized Mozart would know. Many cities had outlawed German music, as well as German literature and German-language studies in schools and universities. In Cincinnati as well as Chicago, she had seen restaurant signs and market labels edited to rename sauerkraut "liberty cabbage" and bratwurst as "liberty sausage." If Marie defied the fervently patriotic trend, would some aggrieved stranger accuse her of disloyalty?

Yet it was music, wonderful music. It was Mozart. He had nothing to do with the kaiser or the war. The aria was in Italian. She could always feign ignorance and claim she thought the composer was Salieri.

"This is for you, Millicent," she said. Then she drew in a breath and began to sing "Voi che sapete" from *The Marriage of Figaro*. Although the role was traditionally performed by a woman soprano, the character was an adolescent boy, Cherubino, who found himself bewildered, intrigued, and alarmed by his first pangs of love and desire. How much of the Italian her listeners grasped, Marie did not know, but she was gratified to see that the sprightly aria seemed to please them.

She had nearly finished when a movement in the corner of her eye drew her attention. Turning her head slightly, she glimpsed two soldiers peering in through the window of the railcar door. One was the redhead who had spoken to them in the station, and the other was his dark-haired, dark-eyed comrade.

Marie's heart thumped, though she did not miss a note. Shifting her gaze back to her rapt audience, she pretended the men were not watching and finished the aria flawlessly. The Signal Corps girls, as well as the other passengers who had unexpectedly found themselves at a concert, rewarded her with generous applause. Glancing to the window as she swept a comical bow toward the girls, she felt heat rise in her cheeks to see the dark-haired soldier smiling and applauding too.

"Encore!" Millicent called out, evoking laughter from the other girls.

"Someone else will have to perform it," Marie replied, waving her off. "This diva needs an intermission." As she left her stage, such as it was, she stole a look to the railcar door again. The redhead was gone, but the dark-haired soldier was still watching her, smiling. Then he inclined his head to indicate the car behind him, raised his eyebrows in a question, and turned away from the window out of sight.

Marie stood still, her gaze fixed on the empty window, as the other girls settled down to chatting or admiring the scenery. "I need a drink of water," she murmured to Louise, who sat nearest. Without giving herself too much time to think it over, she went to the door, paused with her hand on the latch, then crossed into the adjacent railcar.

She found herself in another lounge, this one more filled with passengers than the one the Signal Corps women had claimed. Her gaze swept the room, but although she spied two soldiers in khaki playing checkers at a table in the far corner, neither was the one she sought.

Carefully, swaying with the motion of the train, she passed through the car and exited into the next, which turned out to be a dining car. Over the clattering of the wheels and rails, she heard unseen voices and the faint clink of china from behind a partition at the far end. At a table near it, an older gentleman sat reading a newspaper, a cup of coffee steaming on the table before him, the aroma rich and enticing.

Between them, the dark-haired soldier stood in the aisle, watching the passing scenery through the window. At the sound of the door, he turned, caught her eye, and smiled, relief and delight in his warm brown eyes, as if he had hoped she would follow but had not expected it.

Without a word, they seated themselves on opposite sides of one of the tables, which was spread with a white tablecloth but not yet set for supper. "Hello," the soldier said, after they had sat in silence for a moment, adjusting their chairs, glancing out the window, exchanging hesitant smiles.

"Hello," Marie replied.

His hair was thick and wavy, so dark brown it was almost black, and longer in the front, just within regulation length, but clipped close around the sides. "You have a beautiful voice."

She clasped her hands in her lap. "Thank you."

"I heard music from the other car, and I had to find out who was singing so beautifully in my language." His smile deepened, revealing a dimple in his left cheek. "I thought I would find an Italian girl. You . . . were a pleasant surprise. I never expected to see you again."

His smile warmed her. "You're a fan of opera?"

"My parents love it, and they passed that love along to me. They're very proud that most of the world's most beautiful operas are in Italian." He winced slightly. "Although Mozart—"

"Was Austrian. Yes." Marie hesitated. "You aren't going to report me to the authorities?"

"Of course I am," he said, feigning solemnity. "In a minute, I'm going straight to the conductor."

She laughed, a trifle shakily. "Is there anything I could say to change your mind?"

He shrugged. "You could tell me all about yourself. If I'm distracted long enough, I might forget my mission entirely."

"In that case," said Marie, sitting back in her chair, folding her arms, "I suppose I should give you the long version."

She told him what there was to tell about her life since her family had come to America, her music studies, her work for the telephone company, her decision to join the Signal Corps. When prompted, she divulged more stories of her family, her childhood, her disappointing audition season, her fears that she would arrive in France only to discover that everything she cherished about her homeland had been utterly, irreparably devastated.

"I should mention," she added, realizing that she had not yet told him, "that my name is Marie."

"I'm John," he said, reaching across the table to shake her hand. His fingers were long and elegant, like a pianist's. "Giovanni, actually. Giovanni Rossini. No relation to the composer, much to my father's chagrin."

Marie smiled. "Pleased to meet you." She let her hand linger in his, warm and strong around her own, for as long as she dared. Then she pulled away, interlaced her fingers, and rested her hands on the table. "Now it's your turn, Corporal Giovanni Rossini of the Three Hundred and Seventh Infantry." She had noticed his insignia over the course of their conversation, whenever holding his gaze had become too much and she had needed to rest her eyes elsewhere. "Is Chicago home, or were you just passing through? What awaits you in New York?"

"Another train to Long Island, and then a bus," he replied. "I'm stationed at Camp Upton, in Suffolk County. I was in Chicago on leave, for a wedding." Something in her expression must have revealed her sudden dismay, for he quickly added, "My sister's wedding."

"I see."

"So to answer your other question, I still call Chicago home, but I've lived in New York for the past few years while I've been in college." His smile turned rueful. "I graduated from Columbia in May, and a few months later, I was drafted."

"If you hadn't been, would you have enlisted?"

He hesitated. "I don't know. My parents didn't want me to go. They'd saved for years to send me to college, with the expectation that I'd find work and help support my four younger brothers and sisters. I'd love to impress you with my courage and patriotism and tell you that I was the first to answer when my country called, but—"

"I'm more impressed by honesty than by empty patriotic boasts."

"Glad to hear it. I'll never know what I would have done, because eventually the army decided for me." He gestured to his uniform. "And here I am."

He had more to say about the army, the dream job with a civil engineering firm he hoped they would keep open for him until he returned from the war, his family back in Chicago, and other things both insignificant and consequential. The hours passed, and as the white-coated servers appeared and began to set the tables for dinner service, Marie realized, reluctantly, that she had to go. Millicent and the other girls were no doubt waiting for her and wondering why she had never reappeared after going for that glass of water. Inez could be frantically searching the train for her at that very moment.

Giovanni too seemed to understand that they had to part. "Maybe I'll see you Over There," he said, standing and holding out his hand to her.

She took it and rose. "Or pick up a phone. I might be the girl connecting the call."

He escorted her back to the lounge where she had sung for her friends, who had all departed, replaced by another group of travelers. Just as she was about to bid him goodbye, he pulled her closer, and for a dizzying moment she thought he might kiss her—and then he did. His lips were warm, his kiss tender and searching, and for a moment she could only stand there, closing her eyes and sighing softly in the back of her throat, until a sudden urgency compelled her to press her lips more firmly to his, and to run her fingers through the thick, unexpectedly soft curls at the nape of his neck to draw his face closer to hers.

The train jolted. With a gasp, she pulled away, still clasping his hand, and threw a glance over her shoulder. Her heart thudded with alarm, but no one was watching. No one had seen.

"Marie—"

"Whatever you say next," she broke in, "don't apologize."

He was so surprised he laughed. "Well, if you insist. I won't."

"I'm not sorry, but I don't—" She gestured, flushed, searching for the words. "I don't usually kiss someone I've only just met."

His expression softened. "Neither do I."

"I should go."

"Can I see you again?"

She laughed shakily, her heart pounding, heat rising in her cheeks. "We're on the same train. I think it's almost inevitable."

"I'll take that as a yes." Giovanni smiled, squeezed her hand, and released her. "But in case our paths don't cross, keep your head down Over There. Come home safe."

"You too," she said, breath catching in her throat.

He smiled, inclined his head, and turned away. She watched through the window until he disappeared into the adjacent car.

She returned to the sleeper car, where her companions were preparing for dinner. "Where have you been?" Valerie asked, her tone full of amused insinuation.

"Watching the world go by," Marie replied lightly, searching through her bag for her hairbrush. "Conversing with some of our fellow passengers."

Valerie's eyebrows rose. "Anyone in particular?" When Marie merely shrugged, Valerie grinned, lowered her voice, and said, "I won't tell, but don't let Mrs. Crittenden see you conversing with any gentleman to whom you haven't been properly introduced."

Marie smothered a laugh and thanked her for the warning.

She expected to see Giovanni in the dining car, but none of the soldiers appeared while she and her friends were there. Nor did she see him at breakfast the next morning. She hoped he would seek her in the lounge again, but he never came, at least not when she was present.

It was not such a large train, she told herself, vexed and disappointed. Surely their paths should have crossed again.

It was almost as if he had disembarked, or had never been aboard.

Twenty hours after the *20th Century Limited* departed Chicago, it pulled into Grand Central Terminal in New York City. Disembarking with the other girls, Marie paused for a moment on the platform, suitcase in hand, searching the milling crowd for Giovanni. Twice, at a distance, she spotted two soldiers in khaki and her heart leapt with hope, only to sink again when she noted a different color hair, a shorter stature.

She had hoped, almost expected, that Giovanni would be searching for her on the platform too. Perhaps he'd had only minutes to catch the Long Island train, and had waited as long as he could for her to appear before he'd had to run. Or perhaps it had not occurred to him to look for her. All this time, she had assumed that their unlikely meeting and hours of conversation and wonderful, unexpected kiss had meant as much to him as it had to her. Perhaps she had been mistaken.

She had wanted to tell him goodbye.

"Marie," Berthe called, beckoning. Marie glanced her way and discovered that she had fallen behind the other Signal Corps girls, who were following Inez from the platform in two double lines. With one last, futile glance over her shoulder, she grasped the handle of her suitcase tightly and hurried to catch up with them.

Their destination was less than a mile down Madison Avenue—the opulent fourteen-story Beaux-Arts Prince George Hotel on 28th Street. "Can you believe they're putting us up here?" Millicent marveled as Inez led the way into the grand lobby, which was adorned with rich oak paneling and intricately carved pillars. She became more incredulous yet when they collected their room keys, dispersed to their separate rooms, and learned that they had been assigned two to a suite, each with an in-room bath.

Marie had been paired up with Berthe. They were given a few minutes to inspect their rooms and freshen up before they were to return downstairs and report to the Ladies' Tea Room, where they met another group of recruits, all hailing from the East Coast. Their cohort had been training at AT&T headquarters for weeks, and later that afternoon they proved to be friendly, knowledgeable tour guides when the entire group took the streetcar to the Telephone and Telegraph Building at 195 Broadway.

Inside, they were directed to a lecture hall. After they were seated, an officer took the stage, introduced himself as Captain Ernest Wessen, and welcomed them to New York. "Today you'll meet your chief operators and receive instructions for the days ahead," he said, gesturing to a few other men and women who had assembled in a row behind him. "You should expect to be very busy in the days to come as we prepare to sail, but you'll have time to explore the city as you assemble your kit and obtain your uniforms." His expression grew stern. "I must caution you, however, that you must not speak freely of our mission to strangers. Anyone could be an enemy sympathizer or a spy for the Central Powers. Just as you have sworn never to divulge any information you may hear on the telephone lines, so too should you keep your own orders and deployments to yourselves. Details that may seem insignificant to you could be of great value to the enemy."

Murmurs rose in the air around her, but Marie could not utter a sound as a sudden chill seized her. She had spoken so freely to Giovanni, trusting him implicitly. And then he had vanished—

She took a deep, steadying breath. She must not let her imagination run wild. Nothing she had told him could be of any possible use to the kaiser. She didn't even know the name or number of her own unit or when she might be heading Over There. Nor could she believe that Giovanni Rossini, with those warm, understanding eyes, could be a spy.

Even so, she would never again speak so freely to a man she barely knew, not until the war was safely won.

7

FEBRUARY-MARCH 1918

New York City

GRACE

As recruits from the Midwest and western states arrived in New York, Grace was pleasantly surprised to be appointed chief operator of the First Unit, First Group, the thirty-three telephone operators who were expected to be the first Signal Corps girls sent to France. As she read over the list of those under her command, Grace noted that they hailed from large cities and small towns scattered across the country and ranged in age from nineteen to thirty-five. She had no concerns about the youngest, whom she had observed on the switchboards and knew to be very skilled, but she had definite misgivings about the eldest, whom she had not yet met.

"Thirty-five years old," she lamented to Suzanne Prevot, a fellow New Yorker who had become her best friend among the recruits. "How am I supposed to lead someone so aged? I've always heard that old people are set in their ways. Why would she obey someone who's ten years younger?"

"Because you're her superior officer," said Suzanne reasonably. "A mature woman is more likely than someone younger to understand the need for authority and discipline. I think you have less to worry about from her than from our young Louise LeBreton. Everyone knows that westerners are stubbornly independent and hate to be told what to do, and she's all that in the form of a rebellious teen-ager."

"She's twenty-one. Her sister Raymonde is the teen-ager."

"That's their story, anyway," said Suzanne, skeptical. "Let's not judge the thirty-five-year-old before we get to know her."

"Sound advice." Grace knew, deep down, that her worries were probably groundless. Her supervisory role in the Instructor Department of AT&T had prepared her well for this promotion to leadership, and from what she had observed so far, all of the recruits were absolutely committed to the Signal Corps and to serving their country. Surely no one would jeopardize her place in the unit by defying Grace's authority, especially if she earned their loyalty through her words and deeds.

One of her first responsibilities as chief operator was to see that the thirty-two operators under her command were properly outfitted for overseas service. The army had issued each recruit a footlocker and a list of supplies to purchase, including bandages, a sewing kit, bicarbonate of soda, Lysol, iodine, and other essentials that might be difficult to find in war-torn France.

The operators were also required to purchase their own uniforms, which, since the women were accorded the status of officers, must be in-dividually fitted. Grace took pride in her own uniform, and she enjoyed escorting small groups of girls to a tailor's shop in the city to acquire their own: a high-collared coat and a skirt made of navy blue serge, a tailored shirtwaist of navy blue Palm Beach cloth, tan parade gloves, lace-up heeled boots, an overseas cap, and a straight-brimmed hat of blue felt adorned with the official orange-and-white hat cord of the Sig-nal Corps. On the left coat sleeve, a white whip cord or doeskin insignia displayed the wearer's rank. A telephone transmitter embroidered on a white brassard indicated an operator, and the addition of a laurel wreath below the transmitter signified a supervisor. Grace's insignia also in-cluded a lightning bolt above the transmitter, setting her apart as a chief operator. Mindful that the women would likely encounter mud-choked roads, the War College had designed the skirts to be hemmed nine inches above the ground—daringly short, even though the women's tall boots would conceal their wool stockings. Concerned that an errant gust of wind might reveal a shocking amount of leg, the army added black sateen bloomers to the uniform in order to preserve the operators' modesty. Uncomfortable and embarrassingly old-fashioned, they were the only part of the ensemble that the operators despised.

"I don't mind the bloomers," Inez confided to Grace one morning as they waited for the recruits to assemble in the lobby of the Prince George for the walk to AT&T headquarters. "At least they're sateen rather than thick, scratchy wool. What bothers me is the absence of any indication of rank."

"Our insignia will appear on our left sleeve," Grace reminded her.

Inez shook her head. "That's not what I mean. That indicates our role, but not our *rank*. If we're accorded the status of officers, as we've repeatedly been told, why not give us the corresponding rank as well? There's a world of difference between a lieutenant and a general. Where exactly do we fit into the hierarchy?"

She made a fair point, one Grace had not previously considered. "I don't know, but I assume we're closer to the lieutenant rung of the ladder."

Inez gave a dry laugh. "That's a safe bet, but the army could avoid a lot of confusion and ambiguity by making it official. Women in the navy have a specific rank, yeoman—"

"Yeoman F, for female."

"Right. My point is, why doesn't the army follow suit? They can call me a 'Lieutenant F' if it's important to note that I'm a woman, but give me a rank, a real rank, like the men."

Grace mulled it over as the last of the operators hurried into the lobby with seconds to spare. "I think most of the girls are happy with the title of operator," she said in an undertone. "I don't think they care about a specific military rank, as long as they get to serve Over There."

Inez frowned briefly. "Well, I'm not convinced it's an oversight, and I don't think it bodes well." Without another word, she called the operators to order. Moments later, they were marching off to training.

As soon as their uniforms were ready, the operators were ordered to ship their civilian clothes home, except for their undergarments and pajamas. "You're in the army now," one of their Signal Corps instructors, Lieutenant Hill, told them, his expression making plain that he would not tolerate any wheedling to keep a favorite blouse or pair of silk stockings. "No civilian clothes are allowed."

Grace regretted parting with the soft dove gray cashmere sweater her sister Helen had knit for her. She loved slipping into it back at quarters between the end of a long day of training and bedtime, but orders were orders, and as chief operator, she had to set a good example. As the other girls packed up their boxes, Grace could feel a frisson of wistful excitement circulating among them, the sense that they had put away the accoutrements of their old lives and would thenceforth be fully immersed in the army. It was fortunate that—except for the bloomers—they all adored their uniforms, which made them feel as if they had attained full membership in the American Expeditionary Forces. They stood straighter and lifted their chins proudly when they discovered how their uniforms commanded attention, curiosity, and respect from onlookers whenever they traveled between their lodgings and AT&T headquarters on Broadway. It was there, on the rooftop high above the streets of Manhattan, that each of the groups posed for a formal photograph. The thirty-three women of the First Unit, First Group posed in two rows with Grace front and center, with *Golden Boy* gleaming in the sunlight above them.

On the first full day, the recruits had been fingerprinted and photographed for their passports, and they had also begun a series of inoculations for typhoid and other diseases. "Are you experiencing any symptoms of influenza?" the nurse had asked as she wiped a spot on Grace's shoulder with rubbing alcohol. "Chills, fever, fatigue, coughing?"

"No," Grace answered, averting her eyes as the nurse brought the syringe closer, trying not to flinch as the needle pierced her skin. "Why do you ask?"

"Nothing to worry about," the nurse replied briskly, affixing a bandage to the punctured skin. "A few cases of influenza have shown up on army bases, but not at any of the cantonments you girls trained at." She had gestured for the next recruit. "Next, please?"

A typical day included rigorous practice on the switchboards, including dummy boards where the instructors simulated various calamities that the operators had to work around in order to put their calls through. The recruits attended lectures by Signal Corps officers, including Captain Wessen and Lieutenant Hill, about Signal Corps protocol, communications in modern warfare, the absolute necessity for secrecy and security, and what conditions they should expect during their ocean crossing and upon deployment in France.

Several times a week, they were treated to additional lectures on health and hygiene by the same doctors who conducted their physicals. "You ladies should, as President Wilson exhorted our men in uniform, be 'fit and straight in everything, and pure and clean through and through,'" Dr. Richter told them as he paced back and forth on the stage, hands clasped behind his back, white coat blindingly spotless. He warned them against indulging in alcohol, and absolutely forbade the use of drugs, which he condemned as poison. Grace found the lecture a bit insulting. The recruits had been training diligently for months, and surely they had proven just how seriously they took their responsibilities, how committed they were to their service. Did any of their superiors really think they would throw that away for gin and a smoke?

A female doctor was assigned the unenviable task of delivering a lecture that was as painfully uncomfortable for the recruits to hear as it seemed to be for Dr. Mann to deliver. Striding back and forth across the stage, occasionally pausing to indicate various poster-size illustrations with a pointer, she explained the rudiments of sexual intercourse. "I assume you have heard most of this from your mothers," she began, "but I shall address the subject from a clinical perspective." Grace observed many of the girls exchanging bewildered, alarmed glances as Dr. Mann explained in vague terms how babies were conceived and how only vigilant abstinence would prevent it. She also warned them against "social diseases" without saying what they were or how one contracted them. Grace had read Dickens and Hugo and had studied biology at Barnard, so she thought she grasped the essentials, but she could not vouch for the younger girls.

Later that evening, Berthe Hunt, one of the California operators who had been assigned to First Group, tentatively asked if she could speak to Grace alone. They found a quiet corner away from the others, and as Berthe frowned and fidgeted, Grace patiently waited for her to speak. "Miss Banker," she began, "as you may know, I am married."

"Yes," Grace replied, smiling to put her at ease. "I'm aware."

"Dr. Mann on sex—" Berthe hesitated. "She was fairly good, but not very forcible, and I'm afraid she took too much for granted. She didn't say anything that wasn't correct, but she didn't say all that should have been said, either."

"I see."

"A married woman—especially a doctor's wife, as I am—knows things that a single girl doesn't, unless her mother has been very frank, and most mothers aren't."

Grace wondered where her own mother would fall on the spectrum. Was Grace herself among the uninformed innocent? She didn't know what she didn't know. "Do you think we should ask Dr. Mann to give a second lecture?"

Berthe held up her hands and shook her head to ward off that possibility. "Oh, no, not that. I only meant to offer myself as a resource, in case any of the girls have questions. If anyone seems . . . headed for trouble, or if they're confused and need advice, you could direct them to me. I'd be happy to speak with them, in strictest confidence, of course."

"I think that's a fine idea."

"Inez Crittenden was formerly married. I can't speak for her, but she might be willing to advise girls in the Second Group."

"I'll ask her," said Grace, although she wasn't sure whether she should. In their brief time together, she had found the newly appointed chief operator of the forty-two-member Second Group to be very skilled, confident, and committed to her work, but Grace had heard disgruntled murmurings from girls in both groups about Inez's authoritative manner and strict adherence to the letter of the law. Inez might not be the ideal surrogate older sister for a bewildered young woman far from home.

Inez did have a take-charge attitude that suited the military, Grace thought, and that served her well during the recruits' daily military drill. Every afternoon, in sunshine or wind or snow, they assembled on the roof of the Telephone and Telegraph Building to march in formation, twenty-nine stories above the pavement, streetcars, and unwitting pedestrians. Responding to an officer's commands, they drilled until they had mastered "the elementary commands of the school of a soldier," as Lieutenant Hill put it, marching until perspiration soaked their uniforms, only to have the cold February air chill them until they shivered. "This will prepare you well for the situation in northern Europe," the lieutenant told them stoutly one Friday afternoon as the sun declined in the winter sky. Standing at attention, Grace was proud to observe that her fellow recruits revealed not a flicker of dissent or dismay, true soldiers schooled in discipline and prepared to endure any hardships without complaint.

Only once, after the women were dismissed and they hurried inside, did Grace overhear one lament drift up the stairwell. "Why the roof, though?" someone asked, more bewildered than petulant. "Isn't there a nice park somewhere on the ground where we could march?" Someone snickered, and others hushed them, and that was the last Grace heard of it.

The girls were far freer with their opinions in the last week of February when the First and Second Groups received orders to decamp from the lovely Prince George Hotel to new quarters in Hoboken, New Jersey, in preparation for transport to France.

At first, as they packed up their belongings for the short journey across the Hudson River, they fairly hummed with excitement and anticipation. Their relocation closer to the wharf surely meant that their departure for Over There was imminent. Some especially eager girls had already visited the waterfront on their time off, curious about the mysterious Pier Number Two, which no one was allowed to approach without a military pass, and from whence they expected to put to sea. Though Hoboken was not as exciting as Manhattan, there were still charming restaurants and shops to be found—and the secretive comings and goings of soldiers along the waterfront to observe and speculate about.

The operators expected to be billeted at another hotel like the Prince George, if not quite as grand. Grace was as astonished as everyone else to discover that their new quarters was a single large rectangular room above an old saloon, with bare, unfinished walls, no heat, no windows except for two small square glass panes on either end, and no furnishings except for the neat rows of cots in which they were to sleep.

"What a dump," Valerie exclaimed, letting her suitcase and footlocker slip from her grasp and strike the floor with a pair of dull thuds.

"Where's the radiator?" asked Louise, shivering, her gaze searching the length of the room. "Or the fireplace?"

"There doesn't appear to be either," said Berthe, sizing up the place, hands on her hips. "At least it's clean."

That was true enough. The old wooden floorboards had been swept and scrubbed, and the cots were neatly made up with crisp white sheets, gray woolen blankets, and one flat pillow apiece. Yet it remained a cold and cheerless spot, dimly lit, with odors of dubious origin drifting up through cracks in the floorboards from the saloon below.

"Claim a bed, girls," said Grace, raising her voice to be heard over the murmur of distressed and disgruntled voices. "It's not the Prince George Hotel, but it's not a muddy trench in France, either, so be grateful for small comforts while you have them."

The grumbling subsided as the recruits split off into their usual groups of friends to choose cots near one another. Grace took a cot near the top of the stairs, the better to monitor her soldiers' comings and goings, and slid her bag and footlocker beneath it. Suzanne promptly claimed the cot on one side of Grace's, and Berthe the other. Morale did not improve when Grace went in search of the bathroom facilities mentioned in her instructions, and returned to announce that two toilets, two sinks, and one shower were available on the first floor, in the rear of the building down a corridor that, fortunately, did not pass through the saloon. A few recruits rewarded her with wan smiles when she added that, except when they were at AT&T headquarters training, they would take their meals at a small restaurant around the corner. "I haven't seen it yet," she admitted, "but I can almost guarantee that it will have heat. We'll find out when we march over together for lunch in fifteen minutes. After that, I trust you'll be able to find your own way there and back."

That night, most of the girls followed Grace's example and slept in their union suits and knit wool caps to retain warmth, except for a few like Louise who fretted that a snug cap would flatten her hair. The room was pitch dark except for a patch of moonlight peeking through the south-facing window, and as Grace shivered beneath her gray wool blanket, hoping fervently that she would soon be warm enough to sleep, she heard cots rattling softly as their occupants shivered, a few unhappy sighs, and the soft snores of a particularly hardy soul who apparently could sleep through discomfort. Grace wished she were as fortunate.

In the morning, she woke to dim sunlight and a cold nose. From the sound of things, many of the girls were already awake, but none had dared emerge from beneath the relative warmth of bed to seize the day. A check of her watch, which Grace had left on the floor beside her shoes, told her it was almost seven o'clock, time to rise and make ready if they wanted breakfast before departing for Manhattan and their first training session of the day.

Sometimes, she reflected, one just had to jump into a cold lake to get the shock of it over with rather than prolonging the agony by inching away from the shore into deeper water step by step. Grace flung back her blanket, snatched up her clothes and necessary items, and hurried downstairs for a sponge bath. To her surprise, she found Inez already there, smoothing out invisible wrinkles in her dark blue uniform.

"Good morning," Inez said, smiling brightly. "Do you think we should roust these girls out of bed and send them along to breakfast?"

"They might need a gentle push today," Grace admitted. "When I return upstairs—"

"No, take your time," Inez urged. "I can handle this."

As the other chief operator turned on her heel and strode to the door, Grace called after her, "A *gentle* push, remember." An unsettling vision sprang to mind of Inez overturning a cot, spilling the hapless occupant onto the wooden floor, and declaring in a singsong that it was time to rise and shine. She needn't have worried. By the time Grace returned upstairs, all the cots were upright, and nearly all of the recruits had dutifully emerged from beneath their warm blankets and were preparing for the day.

They moved so sluggishly, however, that Grace called them to assemble for some simple calisthenics to warm them up before they went down to breakfast. In the days that followed, that became an essential part of their morning routine, although she moved it to an earlier spot on the agenda, so that it became known as "pajama drill." Each day they would awaken in the cold, exercise to get the blood flowing, shiver through a wash, pull on their uniforms over goose-flesh skin, and then fortify themselves with coffee, toast, scrambled eggs, and bacon at the corner restaurant before they headed into the city for training.

Given the rudimentary comforts, when the recruits were dismissed at the end of each day, Grace understood completely why most of them preferred to stay in Manhattan to tour a museum or enjoy a hot meal before returning to their chilly, drab quarters, which one of the girls had dubbed Hobo House. Grace was amused when the name stuck, but Inez fretted that Captain Wessen and the other Signal Corps officers might hear of it, and the First Unit would be disgraced. "We'll just say it's an abbreviation for Hoboken," Grace said, but Inez was not reassured.

On their unscheduled hours, the operators were permitted to explore the city, with caveats. Before they set out, they were required to inform their chief operator where they intended to go and with whom, and the chief operator could deny them permission at her discretion. They were also obliged to check in with the Hoboken quarters via telephone once every hour, just in case their unit had received orders to put to sea and they must hurry back to prepare. Finally, they were ordered to behave with dignity at all times, and to do nothing that might disgrace the uniform or embarrass the Signal Corps.

Grace emphasized the last point to the women under her command whenever they went out. "We are the first women in the army," she reminded them. "They recruited us only because the need for our skills was so great. If we want any other women to be accepted after us, we must prove every day that General Pershing and the Signal Corps were right to take a chance on us. If we fail to behave with honor and dignity at all times, we'll ruin it not only for ourselves, but for every little girl out there who wants to be like us when she grows up."

That speech never failed to sober them just as they were heading out to enjoy themselves, so Grace would always add, "Have fun. Remember, safety in numbers. Don't do anything I wouldn't." Their smiles returned, and they set off in pairs or in small groups, and they never failed to return safely, well before curfew.

One Wednesday afternoon, as the First Group was dispersing outside 195 Broadway after a particularly grueling day of marching on the rooftop parade grounds in an intermittent snow squall, Grace saw off the last of her charges and was about to head to a favorite midtown bistro with Suzanne when she was approached by one of the operators from the Second Group—Valerie DeSmedt, tall, slim, and stylish in her uniform, looking as if she had just stepped out of a recruiting poster. "Miss Banker," Valerie began, her usually lively expression grim, "may I speak with you privately for a moment?"

"I'll wait at the corner," Suzanne said, inclining her head that way.

Grace put her hand on Valerie's arm and guided her to a spot behind one of the tall marble columns, a bit of shelter from the swirling snow. "Can I help you with something?" she asked, fervently hoping it wouldn't be a topic better suited for Berthe.

"Yes, at least, I hope you can." Valerie squared her shoulders. "My younger brother, Henri, is a private in the Photographic Section of the Signal Corps. He's currently posted to the school for land photography at Columbia University."

"Is that so?" said Grace. "That's not far from here."

"Less than ten miles, according to the map Lieutenant Hill showed me. But Henri won't be there much longer. In a few weeks, as soon as it opens, he's going to be transferred to the aerial photography school at Eastman Kodak in Rochester." Valerie's voice dropped to a murmur. "And as you know, we ourselves could be sailing any day now."

Grace nodded, although the Second Group wouldn't depart until after the First Group had reached the North Sea; by her estimate, which could be overturned in a second by the demands of the war, Valerie had at least another week in New York and Hoboken, probably longer. "I gather you want to see your brother before you both leave the city."

"Exactly," said Valerie, exasperated. "It's not a bizarre request."

"I don't understand. Is your brother's commander refusing to allow you to see him, even for a brief visit?"

"That's not the problem. Henri easily got a half day's leave. It's Mrs. Crittenden. She refused to give me permission. Millicent Martin offered to come with me, so I wouldn't be strolling through the city alone and helpless"—she rolled her eyes—"but Mrs. Crittenden wouldn't budge."

"Did she say why she refused?"

"She said it was too far to go, considering that our travel orders might come at any moment and I might not make it back to quarters in time. But Second Group won't even board a ship until First Group sets sail, right?"

"That's right." Grace paused, thinking. "Would you like me to speak with her?"

Valerie straightened, arms at her sides, eyes defiant. "I was really hoping you would just grant me permission yourself. I could see my brother tomorrow afternoon, and be back at Hobo House hours before curfew."

"I'm sure you understand why I can't do that," said Grace kindly. "Mrs. Crittenden is my equal in rank, and you're in her group. I can't countermand instructions she's given you."

Valerie heaved a disconsolate sigh. "I was afraid you might say that. It's so stupid. I could have just told her that I was going for a stroll through Central Park, and then gone to see my brother anyway. She never would have known."

"But you wouldn't have done that," said Grace, raising her eyebrows, "because you swore an oath of loyalty to the army and you wouldn't do anything to break or even to bend it."

Valerie hesitated. "No, of course not."

"I'll talk to her," Grace promised, resting a hand on Valerie's shoulder. "I'm sure I can make her see reason. In the meantime, do you want to join Suzanne and me for dinner? I've never been to Southern California, and I'd love to hear all about it."

Valerie managed a forlorn smile. "Sure, that sounds nice."

Over dinner, Grace learned that Valerie was friendly, humorous, exceptionally bright, and deeply committed to their mission, impressions Grace shared with Inez later that night when she beckoned her downstairs to the small back room where the only telephone was installed. As she pled Valerie's case, she skipped over the part where Valerie had sought her out to circumvent Inez, implying that the matter had come up while they were dining. As Grace had expected, at first Inez was a bit put out to have her decisions questioned, but eventually she acknowledged that the Second Group almost certainly wouldn't depart for France in the next two days, and a dutiful operator like Valerie ought to be given the chance to say goodbye to her brother.

"I'd love to see my brother one last time," Grace admitted. "That's impossible, though, since he's at Camp Green in North Carolina. I have no idea when he'll be shipping out, either."

To her surprise, Inez clasped her by the shoulders. "Don't think of it that way, as 'one last time,'" she said earnestly. "You don't *need* to see him now, although of course you'd *like* to, because you're both going to come home safely. You'll see him then."

Grace felt a catch in her throat. "Of course. You're right."

"You might even see him Over There."

"Or I might connect a call, and discover that it's Eugene on the line." It wasn't likely, she knew. For months or years to come, it was almost certain that she would be unable to reach him except by letter. But if Grace couldn't see her brother, at least she could help another girl see hers.

The next morning when the two groups met for training, Valerie caught Grace at the door on her way in. "I don't know what you told Mrs. Crittenden, but thank you," she said in an undertone, beaming. "I'm going to see my brother tomorrow."

"That's wonderful," said Grace. "I'm happy for you."

She was also happy for Inez, who had apparently learned to temper her judgments with common sense. It seemed to Grace that as long as they kept within military regulations, it was better to accommodate the girls' personal requests unless there was a very compelling reason not to do so. If Inez had begun to see the merits of that approach, Grace was sure she would be rewarded with better morale and stronger loyalty from her operators.

The following evening, Grace and Inez both stayed behind at Hobo House while about half of the operators went into the city, some for dinner, some to attend a tea dance. "One last frivolous night on the town before we head Over There," one of the girls declared as they left, after promising to heed all of Grace's usual warnings. Grace was upstairs completing paperwork on her cot, wrapped in a blanket with her knit cap pulled over her thick bob for warmth, while Inez stayed downstairs in the heated office to be near the phone when the girls called for their hourly check-ins.

Grace had almost finished her paperwork and was contemplating an evening stroll along the waterfront, if she could find a companion or two, when suddenly she heard a clatter of bootheels on the stairs. A moment later, five of her First Group operators burst into the room, breathless, eyes wide with excitement that turned to confusion when they looked around the half-empty quarters.

"What's going on?" demanded one of the girls—Marie, the luminous Frenchwoman with the beautiful voice. "Why isn't everyone packing?"

Grace set her papers aside and swung her legs over the side of her cot. "Packing for what?"

"For our departure first thing tomorrow morning." Marie studied Grace's expression, while her companions exchanged puzzled glances. "Didn't our orders come in?"

"Not that I've heard." And Grace surely would have heard. Increasingly suspicious, she shrugged off her blanket and reached for her boots. She had just finished lacing them when Inez entered.

"Mrs. Crittenden," one of Marie's companions gasped. "Where is everyone? Did they leave for the ship without us?"

Marie drew herself up, fixed a steely gaze on Inez, and in a tone just short of insubordination, said, "When we phoned to check in, you told us the First Group had received orders to depart and that we must report back immediately."

"What?" Grace exclaimed.

Marie turned to her. "So it wasn't true?"

"Consider it a trial run," said Inez smoothly. "I wanted to see how long it would take you to return to quarters from the city when our orders actually do come in, so I timed you." She tapped her wristwatch. "Thirty minutes, from the moment you hung up until I heard you on the stairs. That's not bad, but I think you could do better."

As the five young women stirred restlessly, frowning, still breathless from their sprint, Grace closed her eyes and muffled a groan.

"We left a delicious dinner half-eaten on the table," someone muttered. "Bought and paid for."

Grace promptly opened her eyes. "Thank you, Denise. That's enough," she said, a trifle sternly. Denise nodded and looked away, folding her arms. "The restaurant on the corner is still open if you're hungry." Opening her footlocker, she retrieved a packet of vouchers, counted out five, and distributed them to the unhappy women. "My treat—or rather, the Signal Corps's treat."

They murmured their thanks and departed, with more than a few withering sidelong glances for Inez in passing, which she either did not notice or ignored. "Thirty minutes," Inez remarked after the women had gone. "I think they should get that down to twenty, even if it means not venturing into the city quite as far as they like."

Grace sighed, removed her cap, and ran her fingers through her hair. "It *is* good to know how quickly the girls can return in a pinch, but I'd encourage you not to run any more unannounced tests. Remember the Boy Who Cried Wolf."

Inez regarded her, uncomprehending. "Soldiers need to follow orders, quickly and without second-guessing their leaders. Our girls will face far more serious tests Over There than an interrupted dinner."

"Indeed they will," said Grace, nodding. "All the more reason to build trust and loyalty now."

Inez mulled that over, her expression betraying her skepticism, but she agreed that the next time, she would randomly select a group of girls checking in and order them to return so she could time them, but she would explain it was only a drill. They wouldn't like having their fun cut short, but they should understand the need to prepare.

Grace supposed that Inez thought it was appropriate to test the operators not only because the timing information she sought would indeed be valuable, but also because the chief operators themselves were often given impromptu tests on protocol. Sometimes they were not told they were being tested until after the fact. With all of that in mind, Grace could not fault Inez for what she had done, only for the way she had done it. She only hoped she had seen the last of Inez's questionable decisions.

That turned out to be a hope fulfilled only ironically, because although Grace was not an eyewitness to the events that became known as "the Hoboken Incident," it fell to her to help pick up the pieces afterward.

Hobo House was only twelve miles from the Banker residence in Passaic, less than a half hour's journey by the same train Grace had once taken for her daily commute. One Saturday, Grace and Suzanne obtained a half day's leave to visit her family. Grace's parents and sisters admired their smart uniforms; her mother's roast chicken dinner with mashed potatoes, peas and carrots, and butterflake rolls was delicious and satisfying; and it was lovely to be at home once again. If only Eugene had been able to join them, her happiness would have been complete.

When Grace and Suzanne returned to Hoboken later that evening, they found most of the operators glowering and fuming in their Hobo House quarters. When Grace asked about Inez, she was told that her

Second Group counterpart was in the office downstairs, writing a report. Several girls from both groups spoke over one another in their eagerness to tell Grace the story, some of them evidently hoping for sympathy and redress, the others seeking to defend themselves.

As far as Grace was able to piece together, a group of operators didn't have the time or money to head into the city, so they found a vacant storefront down the block on River Street, pushed the abandoned furniture against the walls, set up a borrowed Victrola, and held a dance for themselves, partnering with one another. The sound of music and laughter drifted outside, intriguing several officers who were passing by. The men peered in through the doorway, and then, without any invitation or proper introduction, they entered and asked if they might join the girls for the next dance. The girls cheerfully agreed, the officers helped them push heavy tables aside to widen the dance floor, and for a little while, they all had a jolly time. Then, as luck would have it, Inez too heard the music and came to investigate. Aghast by the abundance of impropriety, she immediately silenced the music, scolded the officers, and swept the operators back to quarters. "Young ladies in this service in many cases would not care to meet, socially and indiscriminately, every officer," she told a lieutenant indignantly in parting.

"Mrs. Crittenden is responsible for the Second Group's reputation," Grace told the disgruntled operators. "As I am, for the First Group's. She had no choice but to intercede if she believed something inappropriate was happening."

"We would never do anything to disgrace the uniform," Valerie protested. "It was all perfectly innocent. We were only dancing with a few army officers, as other young ladies dance with other soldiers at YMCAs both here at home and Over There."

"If the YMCA had organized and had chaperoned this dance," said Grace, knowing Valerie could discern the difference, "I doubt Mrs. Crittenden would be upset."

The girls murmured among themselves, angry and apprehensive, wondering what the chief operator was putting into her report, and what the consequences would be. No matter how Grace tried to reassure them, every girl who had attended the impromptu dance worried that she would be dismissed from the Signal Corps.

In the days that followed, Grace was relieved to learn that Captain Wessen and Mr. Estabrook were less alarmed by the dance than Inez had been, but the incident had provoked important questions about protocol that had not occurred to them earlier. Where exactly did the Signal Corps telephone operators fall on the chain of command? Did any officer or enlisted man have the right to address them if they had not been formally introduced? What should the operators do if they encountered an officer or an enlisted man on the street? If either recognized the other, who should salute first?

Grace and Inez were asked to help devise answers, thoughtfully but with some haste, given their imminent departure. Mr. Estabrook believed that the telephone operators should be considered to have the same status as cadets, above enlisted men but below other officers in rank. Grace was not surprised when Inez seized the opportunity to ask whether the women might be assigned actual military ranks, the same as any other soldier.

Captain Wessen hesitated. "I don't think the army intends to do that."

"Standard ranks would make the operators' status clear to everyone," Inez pointed out. "Eliminating unnecessary ambiguity will help maintain order."

The two men exchanged a look. "I'll pass it up the chain of command," said Captain Wessen, "but don't get your hopes up."

Nevertheless, Grace noted, Inez looked very hopeful indeed, even triumphant, as she nodded and sat back in her chair. Her smile did not fade even when Mr. Estabrook noted that in the meantime, the operators should expect to be addressed by their job title and surname, or by the usual honorifics of "miss," "missus," or "ma'am." "Disrespect from the officers and men will not be tolerated," he assured them. "We'll have no 'honeys' or 'girlies' in uniform Over There. Some of the men may have to learn this the hard way."

That brought them to the more fraught subject of less official interactions between men and women in uniform. Inez strongly recommended that if any officer wanted to meet a Signal Corps woman, he must first inquire with her chief operator. If the petitioner's superior officer was willing to vouch for his character, the superior officer could introduce the petitioner to the young woman's chief operator, who could then, at her discretion, introduce the petitioner to the young woman.

Although Grace did not say so aloud, she thought that Inez's plan was an unnecessarily complicated and archaic way for two people to meet. Yet she agreed with Captain Wessen that it was inevitable that some of the young men and women would become interested in one another, and in the absence of parents and the other usual constraints upon courtship, policies were needed to protect the young ladies' honor. After much discussion, they agreed that the Signal Corps women should keep their acquaintance with both commissioned and enlisted men to a minimum, and that they should "resent and properly report" any undue or unwelcome familiarity. Then, when Inez left the room for a moment, Mr. Estabrook beckoned Grace and Captain Wessen closer and murmured, "The bottom line is, no dancing in front of Mrs. Crittenden in Hoboken."

"I believe I can see to that," said Grace, "as long as we put to sea soon."

Both men regarded her wryly, divulging nothing.

"It was worth a try," said Grace, smiling. "You're going to have to tell me the schedule eventually." She was beginning to think that she might not know when they would be leaving until five minutes before departure.

The two men exchanged a look. Mr. Estabrook shrugged, and Captain Wessen nodded.

"This is strictly confidential," said Mr. Estabrook, leaning forward and lowering his voice. "Say nothing to your operators, nor even to Mrs. Crittenden."

"I understand," said Grace, barely above a murmur.

"The First Group's departure is imminent," said Captain Wessen. "Any day now. If you haven't yet put your affairs in order, do so immediately."

"Yes, sir. The First Group will be ready."

At that moment, Inez returned. Without missing a beat, Captain Wessen said, "Ah, Mrs. Crittenden. We were just saying that, with regard to fraternization, the chief operators will be expected to set an example of utmost discretion and restraint for their operators to follow."

"Of course," said Mrs. Crittenden, resuming her seat. "It would be inappropriate for a chief operator to engage in courtship of any kind while we're Over There. Nothing shall distract our attention from our duties and the girls in our charge. Don't you agree, Miss Banker?"

"Why, yes," said Grace, a bit taken aback by Inez's vehemence. Still, she agreed with her in principle. Grace had joined the Signal Corps to serve her country and defeat the kaiser, not to find a husband.

After the meeting ended, Grace carried the secret of their imminent departure back to quarters with her, anticipation rising. The next morning, she tried to conceal her excitement as she led the girls through pajama drill and on with their day. She picked at her breakfast, the fluttering in her stomach making it impossible to swallow more than a morsel. Rather than draw attention to her lack of appetite, she told Suzanne she would meet them outside, then left the restaurant and walked along the waterfront to work off nervous energy. She paused to study the mysterious Pier Number Two, wondering if the ship docked there was the troop transport vessel that would carry the First Group to France.

While she was taking in the scene, an army captain she did not recognize approached her. "Fine ship," he said, cocking his head toward it.

"Yes, sir," she replied. "She looks quite seaworthy indeed."

"When are you and your hello girls setting sail?"

She shrugged and widened her eyes, feigning ignorance. "I don't know."

He threw back his head and laughed. "Well, of course you really do," he said, gesturing toward her insignia. "You're a chief operator. You know, and so do I. So it's quite all right to tell me. When do you sail?"

"If you know," she said, "then there's no need for me to tell you."

She threw him a cheerful grin over her shoulder and headed back to the corner restaurant to rejoin the others.

Later that day, when Grace went to the censor's office to deliver the First Unit's outgoing mail for clearance, she was startled to encounter the same officer in the hallway. "Captain," she greeted him.

"Miss Banker," he replied, his grin broadening at her surprise that he knew her name. "I'm with G2," he said, startling her anew. The intelligence division. "It's just as well that you didn't answer my question earlier today. I had been sent to test you."

"I assume I passed?"

"With flying colors. Keep it up. You're a fine soldier, for a girl."

Taken aback, Grace nodded and continued on her way. What a shame he had not quit before undercutting the compliment.

On the fifth day of March, the women of the First Group were given another thorough medical exam—weighed, measured, tested, and grilled about symptoms including sore throat, fever, cough, and headaches. They assembled before Captain Wessen and swore the military oath, all of them for at least the second time. Then they were ordered back to Hoboken, with explicit instructions to report in every half hour if they left their quarters.

That evening Grace received word that they would board the troop transport the following morning. She called her thirty-two operators together, gave them their instructions, and reminded them to tell no one. "Get a good night's rest," she added. "You'll be glad you did."

As for herself, she was almost too excited to sleep. She lay awake on her cot for hours, eyes closed, mind racing through a checklist of all the tasks she had to complete before they sailed.

Morning came. One more pajama drill, one more quick wash in the small bathroom, one last breakfast at the restaurant on the corner. Then, impeccably attired in their uniforms, their gear neatly stowed, they hauled their bags and footlockers downstairs and out to the curb, where two soldiers loaded their belongings onto a cart and hauled it away down Pier Number Two.

Grace called them to order, and in two lines of sixteen with Grace in the lead, they marched onto the pier and onto the RMS *Celtic*, one of the famed Big Four, the first ships over twenty thousand tons. Towering above the wharf, its sides camouflaged in a confusion of painted angular shapes in shades of green, blue, and beige, it looked nothing like the former White Star passenger liner it had been before the war.

A cold, gray drizzle began to fall just as the group crossed the deck and reached shelter. Grace directed the girls belowdecks to their assigned cabins, which were all on the side facing the dock. After they stowed their bags and footlockers, many were drawn to the portholes. Thousands of soldiers in khaki uniforms stood in formation on the docks, helmeted and with heavy packs on their backs, waiting to board. From a distance, it was a silent, solemn scene, despite the men's apparent good cheer and the occasional unmistakable flash of a grin.

It seemed hours until the last regiment was on board, but the signal Grace awaited finally came, a whistle blast alerting the crew that it was nearly time to cast off. "Blackout curtains down," Grace ordered while the deep reverberations still rang through the air above them. Quickly the girls scrambled to cover the portholes. They were not permitted to move so much as a corner of the heavy cloth aside, not even for a quick peek, until the captain himself declared it was safe to do so.

Grace checked to make sure that every porthole had been attended to, chatting with her girls as she went from one cabin to the next, offering words of encouragement they hardly seemed to need, so excited were they to be setting off at last.

And finally, the whistle blew again, long and loud. The low hum of the engines rose, intensified; a slight lurch, and then a steady forward motion as the *Celtic* pulled away from the dock, moved out into the Hudson River, south into the bay, and out to sea.

She had truly crossed the Rubicon, Grace thought as she looked around at the young women under her command and the heavy weight of her responsibilities settled upon her shoulders. There was no turning back. She was heading Over There, and she would not come home until the war was won.

God willing, she and all of her girls would be coming home.

8

MARCH 1918

Hoboken, Halifax, and at Sea

VALERIE

In the first days of March, Valerie yearned to be in the First Group so badly that she developed a painful habit of clenching her jaw until her teeth ached whenever she thought of it. It wasn't just because she saw herself as a daring trailblazer rather than a follower, the first one to leap into the pool rather than the tentative girl who dipped a toe first, although that was certainly part of it. Nor was it that she couldn't stand her chief operator and preferred to serve under Grace Banker. That might have been true once, but she and Inez Crittenden had achieved a friendly détente after Inez had reversed her decision forbidding Valerie to visit her brother at Columbia University.

"In hindsight, my objections were overcautious," Inez had said when she finally granted Valerie a half day's leave. "It's safe to assume that we aren't going to sail today, or tomorrow, or even the next day."

Valerie could have hugged her, but a grateful, respectful "Thank you" seemed more appropriate. She admired people who could admit their mistakes and tried to put things right without making excuses or blaming someone else. And although some of the girls groused about Inez's leadership style, Valerie couldn't think of any occasion when their chief operator had acted out of ignorance, malice, or incompetence. Inez simply followed the rules and expected her girls to do the same. As far as Valerie could see, even when Inez's decisions annoyed her operators, she never acted out of self-interest, but always for the good of the unit, the Signal Corps, and the war effort. Inez knew army regulations, she followed them, and she expected her operators to do the same. How could any reasonable person criticize her for that? If Inez broke the rules to benefit herself, Valerie would have been outraged, but Inez didn't ask her girls to do anything she herself refused to do.

All Valerie had wanted was permission to visit Henri, but Inez had thrown in an apology and some vouchers so that she could take him out for a nice dinner. That wasn't necessary, but Valerie certainly appreciated the gesture. After that, warmed by memories of a lovely afternoon with her younger brother, Valerie began defending the chief operator when other girls muttered complaints behind her back—unless their complaints were warranted, in which case Valerie tried to mediate.

So it wasn't that Valerie always had to be first in line, or that she yearned to escape from Inez Crittenden. It was just that she couldn't bear to be stuck in Hoboken—waking for pajama drill, shivering through a sponge bath unless it was her turn for the shower, forcing down another barely palatable meal at the corner restaurant, and spending the day drilling, training, and having her temperature taken and throat examined by inexplicably tense nurses—while other Signal Corps girls set forth on the adventure of a lifetime.

"Why couldn't we all have sailed together?" Valerie lamented on the gray, wet morning of March 6, watching from the wharf with the Second Group as the *Celtic* slowly left the harbor and disappeared into the mist. They had planned to line up along the waterfront and wave white handkerchiefs in farewell as their friends passed by, but when the sailors cast off, blackout shades had descended over all the portholes. The First Group had never even known they were there to see them off, and the Second Group operators were crushed to have their fond farewell spoiled.

Inez cocked her head and studied Valerie as if trying to determine whether it was a rhetorical question. "We can't all go in the same ship," she said. "They have to divide us among several vessels to increase the likelihood that at least some of us make it Over There. What would General Pershing do if we all crossed the ocean on the first ship, a German U-boat sank her, and she went down with all hands?"

Valerie wished she couldn't picture the scene so vividly. "The general would be in quite a pickle," she managed to say.

"He'd also be out several dozen highly skilled telephone operators," Inez pointed out. "Not easily replaced."

"And we'd all be dead at the bottom of the sea," said Millicent, linking her arm through Valerie's. "You're both much too morbid. Come on. Let's get out of this rain before we all catch the influenza."

"One doesn't catch influenza from rain," Inez replied, but she too headed back to Hobo House.

"Our turn will come," Millicent consoled Valerie, squeezing her arm. "We'll have to cool our heels in New Jersey a little while longer, but this time next month, we could be in Paris."

It was a cheering thought. They didn't have any say in where they would be stationed, but from what Valerie had observed and overheard, the heartfelt desire of every girl in the First Unit was to be assigned to a post as close to the front lines as possible. As important as supply units at the rear were—and no one denied that; a war could be won or lost depending upon the expedient delivery of munitions, equipment, and food—they all wanted to be near the fighting, working the switchboards where every call mattered, every second counted, every connection had to be flawlessly made, every translation rendered word perfect. Valerie was no different; she hoped to be assigned to General Pershing's own headquarters and to connect the most consequential calls of the war. And yet if her tour of duty included a month or two in the City of Light, she would not be sorry. The romance, the beauty, the music, the art, the fashion, the cafés, the handsome Frenchmen—all those would console her while her more fortunate friends closer to the battlefields saved the world for democracy.

When they reached Hobo House, Valerie removed her navy blue topcoat and brushed off the raindrops with her palm before draping it over her arm and heading upstairs. She was glad the Signal Corps had included a wool coat with their ensemble, not only for the warmth, but to protect the uniform beneath. Valerie was proud of her uniform, except for those wretched bloomers, and since they would be wearing uniforms every day for the duration of the war, she intended to take very good care of hers. The telephone operators had been required to pay for their own uniforms and supplies, and Valerie's entire kit had cost $300. She could only afford $200, earnings from Pacific Telephone she had brought along in case of emergency. Nor had she been the only operator whose funds came up short. To the relief of those who had been unable to afford the expense, AT&T loaned them the difference, which they would pay back through regular deductions from their army salaries. As an operator, Valerie earned $60 a month—less than she had earned at Pacific Telephone—with supervisors taking in $72 and chief operators a respectable $125. She was not the only Signal Corps girl who had taken a pay cut in order to serve her country, and she hoped to earn a promotion before long.

Their quarters seemed quieter and more spacious without the First Group, but rumor had it that a Third Group would be arriving soon to replace them. Valerie hoped Cora would be among them, but as much as she wanted to see her friend, she also hoped that the Second Group would be on their way Over There before then. Inez could not, or would not, tell them when she expected them to depart. All she would say was that they must continue training and remain vigilant. They should pack their bags and lockers every night before turning in, just in case their orders came without warning while they slept.

A week passed, and another.

One morning, Valerie awoke to the pressure of a hand on her shoulder, someone gently shaking her awake. "Miss DeSmedt," a voice spoke close to her ear, low and urgent. "Wake up."

"Hilde?" she replied groggily, forcing her eyes open. The room was pitch-black, except for a flashlight courteously directed not in her face, but to the floor beside her cot. Her cot—Hobo House. Of course. Her sister never called her Miss DeSmedt, or woke her so gently.

"Mrs. Crittenden," the chief operator corrected. "It's five o'clock. Help me wake everyone. We have a half hour to wash and dress, and then we must report to the dock."

Valerie threw off her blanket, all traces of sleep vanishing. "When do we sail?"

"Six o'clock."

"*Merde*," Valerie murmured under her breath. Working her way down one row of cots while Inez attended to the other, she woke the other girls, warning them that they hadn't a moment to waste. Some of the girls blinked at her sleepily before nodding and climbing from their cots; others gasped, threw back their blankets, and raced off to wash and dress.

If Inez had not instructed them to pack their kit every night before bed, they never would have been ready on time, but at half past five o'clock sharp, they were all dressed, alert, and waiting outside the saloon with their footlockers and bags. While a pair of sailors took charge of their belongings, the operators lined up in two rows and stood for inspection. Inez quickly gave them the once-over, nodded her approval, then instructed them to follow her in silence. In the pale dawn of an early spring morning, they proceeded toward Pier Number Two, soundless but for the rhythmic crunch of their heeled boots on gravel.

Ahead of them, looming high above in the semidarkness, was the RMS *Carmania*, a Cunard Line passenger liner repurposed for wartime service, first as an armed merchant cruiser, and more recently as a troop transport. Peering up, high up, her gaze drawn by the sound of muffled voices, Valerie detected moving figures that must have been doughboys crowding the decks and peering from portholes. Inez quickened their pace as they approached the gangplank, crossed the water, and boarded the ship. "Say nothing to anyone outside of our group," she ordered as they gathered around her on the deck, her voice so low that Valerie could barely hear her over the clanging of metal and the shriek of seabirds.

Inez led them belowdecks, directed them to their cabins, and checked each porthole to be sure the blackout curtains were down. Then she ordered them to remain in their cabins until she returned to tell them otherwise.

"How long do you think that'll be?" asked Millicent after their chief operator had departed, closing the door behind her. She and Valerie had been assigned to a cramped four-berth cabin with two other girls, one from Colorado and the other from Wisconsin. "This will be a long, tedious trip if we can't stroll around on the decks or look out the window or talk to any of the officers."

"I'm sure she'll release us after we clear the harbor," Valerie said. "She'll want us to drill at some point, and we have to eat."

"But why all the secrecy and silence?" asked Martina, the girl from Green Bay, a daughter of Belgian immigrants. "The First Group left in broad daylight to fanfare and applause. Why are we sneaking out like we're stiffing our landlord?"

"To avoid spies and saboteurs?" ventured Kathleen, a pretty redhead from Denver who wore her long curls loosely tied back with a ribbon. She and Martina exchanged an uneasy look.

"That's unlikely," Valerie assured them, feigning more certainty than she felt. "They probably need to get an early start due to tides or currents or trade winds or something, and they want us to keep quiet so we don't disturb the neighbors still asleep in their beds."

Some of the tension left the other girls' faces, but as Millicent stretched out on a top berth, the look she threw Valerie over their heads was deeply skeptical.

They settled in, adjusting to the strange, unsettling sensation that they were simultaneously underground and floating. Eventually the steam whistle sounded, deep and thrilling. "There goes the neighborhood," said Millicent, yawning. "No one could sleep through that, and no spy or saboteur could miss it."

"I think we're moving," Martina exclaimed, grabbing the edge of Valerie's berth, just as they all felt the strange lurching motion and sensed rather than heard a low mechanical rumble from the steam turbine.

"I really wanted to see the Statue of Liberty when we pass," said Kathleen. "Do you think it would be all right if I just take a tiny peek—"

"I wouldn't if I were you," Valerie advised, sympathetic. "Mrs. Crittenden would have you swabbing the deck from here to—well, wherever we're heading." No one had actually told them whether they were going to Great Britain or to France.

"You can see it on your way back after we help General Pershing win the war," said Millicent, letting her arm fall over the edge of her berth and patting Kathleen on the head. Kathleen laughed and swatted her hand away.

They settled in, chatting, joking about how glad they were to be out of Hobo House, and speculating about whether their chief operator was sharing a cabin with three of the other girls or had commandeered a first-class cabin all to herself. They had not yet settled the last question when Inez rapped on the door and opened it without waiting for them to answer. "Your life belts," she announced, handing each of them a contraption of canvas and cork, with straps and armholes and the ship's name in narrow black capital letters down one panel. "Put it on and keep it on. Once you do, you're free to explore the decks, but only in pairs or groups, never alone."

"Can we stroll the decks with an officer as our escort?" asked Millicent, examining her life belt dubiously.

"As long as another girl is with you as chaperone, sure." Inez gave them a brisk smile. "The captain offered to lead a tour of the ship for Second Group at eleven o'clock. We'll assemble on B Deck, so join us if you're interested. Wear your life belts," she reminded them again, and departed.

The four bunkmates had had enough of the cabin for one morning, so they decided to explore a bit before joining the tour. Valerie laughed when she stepped into the corridor to find the rest of Second Group emerging from their cabins in a rush, all as eager as she for a breath of fresh sea air and a glimpse of the shore from afar, if it was still visible. It was, she discovered when she stepped out onto B Deck, a green-blue blur off to the west and north, with only open sea to the east.

The tour was interesting but hardly exhaustive. The captain showed them the bridge, the upper decks, the dining rooms, and the lounges, but not the mechanicals, which Valerie thought would have been fascinating, albeit earsplittingly loud. The tour ended in the largest lounge, where they were introduced to a number of officers, most of them first or second lieutenants with the 302nd Engineers and their attached Field Signal Battalion. How delightful that the operators would enjoy such charming, gallant companions on their ocean voyage—handsome young men, dashing in their uniforms, sincerely happy and relieved that "real American hello girls" would be running the army's switchboards Over There.

Afterward, Inez and a Signal Corps officer, Colonel Hertness, escorted them to the large dining room for luncheon. Everyone on board would eat there, the girls were informed, each group according to their assigned shift, but the telephone operators would dine at certain tables reserved especially for them. Within that section they could sit wherever they liked, eight girls to a table, but they could not invite any of the men to join them, nor could they take a seat among the soldiers. The first meal was a sort of rabbit stew with potatoes, brown bread, and coffee— tolerable, but nothing that encouraged Valerie to send her compliments to the chef.

"*Navire anglais, cuisiniers anglais, la cuisine anglaise,*" said one of the French girls, Albertine, making a face and pushing her plate away with her fingertips.

"You should eat something," advised Martina. "We're going to have English cooks and English cuisine for the entire voyage. They'd be grateful for this in Belgium and France."

Albertine puffed out a breath. "They can have it." But she picked up her fork and managed another few bites.

They spent the afternoon at their leisure, strolling the decks, catching glimpses of the distant shore as the *Carmania* moved northward along the coast, speculating about their two small escort ships whenever they switched positions on their flanks, in the lead, or following behind. Some girls clung to the rails, green with seasickness, while others withdrew to their cabins to rest or write letters home. Dinner that evening was much the same as lunch, and with little else to do, the girls retired early, prompted by Inez's warning that although that day had been unhurried after their early embarkation, the next would be full.

Valerie expected to be roused before dawn, but it was at seven o'clock that Inez, or someone working on her behalf, woke them by pounding on the cabin door. Roll call was on B Deck at 7:45, but it was slightly delayed, since every operator who had forgotten her life preserver was promptly sent running back to her cabin for it. A breakfast of fried eggs, toast with marmalade, and coffee began at eight o'clock, and at nine, they reconvened on the deck for sick call. Immediately afterward, they were ordered to strip down to their blouses and bloomers and assemble for drill, which they were told would be a daily activity, rain or shine. Colonel Hertness led them through a series of strenuous calisthenics, far more difficult than anything they had practiced at AT&T headquarters or during pajama drill.

"I thought the winds on the rooftop of 195 Broadway were bad," Millicent managed to say as the ship rose on an unexpectedly large swell and the operators staggered, fighting to keep their feet.

Valerie was too out of breath to reply, and by the end of the hour her muscles trembled from exhaustion. Panting and perspiring along with the rest of Group Two, she wanted nothing more than to catch her breath, wash, and put on a clean uniform, but to her surprise, stewards bearing silver trays suddenly appeared and offered them bowls of bouillon. Muffling laughter, the girls gathered in small groups to chat as they sipped the hot, flavorful broth. "Like a tea party," said Kathleen, raising her eyebrows as she peered at her friends over the rim of her bowl.

Next, they were dismissed to wash and dress, and then Inez led them as a group to one of the lounges for French practice, with an emphasis on military and telephone jargon. Luncheon followed, where they were served a saltier version of the stew that had been served for lunch the previous day, but with mushy chunks of yellow carrot instead of potato.

On a typical day, Inez informed them, they would have a second session of French practice after lunch, but on that first full day at sea, the captain had ordered them to report for their lifeboat assignments. It was unnerving but necessary, Valerie thought, as they were divided into groups of four and assigned to numbered lifeboats, where they were to take specific seats amid the men. Her muscles still sore from the morning's exercise, she practiced scrambling aboard the lifeboat with her cohort, every motion made awkward by her long skirt and the bulk of her life preserver.

When the sailor in charge of their lifeboat declared them adequately prepared, they were dismissed for the rest of the afternoon. Valerie, Millicent, and most of the other girls trooped wearily back to their cabins, to rest and knead the knots out of their aching limbs and shoulders.

At four o'clock, the entire ship was summoned for retreat.

"Retreat?" Valerie asked as the girls filed from their cabins into the corridor again and up toward daylight. She imagined the captain bellowing an order, a sailor yanking a lever, and the turbines throwing the ship into full reverse with a great shriek of metal.

"It means practicing what we would do if we were hit by a submarine," another girl piped up helpfully.

"Right," said Valerie, through the catch in her throat.

Retreat began for the Second Group on the deck outside their corridor with Inez taking roll call. Next Colonel Hertness taught them their formation, and then, when the retreat signal was sounded, they and everyone else on board marched to their assigned lifeboats. Valerie made sure to memorize the way; the colonel would escort them this time, but he could not lead them in an actual emergency. When everyone had assembled in formation on C Deck, they stood by their lifeboats while a regimental band played "The Star-Spangled Banner." Valerie surmised that was to add dignity to the drill, or give them a sense of elapsed time, but for a moment she imagined fleeing a sinking ship to a musical accompaniment and had to smother a hysterical giggle. She hoped if that terrible moment came, she would remain calm, find her lifeboat, and help herself and others aboard. She had faced hardship and loss in her life, but she had never been confronted with imminent danger, with the sudden likelihood of her own death. She wanted to believe that she would be brave in that moment, but she did not know. This ocean voyage, with the threat of storms above and German U-boats lurking below, might be the first real test of her courage.

A whistle blew, jolting her from her grim reverie. It was time to dress for dinner.

After another unremarkable meal, the girls returned to the officers' lounge, where the band played lively music, and most of the girls danced. The two activities, retreat and dancing, were so incongruous that to Valerie it all seemed a bit surreal. But she loved dancing, and Inez had said that if they attended the dance they could stay up until midnight; otherwise they were ordered to return to their cabins and be in bed by nine o'clock, so it was an easy choice. None of the girls were without a partner for a single dance unless they chose to be, and the officers were so charming and handsome in their uniforms that Valerie quite forgot about the war, or at least, she pushed it to the back of her thoughts for the space of an evening.

On their fourth day out from Hoboken, the *Carmania* arrived at Halifax, Nova Scotia, where the cold, damp air and stiff winds kept Valerie's walks on the deck brief and brisk and gave her a grudging appreciation for the despised sateen bloomers. The scenery was beautiful in an austere way, with low hills rising from the water's edge and forests veiled in the first pale green tulle of spring. For hours, while the girls drilled and studied and lunched, dockworkers and the ship's crew loaded the ship with coal and supplies, and yet more coal and supplies, such an astonishing amount of cargo that Valerie marveled that even the great *Carmania* had room for it all. But of course, their European allies had been at war three years, and everything had been used up or destroyed and was desperately needed.

That afternoon, retreat was conducted quite differently than the previous day. Instead of standing in formation while the national anthem played, they boarded the lifeboats and were lowered into the rough, icy waters of Halifax Harbour. While the soldiers practiced rowing, Valerie and the three other telephone operators aboard her boat huddled together for warmth, instinctively shrinking back from the waves that splashed over the sides. No one offered the girls an oar, which was just as well, considering that Valerie's arms still ached from Colonel Hertness's calisthenics.

"For soldiers, these boys make fine sailors," Millicent said, her mouth close to Valerie's ear. "I think we can rely upon them to save us, if it comes to that."

Valerie smiled, nodded, and hugged her life preserver tightly against her chest. Where would the brave young men row them to, exactly, if the *Carmania* was torpedoed in the middle of the ocean? What good would her life preserver do her if the lifeboat capsized, plunging them into the icy waters of the North Sea? So many of the poor souls aboard the *Titanic*, lost six years before, had not drowned, but had frozen to death before they could be rescued. The Germans would search the wreckage of the ships they destroyed for survivors. Would it be fortunate or disastrous to be taken prisoner?

She was all too glad to leave the lifeboat for the illusory safety of the massive troop transport.

The next morning, Colonel Hertness's drill was much easier to endure since the rocking of the ship in harbor was barely noticeable compared to what they had experienced at sea. At luncheon, rumors spread from table to table that during sick call that morning, a few cases of influenza had been reported among the enlisted men of the 302nd Engineers.

"Those poor boys," said Valerie.

Kathleen shrugged. "It's only the flu."

"Maybe so," Valerie retorted, frowning at the lack of sympathy, "but can you imagine anyplace worse to have the flu than in a third-class berth of a troop transport?"

That afternoon, the ship took on additional crew and passengers, and shortly before dinner, the *Carmania* departed Halifax. The girls who had been disappointed with the lack of fanfare in Hoboken were pleased to discover that there was nothing stealthy about this sailing. Civilian fishing boats and pleasure crafts escorted them from the harbor, sounding their horns; on the pier below, a marching band played lively tunes like "For Me and My Gal" and "La Marseillaise"; adults and children lined the wharf and waterfront, cheering and waving Canadian and American flags. Yet a more somber mood descended when the music and cheering faded behind them as they headed out onto the open sea with their escort. The British warship *King Alfred* led the convoy, which included the *Carmania* and five other ships: two merchant steamers, a destroyer, and two smaller craft, their prewar names painted over with dazzle camouflage. Valerie knew they were fortunate to have two warships to protect them. Escort vessels were in such short supply that many troopships departed North America without them, and met up with an escort only as they approached the British Isles, if at all.

As the sun set in their wake, illuminating the distant clouds from below with gorgeously dappled bands of scarlet, gold, and yellow, strict light discipline came into effect. Smoking on deck was banned; the girls had all heard the fearsome warning that on a clear night at sea, the glow of a cigarette could be spotted from a half mile away. Blackout curtains covered all portholes and windows, even in the dining hall, which gave the evening meal a subdued, confined feeling. When Valerie and her bunkmates returned to their cabin afterward, they navigated the decks and corridors by the weak light of small, discreet blue bulbs, which were said to be less visible from a distance at sea.

The next morning, the sunlight seemed a benediction, the cool breezes refreshing as Colonel Hertness led them through their morning drill. Valerie believed her body was acclimating to the exercise, her muscles becoming stronger, her joints more limber, her lungs better able to sustain her. The sea was beautifully calm that morning, the brilliant sunshine striking the ripples until the surface seemed like a vast piece of shimmering silk.

Suddenly a powerful shock struck the ship, knocking the girls off their feet, sending them sprawling upon the deck. Valerie fell to her hands and knees, dazed, ears ringing with the startled cries of her companions. A second shock followed, stronger than the first. Shaking her head to clear it, Valerie staggered to her feet, clutched a railing for support, and made her way forward, far enough to see black smoke churning from the cruiser just ahead of them.

Alarms pealed. Crew and soldiers sprinted past in all directions, shouting instructions and warnings. From the phrases she snatched from the incoherence Valerie understood that a U-boat, possibly more than one, had attacked the convoy. Glancing over her shoulder, she saw the Second Group helping one another to their feet, clinging together for balance, making their way to the stairs that led to their cabins. "Valerie," Martina called to her, barely audible in the din, gesturing for her to follow, but Valerie held on to the rail and proceeded aft, drawn by a glimpse of a faint plume of black smoke. As she approached, she saw that the merchant steamship directly behind them had been struck and was dropping back.

The captain must have ordered full steam, for the *Carmania* surged ahead, leaving the ailing ship farther behind. Most of the convoy kept pace with them, but two of the smaller, swifter ships began to turn. Dozens of soldiers with no role to play in the defense of the ship poured onto C Deck just below her, eager to see what had happened. A sailor darted past, brushing so close that she was able to seize his arm. "We have to stop and help them," she shouted, the wind carrying her voice away, alarms drowning out even the wind. "We have to tell the captain they can't keep up."

"He knows, miss," the sailor said, freeing himself from her grasp. "We can't stop. It's against standing orders. Picking up survivors is the job of the submarine chasers. Our job is to stay with the *King Alfred* and get out of danger as fast as we can." With that, he sprinted away.

Submarine chasers—those smaller ships, surely. Heart thudding, Valerie clenched the railing tightly with both hands, looking from the cruiser ahead of them—damaged, but less so than the trailing ship—to the thickening plume of smoke behind them, to the smaller craft darting about in a pattern she could not decipher, to the choppy surface of the ocean. She expected at any moment to see a dark conning tower breaking the waves, or the expanding V of white foam marking the path of an approaching torpedo.

Minutes passed. She braced herself for another shock like the two she had felt before, but none came. The *Carmania* steadily gained on the cruiser, then slowly passed it, but, to Valerie's relief, the damaged cruiser remained with the convoy. Eventually the alarms fell silent, the crew resumed their interrupted activities, and even the plume of smoke disappeared from view far behind them.

On trembling legs Valerie made her way belowdecks to her cabin, where she found her three bunkmates engrossed in urgent conversation. They cried out with relief to see her.

"Why did you ignore Mrs. Crittenden's order to return to quarters?" Kathleen demanded.

"I didn't hear it," Valerie said.

When they implored her to tell them what she knew of the attack, she told them all she had seen. Their faces turned pale and solemn when she described the ship that had fallen behind.

"Did the *King Alfred* drop depth charges?" asked Martina. "Is that submarine still stalking us?"

"I don't know." Valerie sank down beside her on the lower berth, too weary to climb up to her own. "I saw nothing to suggest that they hit anything, but whether they found a target and took aim—" She shrugged and shook her head, hands clasped in her lap.

It was only later that evening, after a dinner Valerie could barely choke down, that Inez called them to assemble on B Deck and broke the news that had come over the wireless telegraph. The cruiser had been struck on the left propeller; twelve aboard had been killed. The steamer had sunk soon after it had fallen behind the convoy. All souls aboard were lost.

"We are well into the danger zone now," Inez told them, her steady, firm gaze lingering on each of their faces. "Until the danger passes, you must keep your uniforms on, waking and sleeping, in case the captain sounds retreat."

Valerie expected to hear a murmur of dissatisfaction at that, but there was not the slightest mew of complaint. There was no dancing that night, not that anyone was in the mood for it. Instead they retired to their cabins and tried to distract themselves with conversation, letter writing, or reading until lights out.

The next morning, after sick call, they learned that the convoy had marked another death—Private Walter Little of the 302nd Engineers, who had succumbed to pneumonia overnight. A cold shiver of worry stirred in the back of Valerie's mind; she was sure he had been among the first soldiers with influenza reported on sick call. The captain had ordered a formal burial at sea for the following day.

By the time the Second Group gathered in the lounge for French practice, everyone had heard the rumors that four more soldiers were bedridden from influenza.

The next morning at dawn, the operators assembled on B Deck for the solemn funeral of the young soldier who perished before setting foot on a battlefield. They stood at attention among the officers, while enlisted men filled the deck below, in perfect formations. The captain read the burial service, but the wind carried away his voice and Valerie could not make out a single word. An honor guard fired a three-volley salute as the flag-draped coffin slid into the Atlantic.

"Poor boy," Valerie heard one of the girls sigh. She could not tell who. Tears blurred her vision, and her thoughts turned again and again from the young man whose remains had been consigned to the sea to her own dear brother, Henri, who would soon cross these treacherous waters.

After lunch, when they gathered for their second French practice session of the day, Inez arrived late, carrying a large carton upon which were stacked bundles of white duck cloth and cotton. When she set it on Valerie's table, she glanced inside and found spools of thread, needles, pins, and scissors.

"I want each of you to make yourself at least two face masks," Inez declared, taking something from her pocket that Valerie thought was a handkerchief until the chief operator unfolded it. "This is an example provided by the chief medical officer. I'll leave one on each table for you to use as a model."

A hand flew into the air. "Mrs. Crittenden, I don't know how to sew."

"I'll show you," someone else replied.

"Those who know, teach those who don't," Inez ordered. "You must wear a mask anytime you leave your cabin, except when you're eating. Avoid close contact with any of the enlisted men—yes, I know you're supposed to do that anyway, but now I want you to be even more vigilant. Your mask must cover your nose and mouth, and it should be tied tightly enough to avoid gaps between your face and the cloth."

She began distributing sample masks, one per table. Valerie picked up theirs and examined it. "It looks simple enough," she murmured to Millicent.

"Maybe we should make extras for the crew and the officers," Millicent murmured back, "if there's enough fabric."

Valerie nodded, heart sinking. She had heard vague rumors about outbreaks of influenza at army camps, terrible fevers and pneumonia that could sweep through a regiment in a matter of days. Kathleen might dismiss the illness as "just the flu," but the seasonal flu typically claimed the lives of the very young, the very old, and the infirm. What sort of flu was this, to overpower such strong, vigorous young men?

"This isn't a matter of personal choice or fashion or comfort," Inez declared, looking around the room sternly. "You're in the army, and this is an order. Wear a mask or keep to your cabin for the rest of the crossing."

"You heard her," said Valerie to the girls at her table, rising and pulling the carton closer. "Let's get to work."

She and Millicent took charge of distributing supplies while Inez went from table to table showing how the fabric should be cut and the masks assembled. Martina darted off and soon returned with a bundle of newspapers and a handful of pencils, which she used to create a pattern. Kathleen helped her make multiple copies, and before long everyone was either tracing or cutting or sewing, conversing in murmurs, mostly to request shared tools or to seek help with a difficult seam. As soon as Valerie finished her first mask, she put it on, adjusted the ties, and began another, distracted by the unfamiliar sensation of cloth on her face, the humidity of her breath, the muffled voices of her companions who had also donned their completed masks. When she considered all the hardships and dangers the soldiers endured in the muddy trenches in France, including the cumbersome gas masks they wore to protect their lungs from German gas attacks, a soft piece of cloth seemed a very small thing indeed to complain about. She was proud that none of her comrades did.

From that day forward, the operators spent their former leisure time making masks for the troops and the crew. When they ran out of fabric, a quartermaster procured cotton sheets for them, which they tore into strips and layered before cutting out the pattern, to compensate for its thinness. Every day they grew more uncomfortable, sleeping in their clothes, masks obscuring all but their eyes, hearts sinking with each new sick call and the discovery of more cases of influenza, which had spread from the Engineers to the Field Signal Battalion. The operators could not make masks fast enough, nor was Valerie convinced that the barriers were enough to prevent the spread of illness in such close quarters. Thus far none of the girls had been stricken, but they all flinched whenever a bunkmate sneezed. During French practice, which had resumed, girls would sometimes worriedly ask a friend to feel her forehead, to check for fever. All the while they braced themselves for the pealing of the alarm bell, warning that an enemy submarine had been spotted nearby.

A second soldier perished, and he too was buried at sea. How many more young men—or young women—would follow?

The voyage had begun to feel frighteningly interminable. The ship's whistle blasted at unexpected moments, signaling a lifeboat drill. The captain ordered that not only uniforms but also shoes must be worn at all times, even while sleeping. Valerie and Millicent noticed, and Inez confirmed, that the convoy had adopted a zigzag course, "to avoid mines," Inez explained.

"Are we getting close?" Valerie asked Colonel Hertness one morning after drill, keeping her distance even though they were outdoors, where the winds supposedly dispersed the miasma of the disease.

"We'll be close when we reach the Irish Sea," the colonel replied, his voice muffled by his mask. "You'll know it from the water, the greenest you've ever seen."

"What a relief it will be to see it," said Valerie.

The colonel squared his shoulders, and he seemed to frown behind his mask. "I don't wish to mislead you, Miss DeSmedt. Reaching the Irish Sea means we're closer to our safe harbor, but it's also the most dangerous stretch of our crossing. German subs lie in wait for convoys like ours, determined to keep our troops and supplies from reaching British soil. An escort of British torpedo boats will meet us, but they are not infallible, and a U-boat could evade them."

"I see," said Valerie, unable to keep a tremor from her voice. "Thank you for your honesty."

She knew then that they would not be safe from attack until they had disembarked in Liverpool, and even there, other dangers would follow them ashore. She felt as if they were being stalked by sinister enemies, invisible and deadly, below the water's surface and in the very air they breathed.

There was nothing for it. She was at the mercy of the enemy and the pestilence and the unforgiving sea surrounding the great, fragile ship for miles and miles in every direction.

9

MARCH 1918

Liverpool, Southampton, and Le Havre

MARIE

When Marie disembarked the *Celtic* at Liverpool, even the pungent smells of the waterfront, the rough voices of the dockworkers, and the squawk of seabirds overhead seemed bathed in warmth and light. How grateful she was to be on solid ground again, although she still had her seas legs and the wharf seemed to rock with the swells of the ocean.

In the broadest sense of the term, the *Celtic* had actually landed on solid ground the previous evening. After twelve days at sea—enduring bitter cold air and rough swells, evading German mines and submarines—as the ship had passed New Brighton, where the river Mersey met the Irish Sea, she had run aground on a sandbar. Startled by the impact, the First Group had run from their cabins to the deck, where they had clutched the railing for balance as they had observed the alarming scene below. "What a beautiful target for submarines we are, here in the moonlight," Grace had murmured.

"Do you mean that, Miss Banker?" Raymonde had asked, pensive. "Submarines might attack us even here?"

"I'm sure it's unlikely," the chief operator replied quickly. "Didn't you see all the torpedo boats darting around as we came in? Let's put our trust in them to keep the enemy away, and we may be free before the Germans ever realize we're stuck."

Raymonde and her sister had smiled, apparently reassured, but Marie had exchanged uneasy glances with some of the other girls. They understood, even if the LeBreton sisters did not, that their chief operator had not promised that they would be safe, because she couldn't.

When a hard, full reverse failed to wrench the ship loose, a pair of large cruisers attempted to pull her free, all to no avail. Thwarted, the cruisers abandoned the *Celtic* within sight of Liverpool—or so it would have been, if Liverpool had not been under blackout restrictions and there had been lights for them to see—and escorted the merchant vessels into the harbor. What a tempting target for the Germans they were indeed, stranded, helpless, and loaded with troops and materiel.

As night descended and the operators returned to their cabins, Marie had lain awake in her berth for hours, uneasy and restless, until she had finally drifted off to sleep. The next morning, she was relieved to learn that while she slept, the ship had floated free with the changing tide. The *Celtic* was moving down the Mersey, and they were only minutes away from docking at Liverpool.

With all the troops and supplies to unload, it was noon before the Signal Corps operators could disembark. A member of the crew handed each of them a box lunch before they stepped onto the gangplank, so each tucked her box down the front of her coat or held it tightly under an arm or balanced it on top of her footlocker and bag, making for an awkward descent to the wharf. There they were met by Lieutenant Brunelle, a Signal Corps officer who had been assigned to accompany them to France. With the lieutenant in the lead and their chief operator second, they marched to the train station on unsteady legs, taking in the sights and sounds that, for many of the girls, were their first glimpse of any country other than their own.

Marie had been to Great Britain on tour with her mother years before, but not to Liverpool. Though she had prepared herself for wartime ravages, she was taken aback by the absence of able-bodied men, and by the women laborers who had replaced them as drivers, mechanics, clerks, and other occupations once exclusively the province of men. Their khaki caps and long-waisted, belted greatcoats identified them as members of the Women's Army Auxiliary Corps, but as Marie understood it, they had been "enrolled into service," not sworn in to the military as the Signal Corps girls were. As the First Group marched past, Marie observed the WAACs at work—laboring cheerfully, toiling without complaint—and she was indignant on their behalf. A woman doing a soldier's work deserved a soldier's rank and recognition. Some of the British women looked up with keen interest as the Signal Corps group passed; when they smiled and waved, the Signal Corps girls waved back, and a silent understanding passed between them, a thrill of shared pride. They were all doing what no women before them had done, or had even been permitted to do, and the world would never be the same.

At the railroad yard, where more WAACs were hard at work, Marie and her companions left their baggage in the station house while they awaited their train to Southampton. When they returned outside to find a pleasant spot for a picnic, two women with the British Canteen Service offered them each a cup of hot coffee. Marie was glad to have hers, for although she detected the faint spring scent of freshly tilled earth through the creosote and coal smoke, the day was cool and overcast, and the cup warmed her hands comfortably through her gloves.

She soon discovered that warmth was all it was good for. As they seated themselves on a dry, soft patch of grass, she took a sip of her coffee and immediately recoiled, forcing herself to swallow rather than spit it out. The aroma alone should have warned her that this was ersatz coffee, a concoction of charred barley, saccharine, and other dubious ingredients—edible, but barely tolerable. Marie was thirsty or she would have discreetly poured the brown liquid out upon the grass as most of the other girls were doing. The box lunch was more substantial, a bit of cheese between two slices of brown bread and an apple. Marie ate every crumb. It seemed likely that the ship's fare would be the best meal she would be offered for quite some time.

Their train was not scheduled to depart until nearly four o'clock, so they broke off into small groups to walk along the waterfront and stretch their legs before returning to the station house. Once there, they found the platform packed with doughboys and British soldiers waiting to board, talking and joking with buddies, or standing soberly lost in thought, packs on their backs or on the ground by their feet. Conversations broke off as the thirty-three young women assembled, and Marie could not miss the men's looks of astonishment, their admiring glances. The First Group's usual flirts smiled winsomely back, but others were eyeing their train with some concern.

"Is it just me," asked Cordelia, the lone South Dakotan in the group, "or is this train smaller than the ones back home?"

"It's smaller," Marie confirmed. Except for the greater number of carriages, it reminded her of a Cincinnati streetcar.

"It's quaint," said Louise guardedly. "Surely it isn't meant for long distances?"

"Maybe it's our ride to our real train," said Esther, a New Yorker.

"It would never make it over the Alps," said Raymonde, shaking her head.

"Nor the Rockies," chimed in the group's lone member from Colorado.

"It doesn't have to," said Grace. "This is our train, and it'll get us to Southampton safely, if not in style."

"Watch out there!" a man shouted farther down the platform. Instinctively turning toward the sound, Marie spotted a burly American sergeant confronting a private who was slouching against one of the carriages. "What are you thinking, soldier, leaning against the side of that car? Do you want to knock it over?"

Alarmed, the private bolted upright as the soldiers around him roared with laughter. A moment later, the private hung his head sheepishly and grinned as the sergeant gave him a playful slap on the shoulder.

Just then, the whistle blew, and a conductor began walking the length of the platform calling all aboard. Lieutenant Brunelle guided the First Group aboard through a door near the rear of the train. Someone farther ahead, perhaps Louise, exclaimed in dismay before abruptly falling silent. Soon enough Marie discovered the cause of the involuntary complaint: They were packing into a stifling third-class compartment where several dozen British soldiers had already occupied most of the hard wooden seats. The men quickly made room for the Signal Corps girls, but it was still a tight squeeze, and the air was thick with the odor of cigarette smoke, stale sweat, and unwashed clothes. Whispers began to pass from one girl to another up the aisle, and when the news reached Marie, it wasn't good: There were no washroom facilities, so if they needed to relieve themselves, they could either return to the station now and hope they made it back before the train departed, or hold it together until they reached Southampton and pray that the ride wasn't too bumpy.

It was fortunate that no one dared leave, because the whistle pealed soon thereafter, announcing their imminent departure. The train rattled away from the platform, picking up speed as they headed east out of the city, and then southeast over the Mersey and into the English countryside. Crushed between Cordelia and Suzanne, Marie watched the passing scenery and chatted with her seatmates, but the previous night's poor sleep had left her tired and headachy, and she wished she could rest her head on Cordelia's shoulder and doze the hours away. Some of the girls in the back were enjoying a lively conversation with the soldiers, punctuated with occasional bursts of laughter.

A soft sigh came from the seat behind Marie. "It certainly isn't the *20th Century Limited*," Louise lamented to her sister in an undertone.

It certainly wasn't. Marie adjusted her shoulders to relieve the pressure of the hard wooden slats against her spine, remembering the soft leather chairs in the *20th Century Limited* lounge—and, with a sudden pang of longing that nearly took her breath away, the warm brown eyes and strong hands and sensuous mouth of the man who had been her traveling companion for a few brief hours of her journey from Chicago to New York. She wondered where Giovanni was now. Still training at Camp Upton on Long Island, or at sea, or already Over There? Why had he not sought her out after they had parted that evening? Why had he not waited on the platform in Grand Central Terminal, if only to say goodbye? And why was she still thinking about him, when he had certainly forgotten her weeks ago, apparently before they had even reached New York City? She only remembered him because his rudeness offended her, she told herself firmly. An insult tended to linger in the mind like a bruise upon the skin.

She resolved to think of him no more.

Hours later, after a seemingly interminable ride, the train pulled into the Southampton Central Station. Before they exited the train, their chief operator assigned them quarters according to alphabetical order and told them that their meals would be provided in their boardinghouses, although they were free to dine elsewhere, if they had money to spend. "Stay within a few blocks of quarters," she advised. "Travel in pairs or in groups, and always inform a supervisor before you go."

"Will we be sailing for France tomorrow, Miss Banker?" Raymonde piped up.

Grace regarded her with a look that conveyed both amusement and a warning. "If I knew, should I announce it on a train surrounded by strangers?"

Abashed, Raymonde shook her head. Louise took her hand and murmured something that made her sister press her lips together and nod, eyes downcast.

They gathered their belongings, said cheerful goodbyes to the soldiers who had shared their compartment, and disembarked. Twilight had descended, and the blackout was so complete that Marie saw almost nothing of the port city as the First Group marched to their lodgings, a pair of boardinghouses on either side of a cobblestone street a few blocks from the station. She smelled brine and rotting fish and pine tar, and she felt a mist of salty sea air on her face, but she could see little more than the back of the girl in front of her and a few curbs and other obstacles that had been daubed with luminescent paint for safety.

Marie met up with her bunkmate—Minerva Nadeau, from Denver—in the boardinghouse lobby as they left their baggage at the front desk. After a quick washup, the sixteen weary operators went to the dining room, some of their pep returning in anticipation of a hot meal. Their white-haired hostess treated them like visiting dignitaries. "How extraordinary," she clucked as she showed them to their seats. "Girl soldiers, all the way from America!" She served them hot ersatz coffee, which they all pretended to enjoy, fish soup, and one small bun apiece. The soup was bland, thickened with barley and seasoned with a few sprigs of rosemary, but the bread was so hard that they could not bite it, but had to chip off pieces with their knives and soak them in the coffee before they could chew it.

"What is this bread made of that it would be as hard as granite?" Louise wondered aloud.

"Don't ask," said Marie, nodding pleasantly to their landlady, who was watching them expectantly from the kitchen doorway. "Just eat." Surely it was the best meal the boardinghouse could offer. After four years of war, it was no small accomplishment to have anything to spare for travelers, even allies who had crossed an ocean to fight alongside them.

Their bedrooms were small but immaculate, with narrow, comfortable beds and crisp linens. "I'd almost forgotten how lovely a real bed could be," said Minerva, sighing as she settled in beneath her thick feather comforter. Marie, already nearly asleep, murmured agreement.

The next morning, they woke to thick fog and the cry of seagulls. "We won't sail in this," Marie predicted as they washed and dressed. Sure enough, as they breakfasted on porridge with saccharine, more of the hard bread, and a choice of ersatz coffee or watery tea, Grace came over from the other boardinghouse to confirm that they were fogged in. After drill, they would be free to spend the day as they wished, but they should hurry back to quarters if the weather cleared. "Lieutenant Brunelle says that the local YMCA offers recreational activities for soldiers," she added, "and although they're really here for the men, they've agreed to admit us too. It's not far, and it might be worth a look."

Later that afternoon, after drill and luncheon, when Marie, Minerva, and a few other friends had strolled the waterfront, browsed the shops, and needed another diversion, they decided to wander over to the YMCA and see what it had to offer. The old stone building, tall and narrow, sat at the top of the street on a broad green. A tent had been erected there, the sides open to the breeze, with rows of folding chairs arranged before a screen made from a large white sheet. A poster on an easel announced that the film *The Silent Man* would be presented that evening, free of charge to any member of the Allied armed forces; a calendar below noted the dates and showtimes of other pictures.

Inside the stone building, a smiling volunteer welcomed them and offered them each a cup of hot chocolate, which smelled heavenly and tasted divine. The large room resembled a refurbished warehouse, with two fireplaces at either end; a canteen near the entrance, where another volunteer served coffee, hot chocolate, and doughnuts to a group of grateful soldiers; and tables and chairs arranged to create smaller spaces for various purposes—a modest library, a place to write letters and tables for board games, each occupied by a handful of soldiers. Near the far wall, four rows of folding chairs were arranged in concentric semicircles around an upright piano and a small stage apparently constructed of plywood hammered to a platform of empty vegetable and fruit crates. An American private sat at the piano, plinking out the melody for "Oh! How I Hate to Get Up in the Morning" while an audience of a half dozen doughboys groaned, laughed, and shook their heads. One even plugged his ears.

The soldier plunked his hands down on the keys in a discordant crash. "Don't complain unless you can do better."

"*You* could do better," Minerva said to Marie, nudging her.

"Oh, yes," said Cordelia. "Please, Marie, won't you? It's been ages since you've given us a concert."

"It was only a few days ago aboard the *Celtic*," Marie protested, laughing.

"Those were Sunday hymns. We need real music."

Marie gasped in feigned outrage. "Sacrilege! That was classical repertoire."

"Please, Marie," Minerva implored, inclining her head toward the soldiers wincing at their hapless pianist. "Give the boys a treat."

Marie had promised her mother to practice whenever she could. "All right," she said, smiling. "For the boys."

Her friends trailed after her as Marie approached the private, who was playing a labored version of what might have been "Yankee Doodle" with two fingers. "Excuse me," she said, "may I borrow your piano?"

He did a double take at the sight of the uniformed young women, and a broad grin spread over his face. "It's not my piano to loan, miss," he said, rising and gesturing to the bench, "but why don't we take turns?"

Marie smiled her thanks, smoothing her skirt beneath herself as she sat down and scooted the bench closer. It would have been nice if Millicent were there to play for her, but her friend had been assigned to the Second Group. No matter. Marie was a better singer than a pianist, but she had begun lessons with her father when she was very young, and over time she had become a decent accompanist. She ran her hands up and down the keys, wincing at a particularly flat note, but otherwise she found the instrument sufficiently in tune. She would sing a little louder and play a little softer when she needed that note, and with any luck no one would notice.

She began with "It's a Long Way to Tipperary," which drew all the soldiers over and earned hearty applause, then "Good-bye Broadway, Hello France," which the Brits knew less well but still enjoyed. She sang some beloved traditional French tunes next, and by the time she finished the third, she realized that she had drawn quite a crowd. She concluded with a rousing rendition of "Over There," encouraging the boys to sing along, smiling when they clapped and stomped their feet in time to the music.

Afterward, she rose and swept a graceful bow, pleasantly surprised by the enthusiastic roar of cheers and clapping, so boisterous compared to the decorous applause of her parents' musicales. Her friends beamed proudly, clapping as wildly as the boys, and even the YMCA hostesses paused in their work to applaud. A few minutes later, as Marie and her companions were leaving, the hostess who had offered them hot chocolate stopped her at the door. "Would you please come back tomorrow evening?" she asked.

"We always draw a crowd after supper, and I know the boys would love to hear you."

"I don't know if I'll still be in Southampton then," Marie said vaguely. Even that felt like divulging too much about the First Group's mission.

"She'll be here, if she can," Minerva declared, placing an arm around Marie's shoulders. "We'll see to it."

As her friends chimed in their assurances, the hostess beamed and promised to spread the word of the possibility—only the possibility, no promises—of a special concert.

The next morning the weather was even worse than the previous day, extending their stay in Southampton yet again. The operators were eager to get to France, but they made good use of their time, attending to their laundry and mending, practicing French, reviewing military terms, studying war correspondents' reports in the papers to prepare themselves for Over There, and writing letters home. That evening, Marie returned to the YMCA, this time accompanied by Grace Banker and the rest of the First Group, who had heard Minerva's glowing review of the first concert and were determined not to miss out on the second. To Marie's surprise, when they arrived, more than half of the folding chairs were already occupied, and her companions quickly took those that remained.

She altered the program slightly from the previous day, keeping the rousing war tunes that the soldiers relished, but breaking up the set with a few traditional English folk tunes and, daringly, a Baroque piece by Henry Purcell. She could see from the corner of her eye that the music drew curious passersby to the doorway, and once there, the enthusiasm of the audience lured them inside. If the YMCA had chosen that moment to pass the hat for donations, they would have done quite well.

Afterward, many of the soldiers wanted to meet her, and her companions enjoyed just as much flattering attention. "Come back tomorrow?" the hostess asked again as she departed, hopeful, and Marie gave the same vague reply.

For three more days, thick fog and rain prevented them from leaving port. Marie knew that Grace Banker and Lieutenant Brunelle conferred with their transport's captain several times a day, weighing the risks of a more dangerous crossing against allowing General Pershing's dire need for qualified telephone operators to go unmet. "Be prepared," Grace warned the girls whenever they met for meals or drills. "We will likely sail for France the moment the weather improves."

They kept their baggage packed and never strayed more than a mile from quarters. Every evening, Marie performed at the YMCA, drawing increasingly large audiences as word spread. Sometimes as she took her bows, she recognized faces in the crowd from previous concerts, but for the most part she seemed to sing for an entirely different group of soldiers every night.

When she mused about this to the lead hostess—or secretary, which was the preferred title—the older woman nodded and told her it wasn't her imagination. "So many soldiers pass through the port," she said. "They often don't linger more than a day, barely enough time to enjoy a cup of hot chocolate and to send a postcard home. It's the fog that's kept so many here lately."

Marie had a sudden thought. "Do most soldiers come to the YMCA during their stayover?"

"Oh, I wouldn't say most," the secretary replied modestly. "A very respectable number, I suppose. They know we're here for them if they want anything, from refreshments to a game of checkers or a quiet place to read. The soldiers have other choices here in Southampton—pubs, restaurants, churches for those inclined, and so forth. Over There, on the other hand, sometimes our huts are the only option for hundreds of miles."

"By any chance, would you—" Marie chose her words carefully. "Would you recall if the Three Hundred and Seventh Infantry has passed through Southampton?"

"I don't believe so." The secretary thought for a moment. "They're with the Seventy-Seventh Infantry Division, aren't they?"

"Yes, that's right."

She pondered that, brow furrowing, but then shook her head. "I don't recall seeing any of their insignia, but that doesn't mean they haven't gone Over There. That's what you're really asking, isn't it?"

Marie nodded.

The secretary smiled understandingly. "A sweetheart or a brother?"

"A friend," said Marie quickly. "More of an acquaintance, really."

"Just because I don't recall seeing them doesn't mean the Three-Oh-Seventh haven't passed through Southampton. Sometimes soldiers go directly from the train station to their ships without ever pausing at Camp Romsey. Sometimes I don't notice or don't remember every insignia I see. And, as proud as I am of our club here"—she smiled and glanced around at the soldiers and Signal Girls chatting happily or playing cards, waiting for Marie to return from her break—"not every regiment finds their way to us."

"That's their loss," said Marie lightly, managing a smile. "I'd better get back."

Her hands trembled as she returned to the piano to a smattering of applause. Why had she asked? Why did she care? If Giovanni had wanted to see her again, he would have waited on the platform at Grand Central. He could have written to her in care of AT&T headquarters; she had told him she would be reporting for temporary duty there.

She tried to push all thoughts of him aside and concentrate on the soldiers right in front of her, these young men who wanted only to forget their homesickness and worries for a few hours. It worked, mostly, as the music flowed through her and brought them all together, all of them so far from home and uncertain what tomorrow would bring.

At the end of the night, the secretary hurried to catch Marie at the door before she left. "May I have a word, Miss Miossec?" she asked.

Marie hesitated; most of the First Group had already left, and she didn't want to defy orders and walk back to quarters alone.

"We'll wait," said Cordelia, glancing for confirmation to Minerva, who nodded.

"I won't be long," Marie promised over her shoulder as the secretary led her to a small office next to the canteen.

"I'll get straight to the point," the secretary said, closing the door behind them, shutting out the din. "More troops are arriving in Southampton every week, and the commanding officers of their camps would like us to provide more musical entertainment for them. Would you consider staying on here to serve on our paid staff as a programming director with the YMCA? We'd love for you to continue your concerts a few nights a week, and also to organize other performers for those evenings when you're resting your voice—local bands, children's choirs, and so on."

"Thank you for the offer," said Marie, taken aback, "but I'm afraid I must decline."

"At least think it over," the secretary urged. "Strengthening morale is absolutely essential to victory. You and your staff will not only perform for soldiers going Over There, but also for those who have returned—the recovering wounded, the permanently disabled, the unfortunate men suffering from shell shock. This would be important service."

"I don't doubt it," said Marie, "but, respectfully, I believe my skills as a bilingual telephone operator are more essential to the war effort than my gifts as a singer. Nor am I free to resign from the Signal Corps. I enlisted in the army for the duration of the war."

"I see," said the secretary, visibly disappointed. "Well, we shall be terribly sorry to lose you. May I still count on you to perform as long as you remain in Southampton?"

"Of course," said Marie earnestly. "I've enjoyed these evenings more than I can say." Mindful of her companions still waiting at the door, she thanked the secretary, bade her good night, and hurried away.

"What was all that about?" asked Cordelia as they headed back to the boardinghouse.

"It's absurd," said Marie, shaking her head, managing a small, shaky laugh. "After months of disappointing auditions, I've just declined my second offer to sing professionally in order to keeping working a switchboard. I must be mad."

"Nonsense," protested Minerva, linking her arm through Marie's. "You swore an oath to serve your country in the Signal Corps. General Pershing can't win this war without you."

"He can't win it without *us*," amended Cordelia, taking Marie's other arm.

Marie smiled, warmed by their kind words. She had never for a moment considered resigning, but she had to admit, the offer was flattering after so many rejections. One small misgiving briefly flickered—if she remained in Southampton, she might see Giovanni when the 307th passed through—but she quickly quashed it. Eventually, in a day or a week, she would be on her way to France, to serve where and how she was needed most. That was all that mattered.

In the morning, Marie woke to find dim sunlight peeking through the curtains, so unusual for that hour that at first she assumed she had overslept. The fog had begun to lift, and by noon it had nearly dispersed. No one ventured more than a block from quarters all day, and by teatime, two credible rumors were circling between the two boardinghouses: first, that the Germans had launched a new offensive along the Somme in order to defeat the British army before American troops could reinforce them, and second, that the First Group would sail for France that evening.

A few hours later, Grace Banker confirmed that the second rumor was true.

After a hasty supper, the operators lined up with their baggage and marched to the wharf, where they boarded a small Channel packet boat called the *Normania*. It was already seven o'clock, but even in the dim twilight, as evening mists drifted upon the waterfront, Marie observed that the upper decks were packed with Belgian, British, and French soldiers and French civilians desperate to return home. A stewardess led the operators to their cabins, two decks below, down narrow stairs crowded with more soldiers, and through cramped corridors where more French civilians were curled up on the floor with their belongings, trying to sleep. Marie and her companions picked their way through the tangle of limbs and bags and blankets, stumbling, apologizing in French when they were cursed for stepping on a hand or foot.

"My pal went down on her packet boat last week," Marie overheard the stewardess glumly remark to Grace Banker, somewhere up ahead, obscured in the shadows. "We'll probably get it this time."

Marie inhaled deeply to steady herself, shifting the strap of her bag on her shoulder, adjusting her grip on her footlocker. The air was stifling, foul, with barely a trace of sea air to refresh it. The stewardess divided them between a few cramped cabins, where they were obliged to share bunks. "We won't be on board long," Grace reminded them. "Try to sleep. It's a short crossing, and if the fog holds off, we may be in France before you wake."

Marie and her cabinmates bade her good night and climbed into their berths, head to feet. "I'll be thankful when we're safe in France," someone murmured sleepily.

Another girl snorted derisively. "We'd be safer in war-torn France than on this tub."

That evoked a few wry laughs, but soon the pitch-black cabin fell silent. Marie's last thought before sleeping was to hope that the crew's signals to cast off would not wake her.

Sometime later she woke, disoriented, to find the cabin scarcely lighter than before, the ship barely rocking, floorboards creaking overhead with the weight of footsteps on the upper deck. The packet boat was so still, she thought as she carefully climbed down from her berth without jostling her companion, that they must have already crossed the Channel and docked in Le Havre.

Dressing swiftly, wishing she had water for a wash, she opened her cabin door to discover the French civilians still sprawled out on the floor, dozing. Uneasy, she made her way down the narrow corridor to the stairs and outside. To her dismay, she found the upper deck still crowded with soldiers and civilians, milling about or huddled beneath blankets, as far as she could see—which was not very far, for the ship was swathed in a fog bank. The language and accents of voices that drifted to her from the obscured wharf revealed that they had never left Southampton.

Marie closed her eyes and inhaled deeply, suppressing her exasperation. To think that with all of their modern technology, they remained at the mercy of the capricious weather. She returned to her cabin, where her bunkmates were groggily pulling on their clothes. They groaned aloud when she broke the bad news that they were no closer to France. "We'll feel better after breakfast," she said. "Let's find Miss Banker and ask her what the plan is."

They found the chief operator on the upper deck with several of the other girls, and before long all thirty-three had assembled. Soon Lieutenant Brunelle appeared and led them upstairs to the dining room, where they found several officers and a few enlisted men queued up outside the door. The First Group joined the end of the line, conversing in hushed voices about the cursed weather, joking about how it was probably the kaiser's fault, and wondering what might be on the menu. Marie thought she smelled sausages, but until they drew closer to the entrance, she couldn't be sure.

Then she heard the lieutenant's voice, loud and angry, at the head of their group. "What do you mean, they aren't permitted inside?"

Craning her neck, Marie glimpsed the lieutenant confronting a man in a white coat and toque just outside the doorway. She could not hear the man's reply, but he was holding up his hands, crossing and spreading them sharply to ward off the lieutenant and the women, shaking his head for emphasis. They argued back and forth a bit, but the man in white was resolute. Eventually Grace stepped out of the queue and gestured for the operators to follow her toward the bow. "No American women are permitted in the dining room," she said grimly. "As there is no other food service aboard, this leaves us in a tough spot."

"Don't wander off," said Lieutenant Brunelle, his voice brittle. "I'm going to have words with the captain."

They wished him luck and watched him disappear into the fog. The air was cold and damp, but none of them relished returning belowdecks, so they huddled together for warmth, making wry jokes about the possible reasons for their banishment—in French, and quietly, to avoid offending anyone and making matters worse. It seemed an hour before Lieutenant Brunelle returned, carrying a basket loaded with bread and pieces of hard cheese. "No luck finding the captain," he said, "but we can't have you girls going hungry, so I liberated this from the mess."

Grateful, they thanked him and passed the basket around; there was enough for everyone, but only just. While they ate, Marie saw Grace take the lieutenant aside, and she surreptitiously drew closer so she could overhear. "This is unconscionable," the chief operator was telling him in a low, furious voice. "Our girls have to eat, and I refuse to allow them to spend another night in that rat trap belowdecks." The lieutenant nodded along, arms folded over his chest, frowning.

Soon thereafter, Grace called the First Group together and told them to make themselves as comfortable as they could, "without leaving the *Normania*," she added wryly. Then she and the lieutenant strode off together, heading toward the bridge.

Marie, Cordelia, and Minerva decided to walk around the upper deck to get what fresh air and exercise they could on the crowded, fogbound ship. After a few laps, Cordelia mused aloud that the fog seemed less dense than before, the sun a bit brighter. Marie and Minerva agreed that they had noticed the subtle change as well, and hoped it was not merely wishful thinking.

It was almost noon when they returned to the main deck, where they found several of the other girls gathering around Grace and the lieutenant, who had apparently just returned from a lengthy, heated discussion with the captain. "The captain has relented," Grace announced, with only a slight, triumphant smile revealing what a battle it must have been to persuade him. "We are now welcome in the dining room, and the captain has invited us to move into the unoccupied staterooms on the upper deck. Tell the others, fetch your things, and let's get ourselves settled into our new accommodations as quickly as possible."

There were a few quiet squeals of delight, promptly silenced, as they all hurried off to comply. "They had staterooms going unused all this time, while passengers slept on the floors and in the stairwells?" Cordelia exclaimed once they had reached the privacy of their cabin.

"Let's just be thankful that Miss Banker is looking out for us," said Marie, snapping her footlocker shut and slinging the strap of her bag over her shoulder.

They moved quickly, determined to occupy the staterooms before the captain changed his mind. Lunch service for the officers was nearly over by the time they finished, but they were grateful for the corned beef, buns, and watery tea served in the once forbidden dining room.

By midafternoon, although the fog had not entirely lifted, the *Normania* finally cast off and set forth, southeast on the Southampton Water into the Solent and out past Portsmouth. After supper, Marie and most of the other girls returned to the upper deck to admire the views, thrilled to be at sea at long last, but thick fog descended as night fell, and they could not see more than a meter in front of their faces. Marie heard distant whistles from other ships, obscured by the darkness and gloom, and she hoped the sounds alone would be enough to prevent them from colliding.

"Marie," Cordelia asked, "would you sing for us?"

"No singing," a passing sailor growled, making them all jump. "Nothing carries over the water like music."

Marie felt a knot in her chest. In her concern over crashing into another British ship in that miasma, she had almost forgotten the U-boats lurking below.

As the evening grew colder, some of the girls retired to their staterooms, but Marie and several others, too restless for bed, gathered around a smokestack for warmth. Grace and Lieutenant Brunelle joined them there. "Do you see that lifeboat?" the officer asked, indicating the nearest one, covered in a gray tarpaulin and lashed tightly to the rail. "That's where we'll rendezvous if we're attacked. Understood?"

They all nodded somberly.

"Please spread the word to the other girls," said Grace, smiling reassuringly. She rested her hand lightly on Cordelia's shoulder in passing, then walked off to join Suzanne and a few other girls near the railing.

Despite the late hour, and the cold, and the inability to see anything but the shadowed faces of her nearest companions, Marie remained on the deck rather than withdrawing to the relative warmth and comfort of her berth. After so many years abroad, she was almost home, and if the fog cleared and moonlight illuminated the distant coastline of her beloved France, she could not bear to miss her first chance to glimpse it.

Eventually, Grace and Suzanne left the railing and passed Marie and her companions near the smokestack. "It's midnight, so I'm going to say good night," said Grace. "Try to get some sleep, won't you?"

They promised they would, and wished her and Suzanne good night. "I think they have the right idea," said Cordelia after they parted, yawning enormously. "We may be sorry in the morning if we—"

Suddenly the ship lurched and cut the engines. They looked to one another, alarmed, but before anyone could speak, phosphorescent flares shot skyward and brown posts covered in algae and slime thrust upward from the dark waters. Cordelia cried out, seized Marie's arm, and pointed; turning, Marie gasped in horror to see an imposing shadow looming in the mist, swiftly approaching, its edges resolving into an enormous vessel bearing down on them. At the last moment the destroyer threw its engines in reverse, still striking the *Normania*, but reducing the severity of the blow. Marie and Cordelia clung together for support, staggering, but managing to stay on their feet.

Harsh cries and curses and commands in French rained down on them from the destroyer. As the alarm and confusion subsided, they learned that the *Normania* had been caught in a submarine net, and that a French patrol had raced to confront them, believing they had captured an enemy vessel. How aggrieved the French crew was to discover that a British packet ship had sprung their trap instead, and was now entangled, immobile, unable to proceed or withdraw until a diver cut them loose. Marie's heart plummeted when she overheard one sailor tell another that a qualified diver could not be brought out to them until the fog cleared.

She knew then she would not see her beloved France that night.

Shivering from cold and the aftermath of fear, Marie and the few companions who had lingered on the deck finally withdrew to their cabins, hoping the French destroyer would remain with them to frighten off U-boats until they resumed their journey across the Channel.

Although she had a berth to herself, it was uncomfortable to spend another night in her clothes, shivering beneath a thin wool blanket, preventing her from sinking into peaceful slumber with the oppressive worry that they were trapped in the Channel at the mercy of the weather and the enemy. But somehow, eventually, exhaustion overcame her and she slept.

She woke to sunlight streaming through the porthole, the sensation of movement, and the sound of distant cowbells. Heart pounding with excitement and hope, she rose from her berth, hurried to the window—and gazed, at long last, upon the soft green coast of France.

She was home.

10

MARCH 1918

Le Havre, Paris, and Chaumont

GRACE

When the *Normania* docked at the Port of Le Havre, the civilians on board rushed the gangplank with such steely-eyed determination that Grace told her girls to stand back with their luggage until the deck cleared. Only then did she give the operators the order to follow her down the gangplank to the dock, striding with a proud military bearing that belied their wrinkled clothing and disarrayed hair. They had parted from Lieutenant Brunelle aboard ship, and were met on shore by their new escort, Signal Corps captain William Vivian, a tall, sandy-haired fellow of perhaps forty, whose broad, square-jawed face was made boyish by a sprinkling of freckles.

"Our train won't depart until this afternoon, so we have rooms reserved for you where you can rest in the meantime," the captain said as he led them across a broad cobblestone street along the waterfront and into the seaport town. "First time in France?"

"For me, yes," said Grace, "but some of our girls were born here." She had glimpsed the conflicting emotions on their faces as their ship had come into the harbor, and she could well imagine what a strange homecoming this must be, joyful yet melancholy. However long ago they had left their homeland, and whether they had spent two years away or twenty, they had returned to a very different France than the one they remembered.

"If you or any of your girls are up for a tour, I offer myself as a guide," said Captain Vivian, with a self-deprecating grin. "You're not likely to get lost on your own, but I can show you the most charming streets and scenic views, and still get you to the station on time to meet our train."

"I'll gladly take you up on that," said Grace, "and I'm sure some of the other girls will too. Can you give us time to freshen up first?"

"Certainly. I understand it's been a challenging trip."

"Nothing my girls can't handle," said Grace, smiling. If the captain stayed with them long enough, he would see that for himself.

The hotel was only a block away from the wharf, and while they waited for the proprietor to distribute their room keys, Grace announced the agenda for the day. A few girls nodded eagerly when she mentioned the tour, but even they seemed distracted, their eyes on the innkeeper and the pegboard of keys on the wall behind him. As anxious for a wash and a change of clothes as everyone else, Grace gratefully accepted a key to a room she would share with Suzanne and two other girls. How good it felt, after two days and nights aboard the crowded packet boat, sleeping in her clothes, to feel clean water on her skin, to remove the grime of the journey, and to slip into a fresh uniform!

The soft beds with their plump feather pillows were tempting, but Grace could not resist the lure of curiosity. "I didn't come this far to stay shut up in a room," Suzanne said as they headed downstairs, which was exactly how Grace felt. Soon nearly the entire First Group had gathered in the lobby around Captain Vivian, looking much refreshed and eager to explore.

The captain led them back outside onto the cobblestone street. They followed him down the narrow, winding streets lined by charming houses and shops, some new and freshly painted, others ancient and weathered by the sea air. They listened, fascinated and amused, as he shared stories about various landmarks they passed, all of which had been told to him by a barkeeper or a French soldier or another local resident who was "almost always" a reliable source. If not for the great many Allied soldiers and sailors milling about, the ubiquitous posters exhorting passersby to conserve food and mind what they said around strangers, and the displays in shop windows carefully arranged to disguise the scarcity of goods, Grace could almost forget she was in a country at war.

Captain Vivian's tour took them northwest along the coastal cliffs, where they gazed out at the English Channel as the wind whipped at their hair and skirts, forcing them to clasp their hats to their heads or lose them forever. Eventually they reached Sainte-Adresse, a seaside resort village praised as the Nice of Le Havre. Claude Monet had created more than a dozen beautiful paintings of the town and the seascape, the captain told them, and the celebrated actress Sarah Bernhardt had built a villa there.

"Sainte-Adresse was once the crown jewel of Normandy resorts, but the war put an end to all that fun and frivolity." Captain Vivian gestured to a massive brick building up ahead. "Do you see that imposing neoclassical place over there? That's the Immeuble Dufayel, a former hotel, home to the Belgium government in exile since 1914."

Marie studied the house for a moment before fixing the captain with a level gaze. "King Albert of Belgium has been ruling his country from that hotel since the war began?"

"No, that's not what I meant," the captain replied, shaking his head. "After the Germans invaded, the Belgian prime minister and the cabinet fled Brussels and set up a government here. As for the king, it's said that he believed it would be unconscionable for a sovereign to flee his country at its moment of greatest peril."

Marie's eyebrows rose. "He remained behind?"

"Yes, and as supreme commander of the armed forces, he personally led the Belgian army as it fought off the German advance. Eventually, though, he and his staff were forced to withdraw to the only remaining unoccupied land in Belgium, a small region west of the river Yser in the town of Veurne."

Marie nodded, satisfied. "Good for him, staying to fight."

Grace wasn't so sure. Certainly it was impressive that King Albert had remained while others had fled, that he had chosen to risk his life with his troops rather than flee to safety abroad, but what a blow it would be for the Belgian people if he were captured or killed. It was not for her to say whether he had made the right decision, but she had to admire his courage.

At midday, Captain Vivian led them back to the hotel by another route so they could see more of Le Havre, its picturesque gardens, historic churches, and outdoor markets. The rest of the group were waiting for them in the hotel's dining room when they returned, drawn by enticing aromas they all fervently hoped were not cruelly misleading. They were not disappointed. Exclamations of delight rose from the separate tables when their dishes were set before them, steaming bowls of a delicious stew of mussels and fish in a creamy broth of butter, apple cider, and cream, accompanied by thick slices of fresh, crusty bread and Camembert cheese. They had not eaten so well in weeks, nor had they expected to then.

"One of the benefits of distance from the larger cities and the front," remarked Captain Vivian, seated next to Grace, looking as proud as if he had procured the meal himself. "The Germans have made fishing in the Channel dangerous, but the most stubborn piscators still risk it." He leaned closer and lowered his voice. "On the subject of risk, you should be aware that this new German offensive has not let up—in fact, quite the opposite. Paris is under bombardment. It's nothing like Le Havre there. German artillery shells don't discriminate between soldiers and women and children. The moment your train leaves the station, you and your girls will be heading into grave danger, and there will be no turning back."

Grace's heart thudded, but she did not flinch. "There was no turning back the moment we were sworn in to the army," she reminded him. "We never expected any special protection from danger because we're women."

"The Germans did not spare women and children in Belgium," Marie broke in from the other side of the table, regarding the captain with a level gaze. "We're not naïve. We knew the risks when we enlisted. You must think of us as soldiers first and women second." After a moment, she added, "Sir."

"Our girls are eager to be in the thick of it, Captain," Grace added. "Every one of them has requested to be posted as close to the front as possible."

"Good to know." Captain Vivian nodded thoughtfully as he looked around the table. "Keep in mind, not all of you can be assigned to General Pershing's headquarters. Telephone operators are needed in Paris and at Services of Supply bases at the rear too. You'll get your assignments in Paris." He smiled, adding, "I'm glad it's not up to me to decide."

"We'll serve to the best of our ability wherever we're posted," Grace assured him, and every girl at their table nodded assent.

Later that afternoon when the operators boarded their train to Paris, Grace sensed a new frisson of nervous tension within the group, trepidation about the reported bombardment, to be sure, but with an undercurrent of excitement, a thrill of danger. Most of them had never seen Paris before, and they were eager to experience the city they had heretofore only known through pictures, stories, and schoolbooks. Grace was proud to overhear that, even so, most of their conversations centered on where they might be posted and how soon they would be able to get to work. They understood how badly they were needed, and their lengthy delay in Southampton had made them impatient to begin.

Their train was frequently shunted aside to make way for troop transports heading to the front, so it was long after nightfall when they finally arrived in Paris and disembarked at the Gare du Nord in the Tenth Arrondissement. After Captain Vivian's warnings, Grace had braced herself, and prepared her girls, for the possibility that they might arrive in the middle of a bombardment, but the city was eerily quiet. Hauling their gear, they followed Captain Vivian through streets shrouded in the darkness of blackout protocol, making their way by the dim illumination of blue lamps hooded to direct their light to the ground, making them less visible from above. The few glimpses Grace caught of the cityscape revealed churches, businesses, and statues fortified with sandbags, tenuous protection from the devastation of a German bomb, or so it seemed to her. The few people they encountered along the way eyed them suspiciously, but let them pass without impediment.

More than half an hour later, they reached their destination, a YWCA hostel established in the Hotel Petrograd at 33 Rue de Caumartin. In one glance, the French staff noted their fatigue and hunger and promptly escorted them five flights up to their rooms. After leaving her gear in the chamber she would share with Suzanne, Cordelia, and Marie, Grace went down the hallway, knocking on doors, making sure every operator was accounted for and settling in well. Even before she finished her rounds, staff began delivering simple, cold meals of bread, cheese, grapes, and red wine to each room. Grace returned to her own chamber to find her bunkmates already washed, dressed in their nightgowns, and happily feasting. She quickly followed suit, grateful for the hot water and lavender soap she found at the basin, luxuries she meant to enjoy for as long as she had them.

Soon thereafter, sated and fatigued, Grace and her bunkmates doused the lamp and climbed into bed. The blackout curtains cut off even the thin moonlight, making the darkness complete. Yawning enormously, shifting the pillow into a more comfortable position, Grace closed her eyes and began running through her mental list of everything she had to do the next day, but she sank into sleep long before she reached the end.

Suddenly, an earsplitting wail shattered the darkness.

Grace bolted upright in bed, disoriented. Someone pounded on the door. "*Alerte! Alerte!*" a voice shrilled, barely audible above the alarm.

"Air raid," Suzanne mumbled, stirring beside her.

"Air raid," Grace echoed, climbing out of bed. "Get up, Suzanne," she said, shaking her fully awake, before groping her way to the other bed and waking Cordelia and Marie. "Come on. Let's go."

There was no time to dress, barely time to pull on their shoes. They hurried into the corridor, where they found their comrades stumbling from their rooms in their nightgowns, yawning and stretching, urged on by the increasingly frantic maids, who shoved them toward the stairwell and ordered them to hurry, hurry to the cellar.

The terror in the maids' eyes jolted the girls awake. They fled downstairs, some of them sliding down the banisters in their haste. Grace had reached the third floor when she heard the distant rumble of an explosion; she had almost reached the first floor when a tremendous blast detonated so near that she instinctively crouched on the stairs and covered her head, one arm looped around a baluster for support. The windows rattled; the girls shrieked; plaster dust sifted down on them. All the while the sirens wailed on, like an enormous, terrible beast in distress.

"Keep moving!" Grace shouted. The girls picked themselves up and raced downstairs, stumbling in the darkness, down and down, until they felt the cool damp of the cellar air on their faces. Grace waited until the last of her girls had entered the bomb shelter, and only then followed them inside. Two of the maids held hurricane lamps, and in their dim yellow light, Grace saw that benches had been arranged against the walls of the long, rectangular room, and two rows of chairs filled the space in the middle, with a narrow aisle all around. Nearly every seat was filled. Catching her breath, brushing her hair out of her eyes, Grace swiftly counted heads, came up short, and counted again, making sure to include herself. Both times she tallied only thirty-one. Two girls were missing.

"Roll call," Grace said, but her words were drowned out by another thunderous explosion, not as near as before, but still much too close. "Roll call," she repeated, louder. "Audet."

"Present."

"Boucher."

"Present."

"It's Charlotte and Agnes," Suzanne called out, voice shaking. "Charlotte and Agnes are missing."

Grace inhaled deeply. "Very well," she said, more calmly than she felt. "I'll fetch them."

Ignoring the protests of the hostel staff, she darted out of the bomb shelter and raced back up the darkened staircase, trying to remember which rooms the missing girls had been assigned to, whether they were together or apart. On and on the siren wailed, as she ran upstairs to the third floor, the fourth—and then, on the fifth floor landing, she almost collided with Charlotte, who was stumbling toward the staircase in a nightgown and untied boots. "Have you seen Agnes?" Grace demanded, coughing through the dust.

Charlotte shook her head, wide-eyed. "N-no, I didn't see anyone, I thought it was just a drill—"

Grace looked down the hallway to her left, then to her right, hoping in vain to glimpse Agnes emerging from the darkness. "Get downstairs to the cellar."

"But if Agnes is— I'll help you search."

Rather than waste time in argument, Grace nodded and gestured toward the right, while she hurried off to the left. She pounded on doors, tearing them open, glancing inside, moving on to the next. Then, at the end of the hallway, a door opened and a pale face topped by a cap of dark curls peered out. "Miss Banker?" the voice quavered, taut with alarm. "What's going on?"

"It's an air raid," Grace called back, just as the alarm declined in pitch like a terrible machine in its death throes, gradually falling silent. Her ears rang and her heart pounded. She wished she had thought to ask the hostel staff or Lieutenant Vivian when they had first arrived about air raid protocol, whether silence meant the danger had passed or if they should await an all-clear signal. Why had that not occurred to her? Why had she not planned ahead?

She heard footsteps approaching and turned to find Charlotte hurrying toward her. "You found her," Charlotte said, panting. "Are you all right?"

"I'm fine," said Agnes shakily, her eyes darting guilty to Grace, and then away. "I didn't mean to be any trouble."

"I shouldn't have had to search for you, for either of you," said Grace, looking from one contrite face to the other. "Later today we're going to have a chat about how to conduct oneself during an air raid. You were both very lucky this time. Next time you might not be."

"Yes, Miss Banker," they replied meekly, in unison, thoroughly abashed.

She herded them downstairs in case the danger had not passed, only to meet the rest of the group on their way up. Grace assumed that meant the hostel staff had told them it was safe to return to their rooms, but she sought out the YWCA hostess to confirm it.

"I was very impressed with how your girls conducted themselves," the older woman said, after assuring Grace that, if history was precedent, the German planes were unlikely to return that night. "They evacuated in an orderly fashion, especially considering it was their first air raid. While you were gone, they sat in the dark listening to the bombardment, perfectly composed and patient, every one of them."

Not *every* one, Grace thought, but she thanked the hostess and headed upstairs to bed, wondering how she would ever sleep with her thoughts darting between relief that they had escaped injury and self-reproach that she had not been better prepared. Yet eventually weariness overcame her and she drifted back to sleep.

The air raid had come shortly after midnight, but Grace still woke at first light. Per Captain Vivian's orders, she had her girls up at six o'clock and down to breakfast shortly thereafter. They were assembled in the lobby when the captain and a Signal Corps photographer arrived to escort them to the Signal Corps's central office. "Quite a rude welcome to Paris you had last night," Captain Vivian said, studying Grace closely. "Are your girls holding up all right?"

"Of course," replied Grace, a bit surprised. "No one likes to be jolted out of bed by a pealing alarm, but we've all managed on fewer hours of sleep than this."

The two men exchanged a look. "Have you been outside yet this morning?" the captain asked Grace, his brow furrowing.

"No. Your instructions were to meet you here." Grace looked from one officer to the other. "Why? What is it?"

In reply, the captain asked her to call the girls to order, and with the captain in the lead and the photographer following behind, they filed from the building and down the sidewalk, where Grace halted, stunned. The building that had once stood next door had been reduced to a rubble-strewn crater.

"That explains the dust," she said shakily, heart thudding. Behind her, the other girls gasped and murmured in alarm. "I thought that second explosion sounded awfully close."

"Any closer and that would have been curtains for you girls," the photographer remarked, raising his camera to his eye and clicking off a few shots.

"Corporal," the captain admonished mildly. To Grace he added, "Before we report to the central office, we've been asked to take a photo to commemorate the arrival of the first women U.S. Signal Corps telephone operators in Paris. Corporal Gillespie found an ideal spot just around the corner."

"Right this way, ladies," said the corporal, throwing them a cheerful grin over his shoulder as he led them around the block to the Square de l'Opéra Louis-Jouvet, where an impressive bronze statue of a man astride a winged horse stood on a marble pedestal atop a broad oval base.

"*Le Poète Chevauchant Pégase*," Cordelia announced, reading aloud from a bronze plaque on the pedestal.

"He isn't *Golden Boy*, but he'll do," said Captain Vivian as the photographer began to arrange the operators in three rows in front of the statue. The first group stood on the oval base, a second on the ground before them. Borrowing three chairs from a nearby outdoor café, the corporal placed them in the front and instructed Grace, as chief operator, to take the middle seat, flanked by the two supervisors.

"I hope I can get a copy for my scrapbook," Suzanne murmured somewhere behind Grace, forcing her to stifle a laugh just as the shutter clicked.

The walk to the Signal Corps central office at the Élysées Palace Hotel was quite a bit longer, but no one minded that, for it was a lovely stroll past the Place de la Concorde and the Jardin des Tuileries and down the Champs-Élysées toward the Arc de Triomphe. When they reached the lavishly ornamented Beaux-Arts edifice, six stories tall and stretching the entire length of the block, the captain led them through the elegant lobby to a meeting room, where several Signal Corps officers introduced themselves and welcomed them to Paris. Next, a lieutenant stepped forward, and when Suzanne suddenly seized her arm, Grace knew the document he held was the roster of their assignments.

"You have been divided into three groups," the lieutenant announced. "The first will remain here in Paris. Another will be dispatched to Tours, one of our most important Services of Supply bases. The third group will be sent to the headquarters of the Advance Section in Chaumont, Haute-Marne."

Chaumont. Grace felt a shiver of anticipation as the name passed in whispers from one girl to the next. She thought back to the maps they had studied during training and pictured a nexus of several roads and railway routes in a town about 150 miles southeast of Paris. That was where the real action was, where they all wanted to be. She clasped her hands together and assumed an expression of calm interest. Every position was essential, she reminded herself. It didn't matter where she served, only that she did so honorably.

"Miss Grace Banker, Miss Louise LeBreton, Miss Suzanne Prevot," the lieutenant began, reading off eight more names. "Tomorrow you will depart for Chaumont."

Overcome with relief and elation, Grace barely heard the eleven names announced for Tours, and the eleven for Paris. She was going to General Pershing's headquarters, to the very center of the action, exactly as she had hoped. All around her she heard muffled exclamations of delight and saw a few tight smiles and nods of acceptance.

The officer in charge dismissed them with orders to spend the day in Paris as they pleased, to mind the air raid sirens, and to report back to the hostel before curfew. As the group began to disperse, Suzanne seized Grace's hands, beaming. "We're going to the bombing zone," she murmured, her voice trembling from the effort to suppress her delight. She was too kind to gloat in front of the girls who had been assigned to less exciting posts at the rear.

Before Grace could reply, she heard her name and felt a tug on her sleeve. Turning, she found Louise and Raymonde standing before her, arm in arm, eyes shining with unshed tears. "Miss Banker, there's been a terrible mistake," Louise said, as Raymonde gulped and nodded. "I've been assigned to Chaumont, but Raymonde has been posted to Tours."

"Our mother only gave us permission to enlist on the condition that we stay together," said Raymonde, her lower lip trembling.

"I'll swap with someone assigned to Tours," said Louise. "Surely one of those girls would rather go to Chaumont."

"All of them, I would imagine," said Suzanne.

Grace muffled a sigh. "Let me see what I can do." The sisters nodded, their expressions beseeching and hopeful.

Grace caught up with the lieutenant who had read the roster just as he was about to leave the room. She explained the situation, omitting the part about Mrs. LeBreton, but even before she finished, he was shaking his head. "You'd be surprised how many pairs of sisters have been accepted into the Signal Corps," he said. "Invariably they all ask to serve together, but just like the LeBreton girls, they will all be separated."

"May I ask why, sir?" It seemed oddly unkind to deny a request that would do so much to boost morale.

He hesitated, grimacing. "Miss Banker, I shouldn't need to remind you that this is war. Your group already survived one attack. There will be more. It would be bad enough if, God forbid, we ever have to ask a family to sacrifice one daughter, let alone two on the same day, as a result of the same misfortune."

"I understand," said Grace, chagrined. "I'll explain it to them."

He nodded curtly and continued on his way. Grace returned to Louise and Raymonde, who grew somber as she explained why it would be best for them to be apart. She had braced herself for more cajoling, but to her relief, they agreed that it was a prudent measure, for their mother's sake. If she became upset when they sent letters home from different locations, they could tell her honestly that they had asked to be posted together, but the army had decided against it, and they must obey orders.

"Make the most of your time together today," Grace urged them, and they assured her they would. The sisters intended to visit family and friends in the city, assuming they had not evacuated.

Grace knew some of the other French girls had similar plans. Marie Miossec, a Parisienne herself, had brought a key to her family's apartment on the Rue de Naples in the Eighth Arrondissement, and her eyes were bright with anticipation as she hurried off to see it. Once Grace had overheard her mention that her parents had intended to work in Cincinnati for only a few years, but the war had forced them to extend their stay. The concierge had agreed to look after the family's apartment in their absence, but Marie could not pass up the opportunity to visit to see it for herself. Grace understood her urgency. Marie had been assigned to Tours, and this might be her only chance until the end of the war to reacquaint herself with her old home.

As for Grace, she spent the day strolling through Paris with Suzanne and Cordelia, admiring the picturesque scenes, marveling at the beauty that endured despite the all too obvious signs of war. They returned to the Hotel Petrograd well before curfew and were surprised to discover that they were among the last girls to check in. Everyone was anxious about the possibility of a new attack, Grace surmised, and the YWCA hostel probably felt like the safest place to be.

"Lightning doesn't strike in the same place twice," Cordelia noted cheerfully.

"Actually, it can and does," said Suzanne. "The Telephone and Telegraph Building in New York has been struck several times."

"What?" Cordelia exclaimed. "And they had us drilling on the rooftop?"

"Never in a thunderstorm," Grace pointed out.

"Only in a snow squall or two," Suzanne added, shrugging.

But despite their lighthearted teasing, when Grace caught Suzanne's eye, she knew that her friend dreaded nightfall as much as she did, with its potential for a renewed assault, the drone of German planes, the thunder of long-range guns.

Only one operator failed to return on time—Marie, who rushed in ten minutes after curfew, breathless and chagrined, offering sincere, disarming apologies before Grace could reprimand her. When Marie had arrived at her family's apartment, she explained, she had discovered her aunt and uncle—her father's elder sister and her husband—and their two children living there. "They were as astonished and delighted to see me as I was to see them," she said, gracefully unwinding her scarf. "They evacuated Nancy a year ago, when daily life there became too harrowing, and their first thought was to come to our place, though they knew we were in the States. The concierge recognized them, and he assumed, quite correctly, that my parents would want him to let them in."

"My goodness," Grace exclaimed, imagining the scene: Marie unlocking the door and walking in on her unexpecting relatives, their mutual surprise and joy. "All this time, and your parents never knew?"

Marie shook her head. "They fled their home so quickly that they didn't think to bring our address. My aunt remembered only that my parents were on the faculty of a conservatory in the Midwest, so she sent a few letters to the American Conservatory of Music—which is in Chicago."

"So the letters were returned," Grace guessed.

"Unopened." Marie frowned slightly. "Forgive me for boasting, but my parents are quite well known, and the classical music world in the States is rather small. Someone should have known to forward my aunt's letters to the Cincinnati Conservatory." She inhaled sharply and lifted her chin. "*C'est rien*. My aunt and uncle and cousins are safe, our apartment is well looked after, and the family can be in touch once again."

"I'm very pleased for you," said Grace, smiling knowingly, "but that doesn't explain why you missed curfew."

"Of course it doesn't, and I make no excuse, but after they kissed me and fussed over me—and lamented to see me so unfashionably attired in a stiff, dark uniform with these appalling bloomers—my aunt insisted upon ringing all of our other relations who had fled to Paris. She commanded them to appear at once to give me a proper welcome, and before I knew it, a crowd had swept in, full of questions and praise and admonishments. They were about equally divided between those who admired my courage and those who declared I was *une imbécile complète* to have returned to France at such a dangerous time."

Grace's smile broadened. "Your aunt rang your other relations?"

Marie paused. "Yes," she said, abashed. "Our apartment does have a phone. I should have called you when I realized I would be late. That is not a mistake I will ever repeat, I swear it."

Her vow was so fervently delivered that Grace had to smother a laugh. "I'm sure you won't. Now, off to bed."

Marie nodded and hurried on her way.

With all of her operators accounted for, Grace too went to bed. Sleep did not come easily, but the night was blessedly peaceful, and in the morning she woke, rested and refreshed, full of anticipation for the day ahead. The other girls seemed to share her mood, those who were packing their bags for Tours and Chaumont, as well as those who were staying in Paris and were eagerly looking forward to their first day on the switchboards at the U.S. Headquarters. Grace had not anticipated the tearful farewells in the hostel lobby when it was time to depart for the train station, but it was only natural, considering how long the First Group had been together, how much they had endured and shared. It was strange and unnerving to see how easily and arbitrarily they could be divided up and scattered, but good soldiers followed orders without complaint.

The operators departing Paris traveled to the Gare de l'Est together, only to separate on the platform, eleven boarding the train heading southwest, and eleven more, including Grace, awaiting one bearing southeast. For the first time they were quite on their own. Captain Vivian had left with Marie, Raymonde, and the other girls assigned to Services of Supply; after escorting them to Tours, he would set out for Le Havre to meet the Second Group, who had almost caught up with them thanks to the First Group's lengthy delay in Southampton. In his absence, as chief operator, Grace was now the ranking officer in charge of the Chaumont girls, not that she anticipated needing to order them about while they traveled. Her ten operators were smart, poised, and capable of looking out for themselves. Even Louise, who had been so tearful the day before, had reconciled herself to her younger sister's absence and seemed as determined as any of them to do her bit proudly.

They crowded aboard the train, into a car already packed with French soldiers and civilians. By that time it was standing room only, so as the whistle shrilled and the train left the station, they stowed their luggage and clung to whatever straps and bars were within reach, craning their necks to watch the passing scenery, gasping and muffling laughter whenever a particularly hard jolt jostled them against one another.

They sped through the French countryside, through rolling hills and green pastures, past farms and quaint villages. The train stopped infrequently, but whenever seats were abandoned, the girls promptly claimed them, and eventually they all managed to find a place, even when it meant squeezing four onto a seat for three.

Several hours and 150 miles later, the train chugged to a stop at the station at Chaumont-sur-Haute-Marne, which, from the scenes they had glimpsed through the windows, appeared to be a charming village on a high hill, with breathtaking views of the beautiful river valleys of the Suize and the Marne below. The eleven operators collected their gear, disembarked, and gathered on the far side of the platform, searching the crowd expectantly for their escort, nodding pleasantly to the soldiers who threw them curious glances and astonished grins in passing. Always before, in Liverpool, in Le Havre, a Signal Corps officer had met them upon arrival, identifying them at a glance by their uniforms, by the fact that they were a group of women where none were expected to be. Each time, their escort had promptly approached them, had introduced himself, and had led them through the next stage of their journey, but now Grace had only an officer's name but no one to match it to. Perhaps she had misunderstood her instructions and the officer had never intended to meet them at the station, or he had meant to come but some emergency had detained him. Either way, he was not there, and she would have to seek him out.

She glanced around the platform and spotted an amiable-looking corporal. "Excuse me, soldier," she said. "Where can I find Lieutenant Riser?"

"This time of day? The Signal Corps office in the caserne, I guess."
The soldier gestured toward the station house, then to the right. "Exit
through the building, then head up the hill. All of the American army
offices are in the caserne—the old stone barracks, three wings around a
courtyard, surrounded by a tall iron fence. You can't miss it."

"Thank you."

"Wait, miss," said the corporal as she turned back to her girls. "Are
you our hello girls?"

She smiled at him over her shoulder. "We're telephone operators,
yes."

If he caught the gentle correction, his broad smile gave no sign of
offense. "Oh, miss, you have no idea how glad everyone is going to be to
see you. What a relief it's going to be to have real American hello girls
on the switchboards!"

"Thank you, soldier," said Grace, touched. "We're glad to be here."

She turned back to the girls to find that they had already lined up in
two columns with their gear, awaiting her order to depart. Evidently she
was not alone in wondering why no one had met them, or in deciding
to think nothing of it. They had passed through grueling examinations,
had endured exhaustive training, and had crossed an ocean to do their
bit. They could certainly find their way through a small French village
to present themselves to their commanding officer.

They marched through the station house and outside to the cobblestone street, eyes forward, aware of the stares and double takes and
astonished grins of the great many American soldiers from all branches
of the AEF filling the streets and sidewalks, hurrying by on what Grace
assumed must be important military business. Of course Lieutenant
Riser could not spare time to meet them at the station. She should take
it as a sign of his confidence in them that he had not considered it necessary.

Even with the military presence, Chaumont was as charming as
it had appeared from the train, with picturesque buildings arranged
around well-tended squares and cobblestone streets, all bathed in sunlight streaming through fleecy white clouds in a perfect blue sky. Grace

found the ancient gray stone barracks exactly as the corporal had described it, but with a small group of soldiers drilling in the courtyard, and guards posted at the imposing front entrance.

"Wait here," she told the girls. Nodding, they set down their gear and took in the scene, their faces alight with interest, some of them rubbing their shoulders and necks to loosen stiff muscles. Alone, Grace approached the guards, identified herself, and told them of her orders to report to Lieutenant Riser. They told her where to find him, not in the small telephone room on the first floor, where she and her girls would soon take over the switchboards, but in his office on the second floor.

She pretended not to notice the startled glances she collected as she made her way to the stairwell and climbed to the second floor. Brass nameplates beside each door identified the occupant; Lieutenant Riser's door was open, and when she peered through the doorway she glimpsed two officers engrossed in conversation, one seated casually on the edge of the desk with his arms folded over his chest, the other standing.

Grace cleared her throat and rapped on the doorframe. "Lieutenant Riser?" she asked.

Both men turned toward the door, and the one sitting on the desk rose. "Yes?" snapped the lieutenant, a tall, athletic man in his early forties with light brown curly hair. His companion, a captain, was slightly shorter and about five years younger, with wavy dark brown hair and blue eyes and a friendly, curious smile, a welcome contrast to the lieutenant's frown. His khaki shirt, jodhpurs, and slouch hat marked him as an Australian. Intrigued, Grace let her gaze linger on him a moment. Could he be one of the heroes of Gallipoli? Australians, she had heard, were famously informal and nonchalant. He probably would not mind if she asked—but now was not the time.

Quickly she returned her attention to the lieutenant. "I'm Miss Grace Banker," she said, "chief operator of the First Unit, First Group of the U.S. Signal Corps telephone operators. I was instructed to report to you upon our arrival."

"Come on in, then," he said, gesturing impatiently. She entered, withdrew her orders from her coat pocket, and handed them to him. He looked them over, grimacing and shaking his head.

"Is something wrong, sir?" asked Grace.

"Wrong?" he muttered as if to himself, gaze fixed on the papers. "Where do I begin?"

The captain threw the lieutenant a quizzical look, then offered Grace a bemused shrug. "Welcome to Chaumont, Miss Banker," he said, his accent relaxed and charming. "I think that's what Lieutenant Riser meant to say."

"Yes, welcome," said the lieutenant, sighing in resignation and tossing her documents on his desk. "You might as well get settled into your quarters. The YWCA has set up a house for you on the Rue Brûle. Just follow the main road south, almost to the edge of town, and you'll see the sign. The staff there will provide all your meals. Tomorrow morning at seven o'clock, report to Corporal Farmer, the chief operator for the night shift. You'll find him in the telephone room on the first floor."

Grace clasped her hands behind her back. "If it's all right, sir, my operators are ready and eager to see the switchboards right away."

"How nice, but they're going to have to wait," he replied, his voice clipped. "We have qualified soldiers on duty at the moment, and I'm not going to pull them in the middle of a shift and disrupt operations at one of the busiest times of the day."

"Understood, sir," said Grace, although she hadn't intended anything of the sort. "Seven o'clock tomorrow morning it is."

The lieutenant had already turned away and was busying himself with some papers on his desk. "Get settled in," he said, gesturing vaguely toward the south. "Have something to eat. Get your beauty rest. Do whatever it is army girls do when they're off duty. Dismissed."

Inwardly, Grace bristled, but she kept her expression impassive. "Yes, sir." Nodding politely to the Australian captain, she turned on her heel and left the office. Once outside and alone, she inhaled deeply and puffed out her cheeks. So much for the corporal's prediction that everyone would be happy to see them.

Suzanne spotted her crossing the courtyard and left the other girls to meet her halfway. "How did it go?" her friend asked warily, falling in step beside her.

Grace managed a laugh. "I don't think the lieutenant likes women very much."

"Maybe he just doesn't like women in his army."

"That's probably it." As they approached the others, Grace raised a hand to get their attention. "I've met with our commanding officer, and he welcomes us to Chaumont. He understands that we're eager to get started, but they won't need us at the switchboards until tomorrow morning, so we're to settle into our quarters." When a murmur of disappointment and surprise arose, she waved it off, smiling. "I know, I know, but orders are orders. Enjoy the free time while you can. I doubt we'll have much of it in the days to come."

Gathering up their gear, they formed two lines and marched away from the barracks. They had not gone far down the main road when a vehicle approaching from behind passed them and halted at the curb. The passenger door opened, and out stepped the dark-haired captain. "G'day, Miss Banker," he said. "Need a lift? It's a long way to haul all that gear."

Grace sized up the truck. "That's kind of you, but I don't think we'll all fit. Could you take our gear, and we'll follow along on foot?"

"Easily done," he said cheerfully. After a quick word with the driver, both men loaded the operators' footlockers and bags into the back, and then, as the driver sped off, the captain joined Grace at the head of the column and walked along with the group. "Wilberforce MacIntyre," he said, extending his hand, which she shook, his palm broad and callused in hers. "My friends call me Mack."

"Pleased to meet you, Captain Mack," she said, not quite ready to dispense with all formalities.

"Don't mind the lieutenant," he said. "He's not always so gruff. Just do your job well and mind the rules, and he'll warm up to you girls soon enough."

Grace certainly hoped so. "Thanks for the advice." She glanced at his insignia. "You're with the First Australian Imperial Force?"

"That's right. Special liaison officer to the AEF." As the truck slowed to a stop several yards ahead, he gestured to a large, three-story, white stone house on a small rise surrounded by linden and chestnut trees. "This is the place, your country estate in France. It was originally furnished for AEF officers, quite comfortably, or so I'm told. Puts my barracks to shame."

"It's lovely," said Grace. "I hope no one was evicted on our account."

"Don't lose sleep over it. It could be the former residents moved someplace better." Captain Mack inclined his head back in the direction they had come. "Maybe into the chateau with General Pershing."

Grace laughed. "I hope it's something like that." She wondered if she and her girls would have the entire house to themselves. More operators were on the way, of course, but this gracious residence seemed too grand, too luxurious for wartime.

The captain and the driver unloaded their gear and accepted the operators' thanks good-naturedly. "See you around, Miss Banker," the captain said as he climbed back into the truck. She smiled and waved as they drove off, hoping that the captain's friendliness would prove to be more typical of the officers at Chaumont, and the lieutenant's curtness an anomaly.

As the other girls carried their gear inside, Suzanne planted herself in front of Grace and regarded her knowingly, eyebrows arched. "That was interesting."

Grace slung the strap of her bag over her shoulder. "What was interesting?"

"'See you around, Miss Banker.'"

"Don't be silly." Grace felt warmth rising in her cheeks. "He was just being friendly."

"Maybe." Suzanne shrugged, balancing her footlocker on her hip. "*I* think it was a promise."

Could it have been? Pleasantly flustered, Grace pulled a face, feigned exasperation, and entered the house. Inside the charming foyer, she found her operators gazing about in admiration and marveling at their good fortune, since many had expected to be quartered in a French version of Hobo House. The YWCA hostess, the cook, and two house-maids hurried out to greet them, and as the staff showed the other operators to their rooms, the hostess led Grace on a brief tour of the common areas—the kitchen, dining room, library, and parlor, where there was a piano.

"It took quite a bit of haggling to bring home that prize," said the hostess proudly. Mrs. Ivey was a small, plump, dark-haired woman in her early fifties, with rosy cheeks and bright, sparkling brown eyes. "Do you play?"

"Not I, but some of our girls do."

"They say there are five bathtubs in Chaumont, and we have three of them." Mrs. Ivey hesitated before adding, "Granted, sometimes there are water shortages, but when it is plentiful, you can usually count on a hot bath at the end of a long day."

Grace could hardly believe their luck. Thanking their hostess, she gathered her belongings and climbed up two flights to the room she had been assigned, a bright, clean chamber with two twin beds and a nightstand between them. Suzanne was already stretched out on one of the mattresses, hugging a plump pillow to her chest and sighing in contentment.

The girls spent the afternoon unpacking, washing clothes, and exploring the neighborhood, reconvening in the dining room at suppertime. Though the portions were small, the meal was tasty and filling—chicken in a cream sauce, a stewed cabbage dish, strong-flavored cheeses, and crusty bread. Breakfast the next morning was equally delicious, but afterward Mrs. Ivey took Grace aside and confided that rations varied from week to week, and although her staff was creative, the girls should not expect to eat this well every day.

"We understand," Grace assured her. "We'll be grateful for anything, and we won't waste a morsel."

Soon thereafter, Grace called the girls to order and led them back to the stone barracks, past dozens of soldiers who stopped what they were doing to watch them march by, some looking on with admiration or astonishment, others with deep skepticism. It was difficult not to tense up knowing that they were the object of so much scrutiny, but Grace kept her eyes forward and head high, confident that the girls would follow her example. Every one of them was aware that they had much to prove, not only about themselves and their profession, but for all women everywhere who had ever been dismissed as too weak, too emotional, too frivolous, or too timid to contribute to a cause as daunting and consequential as victory in war.

They marched through the iron gates, across the courtyard, past the guards, and through the main entrance, arriving at the telephone office precisely at half past six. Reporting a half hour early had been Grace's idea, one that she would have discussed with Lieutenant Riser the previous day, had he not dismissed her so peremptorily. She and her operators had no idea how these switchboards would be arranged, or even what type of equipment was installed. Grace had instructed each of her girls to choose a night shift operator and observe him at his station, familiarizing herself with the switchboard and noting any particular quirks or weaknesses before she replaced him. Such preparation would allow for a smoother transition between shifts, reducing the likelihood of dropped calls, delays, or incorrect connections. It was a prudent plan, and Grace was confident the chief operator of the night shift would agree to it.

But before she could seek out Corporal Farmer, as soon as she entered the telephone room, she found Lieutenant Riser standing just inside the doorway.

"Miss Banker," he greeted her, surprised. "You're early."

"I hope that isn't a problem, sir," she replied, discomfited. "I wanted my girls to have time to observe the night shift operators at work before they take over at seven o'clock."

He folded his arms and regarded her for a moment, the barest trace of a smile on his face. "The shift change is actually at eight. I built in time for your girls to observe our operators when I told you to report at seven."

"I see." She could feel her cheeks growing warm. "Very good. Ninety minutes to observe is even better than thirty."

"All the same, you could have slept in, if you'd followed orders."

She would have done so, if she had known, if he had seen fit to tell her. "We're perfectly well rested now, sir, and eager to get to work."

His gaze shifted to the ten other women, who had already dispersed to different stations and were studying the switchboards. "I see that." He turned back to her. "I suppose I could have saved us both some trouble by letting you observe the switchboards yesterday. I assume that's what you were really asking to do."

"Yes, sir, but I don't think there's any permanent harm done."

He cleared his throat roughly, as if he were trying to disguise a laugh. "I agree, Miss Banker. Carry on. If you or your girls have any questions, don't hesitate to ask."

The lieutenant walked off down the aisle between the switchboards, hands clasped behind his back. He had referred to the women as "your girls," she thought ruefully, while the men of the night shift were "our operators." She hoped he wouldn't insist on such distinctions much longer.

At eight o'clock, Grace approached Corporal Farmer. "I'm here to relieve you," she said.

Grinning, he rose, removed his headset, and handed it to her. "I stand relieved. Congratulations, miss."

She smiled and thanked him. Taking his place at the station, she slipped on the headset, adjusted the mouthpiece, and scanned the rows of tiny lightbulbs and numbered jacks and keys. She barely had time to glance around the room to make sure the other operators were settling in when a bulb at her station lit up, signaling an incoming call. Swiftly she took a flexible black cord in hand, located the corresponding jack from among the many arranged in rows at the bottom of the switchboard, and plugged it firmly into place.

"Number, please?" she inquired.

No reply. She heard a faint sound, like a gasp, enough to tell her that the line was not dead. "Number, please?" she repeated, louder.

"I'm sorry, miss," a man replied, a bit hoarsely. "When you said, 'Number, please,' I couldn't answer. There was a lump in my throat. For a moment, I thought I was back home in Albany."

Grace smiled. "Sir, I can tell from my switchboard that you aren't. Other than that, how can I assist you?"

"Yes, of course, let's get to it." His voice trembled slightly as he gave her the number. Swiftly she connected the call, listened in a moment to make sure the two parties were engaged, and released the call just as another light flashed on her switchboard.

Another cord, another jack. "Number, please?"

It was another astonished caller, who stammered a bit as he gave her his party's number, and said, "God bless you girls," after she connected his call.

All around her, she heard the other girls connecting calls, graciously accepting thanks from the astonished and relieved soldiers, unfailingly efficient and professional as they warmly reassured the soldiers that, yes, "real American hello girls" were on the job and had everything well in hand.

Grace felt a heady rush of gratitude that she had found her way there, to France, to Chaumont, to the place where she was most needed.

She was truly a switchboard soldier now.

11

APRIL 1918

Le Havre and Paris

VALERIE

When the Second Group's ship finally docked in Liverpool, Valerie was so grateful to step onto British soil that tears filled her eyes. Although Colonel Hertness had warned her that the Irish Sea would be the most dangerous part of their voyage, to the relief of everyone on board, the *Carmania* had passed through the emerald green waters untroubled by German U-boats. No one else had succumbed to influenza after the first two tragic deaths, but several afflicted soldiers who had seemed perfectly healthy only days before had been carried from the ship on stretchers and immediately transferred to quarantine. None of the telephone operators had fallen ill, but Mrs. Crittenden's constant insistence upon mask-wearing and her threats to issue demerits to "mask slackers" had set many of the girls' nerves on edge. As soon as they descended the gangplank in Liverpool, several operators snatched off their masks and inhaled deeply, filling their lungs as they claimed they never could while wearing a mask, shooting furtive looks at Mrs. Crittenden as if daring her to enforce her mask requirement on land. Mrs. Crittenden did not take the bait, not even when a few girls tossed their masks into the nearest rubbish bin.

"I wouldn't do that if I were you," Valerie warned as one of the operators prepared to discard hers.

"Why not?" she retorted. "We don't need these anymore. We left the influenza behind us on that ship."

"You don't know that for certain."

But the girl just sniffed disparagingly and flung her mask in the bin. As for Valerie, she had removed hers and had tucked it away in her kit with her spares. She hoped she would never need them again, but why let all that sewing go to waste, and why tempt fate?

Shortly after disembarking, they were met at the pier by Major Chandler, the Signal Corps officer assigned to escort them across England. During the long, uncomfortable train ride to Southampton, Major Chandler chatted with each of the girls for at least a few minutes, inquiring after their needs and offering to assist them whenever they mentioned a problem with one thing or another. Valerie quite liked him until, after she described the attack on the *Carmania*, he confided that he believed the operators had risked their lives in vain, for the war was already lost.

"There is no hope for the Allies," he told her morosely. "Soon Germany will emerge triumphant, and Great Britain will be wiped off the map."

"I suppose our American boys will have something to say about that," Valerie retorted, shifting in her seat, turning her back on him. He tried to explain that he had simply stated the facts as he observed them, but Valerie was too outraged to listen. How dare he spread such defeatist, demoralizing talk just as they were about to sail for France? If he kept that up, the kaiser ought to put him on the Boche payroll.

She was glad to see the last of Captain Chandler after he escorted their group to their boardinghouse. Leaving their gear in their rooms, the operators regrouped for lunch in the dining room, where Valerie forced down quite possibly the worst meal she had ever tasted in her life—boiled dandelion greens, ersatz coffee, granite-hard bread, and a strange, watery dessert sweetened with saccharine. Afterward, Mrs. Crittenden granted them permission to explore Southampton until curfew, so Valerie, Millicent, and a few other girls found their way to a YMCA hut, where an angel disguised as a YMCA hostess offered them doughnuts and cups of rich, steaming hot chocolate. A few soldiers played board games in one nook or read books in another, but a piano at the far end of the room sat idle. Urged on by her friends, Millicent flexed her hands, sat down at the keyboard, and soon had the doughboys singing along as she played all the favorite war tunes: "Over There," "It's a Long Way to Tipperary," and "Keep the Home Fires Burning."

"Another Signal Corps telephone girl passed through here not long ago," the YMCA secretary mused to Valerie when she returned to the canteen to refresh her cup. "Her group's packet boat was fogbound for a week, and she came here almost every night to entertain the soldiers. She had the most wonderful voice."

Valerie smiled. "Marie Miossec, I presume?"

"Why, yes," the secretary exclaimed, astonished, and then she laughed at herself. "I shouldn't be surprised. All you Signal Corps girls must know one another."

"Those of us in the First and Second Groups do, anyway. We trained together in New York."

"Do you think you'll see Marie again Over There?"

Valerie shrugged. "It's possible. If we're stationed in the same place, sure, but I have no idea where she is or where I'll be."

"Well, if you do see her—" The secretary hesitated. "The night before she sailed for France, she asked me if I knew whether the Three Hundred and Seventh Infantry had passed through Southampton."

"Oh, she did, did she?" said Valerie, recalling the handsome dark-haired soldier who had stolen Marie away after her impromptu concert in the lounge car.

"Yes." The secretary allowed a knowing smile. "She said she had an acquaintance in the division, but I suspect he's something more than that. If you see her, tell her they haven't been through Southampton yet, and I've been keeping an eye out."

"I'll tell her," Valerie promised, and then a thought came to her.

"Could you keep an eye out for a soldier for me too? My brother, Henri DeSmedt, is with the Signal Corps Photographic Section. I don't know which unit he'll be assigned to after his training, but—" From her inside breast pocket, she withdrew a small folder she had made from stiff cardboard to keep precious photos safe and close to her heart. Removing Henri's portrait, she gazed at it for a moment before passing it to the secretary. "I don't know exactly what I want you to do, if he does pass this way. Tell him—" *Tell him I love him and miss him desperately*, she thought. "Tell him his big sister got to France first."

"I'm afraid you're too late for that," said the secretary, brow furrowing as she studied the photo. "He's already Over There."

For a moment Valerie merely stared at her, uncomprehending. "No he isn't. He's back in upstate New York, training with the aerial photography school."

The secretary's glance shifted to Valerie, then back to the photo in her hand. "I suppose I don't really know whether he's gone Over There," she said, shaking her head as she returned the photo, "but I'm quite certain he isn't in New York. He passed through Southampton with a Signal Corps unit less than a fortnight ago. You said his name is Henry, right?"

"No." Feeling slightly foolish, Valerie amended, "It's Henri, actually."

"From what I overheard, he's going by Henry among his buddies." The secretary smiled, remembering. "Sometimes they called him Hollywood Hank."

"Hollywood Hank?"

"A friendly nickname. It seemed to suit a fellow in filmography. He always carried a still camera, too." The secretary regarded her thoughtfully. "Is your family from Hollywood?"

"Los Angeles," Valerie replied, heart thudding. "Brussels and New York before that." The details—the soldier's name, his hometown— differed enough to suggest that there were two soldiers, but what were the odds that they would both be assigned to the Signal Corps, and that a photograph of one could be mistaken for the other? That was simply too improbable for Valerie's mathematical mind to dismiss as mere co-incidence.

"I don't understand," she said, mostly to herself. "When I saw Henri in New York, he told me he was going to be transferred to the aerial photography school. How could he have shipped out before I did? Why didn't he tell me?"

"Perhaps his orders came so suddenly that he couldn't write until after they set sail," the secretary said. "Or perhaps he did write, but you shipped out before his letter arrived."

Valerie envisioned a battered envelope abandoned on the floor of their quarters at Hobo House, her name in her brother's handwriting, the ink smeared where the rain had touched it, traces of muddy foot-prints suggesting a wayward journey through the post. "All this time, I've assumed he's still safe."

"Oh, let's not have any of that, now." The secretary clasped her hand and gave it a reassuring squeeze. "Your brother might not be where you thought he was, but that doesn't mean he isn't safe. And wouldn't he be safer filming parades in Paris than training for aerial photography? It must be terribly dangerous to fly over enemy territory and take photo-graphs of their entrenchments."

Valerie felt a chill imaging her brother's fragile plane flying above no-man's-land while a German gunner fixed him in his sights. Of course she didn't want Henri soaring through enemy skies, a defenseless target; she wanted him safe back in Rochester, training for a role he would never need to perform if the war ended before he qualified.

"I don't suppose you remember what unit this Hollywood Hank fel-low was in?" Valerie asked, managing a wan smile.

"I'm sorry, but I don't." The secretary sighed and patted her hand. "I'm sure you'll hear from him soon. His letters will catch up with you eventually, if you stay in one place long enough."

Valerie hoped so. She reassured herself with the thought that even if his hypothetical last letter to Hobo House had landed in some dead-letter office, he also would have written to their mother and Hilde, and they would send word to her.

Thanking the secretary, she returned to the piano just as Millicent finished an especially lively rendition of "Good-bye-ee!" At the same moment, a corporal approached and rested his elbow on the piano. "Would you play me some ragtime, miss?" he asked, his expression plaintive. "What's new back home in the States?"

Millicent thought for a moment, and then began to play "When Alexander Takes His Ragtime Band to France." She smiled up at the soldier, eyebrows raised, expecting a smile in return.

Instead the corporal scowled and shook his head. "Not that. That's old! I heard that two weeks ago."

He stalked off, annoyed, but Millicent merely shrugged and played on. When she finished, she lifted her hands from the keys and turned around on the bench to face Valerie. "I feel like I've utterly disgraced myself as far as my up-to-date American-girlness is concerned."

"Don't mind him." Valerie inclined her head toward the audience, whose applause had barely faded. "Everyone else enjoyed it."

A few soldiers called out requests for another tune, but Millicent declined. The hours had passed swiftly, and if the operators didn't hurry, they wouldn't make it back to the boardinghouse in time for supper and curfew.

Mrs. Crittenden was waiting for them in the foyer with news. "If you've unpacked, repack," she told them. "If this fair weather holds, we'll be sailing for France tomorrow morning, first thing after breakfast."

Millicent gasped with excitement and clutched Valerie's arm. "We'll be ready," Valerie promised. She would be willing to skip breakfast, and dinner too if either meal resembled that barely palatable lunch, but she didn't say so aloud.

The next morning dawned clear, fresh, and sunny, good weather for a smooth Channel crossing, but with no cloud cover or fog to conceal them from German aircraft. Their sturdy packet boat—fairly bursting with telephone operators, French civilians, Allied soldiers, and Red Cross officers—departed Southampton as stealthily as it could in the bright sunshine. Valerie did not know whether to be impressed or apprehensive when a member of the crew told her proudly that their boat had sunk a German submarine on her last outing, but she was relieved when a Royal Air Force airplane joined them as an escort when they passed Portsmouth.

After their adventures aboard the *Carmania*, Valerie and her friends had braced themselves for another nerve-racking voyage, but the crossing was blessedly uneventful, and they arrived at Le Havre unharmed. A Signal Corps officer, Captain William Vivian, met them when they disembarked, and after escorting them to a charming hotel for lunch, he offered to lead them on a sightseeing tour of the seaside town. "I feel like we're children on a school outing," Millicent murmured as he led them through the winding cobblestone streets and pointed out the various places of interest. Valerie smothered a laugh, but she rather enjoyed the tour, and she certainly liked the sympathetic, courteous Captain Vivian more than prophet of doom Major Chandler.

Captain Vivian accompanied them aboard their train to Paris, which departed Le Havre in the late afternoon. "Paris," Drusilla exclaimed, sighing, conveying in a single word the anticipation Valerie and her friends all felt as they approached *la Ville Lumière*. They chatted excitedly as the train carried them southeast through the French countryside, each sharing what she looked forward to seeing most—the Eiffel Tower, the lively theaters, the lovely boulevards and gardens, the splendid architecture, the charming shops and markets. Overhearing them in passing, Captain Vivian paused, brow furrowing. "Remember, Paris is under bombardment," he said. "It isn't the city you've admired on postcards, not at the moment, and we aren't tourists on holiday. On their first night, your friends in the First Group narrowly escaped being struck by a German aerial shell."

A few girls exchanged alarmed glances, but Millicent declared, "Bombs or no bombs, Paris is still Paris." When several other girls chimed in their assent, Captain Vivian smiled ruefully, shook his head, and continued down the aisle.

"I hope we arrive before dark," said Drusilla. "Wouldn't it be wonderful to get our first glimpse of Paris at sunset, with the blues of the evening sky and the gold and reds of the fading sun glistening on the Seine?"

"Yes," said Millicent, eyes shining, "and with the Eiffel Tower gleaming in the last rays of the sun, rising above the city like a sentinel guarding the inhabitants!"

They all agreed it would be glorious, but as the hours passed and darkness overtook them, it became apparent that they would not arrive until well after nightfall. At half past eleven, the darkness was so complete that only the slowing of the train alerted them that they were approaching their destination. When they disembarked onto the platform, they looked around in utter disbelief. If not for the tiny blue lightbulbs illuminating the entrance to the station house, they could have been in the open countryside rather than in the heart of a city.

"We could be in Waterloo, Iowa, for all the nightlife here," Drusilla lamented.

A smattering of giggles followed. "Blackout protocols," Inez pronounced, smothering their mirth. "You can admire the city tomorrow after sunrise."

Just then, a man emerged from the shadows, startling them until he drew closer and they recognized his Signal Corps uniform. He introduced himself as Lieutenant Highland, their escort to quarters. Captain Vivian fell in step beside him as they passed through the station and outside to the street, where the darkness was so complete that Valerie, Millicent, and Drusilla linked elbows for safety.

Several automobiles were parked at the curb, which, thanks to a thin coat of luminescent paint, Valerie glimpsed just before she would have tumbled into the street. She climbed aboard the lead vehicle with Millicent, Drusilla, and two other girls, and after making sure everyone was accounted for, Lieutenant Highland took the wheel and slowly drove off through the deserted *arrondissement*.

Valerie was exhausted from the long day of travel, and her companions' drooping eyelids and stifled yawns told her they felt the same, but Lieutenant Highland was wide awake and talkative. After inquiring about their journey, he began narrating the drive as if they were on a sightseeing tour.

"Here's where Big Bertha struck last week and killed sixty-eight people," he said cheerfully, pointing out the window into the darkness. Instinctively they turned their heads to see, but they couldn't make out anything beyond the tip of his finger.

"Big Bertha?" one of the girls asked, voice quavering.

"A massive German howitzer, named after the manufacturer's wife," the lieutenant replied, with unsettling enthusiasm. "It can fire projectiles almost two tons in weight a distance of nearly six miles. The Germans' favorite shell uses a delayed-action fuse. It can plow through forty feet of concrete and rock before exploding, and let me tell you, if one of those hits the ground nearby, you really feel it."

"That's . . . impressive," Valerie managed to say.

Drusilla tugged on her sleeve. "Do you think the Signal Corps will issue us helmets?" she whispered.

"I don't think a helmet would help much if a shell like that hits," Millicent murmured back.

Valerie shook her head and shrugged, instinctively straining her ears for the sound of distant artillery fire, not that she would recognize the sound of an incoming shell or would know where to flee for safety in the unfamiliar city.

The captain continued his lively, harrowing narration until they arrived at their hotel, fatigue and trepidation having supplanted nearly all their earlier excitement. Valerie received her key, hauled her gear to the third-floor room she would share with Drusilla, spared a few moments to wash and undress, and collapsed into bed.

She slept deeply through the night, until a tiny filament of sunlight peeped in beneath the blackout curtains and woke her. That told her two things: first, that they had not drawn the blackout curtains well enough, because if light could slip in through a crack, it could slip out, and second, that it was morning, and within a few hours they would receive their long-awaited assignments. She fervently hoped she could stay in Paris, not only because she was travel weary, but because she longed to take her place at a switchboard without further delay and start doing her part to win the war.

She woke Drusilla, who mumbled drowsily until Valerie raised her voice and gave her a good shake, a role reversal that would have astonished her elder sister. They washed, arranged their hair, dressed in their cleanest uniforms, and hurried downstairs to join the rest of the Second Group in the dining room for a breakfast of toast, jam or honey, and ersatz coffee with cream. Afterward, Inez led them down the hall to a parlor to await the arrival of the Signal Corps officer who was on his way from AEF headquarters with their assignments.

The room buzzed with excitement and nervous speculation. Valerie tried to relax by strolling around the elegant room, admiring the rococo architecture and antique furnishings, gazing out the windows at passersby—the young women so effortlessly beautiful even in wartime; the matrons with their market baskets; the Allied soldiers, some grinning and craning their necks, on leave, no doubt, eager to see everything before they returned to the fight; others intent and purposeful as they went about their duties. The building directly across the narrow street appeared to be another hotel, six stories of white stone with an arched frontispiece embellished with sculpted cherubs. She was wondering whether their own accommodations were similarly elaborately adorned when a Signal Corps lieutenant strode into the room carrying a thin sheaf of papers. Inez hurried forward to meet him, and while they conferred quietly, the operators quickly assembled into four rows of seven and stood at attention.

Valerie's heart pounded as Inez introduced the officer as Lieutenant Baker. He made a few brief remarks, welcoming them to Paris and thanking them for volunteering for such important service. Valerie barely heard him, impatiently willing him to get to the list in his hand. Eventually, after an interminable few minutes, he read off the names; she waited, holding her breath until he came to her own, rejoicing in his use of alphabetical order, which meant she would not wait long.

Paris. She exhaled, a long sigh of relief, and drew in a breath, closing her eyes, weak-kneed from gratitude. She had been assigned to Paris.

Millicent and Drusilla had too, as had Inez, as their chief operator, but Martina had been sent to Tours, and others to Chaumont. They hardly had time to say proper goodbyes, as the operators departing Paris were sent back to their rooms for their gear and the Paris contingent were instructed to follow Lieutenant Baker to the Signal Corps central office at the Élysées Palace Hotel. Just as Valerie had hoped, they would begin work immediately.

What a marvelous walk it was, the sun shining, the gentle breeze carrying the fragrance of spring flowers, with only the passing soldiers and the brown sandbags stacked against foundations and the occasional rubble-strewn vacant lot reminding them of the war. They passed behind the Élysées Palace, the eighteenth-century French classical presidential residence, and glimpsed the Arc de Triomphe and the Eiffel Tower not far away. The Élysées Palace Hotel was a Beaux-Arts marvel, its lavish beauty little marred by sandbags outside and blackout curtains within, but Valerie and her companions were most eager to see the telephone rooms.

They arrived just before the shift change, when the highly skilled women would take over for the slower, less experienced male soldiers who worked the easier night shift. In the few moments before the American girls took over the switchboards, Valerie and her companions enjoyed a happy reunion with their friends from the First Group, exclaiming with delight, embracing, sharing bits of news.

Valerie was most pleased to see Cordelia again. "Is Marie Miossec here in Paris?" Valerie asked after they shared a fond hug. "I have a message for her."

Cordelia shook her head. "No, she was sent to Tours."

"Tours?" Valerie glanced at a switchboard station. "I suppose I could call her."

"Only if it's official Signal Corps business," Cordelia warned. "You'll get written up if you're caught making a personal call."

"In that case, I suppose I can be good, or I can be quick."

As Cordelia gaped at her, shocked, Inez clapped her hands for attention. "A little decorum, please," she said, exasperated. "Remember, you are soldiers, not schoolgirls, and everyone is watching us."

Abashed, they murmured apologies and prepared to take their stations. Valerie was pleasantly surprised to see that the switchboards appeared to be just off the assembly line, the most advanced technology and practically gleaming with newness. What a thrill it was to replace a weary soldier at his station, to don her headphones and mouthpiece, and to begin connecting calls! Quartermasters in the city wanted to contact their counterparts at Services of Supply, intelligence officers at AEF headquarters needed to reach colonels at the Advance Section in Chaumont, and so on, one call after another in quick succession.

"Number, please," Valerie said a few hours into her shift.

"Oh!" a deep-voiced man exclaimed. "Thank heaven you girls are here at last!" He asked to speak to the American ambassador, and Valerie swiftly connected him. "God bless you," he added before she withdrew from the call.

Reactions such as his were quite common, and each time they made her smile. How glad she was to be plugging away at a switchboard again, serving her country—countries, she supposed, the United States as well as Belgium—in a time of such profound crisis. None of the dangers and hardships of the voyage mattered anymore, now that she was here doing her bit. Every call was important, each operator performed efficiently and accurately, the room hummed with activity, and the new switchboard worked like a dream.

It wasn't until hours later on her lunch break, which the operators took in small groups in overlapping thirty-minute shifts, that Valerie learned that this was a recent, necessary, and very welcome development.

"We've been in this building less than a week," Cordelia told her as they shared a bench in a nearby park, nibbling their lunches and keeping an eye on their wristwatches. "Before then, we worked out of the American headquarters in the Hotel Mediterranée on old magneto boards installed for the Exposition of 1900. Some of them were constructed so awkwardly that sometimes we had to climb a ladder to make a connection."

"You're joking," said Valerie, astonished.

"God's honest truth."

"I suppose that explains why French operators are so much slower than us on the boards, if those rumors are true and they haven't been unfairly maligned."

"How can I put this nicely?" Cordelia paused to think. "The French girls—well, let's just say we have philosophical and cultural differences in our approach to the job. Some of them have been telephone operators for decades, and they're very set in their ways. They were *extremely* displeased when we showed up to replace some of them. Those that were sacked kicked up quite a fuss, shouting and demanding to keep their jobs even as they were being shown to the door. Those that remained have resented us ever since out of loyalty to their friends. They absolutely refuse to learn from us. I can tell you from personal experience, woe be it to the American girl who encourages her new French colleague to be more efficient and to put a smile in her voice."

Valerie winced. "Maybe that sort of encouragement is best left to the chief operators."

"Yes. Lesson learned." Cordelia sighed. "One thing's for sure, their conduct would never be tolerated back in South Dakota, or really anywhere in the States. Our offices are quiet and businesslike, but the French girls raise their voices to the callers and gesture frantically with their hands while they're speaking, and they have constant, ongoing conversations and arguments with one another."

"During their shifts? While they're working?"

"From the moment they sit down to the time they remove their headsets. It never ends. The din is enough to give you a headache."

"How do they manage to connect their calls?"

"That's precisely the problem. They don't manage it. They make mistakes and they're slow. When we shared space at the Hotel Mediterranée, I saw girls shout at one another and forget to stop shouting when a caller rang. *J'écoute! J'écoute!*' they scream at some hapless medic trying to order a shipment of splints and bandages."

Dismayed, Valerie nonetheless couldn't help laughing at Cordelia's comical delivery. "I bet you're glad you're not sharing space with them any longer."

"Yes, but we still have to work with them, so we're still obliged to tiptoe around their whims and tempers." Cordelia pressed a hand to her brow and shook her head. "Most of our toll calls still have to go over French lines, and you'll soon find out how trying that can be. First, you have to connect to the French line and say '*J'écoute.*' Then, after about fifteen minutes, someone will respond, and you'll have to begin an exchange of pleasantries. 'Good morning, how are you? How is your family? Is it raining there? Did you have a nice lunch? If you please, I should like to get—' And only then can you bring up the name of the town you're trying to reach. All of this must be conveyed in honeyed tones, or you're finished before you've begun. If you've done well so far, the mademoiselle may reply, '*Ah, oui,*' in a languid sort of way, as if your call has no particular urgency, but she might as well handle it, since she doesn't have anything better to do at the moment."

"They can't possibly be so indifferent," Valerie protested, laughing.

"You'll find out for yourself soon enough. What's more, if you request the same location too often, you'll infuriate them, and they'll shout something like, 'You are unbearable, you ring too much, it gets on my nerves! *Je coupe!*' and—bing, the call is disconnected and that's the end of that."

"I really hope you're exaggerating," said Valerie, glancing at her watch and gathering up her things. "We have French girls in the First Unit, and they don't behave anything like this. Marie, Louise, Raymonde—"

"Yes, but the difference is that our girls were born in France, but they were trained in America." Cordelia rose and fell in step with Valerie as they walked back to the Élysées Palace Hotel.

"Maybe our French girls can talk to the French operators on our behalf," Valerie suggested. "They could be our diplomats, and reach out to the French operators in the spirit of friendship and cooperation."

"They could try," said Cordelia, dubious. "Personally, I'd be afraid of making matters worse. So far, when any of us has approached them and tried to make peace, they've rebuffed us. They think *we're* the ones at fault, that we're curt, unfriendly, and rude. They don't think they need to change, to be more efficient and professional."

"Maybe the olive branch would be more appealing if it came from a French messenger," said Valerie. "Especially if our suggestions were phrased more tactfully."

Cordelia shrugged. "Maybe you should be our diplomat. After all, you're Belgian, right? You're neutral. You can be impartial and work for the good of all."

Valerie had to laugh. "I'm wearing a United States Signal Corps uniform. I think most people will assume I've taken sides."

Still, someone had to do something. No good could come of this animosity between the American operators and the French. They would have to learn to work together if they hoped to win the war.

12

APRIL 1918

Tours

MARIE

Marie had been in Tours three weeks when her mail finally caught up with her.

She had not heard from her family since Hoboken, and the bundle of letters arrived as a much welcome surprise. It seemed almost miraculous that the fragile pieces of paper could have survived the same difficult overseas journey she had taken, and that with all the disruption of the war, and the logistics involved in shifting materiel and men from this port to that encampment, the AEF had spared resources to bring her long-awaited, loving words from home.

Soldiers posted elsewhere might have taken the successful delivery of the mail for granted, but not Marie. She had learned a great deal about shipments and cargo—and all that could go wrong with them—during her brief tenure at the Services of Supply base.

For Marie's cohort, simply reaching Tours had been challenging. She had visited the lovely medieval town on the Loire known as *le Jardin de la France* years before, but she did not remember the journey from Paris being quite so long and arduous. So boundless was her joy to be back in France, even a France at war, that somehow she had expected the trip to be swift and comfortable, especially considering that they had been heading away from the front, unlike the girls posted to Chaumont, who were cheerfully speeding toward danger.

Captain Vivian had accompanied their group of eleven aboard the train that carried them 240 kilometers southwest of Paris, but theirs had not been a swift, straightforward route. Their train had frequently been sidetracked, required to pull over at a station and hold for hours to make way for urgent medical transports carrying wounded out of range of the massive guns hurling shells upon Paris. On several occasions they passed locomotives heading in the opposite direction, slower freight trains hauling supplies to the city and bases farther east, and similar freight trains—not passenger cars—packed with American doughboys on their way to the front. Each time, the telephone operators waved and cheered to the boys, and some brandished little American flags through the windows. The soldiers always waved back, grinning and whistling and waving their caps. Each time, too, Marie searched for a pair of familiar, warm dark eyes, but the trains passed too swiftly for her to distinguish one young man's face from another.

They finally reached Tours at eleven o'clock, but as in Paris, the blackout was so strictly enforced that only blue bulbs, fluorescent paint, and faint starlight illuminated the depot. Hauling their gear, shivering in the unexpected cold, trusting in Captain Vivian's navigation, they made their cautious, uncertain way through the town to the front portico of a convent. A long bell-pull hung to the right of the tall double doors; Captain Vivian pulled the rope, and before long the door swung open with a soft groan and an elderly nun emerged from the darkness carrying an old-fashioned oil lamp. Greeting the girls in French, she ushered them inside, bade the captain good night, and shut the door firmly, leaving him on the doorstep. A few of the girls giggled nervously to see the officer who had safely shepherded them many hundreds of miles so peremptorily dismissed, but no one opened the door to say a proper, respectful goodbye. Instead they stayed close to the circle of light cast by the lamp as the nun led them upstairs to their quarters.

Their residence in Tours turned out to be a large dormitory chamber with plain stone walls, unadorned except for a single crucifix at the far end. Blackout curtains covered the high, tall windows, and several narrow beds arranged in two long rows were enticingly made up with thick wool blankets and soft pillows. Too weary to be particular, Marie claimed the first unoccupied bed she came to and stowed her footlocker and bag underneath. Too tired and cold for conversation, the girls washed in basins along the far wall, undressed quickly, and sank into their beds, shivering, until they eventually grew warm enough to sleep.

In the morning, Marie woke to the sound of a heavy door swinging open and golden shafts of sunlight illuminating the edges of the blackout curtains. A dainty, elderly nun entered the room, immaculately dressed in a crisp black habit and white wimple, bearing a tray loaded down with so many dishes that Marie had marveled she could lift it. The nun caught her eye and smiled, but before Marie could climb out of bed and hurry to assist, the nun set down the tray on a table near the door. "Good morning, child," she said warmly, bringing Marie two dishes from the tray—a bowl of steaming, rich hot chocolate and a plate with two slices of baguette and a thick pat of fresh, creamy butter. Astounded, Marie murmured her thanks, suddenly ravenous, remembering only then that she had had no supper the night before.

Enticed awake by the delicious aromas, the other girls soon sat up in bed, rubbed their eyes, and gaped in astonishment as the sweet, smiling nun served them breakfast in bed. They delighted in that first delicious meal in Tours, but they were obliged to eat quickly rather than savoring it, for their first shift would begin promptly at nine o'clock.

After they had washed and dressed, they descended to the convent foyer, where Captain Vivian waited to escort them to Signal Corps headquarters. Marie felt overwhelmed with a sense of homecoming as they marched through the narrow streets, past the half-timbered buildings of *le Vieux Tours* and the more numerous white cut-stone buildings with blue slate *ardoise* roofs. The Signal Corps had established their main offices in a former cloth merchant's warehouse, with large, open rooms on the ground floor and smaller offices above. When Captain Vivian showed them to the telephone room, the operators were relieved to discover modern switchboards as up-to-date as those they had used back in the States. Their training had prepared them for anything from antique to modern, and they had worried that Services of Supply, so far to the rear, would have been stuck with old hand-crank models, which were ideal for locations that lacked electricity, but were slower, cumbersome, and prone to indistinct connections.

Marie and her cohort had observed the men on duty as they finished up the night shift, familiarizing themselves with the switchboards, selecting their stations. When the time came for the women to take over, the soldier Marie had been observing handed her the headset, comically dusted off the chair, and gestured to it as if he were a maître d'hôtel seating her at a fine restaurant. "It's all yours, and you're welcome to it," he declared. "I'm a telegraph operator. It must have been someone's idea of a joke to give me this job. How do you girls put up with callers' complaints and demands and bad tempers day in and day out?"

"One becomes accustomed to it," Marie replied, smoothing her skirt beneath her as she gracefully seated herself. "It helps to remember that the one who loses their temper has relinquished control of a situation. The one who remains calm controls the outcome."

The soldier nodded thoughtfully, but a buzz and a flashing bulb on Marie's panel brought the discussion to an abrupt end. She had connected that call, helping a quartermaster in Tours speak with a clerk in Le Havre; no sooner had she withdrawn herself than another call came in, and another, in an unceasing, urgent flurry. She was startled, the first time she connected a call with a soldier at the front, to hear explosions in the none-too-distant background, but she soon became accustomed to the frightening sound; sometimes she and the other girls were obliged to shout into their mouthpieces in order to be heard over the artillery fire on the receiver's end. By the end of her first shift, Marie surmised that she had connected calls from soldiers serving along every part of the supply chain, from ports to storage depots, from regulation stations to divisions at the front.

In the days that followed, Marie and her friends discovered that a Services of Supply base was a curious amalgam of military encampment, manufacturing town, and rehabilitation asylum, adjacent to a pictur-esque French town. In some cases, the AEF's various production plants, storehouses, and offices moved into existing buildings, but when no suitable premises could be found, new facilities had been built on the outskirts of town, their straightforward, functional, American newness looking jarringly out of place next to the existing French architecture.

The inhabitants of wartime Tours were an unusual mix as well. Most of the men assigned to Services of Supply had been posted there because of their professional skills. Most had left their civilian jobs to enlist in the military because recruiters had specifically appealed for work-ers from their trades and occupations. They could do the same work they did at home, but by signing up to do their bit with the AEF, they could see France, strike a blow against the kaiser, and fight for democ-racy abroad at the same time. Unlike the recruits in the infantry units, who were ideally between eighteen and thirty, these soldiers were just as likely to be well into their thirties or even middle-aged, with experi-ence in fields that were, to Marie at least, surprising in their variety. Of course the army needed mechanics and stevedores, but it never would have occurred to her that it also needed purchasing agents, accountants, and warehouse managers. After a few days at the base, however, she had a new appreciation for just how vital men with those skills were.

She supposed General Pershing and his advisors had made the same assumption about skilled telephone operators, until they came to France and found themselves stymied and frustrated by the antique technology and inadequate service.

One important difference Marie soon observed between the tele-phone girls and the male soldiers serving in Tours was that the women without exception felt proud of their role and appreciated for their work, but the morale of the men varied widely. Some draftees who had never wanted to fight were relieved to be posted more than two hundred miles from the front, managing inventory or fixing engines for the duration without any real fear of losing their lives. Others who had yearned to win glory on the battlefield were frustrated that their ambitions had been thwarted, and some worried that the folks back home would question their courage. They often had to be reminded that their service was equally honorable and was absolutely essential to victory.

The last group, the most unfortunate, consisted of officers who had been transferred to SOS after some failure at the front—ineffective leadership, reckless behavior, dangerously poor decision making. Sometimes it was rumored that an officer had "succumbed to the physical strain of the front," which could mean that he struggled with insomnia, or had contracted hysterical laryngitis because he could no longer bear to give an order that would send his boys over the top to their deaths, or had simply collapsed from exhaustion and strain. These unfortunate men saw their reassignment as a disgrace and a punishment, and there was no convincing them otherwise—in part because they refused to discuss it at all.

One division of labor disturbed and angered Marie more than any other. She had been in Tours more than two weeks before she discovered that Black men were also serving in the U.S. Army, but only in the most menial tasks and often out of sight. That discovery had come purely by chance. One afternoon when they were off duty, Marie and a few friends were hiking through a leafy wood when they stumbled upon a lumberjack crew on their dinner break. Marie greeted them in French before she realized they were Americans—most of them had removed their shirts in the heat, and had hastily pulled them on when the women arrived. Some of the men eyed them warily and nodded, but a few smiled and returned her greeting in English or fairly passable French.

"We're going to get back to logging soon," one of the men said, gesturing to a stand of trees that had been marked with chalk. "You should be sure to head back the way you came, and stay clear of this section."

"Thank you for the warning," said Marie. "Our apologies for getting in the way."

The women retraced their steps along the cleared trail, speculating about the men. "Should we have spoken to them?" Martina wondered aloud.

"Why not?" said Raymonde sharply. "Because they're Black?"

"No," Martina replied, offended. "Because they're enlisted men. We're not supposed to fraternize with them, only officers."

"We're permitted to *speak* to enlisted men," said Marie, crunching leaves underfoot as she moved into the lead. "We just aren't supposed to dance with them, or to accept their dinner invitations, and so forth."

It occurred to her that she had never seen any Black men at the YMCA hut, or at any of the dances they hosted, or at any of the cafés or restaurants in Tours, or even simply walking along the streets of the town. Could it be that the U.S. Army was as segregated as many of the country's cities and states? Had the Americans brought their irrational race hatred with them to France along with their doughboys and advanced telephone technology? If so, they would soon discover that the French would not indulge their intolerance.

Marie hoped her American friends were at least embarrassed if not outraged by their hypocritical president, who loudly proclaimed the righteousness of fighting for democracy abroad while denying it to people in his own country, not only to Blacks who were denied the rights of full citizenship, but also to women who were denied the right to vote.

She wanted to investigate the Black soldiers' circumstances, but she had little time to pursue the matter. From the moment the Signal Corps girls reported for duty, they had worked tirelessly, seven days a week, encouraged by the appreciation their grateful callers expressed on the line, and by their supervisors' promises that as soon as additional operators from the Second Group arrived, they would be allowed one day off each week. Despite their demanding schedule, Marie and her friends found time to explore Tours, which had retained much of the beauty and charm she remembered despite the overwhelming military presence. They attended dances and movies at the YMCA hut, enjoyed long walks along the Loire or the Cher in fair weather, visited cathedrals and botanical gardens, and explored the shops and cafés that remained resolutely open despite the scarcity of essential goods and most luxuries.

Marie, Raymonde, and some of the other French girls spent many of their spare hours looking up family and friends with whom they had lost contact after the German invasion. Marie had seen several of her relatives at her family's apartment during her brief stay in Paris, and with the help of the Red Cross, she had been able to track down new addresses for others who had fled the occupied territory. She had written to each family, and hoped for swift replies, and when she received a bundle of letters in the third week of April, she assumed that was what had come. Much to her surprise, she instead glimpsed a Cincinnati postmark and recognized her mother's handwriting on the first envelope, and on two of the four beneath it. It was perhaps a month's worth of news from home, and as soon as she completed her shift and finished supper with her friends, she returned to the convent and curled up to read them in a secluded stone alcove with a tall window composed of many translucent, diamond-shaped panes. As rain pattered on the glass, she arranged the envelopes in chronological order and opened the one on top.

How wonderful it was to hear her mother's voice through her written words, and how reassuring to learn that her parents and younger sisters were safe and healthy! The first letter contained news from the family and the neighborhood, as well as mild admonishments for Marie to be wary of danger, to take care of her voice, and to avoid the infamous Parisian salons, if she should be invited to any. "Paris is beautiful and sensual, but it can be frivolous and decadent too," her mother warned. "The aristocracy may pay for our time and talent, but we singers dare not adopt their indulgent, self-destructive habits."

Marie had to laugh. She had already left Paris; she could not imagine anyone from the *beau monde* deigning to invite her to a salon, infamous or not; and she had no time and little inclination to attend anyway. Yet she basked in the warmth of her mother's admonitions, recognizing the love and concern for her well-being that had prompted them.

The second letter was from her sisters, full of schoolgirl gossip, questions about army life, and assurances that they were praying for her every day. Marie would be sure to tell them that their Paris apartment was safe and sound, and that their aunts, uncles, and cousins sent their love.

The third letter, dated a week after the first, was more somber in tone, and the news was unsettling. The family was fine, her mother hastened to assure her, but anti-German prejudice and paranoia were on the rise back home. Dr. Kunwald had been arrested under the Alien Enemies Act, and both he and his wife had been imprisoned at Fort Oglethorpe in Georgia. No one knew precisely what the charges against him were. Mutual friends with legal expertise believed that Dr. Kunwald had been accused of conducting German music and publicly demonstrating too much pride in his Austrian homeland, but that did not explain why his wife had been detained. Then, in early April, the Cincinnati City Council had passed an ordinance changing the names of fourteen streets whose names had Germanic origins.

"This will be as annoying to get used to as it is difficult to stomach," her mother wrote. "Berlin Street will become Woodrow Street in honor of the American president. Bremen Street will become Republic, and Frankfort Avenue will become Connecticut Avenue. Schumann Street will henceforth be called Beredith Place; who this Mr. Beredith is and why he deserves to be honored more than the great composer, I cannot say." It remained to be seen, Marie's mother added, whether the Over-the-Rhine neighborhood would be permitted to retain that fond moniker much longer. As for why these changes had been implemented, Marie's mother quoted the explanation one councilman had given to the *Cincinnati Enquirer*: "American victories are not won by armies alone, but by armies backed up by a national spirit," a Mr. Murdock had declared. "We councilmen can do our bit by ridding Cincinnati of every reminder of German propaganda. We should have names on every street corner that are an inspiration to children and adults, and not names that indicate the Hun and his devilish actions and contrivances."

Marie would have felt thoroughly sickened had her mother not added that another councilman had dismissed the name changes as foolish, unhelpful, and a waste of time. If the United States had a falling-out with Ireland next week, or the Netherlands the week after that, would more street names be discarded? "The Germans of Cincinnati are patriotic," a Mr. Mullen had declared. "They have subscribed liberally to Liberty Loan programs, the Red Cross, and other war funds. Many of them are better Americans than those who were born in this country."

Marie sighed and returned the letter to the envelope, wondering how it had slipped past the censors. Perhaps she should warn her mother to be more circumspect or risk being labeled a German sympathizer. After all, the French had made similar changes to the streets of Paris; Avenue de l'Allemagne had been renamed Avenue Jean-Jaurès, and the Rue de Berlin had become the Rue de Liège. But no sooner had the thought come to her than Marie banished it. Changing street names was one thing; persecuting immigrants of German descent was quite another. She would never ask her mother to remain silent if she witnessed injustice, nor would she ever ignore injustice herself.

The next letter cheered her up immensely. It was a lighthearted note from her friend Ethel, full of gossipy anecdotes about their coworkers at the Valley Exchange in Hartwell, including a comic narration of how one new girl was fired on her first day after sneaking a cup of coffee into the telephone room and accidentally spilling it all over the switchboard. "We're lucky she didn't electrocute us all," Ethel remarked, which Marie hoped was an exaggeration.

She was still smiling as she returned Ethel's letter to its envelope and picked up the fifth and last, pausing for a moment to ponder the unfamiliar handwriting. The postmark said New York, New York; perhaps one of her instructors at AT&T headquarters had written to check in. Curious, she carefully tore open the envelope, removed a single sheet of white paper, smoothed the creases, glanced at the first line, and gasped aloud.

"*Bonjour*, Cherubino!" the author greeted her.

Her gaze immediately darted to the closing, but the signature only confirmed what she already knew. After weeks of silence, Giovanni had written to her.

It was a brief letter, warm and funny, but apologetic too. He had enjoyed meeting her on the train, he wrote. Her beautiful voice and interesting conversation had made the miles pass swiftly. "I regret that I did not see you again, so I could say a proper goodbye and ask permission to write to you," he said. "You may remember my buddy Charles, the redhead who spied on your concert through the lounge car window with me. I'm sorry to say he came down with appendicitis later that night—he's fine now, never fear—but I couldn't leave him, and as soon as the train halted, we had to rush him off ahead of the crowd and put him in a taxi to the hospital. Another buddy rode along with him so I could run back to the platform, but I was too late. You were nowhere to be seen."

Marie pressed a hand to her lips, heart pounding. This was the logical explanation she had hoped for. Giovanni had not vanished into thin air after all, nor had he forgotten her, and he was almost certainly not a German spy.

He was too discreet to mention the kiss, and she was grateful for that. It was not a moment she wanted to share with the censors.

"It's not likely that I can get leave again so soon after going to Chicago," he continued, "but if we have any time in the city before we ship out, I would like to see you again, if you're willing, and if they let you. I tried to reach you by phone at AT&T headquarters, but the girl who picked up said that she wasn't allowed to tell me that you weren't on duty at the moment. She sounded like she might have said more, but another girl suddenly came on the line and primly told me that under no circumstances was a telephone operator allowed to accept personal calls while on duty, and if I made a second attempt, she would report me to my superiors. She pulled the plug before I could apologize. My only saving grace was that I never had the chance to give either of them my name, only yours. I hope I didn't get you into trouble."

Marie inhaled sharply, pressing her lips together, indignation smoldering. Secrecy was the official policy; the operator who had first taken the call had bent the rules to tell Giovanni the little she had revealed. One of the chief operators must have overheard her, and had taken over the call. But who? Grace Banker was dutiful and responsible, but also reasonable and kind, and no one would ever describe her as prim. It must have been Inez Crittenden who had hung up on Giovanni and never told Marie about the call. Marie would have known who the unnamed man was, and her worries could have been put to rest if only Mrs. Crittenden had seen fit to—

She shook her head to dispel her outrage, resigned. What was done was done. Of course Mrs. Crittenden had refused to answer Giovanni's query; it would never occur to her to make an exception to any rule. If Mrs. Crittenden's reaction to the Hoboken Incident was any indication, she probably thought she was protecting Marie from unwanted male attention. In hindsight, it probably would have been impossible for Marie and Giovanni to meet in the city before the First Group departed for France, so she could not condemn the chief operator for denying her that chance. At least now Marie knew that Giovanni had tried to reach her, and that he wanted to see her again.

She could write to him, now that she knew he would welcome her letters. She was strictly forbidden to tell anyone where she was posted, but if she mentioned that her mother would be pleased if she knew how far away from the front she was, Giovanni could easily narrow down the options. And if she dared mention that she was Operator Four, and if he could somehow gain access to his unit's phone, he might call her—but she shouldn't hope for him to do anything that might get him in trouble. Letters that could pass the censor's scrutiny would have to suffice, for now. Perhaps they would have another opportunity to reunite, although at the moment she could not imagine how or where or when.

Marie sat lost in thought, the letter clasped to her heart, when suddenly something small and quick darted past below the alcove, a patter of feet on stone, a rustle of muslin, a soft gasp as someone spotted her and darted off before being seen in turn. Quickly gathering up her letters, Marie slipped down from the alcove and glanced up and down the corridor. She glimpsed what seemed to be the hem of a skirt seconds before it disappeared around the corridor.

Curious, Marie hurried in pursuit, following the sounds of light footsteps, turning the corner in time to spy a small figure darting through an arched doorway. Following, she found herself in a small chapel, where sunlight streamed through a pair of stained glass windows depicting Saint Ursula and her companions. Tapestries adorned the walls, and as Marie quietly moved into the center of the room and slowly turned in place, she noticed two small shoes and two white stockings peeping out from beneath one of the woven artworks, which bulged suspiciously.

Marie drew closer, suppressing a laugh when the tapestry trembled. Tucking her skirt beneath her, she sat on the cold, smooth stone floor. "*Bonjour, ma petite*," she said gently.

The tapestry held perfectly still.

"*Je m'appelle Marie. Comment t'appelles-tu?*"

There was no reply, although one of the feet shifted.

Marie tried again. "*Au clair de la lune*," she sang softly, "*mon ami Pierrot, prête moi ta plume pour écrire—*" She paused. "*Prête moi ta plume pour écrire . . . pour écrire . . .*"

"*Prête moi ta plume pour écrire un mot*," a sweet treble voice sang, muffled by the tapestry.

Slowly, carefully, Marie lifted the edge of the tapestry aside. There stood a girl of perhaps four years old, her back pressed against the wall, her large, dark brown eyes gazing solemnly into Marie's. She wore a gray pinafore over a white blouse, and her light brown hair had been done up in two braids, one of which was tied with a slender white ribbon. The other had no fastener and was coming undone.

"Oh, what do we have here?" Marie exclaimed softly in French, indicating the unruly braid. The child glanced down at the loose strands of hair spilling over her shoulder, then back up at Marie, her lower lip quivering. "Shall I tend to that for you?" When the child nodded, Marie checked her pockets, remembering a scrap of fine yarn she had saved after darning a stocking that morning. Holding it up between her thumb and forefinger, she held out her other hand to the girl, beckoning. "Would you come closer, please? I can't reach from here."

The girl hesitated for a moment, then took Marie's hand and let her draw her out from behind the tapestry. "This will take only a moment," said Marie, finger-combing the ends of the braid, neatly plaiting it again, and tying the yarn in a bow around the end to secure it. "There. All finished. How pretty you are!"

The little girl smiled shyly but said nothing.

Marie took both of the girl's hands in hers. "I'm sure there's someone missing you and wondering where you are," she said. "We should tell them you're safe so they won't worry. Could you lead the way?"

The little girl mulled that over, then nodded.

"Good," said Marie. "One more thing: Could you help me up?"

Smiling, the girl planted her feet and pulled. Marie groaned through clenched teeth as she slowly rose, staggering a bit as she found her feet. "You're very strong," she declared. "Thank goodness you were here! Without your help, I might have been stuck sitting on that floor forever."

The girl giggled and shook her head.

Marie released one of her hands and squeezed the other playfully. "Shall we?"

The girl nodded and led her off, down one hallway and then another, into a part of the convent Marie had not seen before. From a distance she heard children laughing and chattering. The happy sound grew louder until they came to a spacious rectangular room with a high ceiling, where sunlight streamed through tall windows upon several long tables with benches arrayed before them. Here and there, several nuns watched over at least two dozen children at play, some skipping rope, others leafing through books, some bouncing a ball back and forth, a few cuddling dolls or pushing wooden trucks across the stone floor.

One of the nuns, Sister Agnès, glanced their way, gave a start, and hurried to meet them. "You brought our Gisèle back to us," she exclaimed. "Two of our sisters are still searching."

"She brought me," said Marie, smiling down upon the young girl. "So your name is Gisèle. Such a lovely name for a girl with a lovely voice."

The nun regarded Marie briefly, bemused, but she quickly turned her attention to Gisèle. "Run along and play with your friends, child," she said kindly. "As I said before, we will go outside to play tomorrow, after the rain has passed."

The little girl pouted for a moment, but then she waved shyly to Marie and darted off.

"I didn't realize children were staying at the convent," said Marie as she and the nun watched Gisèle join the girls skipping rope. "I'm surprised I haven't heard them."

"They arrived only a few hours ago, and they took their supper here," Sister Agnès replied, indicating the long dining tables. "These children are orphans and refugees who had found sanctuary in a convent in Château-Thierry. After the *Kaiserschlacht* began, it was far too dangerous for them to remain, so the sisters asked us to take them in."

"The poor dears," Marie murmured, her gaze traveling around the room. They were all so young. Most of them probably did not remember a time when France was not at war. "Where are their parents—of those who have not been orphaned, I mean?"

"We have names, and some addresses, but with few exceptions, we don't know. We simply trust that the Lord will guide them back to their children after the war." Sister Agnès sighed, then fixed an appraising look on Marie. "I don't understand why you said that Gisèle has a lovely voice. You must have realized that she doesn't speak."

"She may not speak, but she does sing," said Marie, surprised. "I assumed she was shy around strangers."

The nun shook her head. "She hasn't said a word since she arrived, at least not when I or my sisters could overhear." Brow furrowing, she studied Gisèle for a long moment before turning back to Marie. "Would you indulge me? Could you encourage her to sing again?"

"Of course."

They made their way across the room and watched the girls jump rope for a while. When they paused to switch places, Marie said, "Gisèle, I've forgotten the words to our song again. Could you please help me?" She frowned as if struggling to remember. "*Au clair de la lune, mon ami Pierrot*—"

Gisèle joined in, and together they sang, "*Prête moi ta plume pour écrire un mot.*"

"Well done," Marie praised, smiling.

"You remembered all by yourself," said Gisèle. "You're a good singer."

"Thank you, Gisèle. You are too."

Sister Agnès clasped her hands in prayer, her lips moving silently.

"But that's so easy," declared a girl holding one end of the jump rope, shaking her bobbed blonde curls. "Everyone knows that song."

She began to sing, her voice a pretty alto. Gisèle promptly joined in, and soon, one by one, most of the other children had too. They apparently knew all the verses, and to Marie's amusement, they sang them all, abandoning their toys and games, drawing closer until they had formed a lopsided semicircle around Marie and Sister Agnès.

If they were standing on risers, Marie thought, one might mistake them for a choir—a very young and untrained choir, but even so.

"Let's do another," a little boy cried out when they had finished. "*J'ai vu le loup!*"

"An excellent choice," said Marie, and after humming the first note, she led them in the song. Nearly all the children knew the melody, and those who were too young to sing more than a few repeated phrases clapped their hands or bounced up and down in time with the music. They reminded Marie of her sisters—when they were much younger, of course—which both charmed her and made the pain of their absence all the more acute.

One song led to another, until Sister Agnès clapped her hands for attention and told the children that it was time for prayers and bed. Crestfallen, the children mumbled assent.

"Let us thank Mademoiselle Marie for singing with us this evening," said Sister Agnès, turning from the children to Marie, smiling hopefully. "Perhaps she will join us again?"

All the children chimed in, begging her to come back. A few of the girls even darted forward to take her hands, as if they would hold her there, and the one with the bobbed blonde curls flung her arms around her waist. Gisèle hung back, too shy to push her way to the front of the crowd, but she peered up at Marie hopefully, her eyes shining.

"Of course I'll come back," said Marie, and laughed aloud in sheer surprise when the children cheered. A bit overwhelmed, she looked over their heads to Sister Agnès and the other nuns, who smiled and nodded in approval.

Apparently she had come to France to become a children's choirmistress. Well, why not? They were all living beneath the same roof, so it was hardly an inconvenience, and it would be a small repayment to the sisters for their generous hospitality. Her mother would be delighted to hear that she would be singing regularly, even if it was not her usual repertoire.

Marie only hoped that through music, she could help the children find consolation—and if she dared hope for so much, even joy—amid the wretchedness of war.

13

APRIL–MAY 1918

Chaumont

GRACE

By the time a cohort of operators from the Second Group arrived in Chaumont, Grace had become accustomed to the routine of General Pershing's First Army Headquarters. The sight of trenches and air raid shelters no longer immediately evoked trepidation and grim thoughts of the dangers that made the installations necessary. On the three-mile trek down the muddy road from her quarters to the telephone office in the caserne, she no longer did a double take if she passed columns of German prisoners of war, disconsolate or defiant, marching to work— digging ditches, clearing debris, shoveling coal—grueling, essential labor that was not unduly dangerous and would not give the prisoners an opportunity to jeopardize the war effort. The sight of troop trains packed with Allied infantry chugging past Chaumont en route to the front still made her pause and reflect, but she had resigned herself to the grim truth that some of them would return gravely wounded, and far too many would not return at all. She still flinched if an errant German shell exploded unexpectedly close, or woke, heart pounding and breathless, when the air raid siren shrieked in the middle of the night, but that was only because of the sudden jolt to her senses. She would be a fool to lose her respect for German artillery no matter how familiar she became with the devastation an attack could inflict.

Most of the time, she was much too busy to brood over potential dangers to her own safety, or even to her life. From the time her shift began in the morning until she was relieved in the late afternoon, she and her fellow operators worked tirelessly connecting calls, constructing long-distance relays, instantaneously translating from English to French and back again for callers who could not comprehend each other, and the myriad other tasks required of them. Every command to attack or withdraw, every order to shift troops from this flank to that line, every report from the front, every urgent message communicating vital intelligence to commanders in the field—every call was routed through the switchboard in the old stone barracks. At the end of her shift, Grace invariably felt both exhausted and exhilarated, knowing that with every call she connected, she was striking a blow for the Allies, bringing them one day closer to victory.

Yet while Grace firmly believed that the Allies would ultimately triumph, the classified reports she overheard on the lines revealed unexpected discord between the Allied countries' commanding generals, disagreements they were careful to conceal from the public and the troops. Only days before Grace's cohort arrived in Chaumont, French marshal Ferdinand Foch had been appointed Supreme Allied Commander, and a few weeks later, he had been named Commander in Chief of the Allied Armies. The French had long considered the inexperienced U.S. Army to be a "weak asset," and General Foch believed that AEF troops should be dispersed among the French and British armies, reinforcing seasoned divisions whose numbers had been depleted due to heavy casualties. While General Pershing allowed certain American units to rotate through the French and British forces to give them experience, he adamantly resisted proposals to use his troops only to fill gaps in his allies' regiments. For the most part, the U.S. Army continued to assemble and train in Lorraine, about 370 kilometers east of Paris near the German border. From what Grace could discern, General Pershing's intention seemed to be to prepare his soldiers until they numbered one million strong and could take to the battlefield as a unified, independent American army capable of launching a crushing offensive that would destroy the German defenses.

That was not to say that American doughboys were not yet serving on the front lines. Troops attached to Allied divisions were fighting and dying in the trenches alongside French and British soldiers. U.S. Signal Corps units had been working at the front for nearly a year, taking heavy fire while laying telephone lines, swiftly and steadily building a communications network from Le Havre to Marseille and from the front to Bordeaux. Grace was still haunted by the call she had connected from a sergeant reporting to AEF headquarters that his Signal Corps unit had been attacked by German chemical troops while repairing broken telephone wires along the edge of no-man's-land. For sixteen hours the soldiers had labored with their gas masks on, repairing one line and moving on to the next, as one man after another collapsed to the muddy ground, skin covered in blisters from mustard gas.

The *Kaiserschlacht*—the Germans' fierce Spring Offensive, whose launch had coincided with the First Group's arrival in Le Havre—marked a significant change in strategy from the trench warfare of the previous four years. German heavy artillery and aerial units fiercely bombarded the British lines, creating gaps through which the kaiser's *Sturmtruppen* assault units swiftly advanced, wielding mortars, lightweight machine guns, grenades, and flamethrowers to capture positions behind Allied lines, with the aim of severing the British forces from the French. The German army sometimes advanced so quickly that they outran their supply lines and had to fall back to more defensible positions. Thousands of troops on both sides were being killed or wounded every day. Desperate civilians were fleeing for the relative safety of the west, while the citizens of Paris, weary from enduring relentless bombardment from the Big Berthas and the Paris Gun, prepared for invasion.

For months Grace and her operators had trained to work in such conditions, but now that she was in the thick of it, she couldn't say whether any lecture or lesson could have fully prepared them. What she did know was that her girls did everything asked of them and then some, performing beyond the Signal Corps's most optimistic expectations. Lieutenant Riser had needed only a week to warm up to them, as Captain Mack had predicted he eventually would, and since then he had become one of their most loyal admirers and staunchest advocates. "I was angry when I was first informed that I would be commanding a lot of female operators," he confided one day as he, Suzanne, and Grace walked to lunch at the mess hall, "but you ladies have completely converted me."

Grace and Suzanne exchanged a look, hid their smiles, and thanked him. They had both noticed his change of heart; he had never tried to hide his irritable scowls or soften his sardonic remarks, and their gradual easing had made the women's workplace much more pleasant. Only the previous afternoon, he had fairly burst with pride when a colonel touring the caserne had strolled the aisles of the telephone room, observed the women at work, and remarked to the lieutenant, "Your operators have lots of pep. They're regular soldiers."

"We're simply doing our jobs, Lieutenant," said Grace, "like every other soldier here."

He snorted and gave her a sidelong look. "We both know there's nothing simple about it, especially when you run into grumpy intransigents like me."

Grace had to laugh. Fortunately, they rarely had to contend with skeptics and detractors anymore, since they had proven themselves to be diligent, capable, and levelheaded in a crisis. Their performance spoke for itself, through the steadily increasing volume of calls connected each day and their significantly improved accuracy compared to their male counterparts. Even the men they had replaced were more relieved than insulted. In fact, and quite unexpectedly, Grace and her operators encountered less interference from chauvinist critics than from excessively enthusiastic soldiers. A caller astonished to hear a woman's voice on the line might try to prolong the conversation, asking for her name and where she was posted, details she was absolutely forbidden to divulge for security reasons. Once, Grace had to take over a call when she overheard one of her girls contending with a soldier who was so delighted to hear a female voice in a familiar accent that he had apparently forgotten whatever urgent matter had prompted him to pick up the phone.

"He asked if I was American, I told him I was, and I repeated, 'Number, please,'" Esther told Grace afterward, exasperated. "Next thing I know, he's shouting to someone nearby, 'Come here, Jim, I'm talking to a real live American female woman!' They both insisted that I say, 'I am a sure-to-goodness American,' and then some other fellows crowded near the phone and I had to repeat it for them. Next the whole gang threw questions at me all at once—my name, where I'm posted, if I would introduce them to my friends. That's when you stepped in, and you know the rest." Esther lifted her hands and let them fall to her lap, frustrated. "The caller simply could not move along and tell me what party he was trying to reach. What should I have done, pulled the plug?"

"Tempting, but no. That's against protocol." All acceptable verbal responses and procedures for every scenario were clearly established in the handbook *Military Telephone Regulations*, which each recruit had received when she reported for advanced training. Signal Corps procedures closely followed those used by domestic telephone companies, which made them quick and easy for the experienced operators to learn, even where certain crucial adaptations had been made for military purposes. As always, operators were instructed to "cultivate a distinct, clear, and cheerful tone of voice," and use only the specific phrases stipulated for a particular request, such as beginning every call with "Number, please," or "*J'écoute*" if the French was needed. The timing and number of rings was strictly regulated as well; when an operator attempted to reach a party, rings were to last two seconds, and if no one answered, she was to continue to ring every ten seconds for a period of ninety seconds. Operators were required to be concise when they spoke to callers, even if the callers themselves were not. And unlike their French counterparts, American operators were forbidden to disconnect any call before the parties stopped talking—unless General Pershing himself wanted to place a call and all the jacks and cables were in use. Only then could an operator take a deep breath and disconnect another call in progress, fervently hoping that by a stroke of good luck, she had chosen the least important conversation on the switchboard.

Grace had learned all too well that French operators did not concern themselves with such scruples. If they or one of their friends required an open line, they would simply yank out a plug without a second thought. Their response was the same whenever they felt that American operators were needlessly tying up their circuits. "Mademoiselle," as the American girls referred to their counterparts at French Central, even those who were quite elderly, were generally understood to be impatient, temperamental, and exasperating. Although Grace tried very hard to admire their easy nonchalance, when urgent calls absolutely had to be put through without delay, their cool insouciance was mystifying.

Yet not all French operators approached the job with such indifference. French officers working the relays near the front always put the American girls' calls through swiftly, perhaps because they understood all too well what a difference a few minutes could make.

Grace reassured Esther that she had handled the situation exactly as she should have, not only by resisting the urge to disconnect the call out of pique, but also by refusing to divulge her name or location or whether she had any friends anywhere in France. Even if a superior officer on the line demanded an operator's name, she was permitted to identify herself by her operator number alone. The absolute importance of confidentiality had been drilled into them from the first day of training. Any detail, however ostensibly trivial, could be exploited by the enemy, from a description of the weather outside their window to an offhand remark about the unusual number of calls made to a particular city on a given day.

Nor was the danger of a security breach limited to callers they knew were on the line. If advancing Germans chanced upon a Signal Corps ground line, they could tap into the wire, eavesdrop, and gather crucial intelligence, with disastrous consequences for the Allies. The operators had been warned to listen for a peculiar dull quality on the lines, which could indicate that they had been tapped. To further thwart spies and to help disguise troop movements, locations were identified by code names, which were changed frequently. A town might be known as "Po-dunk" one day and "Wabash" the next; one division could be "Nemo," and another "Waterfall." All communications were to be handled with utmost secrecy, for thousands of soldiers' lives and the outcome of the war could depend upon the operators' discretion. "We must keep our mouths shut, ask no questions, and never discuss anything," Grace occasionally reminded the girls under her command, breaking down that particular section of *Military Telephone Regulations* into its simplest, most essential truths. Any one of them, including Grace herself, could face a court-martial if they divulged any information about communications to anyone except for the proper authorities through designated military channels. Grace was absolutely certain that none of her girls would violate that rule intentionally. It was up to her to train and supervise them properly so they would never do so unwittingly either.

As the weeks passed, Grace observed her girls adapting well to life at Chaumont, settling into a routine and gaining confidence as their accomplishments earned them respect. Even so, many of the girls struggled with homesickness, or with constant fatigue due to their long, arduous workdays, or with stress brought on by their daunting responsibilities. Some especially tenderhearted girls contended with all three. Without drawing attention to any individual girl's troubles, Grace was always there to offer a shoulder to cry on or a listening ear. She was pleased to see how the girls looked out for one another, boosting their buddies' spirits, keeping morale high. As for herself, exhaustion was her greatest nemesis. Most days she felt as if she worked and worked, and managed and managed, collapsing into bed at night thoroughly spent.

And yet she wouldn't be completely honest if she didn't admit that she too felt an occasional pang of homesickness, especially on Sunday afternoons, when she might have been at home with her family enjoying their traditional Sunday dinner, perhaps her mother's scrumptious roast chicken with all the trimmings. Letters from her parents and sisters comforted her, transporting her home in spirit across the miles, drawing her closer to loved ones and friends and her most favorite places. She wished she heard from her brother more often, but she supposed

Eugene's schedule was as relentless as her own, leaving him little spare time for writing letters. The last she had heard, he was still training at Camp Green in North Carolina, and he still didn't know when his division might ship out. But that news was weeks old; he might be crossing the ocean at that very moment, or he might have already joined Grace in France. Eventually, she trusted, her letters would find him.

While the arrival of reinforcements from the Second Group could not ease Grace's longing for home and family, it certainly lightened her other burdens. The girls from the First Group enjoyed a happy reunion with the friends they had made in New York, and they all cheered when Lieutenant Riser announced that, thanks to their increased numbers, their shifts would be shortened and they would be permitted occasional days off. Equally welcome was the news that a fully trained Third Group had already departed New York and was expected to reach Liverpool in the first week of May.

Grace resolved to make the most of her days off, which back home she would have accepted as her rightful due, but which in Chaumont, where the work of war never ceased, felt like an indulgence. First she caught up on her sleep, and then she became better acquainted with Chaumont. With Suzanne and Esther, she explored the town's museums, shops, and cafés, where they fell in love with a local delicacy, *idéal chaumontais*, a meringue cake with almonds and praline cream. They toured the Basilique Saint-Jean-Baptiste, a magnificent thirteenth-century Gothic church in the oldest part of the city, and admired the views of the Suize river valley from the pedestrian path of the Viaduc de Chaumont, a nineteenth-century railroad bridge composed of three rows of stacked masonry arches towering fifty-two meters above the countryside. They visited the Keep, all that remained of the medieval castle of the Counts of Champagne, and spent many pleasant hours enjoying the charms of the Place de la Concorde. For safety in numbers as well as companionship, they invited more friends to join them on hikes along the Marne and along the trails that wound through the surrounding forests. When the weather was especially fine and the German guns were quiet, if they had an entire day to themselves, Grace and her friends would rent or borrow bicycles and ride out into the beautiful French countryside, delighting in the valleys full of spring wildflowers and the quaint stone farm cottages amid newly sown fields.

In addition to outings with her girlfriends, Grace also spent time with Captain Mack, who sought her out whenever he returned from the front. He disclosed almost nothing about the missions that often called him away for weeks at a time, and she knew better than to pry. Although when they first met he had told her he was a special liaison officer to the AEF, even after they had become better acquainted, he had not explained what his duties actually were, and she had begun to suspect that he worked in military intelligence. Although she would not admit it aloud—not even to Suzanne, whose knowing gaze missed nothing—Grace had become quite fond of him. He was awfully good-looking, with his thick, dark brown hair, broad shoulders, and smiling blue eyes. His easy, friendly manners charmed her, and his heroic war record spoke of his courage and strength of character.

With Suzanne or Esther along as chaperone, Captain Mack invited Grace on excursions unique to a war zone, showing her around experimental gas fields, or touring an airfield to observe new aircraft taking flight. She felt a quickening thrill whenever he took her hand to help her over obstacles in their path, a sensation that intensified dizzyingly whenever he partnered her at YMCA dances. On one especially enjoyable afternoon, they had gone horseback riding along a safe region of the Marne, where she had delighted in their swift horses' powerful grace, the wind in her hair, the lovely scenery, all sun-bathed rolling green hills and verdant forests, and of course, the captain's company. Sometimes he took her out to dinner at the Hôtel de France or the officers' club, where he entertained her with stories of his childhood in Melbourne, when a perfect summer day meant exploring the Yarra Ranges or sailing in the Bass Strait.

Once, as they were strolling alone through the outskirts of Chaumont, a trench mortar suddenly exploded nearby, and as the shrapnel and debris fell all around them, he instinctively pulled her close against his chest beneath the shelter of his arm, knocking off her hat, and held her there even after the danger had passed. A warm, sparking current flowed through her as she felt his chest rise and fall against her cheek and the palm of her hand, as she breathed in his scent of leather and wool and shaving soap. She could not bear to move and break the spell and remind him that they ought not to stand there practically embracing where any passerby might see them, but eventually she could not resist turning her face up to his to read his expression. He was gazing at her with an intensity and warmth she had never glimpsed in a man's eyes before, but as she watched him, heart thudding, trying to think of something clever and charming to say, he suddenly kissed her. For the barest of moments she stiffened, but then she melted into him, closing her eyes, pressing her lips to his, reaching up to entwine her arms around his neck—until, with a sudden gasp as if she had plunged into cold water, she pulled away, instinctively raising the back of her fingers to her lips.

"Sorry," he said huskily, brow furrowing in concern. "I thought you wanted—"

"I did." Quickly she let her hand fall to her side. "I did. But—not here." Where, then? She fervently hoped he would not ask, for she had no idea. She couldn't allow herself to be seen kissing him, or anyone, or doing anything that might suggest she allowed him to kiss her when no one was watching—

She took a deep, steadying breath, and when she realized he was studying her, curious, a small, puzzled smile playing in the corners of his mouth, she managed a smile and suggested they continue their walk. He agreed, and as they proceeded along, she noticed that he kept a respectful amount of space between them. She almost wished he wouldn't, but as they chatted and exchanged occasional glances and his eyes seemed to invite her to draw closer, she dared not close the distance.

None of the young men back home in New Jersey had ever courted her in such unusual fashion—if Captain Mack was courting her. She wasn't quite sure, and she was uncomfortably uncertain how she should respond if he made his intentions to court her clear. Back in New York, Captain Wessen and Mr. Estabrook had made it very clear that chief operators must set an example of utmost discretion and restraint as far as fraternization was concerned. At the time, Grace had agreed with them, and with Inez Crittenden, that it would be best to avoid any romantic entanglements. Now she wasn't so sure. Had she already become entangled? She wasn't sure about that either.

She decided it would be silly to avoid Captain Mack while she sorted out her feelings, so she continued to accept his invitations to dinner and on excursions into the countryside. She also saw him at parties arranged by the YWCA at the women's residences, or by individual army units and other organizations. They were each other's favorite partner at dances the YMCA hosted most weekends for the officers, telephone operators, and nurses stationed in Chaumont. The dances were scrupulously chaperoned and very well attended, and they were so much fun that Grace went with her girlfriends even when she knew Captain Mack wouldn't be there. The men outnumbered the women several times over, so the women were asked to halve, and sometimes even quarter their dances so that each man would eventually get a dance, if not for the duration of an entire song.

It was at one of these dances where Grace first heard the rumor that the army nurses fervently disliked the telephone girls.

"Did we offend them somehow?" Grace asked the operator who had first mentioned it. Grace had advertently prompted Esther's remark when, thinking aloud, she had observed that the nurses tended to stake out their territory along one side of the room, mingling freely and cheerfully with the officers on the dance floor and near the refreshment table, but staying well clear of the places where the operators gathered.

"Did we offend them?" echoed Esther dryly, folding her arms. "Only by coming to France."

"Surely that can't be so," said Grace, but even as she spoke, memories arose of several peculiar encounters she'd had with nurses during her time in Chaumont. A few days after her arrival, she had greeted a group of nurses when they passed on the street, but the nurses had not paused to introduce themselves, which was a bit unfriendly considering how few American women there were in the town. She had not taken offense, but rather assumed that she had interrupted them on urgent medical business, and she had thought nothing more of it.

The following week, Grace and her YWCA hostess had called on the nurses at their YWCA residence, which the operators passed every day on their way to and from work. Mrs. Ivey had suggested that the operators invite the nurses to tea so they could get to know one another, in hopes that the nurses, who had been in Chaumont longer, would share what they had learned about life at First Army Headquarters with the newcomers. The nurses' YWCA hostess had been delighted to welcome them into their parlor, but only three nurses of the dozens residing there had joined them. Despite Grace's best attempts to be friendly, the conversation was stilted and the nurses had given only a noncommittal reply to her invitation to tea. "The best way to learn a new city is to explore it on your own," the senior nurse had remarked, and her companions had nodded.

"I don't think that was an outright refusal," Mrs. Ivey had said hesitantly as she and Grace walked back to the house on Rue Brûle. "Perhaps they didn't know who would be on duty that day and who would be free to attend, and they plan to send a note later to RSVP."

"That's possible," Grace agreed, but when a week passed with no word from the nurses, she concluded that they were too busy to attend and had forgotten to formally decline the invitation. She was disappointed, but once more, she hadn't taken offense. She was never one to hold a grudge, and it was hard to imagine anyone who deserved to have an inadvertent social blunder forgiven and forgotten more than army nurses in wartime did.

The two YWCA hostesses must have conferred privately, for although plans for a tea had been abandoned, a few weeks later, several nurses called at the operators' residence, a perfunctory courtesy to reciprocate Grace's visit. Even then Grace was baffled by the strangely cold and formal spirit of their visit, and she was astonished when, exactly four and a half minutes after they arrived, the nurses departed.

Perhaps Grace had ignored the signs that had been right in front of her all along, but Esther's dry remark was the first specific report she had heard of any hard feelings between the operators and the nurses. "I don't understand," she said. "Why would they dislike us? We haven't done anything to them that I'm aware of, and we're here to serve our country, the same as they are."

Raymonde sighed and planted a hand on her hip. "It must be because we're younger and prettier," she said, nodding for emphasis as she studied the nurses from a safe distance.

"That can't be it," said Winifred, the eldest of the operators, who Grace had once feared would be inflexible and resistant to authority due to her advanced age. How ludicrous such worries seemed now.

"They think they're better than we are," Esther said. "They're all educated ladies who have taken up nursing out of noblesse oblige, and we're just humble working girls."

Some of the girls nodded, frowning, but Grace would have none of it. "Many of us are college girls too, just as I'm sure many of them first became nurses to earn a living, before the war."

"It's not our imagination," another girl chimed in. "I've heard it straight from some of the wounded soldiers who have come into town after they've been discharged from the hospital. 'Gee, how those nurses do hate you,' one of them said. Those were his exact words."

Several other girls nodded.

"Maybe that's how it all started," Suzanne said. "One of the soldiers made an offhand remark, trying to be funny or clever, and our girls took offense. The next time a group of operators crossed paths with a group of nurses, our girls gave them the cold shoulder, and the nurses decided we were rude and not worth befriending."

It was as plausible an explanation as any, but Grace knew it would be impossible to trace the rivalry back to its roots and pull it up. The best she could do now would be to prune it back. "Let's give the nurses the benefit of the doubt," she said, her voice conveying that it was an order. "Every day they witness horrors we hardly dare to imagine. Who could blame them if they envy us our relatively easy lives?"

"And our youth and beauty," Raymonde chimed in.

"Let's take the high road," said Grace, directing her remark to Raymonde, but speaking to all of them. "If the nurses snub us or scowl at us, we'll repay them with kind words and friendly smiles. We may win them over yet."

Most of the girls looked dubious, but they all agreed to try.

Grace hoped it would make a difference. There was too much at stake for any of them—American telephone operators, French operators, nurses—to waste time indulging in petty rivalries. They were all Allied women working on behalf of the same righteous cause, and they ought to rally around their common goals and shared values. Grace saw no other way that they could win the war if not together.

14

MAY 1918

Paris

VALERIE

The operators working the switchboards at the Élysées Palace Hotel were delighted when a cohort from Group Three reported for duty in mid-May. With more operators, they could increase their volume of calls even as they lightened each girl's workload. That would have been enough to satisfy Valerie, but soon thereafter she learned that more telephone operators meant an additional supervisor was required, and Inez Crittenden had recommended her for the job.

"Me?" Valerie asked as the chief operator presented her with a laurel wreath patch to add to the insignia on her left coat sleeve. "You want me to be a supervisor?"

"Why not?" Inez asked, smiling, a bit puzzled. "You've been doing the work—keeping everyone on task, solving problems, filling in wherever help is needed. You might as well have the title and the raise in salary too. You've also shown that you can take orders and lead by example. Aboard the *Carmania*, for example, when I instructed the group to wear masks, you put yours on and kept it on, without a single moan of complaint. I appreciated that, and I haven't forgotten."

"To be perfectly honest," said Valerie, "that wasn't obedience. That was pure self-interest. I didn't want to get sick and die."

"Be that as it may, you did it, you encouraged other girls to follow suit, and you surely saved lives." Inez studied her, bemused. "I'd like to reward you with a promotion, but only if you're willing."

"Far be it for me to talk you out of it," said Valerie, accepting the patch. She was grateful for the promotion and the raise, and she supposed she did tend to step up and take charge when it was necessary, but Inez's praise had caught her entirely off guard. Supervisor roles usually went to people like her sister, Hilde—responsible, serious, a bit strict—not fun-loving girls like herself. Maybe there were other acceptable ways to be a leader, Valerie mused, or perhaps she wasn't as frivolous as she used to be.

Their commanding officer preferred to mingle the different cohorts so that newcomers could learn the ropes alongside more experienced girls, and thus the ten girls placed under Valerie's command included three from Group One, three from Group Two, and four from Group Three. On their lunch break, Valerie invited her four novices to join her at Jambon et Deux Oeufs, a nearby café that had become a Signal Corps favorite, so she could get to know them. By the end of the meal, she was absolutely delighted that they had been assigned to Paris, and to her cohort in particular. They seemed smart, capable, brave, and proud to do their bit; two were American, one French Canadian, and one a native of France who had immigrated to the United States with her parents as a young child. They were full of questions about their new roles and workplace, and Valerie gave them candid answers. Yes, Paris was occasionally bombarded; no, she personally did not fear the city would be invaded. Yes, French telephone operators could be difficult to work with, but no, they were not as bad as the worst rumors about them claimed.

Over the next few days, as the early arrivals and the newcomers became better acquainted, the First and Second Group girls were surprised to learn that beginning with the Third Group, recruits were quartered in New York City throughout their training, and did not venture across the river to Hoboken until the day they boarded their ship.

"No more suffering in Hobo House with no heat, flimsy cots, and thirty girls sharing a single shower?" Millicent exclaimed, indignant. "You had it easy!"

When the newcomers looked chagrined, Valerie said, "We're happy for you, really. We're just a tiny bit jealous."

"Speak for yourself," said Drusilla, smiling. "I wouldn't have changed a thing. Roughing it together helped us build camaraderie and character."

The Third Group had certainly roughed it at sea. Although no one on board had come down with influenza, their ship, the *Baltic*, had been tormented by storms and rough seas throughout their voyage, and their convoy had been attacked as they approached the British Isles. Forced to alter course around the northern coast of Ireland to avoid a German submarine that had been stalking them, they had believed the danger was behind them when the convoy finally moved south between Ireland and Scotland surrounded by a protective escort of destroyers and torpedo boats. One fateful day, most of the girls were resting in their cabins after lunch when suddenly the *Baltic* shook from a massive blow. Hurrying out onto the deck, the operators arrived in time to witness British destroyers firing on a periscope protruding from the waves. Suddenly an explosion off the bow sent an enormous spray of water over the women's heads, soaking their shoulders and faces. Black water roiled to the surface, a geyser of oil and air bubbles, a sure sign that a destroyer's depth charge had struck something only a few hundred yards away—a U-boat, probably, though no debris surfaced to confirm it.

"It's a relief to be safe on land at last," one of the new girls said with a shudder, wrapping her arms around herself as if she felt a chill. Valerie, Millicent, and Drusilla exchanged wary looks. The German bombardment of Paris had relented in recent days, but no one expected the respite to last forever. Valerie knew it was her responsibility to make sure the newcomers knew what to do when the onslaught resumed, as it surely would.

Nor was that dreaded day far off, Valerie suspected. Based upon the details she gleaned from the increasingly urgent calls flying between Paris and Chaumont, she was certain General Pershing intended to launch a major offensive with his Allied counterparts within a matter of days. This would be the U.S. Army's first significant battle of the war, and from what Valerie had been able to piece together, it seemed that they would take the field as a cohesive American force rather than being dispersed among the French and British units, just as General Pershing had wanted all along. She had no idea where Pershing's forces would engage the enemy or when, only that the objective was to halt the German advance upon Paris.

Valerie fended off an annoying sense of impending doom by diving headlong into her new responsibilities, and bringing the new girls up to speed comprised an important part of that. One minor obstacle, particularly for the girls who were not native French speakers, was the difference between how American and French callers recited four-digit phone numbers. If an American wanted to reach number 7534, they would pronounce each digit separately, as in "seven-five-three-four," but the French preferred to say "seven thousand, five hundred, and thirty-four." For most of the Signal Corps girls, the shift was simply a matter of remembering to follow the preferred format, but for the American-born girls who had learned French in school, precious seconds were lost as they composed the numbers in their heads before saying them aloud. The difference was so slight that no one except the operators themselves or an extremely impatient caller would notice a delay, but there were many impatient callers, and the girls, who prided themselves on flawless service, could not bear to disappoint anyone.

Valerie enjoyed more entertaining distractions when she was off duty. It was great fun to introduce the new girls to the operators' favorite cafés, parks, and historical landmarks, and to escort them to the dances, films, and performances the YMCA provided at their huts, as their offices were called, even when they were located in perfectly sturdy stone buildings.

Recreation and sightseeing helped relieve the stress of their demanding jobs, but sometimes such simple measures did not suffice. "You should try to find some lightheartedness and beauty in the world around you whenever you can," Valerie urged her girls whenever the grim reality of wartime threatened to overwhelm them. She knew that since every stroll from their quarters to their workplace and back plunged them into the sights and sounds of war—piles of rubble where charming shops and homes had once stood, desperate refugees lining up for food and clothing at a Red Cross tent, truckloads of wounded soldiers speeding past on their way to hospitals—melancholy and fear could consume them if they were not careful.

Too often, she struggled to follow her own advice. Sometimes when she went to a favorite café, instead of reveling in that time-honored tourist pastime of observing the Parisians who passed by her sidewalk table, she brooded over the boarded-up windows and the paltry menu, restricted by severe shortages of cream, butter, eggs, and sugar. While strolling with friends through a park, instead of being grateful for the benevolent sunshine, the soft breezes, the green grass, and the fragrant flowers, she saw only the bomb craters in the once verdant lawns and the gaps where magnificent chestnut trees had been cut down for firewood. Once, at a concert hosted by the YMCA, she looked around at the grinning, cheering doughboys fresh off the ships from America, stomping their feet and clapping in time to the music, and her heart sank with dismay. She knew what lay ahead of them better than they did, and those very soldiers who were reveling now could be killed by German artillery before the week was out, perhaps in the imminent battle she knew, but they did not, that General Pershing intended to launch within days.

But now Valerie had an even stronger impetus to keep her spirits up. She had become a supervisor, and the girls under her command would look to her to set the tone. If she was brave and optimistic, they would find it easier to be so too.

One Monday morning at the end of May, after a particularly lovely, quiet Sunday, Valerie woke at six o'clock and began preparing for her shift. A half hour later, clad in a freshly pressed uniform, she made the rounds of her floor, knocking on the doors of her most notorious sleepyheads to make sure they were out of bed.

She was just about to descend the stairs to breakfast when a thunderous explosion shook the building.

Gasping, she seized the railing to steady herself as sirens began to wail overhead and alarm bells rang on every floor. All along the corridor, doors flew open and people spilled out in various states of dress, faces pale, eyes wide with shock and fear. Valerie hurried back the way she had come, pounding on the doors. "Let's go!" she shouted, again and again, gesturing toward the stairwell as the girls sped swiftly past. "Air raid! Let's go!" When she was as sure as she could be that all the operators on her floor had evacuated, she descended the stairs after them.

The stairwell was packed with other fleeing guests, hurrying and stumbling downward, some carrying suitcases or blankets or small children. On the lower levels, guests clustered in small groups, their backs pressed against the wall, or they huddled in corners, shielding their heads with their arms. "Keep going," she shouted to her girls, even though she could not see too far ahead, hoping they could hear her over the sirens and the bells. Eventually they reached the ground floor and exited the building onto a sheltered courtyard called an *abri*. Many guests had congregated there and were milling about, eyes turned warily upward. Valerie spotted a few of her girls on the far side and went to join them, and as the minutes passed, more operators found their way to the group.

"This doesn't feel safe," said Drusilla, shaking her head. "This shelter could never withstand a direct hit. It could barely protect us from a thunderstorm."

Eyeing the thin metal ceiling, Valerie had to agree. "Let's try to reach the basement," she said. "Stick together."

They made their way back into the hotel and down a service corridor to another staircase, one not intended for guests. They descended to the cellar, which was filled with wine barrels, cobwebs, several Signal Corps girls including Inez Crittenden, and numerous uniformed staff, who looked more annoyed by the interruption of their work than frightened by the attack. The staff did not object when Valerie's group burst in, but nodded curtly and moved aside to make room for them.

Just then, another tremendous boom rattled the shelves. Several girls gasped and instinctively clutched the arm of the girl next to them as dust sifted down from the ceiling. A moment later, realizing they were unharmed, the jumpy girls laughed self-consciously and released their grip.

"That's not a Big Bertha," said Inez, head cocked to one side as she listened. "That's the Paris Gun."

Valerie wondered how she could tell the difference. The sirens and alarm bells were more difficult to discern from the cellar, but Valerie could still hear them, which told her the danger had not passed. Fifteen minutes later, another explosion boomed, but this time the girls barely jumped. The next time a distant boom rattled the shelves, Valerie checked her watch and confirmed her hunch. "They're firing every fifteen minutes," she said in French, not knowing whether the staff spoke English and not wanting to exclude them.

"The Germans hope to demoralize us," said Inez. "They're not trying to crush the city, only our spirits."

Valerie looked around for a seat, overturned a sturdy bushel basket, and settled down upon it gingerly until she was sure it would bear her weight. "Sounds like they're taking down a good part of the city nonetheless."

Another hour passed. Every fifteen minutes, the German gun hurled another shell.

"Mrs. Crittenden? Miss DeSmedt?" Martina ventured. "We're supposed to report for duty soon. What should we do?"

"We should go," said one of the new girls. "Who will connect the calls if we're not at the switchboard?"

As the girls murmured in worry, Valerie held up a hand for quiet. "The night shift operators will remain at their posts until we relieve them," she said. "It'll be fine."

"I'd rather be at my post than here," another girl declared, evoking a chorus of assent.

Valerie looked to Inez and raised her eyebrows in a question. Inez shrugged and tapped her wristwatch, a gesture Valerie interpreted to mean that they should wait and see. Another half hour passed, bringing one explosion every fifteen minutes. Eventually the sirens and alarm bells fell silent, yet another shell fell right on cue. On the other side of the cellar, a chef muttered to two younger men dressed in cook's attire; they nodded in reply, and all three men left, presumably to return to work. Without interrupting their hushed conversations, the operators watched them go. A few girls stole glances at Valerie and Inez, but although none asked if they could follow, Valerie knew they wanted to. *She* wanted to.

She rose, dusted off her skirt, and sat down beside Inez on a long wooden crate. "Headquarters is less than a mile away," she said quietly. "We could easily run that distance between the bombs."

Inez hesitated. "We'd be taking quite a risk."

"We're taking quite a risk simply being in France," Valerie pointed out, lowering her voice as the girls began to look on with interest. "We could get hit if we run. Or the next bomb could land right on top of this hotel. We are awfully close to the president's residence."

Inez paused, thinking. "We could ask for volunteers," she said, after another shell exploded, somewhat more distant than before. "Anyone who doesn't think she can make it, or who doesn't want to try, may stay behind."

When Valerie nodded agreement, Inez rose and explained the plan. She had barely finished speaking when every girl shot her hand in the air to volunteer.

They climbed the stairs to the first floor and gathered near the front entrance. "I'll take the lead," Valerie announced, as she and Inez had agreed. "Mrs. Crittenden will bring up the rear. Stay with the group, even if you have the speed of an Olympic sprinter."

"Not in these shoes," said Drusilla. A few nervous giggles arose.

"On my mark," Valerie said, glancing around at the group, then back to her watch. On the quarter hour, she held up a finger; a few seconds later, an explosion thundered, perhaps a mile to the east. "Now!"

She ran outside, bearing right down the sidewalk, turning right again at the end of the block. She heard footfalls behind her and hoped all the girls were keeping up, trusting that Inez would not let anyone fall behind. She had expected the streets to be deserted, but small bands of soldiers were running in formation, a few vehicles were speeding past on the boulevard, and numerous civilians were taking advantage of the lull between explosions just as the operators were to move from one safe haven to another.

"Five minutes," Inez called out from the rear as Valerie led them left on Rue la Boétie, and then right onto the Champs-Élysées. In the distance she glimpsed the Arc de Triomphe, eerily silhouetted by the sun in a cloud of dust and smoke. Behind her someone stumbled and muttered a curse, but when no one called out for help, Valerie ran on.

"Ten," Inez shouted, just as the Beaux-Arts façade of the Élysées Palace Hotel came into view. When Valerie reached the front entrance, she pulled the door open and motioned for the others to hurry inside ahead of her. After Inez entered, Valerie scanned the boulevard to confirm that everyone had made it, then ducked inside and closed the door firmly behind her.

She joined the others in the center of the lobby and stood bent over with her hands on her knees, catching her breath. "We made it," Millicent gasped. "Let's get to work."

An explosion rattled the windows. The girls jumped and shrieked.

"Fifteen," said Inez.

Valerie looked at her and started laughing. Inez grinned back, and a few of the other girls joined in weakly. "Millicent's right," said Valerie, rubbing her side where a cramp pinched. "Let's go."

Straightening their jackets, tucking in their blouses, removing their hats and smoothing loose strands of hair back into their coiffures, they made their way to the telephone room, where the commanding officer regarded them in astonishment.

"Sorry we're late," said Inez, gesturing for the operators to take their usual stations.

"We weren't expecting to see you at all," the commanding officer said. "Are you ladies all right?"

"Of course," said Inez. "This isn't our first bombardment."

"I'm here to relieve you, Corporal," Valerie told her night shift counterpart.

"Glad you could make it, miss," he said, handing her the headset. "The army doesn't pay overtime. Nice of you to come out in this German hailstorm."

"I figured you needed your beauty sleep," she replied airily as she took the chair. "Be careful out there. The bombs are coming—"

"Every fifteen minutes," he finished, nodding. "Yeah, we noticed. Listen, we've had intermittent outages at Robin and Cyclone all morning. Crews are working on the lines, but it's touch and go."

"Good to know. Thanks." The corporal nodded in parting as she put on the headset and adjusted the mouthpiece. "Keep your head down," she called over her shoulder, turning back to the switchboard just as a light flashed, signaling an incoming call from the French exchange. Quickly she inserted the cable into the jack. "*J'écoute.*"

The bombings continued on the quarter hour throughout the morning, then, curiously, went on hiatus over the noon hour, then resumed at one o'clock and persisted throughout the day. The gun fell silent in the late afternoon, just as the women finished their shift, so they walked back to quarters rather than making a run for it, wary, bracing themselves for another barrage. Along the way, Valerie noted with relief that all of the buildings on their route seemed to have survived unscathed. Her heart went out to the weary, besieged Parisians they passed, women, mostly, who had emerged from their homes to hurry through their delayed errands before sunset.

The night was blessedly calm, but at half past five o'clock the next morning, Valerie was jolted awake by a distant explosion. Belatedly, the siren began to wail. With all hope of sleep banished, she dragged herself from bed and made ready for the day, wincing at the explosions that followed, each precisely on the quarter hour. This time the operators knew what to expect, so they timed their sprint to the Élysées Palace Hotel perfectly and arrived for their shift with minutes to spare. Again the German gunners took a lunch break, which Valerie found darkly amusing, and again they resumed the assault throughout the afternoon. The next day brought more of the same, although that night their sleep was rudely interrupted by an air raid. They were groggy the next morning, but adrenaline and sheer determination kept them alert at the switchboard.

In late May, their commanding officer instructed them to prepare for immediate evacuation, but the operators protested. "We'll stay at our posts as long as the men do, sir," Inez replied firmly. "With this drive going on, if you put less experienced boys in our places, it could prove disastrous."

It was not boasting, but simple fact, and the Signal Corps officer relented.

By then Valerie had learned that the U.S. Army's 1st Infantry Division had launched the first American offensive at Cantigny, an evacuated farming village on a ridge in the Picardy region of northern France. On May 30, the Germans had fallen back, giving General Pershing his first victory; that same day, the general had ordered the army's 3rd Infantry Division to Château-Thierry, a small industrial town on the Marne, joining with French divisions to prevent the Germans from crossing the river. On the first day of June, chilling news came through the wires that German troops had entered Château-Thierry, but eventually the American and French forces pushed them back across the river and held them there.

For two weeks, the bombardment of Paris continued as the Allied forces fought along the Marne. One day in early June, shell fragments shattered a window of the telephone room, prompting a Signal Corps officer to urge the operators to take cover in the basement bomb shelter.

"We will not abandon our posts," Valerie replied, shocked by the very thought of allowing all those urgent calls to go unanswered. What terrible consequence would befall the Allied forces if communications abruptly ceased? "We will stay until the last man leaves."

She expected to be reprimanded, but the officer knew she was right, and he did not repeat his order. He knew as well as they did that the Signal Corps needed them at the switchboards in the chaos and destruction of battle more than at any other time. The switchboard soldiers could hold out as long as the men did, and they would prove it.

15

JUNE 1918

Tours

MARIE

In early June, Marie gleaned from calls she placed between certain divisions at the front, requisition offices, and munitions depots that U.S. Marines had engaged German forces at Belleau Wood. The increasing volume of calls told her that the battle was intense, the number of casualties horrifying, and victory uncertain. Every officer Marie spoke to agreed that the war had entered its most crucial period, where the eventual conclusion could depend upon the outcome of a single battle. They would not know which one until it was all over.

And yet when Marie strolled around Tours, if she avoided the military installations and the parts of town where soldiers congregated, she could almost forget that France was at war. The sun still shone brilliantly in an azure sky, the green, rolling hills soothed her with their beauty, the deep forests evoked quiet wonder, the Loire and the Cher flowed ever freely, and farmers' fields thrust green and golden shoots to the sky to quench themselves in gentle rains.

Then she would walk along the outskirts of the town and observe the soldiers racing to load trains with armaments and supplies for the front, or maimed or shell-shocked soldiers recuperating beneath the watchful eye of Red Cross nurses, or refugees slowly wandering into town carrying their meager possessions in small bundles on their backs, their clothing tattered and shoes worn through, their expressions grim and eyes defiant. Instinctively Marie would search their gaunt faces for a glimpse of a missing cousin or a long-lost friend, but she never recognized anyone she knew. She always shared whatever food or coin she happened to have on her, and she was often rewarded with news from the occupied territories in the east. Whenever she came upon families with small children, she quietly told them that they could find a hot meal, clean clothing, and perhaps even shoes for the children at the convent. Marie knew the generous sisters would never turn anyone away.

The nuns had taken in at least twenty more orphans since Marie had met Gisèle and the others, and more than half of the newcomers had joined the children's chorus after hearing them perform.

Marie's friends fondly teased her about how many of her off-duty hours she devoted to the choir. She led all the children in musical games on Tuesday and Thursday evenings for an hour after supper, and those who especially loved to sing gathered on Wednesday evenings and Saturday afternoons to practice songs composed for treble choir. Marie had begun with the favorite tunes they had sung together that first day, and had soon moved on to instruction in solfège and pieces with simple two-part harmonies. After a few weeks of rehearsal, the choir began performing at Sunday morning mass each week in the convent's chapel, which delighted the nuns. Somehow word spread to an army chaplain, who asked Sister Agnès if the children could provide music for a special mass for wounded soldiers. Sister Agnès brought the request to Marie, who had misgivings. "I don't want to put the children on display," she said. "Some of them are still so very shy."

She was thinking of Gisèle, of course, but Sister Agnès needed no explanation. "Why don't you ask the children if they would like to sing?" she proposed. "Think of this not as a performance, but as a ministry. So many of these men bear wounds of the spirit as well as the flesh. The sound of children's voices, the reminder of innocence and how we are all God's children, may bring them great comfort."

Marie understood well the healing power of music, and it occurred to her that the children's own invisible wounds might be soothed if they saw how much joy and comfort they brought to others. When she asked the children if they wanted to sing for the wounded soldiers, they all agreed, some with great excitement, some with trepidation, but none wanted to be left behind while the rest of the choir sang.

The army chaplain arranged for vehicles to carry the children, Marie, and several of the nuns to a fifteenth-century chateau on the outskirts of Tours that had been transformed into a convalescent hospital. The estate boasted a modest white stone chapel, which steadily filled, first with the walking wounded, who entered in pairs or alone, seated themselves in the pews, and knelt to pray or chatted quietly with their companions. Most of the seats had been taken when the nurses began escorting in the shell-shock patients, their gaze distant and melancholic. At the same time, attendants wheeled in the amputees and the men burned or blinded by gas, all swathed in white bandages, all unsettlingly quiet.

Marie viewed this from the corner of her eye as she arranged the children in their usual rows in the transept to the right of the altar. The children fidgeted, eyeing the wounded men and whispering to one another. But as soon as the service began, they were perfectly angelic, following the liturgy as dutifully as they did at the convent, and as they probably had under their parents' watchful eyes in the villages they had fled. Their sweet treble voices filled the chapel with simple hymns in French and Latin, their music beautiful not because it was flawlessly performed, but because wherever children were loved and cared for and could lift their voices in song unafraid, there was hope for a better world.

Marie was not surprised to see many of the men moved to tears.

After the final benediction, as the gathering dispersed, several of the soldiers came over to meet the children, offering a gentle pat on the head, a smile, or a few words of thanks in French. Afterward, two men in Signal Corps uniforms with photography unit insignia, one carrying a camera and tripod, the other a notebook and pen, asked Marie if she and the choir would mind posing for a photograph. Marie glanced to

Sister Agnès, uncertain, but when the nun nodded and smiled, Marie consented. While the soldier with the notebook asked Sister Agnès a few questions about the choir, the soldier with the camera helped Marie arrange the children in two rows on the steps to the altar, with Marie standing to one side, and after making a few adjustments here and there to make sure every child's face could be seen, he took the photo.

"I'll make sure to send a few prints to the convent," he promised, smiling. Some of the children jumped up and down and squealed with excitement, but Marie calmed them with a reminder that they were in a chapel. She prompted the children to thank the two soldiers, adding her own thanks as well.

Marie and the sisters led the children outside to the vehicles, where the chaplain presented Sister Agnès with a small leather bag. "The soldiers took up a collection," he explained with a grin as he climbed into the driver's seat of the lead automobile.

Marie was mystified. Even the walking wounded had been dressed in hospital attire, except for their shoes. Where had any of them carried a billfold or loose change?

"Perhaps the chaplain meant other soldiers in his congregation, not only the patients we saw today," Sister Agnès mused later, back at the convent, as she counted the coins and bills, American and French. "That would account for this abundance. This should be enough to keep the children fed and clothed throughout the summer."

"Perhaps we should have the children sing at the cathedral on the Feast of the Assumption," Marie said. "That might take care of autumn. A Christmas concert in December might see them through the entire winter."

Sister Agnès laughed lightly. "Perhaps we should, my dear." She gave Marie an appraising glance. "As long as you're willing to stay on as choirmistress."

"I wouldn't dream of giving up my baton," Marie assured her, smiling. "I'm here for the duration. The army said so."

How could she give up working with the children when those precious hours offered her such respite from the war?

Marie did spend her time off duty in other ways as well, of course, sipping ersatz coffee at cafés with her girlfriends, walking along the Loire, or hiking through the leafy woods, delighting in the birdsong she remembered from childhood, and the sights and fragrances of the trees and flowers she would always associate with home. She and her friends never again stumbled upon the team of lumberjacks, nor heard the sound of saws or timber falling. Marie assumed the men had either moved deeper into the forest or had completed their work and been reassigned to other crews.

In the evenings, the girls attended parties and dinners hosted by the YWCA, and dances and concerts at the officers' club and the YMCA. The YMCA hospitality hut had a piano, and one Saturday night, friends who had enjoyed Marie's singing back in Southampton persuaded her to put on a concert. A sergeant with one of the Engineer Service Battalions accompanied her as she performed the usual favorite military tunes, interspersed with a few French traditional songs. The sergeant was not familiar with them, but he was skilled enough to pick up the melody and play the appropriate chords.

"Do you know the one about the switchboard soldiers?" a private called out when they returned from a break.

Marie shook her head. "I'm sorry, no."

"Sure you do," he protested. "You must. You're a hello girl yourself."

"Some fellow sang it at the YMCA in Southampton," another private seated next to him chimed in. "He wasn't half as good as you, though. It went something like this." He began to hum, dreadfully off-key, then nudged his buddy, who joined in, further muddling the tune. Occasionally they tried to substitute some lyrics for the humming, but the only words they seemed to know were "switchboard soldiers."

"The melody sounds vaguely familiar, but I'm sure I've never heard the song before," said Marie, suppressing a smile. "Is it Gershwin?"

The pianist choked back laughter, but the first soldier just shook his head. "No, the fellow wrote it himself."

"I see. Well, that explains why I don't know it." She wished she did, since it was apparently a tribute to her and her friends. They would be amused—and flattered too, no doubt—to hear that their fame had spread so far and wide that admirers were composing songs in their honor.

After the set, she joined her friends at a table, where they were drinking lemonade and chatting with a trio of admiring officers. Just as Marie seated herself in the last empty chair, a Signal Corps corporal approached her. He looked familiar, but she could not quite place him.

"Excuse me, miss," he said, removing his cap to reveal boyishly thick blond curls. "I overheard you tell that other fellow that you're a hello girl."

Suddenly Marie remembered where she had seen him before, and after craning her neck to glimpse the insignia on his sleeve, she was certain. He was the photographer who had taken a picture of the children's choir at the convalescent hospital.

"Any girl who works a switchboard can be called a hello girl," Cordelia broke in, smiling up at the handsome young man with dark blue eyes. "*We* are Signal Corps telephone operators."

"Of course. I meant no disrespect." He smiled apologetically, looking around the table to include the other girls, who had broken off their conversations to listen in. "I see from your uniforms that you're all telephone operators. My sister is too, and I was hoping you might know if she's posted here. Her name is Valerie DeSmedt."

"You're Henri," said Marie, astonished, as the other girls brightened at the sound of the familiar name.

"Yes, I am," he replied eagerly, pulling up a chair from an adjacent table and sitting down beside her. "You know my sister! Is she here?"

"Of course we know Valerie. We all trained together in New York." Then Marie shook her head, regretful. "I'm so sorry. She isn't here. She wasn't posted to Tours."

His face fell. "Do you know where she is?"

"I'm afraid I don't. Her group sailed after mine did, so I wasn't there when she received her assignment. All I can tell you is that she arrived in France in early April." She glanced around the table, raising her eyebrows inquisitively, but the other girls merely shook their heads and shrugged sympathetically. "I wish we knew more."

"That's all right." He managed a smile. "Just knowing that she made it to France safely is a relief." He rose and put on his cap. "I'm with the Photographic Section, and we travel around a lot. That makes it harder to get mail, but maybe I'll run into her somewhere along the way."

"*Bonne chance*," said Marie. "If I do happen to speak with Valerie, I'll tell her we met, and that you send all your love."

"We all will," said Cordelia, and the other girls nodded.

"Thank you, ladies. Have a good evening." Henri inclined his head in farewell and departed.

"Poor fellow," said Cordelia. "Well, at least we can try to pass on his message. It shouldn't be too hard to find out where Valerie was posted."

"She's in Paris," said Martina, sipping her lemonade.

They all turned to her. "You knew, and you said nothing?" Marie said, astounded.

"We're not supposed to divulge any details about where anyone is posted," Martina reminded her. "Nothing is more important than secrecy, remember? We don't know anything, we don't say anything."

"But that was Valerie's brother!"

"He could've been a spy," said Cordelia, shrugging.

"No, he's definitely her brother," said Martina, nodding for emphasis. "Valerie carries family photos around in a little cardboard folder in her jacket pocket. She was always showing the girls in Second Group his picture, at least once a day the whole time we were at sea. Well, maybe not *that* often, but enough that I definitely recognize him."

"He could be her brother *and* a spy," Cordelia mused.

"Oh, Martina." Sighing, Marie pushed back her chair and rose. "It is possible to be *too* vigilant."

She hurried after Henri, but the men's uniforms were so similar that she quickly lost him in the crowd. She reached the door without seeing him, so she went outside and glanced up and down the street, but night had fallen, and if he was out there, the blackout had enveloped him.

She returned inside and scanned the crowd from a clear space near the canteen, but he was nowhere to be seen. Sighing, she sat down on a high stool at the counter, wondering how to proceed.

"You look rather downcast for someone who just finished enchanting hundreds of soldiers with her lovely voice," a woman remarked from behind the counter. "Anything I can do to help?"

Turning, Marie discovered one of the YMCA hostesses regarding her with sympathetic curiosity. "I was just speaking to the brother of a friend," Marie said. "As soon as he left, I realized I had something important to tell him, but I couldn't find him."

"That's too bad," the hostess said, sighing. "You never know. He might come back. Many of the soldiers stationed here drop by two or three times a week."

"That's part of the problem. He isn't stationed in Tours. How long he'll be in town and how to reach him after he leaves, I have no idea." Perhaps because she was exasperated with Martina, perhaps because the question had been troubling her for weeks, Marie said, "Could you help me with something else? As you've said, this is a very popular place among the soldiers, but I've never seen any Black American troops here. I know there are some in Tours, but I never see them around the town either. Do they not feel welcome—or it is worse than that? Do they feel unsafe, or are they forbidden to come?"

"Well—" The hostess drew herself up, mouth pursed, expression guarded. "I can't speak for the entire town, of course—I'm not *from* here, obviously, I'm not French—but with regard to our organization, the colored men have their own hospitality huts closer to their quarters, staffed by colored women. Rest assured, their huts are just as well supplied and maintained as ours."

"I see," said Marie flatly. "Theirs and ours. Equal, but separate."

The hostess flushed. "You don't understand. It's only meant to make everyone as comfortable as possible. I'm sure they prefer to have their own gathering places, where they can relax and enjoy themselves among their own kind, just as we do."

"Have you asked them?"

"Well, no, but that's not really my place." Flustered, she wrung her hands, then spread them in an appeal. "You must understand—"

"Thank you," Marie said coolly, "but I believe I understand perfectly." She descended from the stool and returned to her friends' table.

"Any luck?" asked Cordelia as she sat down.

"None at all," said Marie. "I couldn't find him. Tell me, were all of you aware that there are Black American soldiers stationed here at Tours, and that apparently they aren't welcome in this hut?"

"That they're in Tours, yes," said Cordelia, who had been with her that day in the forest. "That they're not welcome in here, no. I thought the YMCA was open to all soldiers."

"The colored soldiers have their own hut," said one of the officers, a stout fellow with flushed cheeks. He meant it to be reassuring, but Marie, Cordelia, and two of the other girls shot him a sharp look.

"Their own hut and a raw deal," said another officer, the youngest of the three, frowning. He leaned forward and rested his elbows on the table. "Thousands of colored men enlisted thinking they'd be going Over There to fight the Hun. They trained as combat troops back home, only to come here and find themselves assigned to manual labor for the duration."

"Not all of them," said the third officer, who had a deep bass voice. "The Three Hundred and Sixty-Ninth Infantry was assigned to a French division since May—the Sixteenth, I believe. They went into battle at Château-Thierry and have been fighting ever since."

"To the Black Rattlers," said the youngest officer, raising his glass.

"To the Harlem Hell Fighters," said the basso profundo, clinking his glass against his buddy's. Marie quickly raised her own glass, which only had a few drops of lemonade left, and echoed the toast. Her friends cheerfully did the same.

The stout officer's flushed cheeks reddened further as he looked around the table. "Someone has to do the grunt work of this war," he said. "We in Services of Supply know that better than anyone. We can't win this war without men to unload ships, and to lay railroad tracks, and to work as lumberjacks and stevedores—"

"Yes, but think of how you would feel in their place," Marie interrupted. "I know how I would feel if I had joined the Signal Corps because I'm a skilled telephone operator, only to arrive in France and be put to work peeling potatoes because I'm a woman."

The girls nodded, and Cordelia even applauded, but the stout officer shook his head. "I bet if that had happened," he said, fixing Marie with a pointed look, "you'd still be doing your bit, peeling potatoes for your country."

"I'm sure I would be," Marie retorted, "just as these Black soldiers, your fellow Americans, are doing *their* bit. And as American soldiers, when they're off duty they ought to be allowed to relax here, or anywhere else you soldiers are permitted."

"Many of us agree with you," the basso profundo said, and the youngest officer nodded earnestly.

The stout officer smiled slightly, as if suddenly understanding the reason for her indignation. "You're French, aren't you, mademoiselle? See, you just don't understand how things work in the United States."

She was about to tell him just how much she understood when all at once the fire went out of her. She had so enjoyed singing there for the soldiers and her friends, but she did not know how she could ever bring herself to do so again, knowing that brave men had been excluded because of their race. Not only that, she could not bear to remain in the hut another moment longer.

"Please excuse me," she said, smiling apologetically to the youngest officer and the basso profundo. "I believe I've spoiled the mood of what had been a very pleasant evening. I'll say good night." She rose, and the three officers quickly did so too, the youngest shooting a glare at his stout buddy. When her friends began to rise too, she urged them to stay and enjoy themselves. All of them did except for Cordelia, who insisted on accompanying her back to the convent so she would not have to walk in the blackout alone. Good friend that she was, she also very kindly put up with Marie's fuming and muttering disparagements in French under her breath the entire way.

The next morning, refreshed by a good night's sleep, Marie decided that if she could not fix all the injustices in the world, she could at least reassure one comrade. She reported for her shift as usual, and as soon as there was a lull in the flow of calls, she quickly rang the Signal Corps headquarters in Paris. "This is Operator Four at the Burrow," she said crisply when the operator picked up. "If you have an operator named Valerie, tell her that her brother is currently here, safe and sound." Without waiting for an acknowledgment, she disconnected the call. That was the most she could do, and it was probably more than she should have done, according to protocol. She hoped Valerie would get the message.

A few days later, she had just ended a call between a quartermaster in Tours and his counterpart in Neufchâteau when one of the girls called out, "Operator Four, take over jack seven-two-one."

Marie's heart thumped. Surely the caller was Valerie from Paris, replying to her message. Swiftly she made the connection. "Number, please."

"Cherubino," a warm baritone voice replied. "Is that you?"

"Giovanni," she gasped. "You—you—"

"I got your letter."

"Yes." She felt blood rising in her cheeks at the memory of his kiss. "Where are you? No, don't say it, you can't tell me." She glanced at the switchboard. Pas-de-Calais. The 307th must be attached to a British division for training. "Are you all right?"

"Yes, yes, I'm fine. How are you?"

"I'm fine too." Fine? How banal she sounded. It was a wonder he didn't disconnect from sheer boredom. She was overwhelmed with relief, overjoyed—but how could she tell him that? "You needn't fear for me. I'm completely out of harm's way."

"You have no idea how relieved I am to hear that," he said. "Look, I don't have long to talk, and I don't know if I'll be able to call again. I only managed it this time because a buddy owed me a favor."

She laughed tremulously, heart pounding. "Now *I* owe *him* one."

"I just wanted to hear your voice."

"It's so good to hear yours." She took a steadying breath and kept her voice carefully neutral. None of the other girls could know that this was anything more than an ordinary call. "I'm so glad you called. Write to me. Keep your head down. Stay safe."

"I will. You too."

A light flashed on the switchboard. She had to disconnect, but not before— "If you can get leave, call me again," she said quickly. "I'll meet you, somehow, in Paris, anywhere—"

"Yes, I will. Marie—"

"I'm so sorry, I have to go—"

"I understand. It's all right. Take care, my Cherubino."

"*Au revoir*, Giovanni." She yanked the plug and the line went silent. Drawing in a shaky breath, she inserted a plug into the new caller's jack. "Number, please?"

Somehow she completed the rest of her shift, her heart aching and soaring. Giovanni was alive. He was in danger. She had heard his voice. He was hundreds of miles away.

She might not hear from him again for weeks, or months, but she could not let that distract her. Too much depended upon her doing her job and doing it well. Her young singers needed and deserved her full attention when she was with them.

She must try not to think of him, even though the simple fact that they were both alive in the world at the same time seemed like a glorious miracle.

The days passed. She sang with the children. She wrote Giovanni a long letter. She tore it up and wrote another.

A week after she and Giovanni spoke, Marie's supervisor caught her at the door when she was about to leave for the day. "Major Rodriguez wants to speak with you," she said. "He's waiting in his office."

Marie's heart plummeted. The major must have discovered the illicit calls—hers to Valerie, Giovanni's to her. She would be dishonorably discharged or even court-martialed. She would be sent back to America in disgrace, or, since she was not a citizen, be cast out and left to fend for herself in war-torn France, with no way to return to her family.

If that was her fate, so be it. The nuns might permit her to stay on at the convent and help care for the children. If not, she would return to her family's Paris apartment and find another way to fight the Germans. She regretted nothing.

She murmured a reply to her supervisor and set out for the major's office. Her hands trembled; she clasped them together to still them, then clenched them into fists and held them rigidly at her sides. The Signal Corps needed her—that was her one saving grace. She would acknowledge her wrongdoing, promise never to disregard protocol again, and throw herself on his mercy. It was the only chance she had.

"Major Rodriguez?" she said, lingering in the open doorway. "You summoned me?"

"Ah, Miss Miossec," the major greeted her, surprisingly pleasant. He gestured to a chair in front of his desk, and after crossing the room on trembling legs, she sank into it. "How are the new girls working out?"

For a moment Marie was rendered speechless. "Very well, sir," she said warily. "They are all capable operators with excellent attitudes and esprit de corps." She hesitated. "A few need to perfect their schoolbook French, but I'm sure they'll increase their fluency after they've lived among native speakers for a while."

"Your supervisor said much the same," he said. "And that brings us to the reason I summoned you. Now that we have more, albeit less experienced, operators here at Services of Supply, your exceptional skills and bilingual fluency are required elsewhere. We'll be sorry to lose you, but you've been transferred closer to the front."

Marie regarded him numbly. "To Chaumont?"

"Closer to the front," he repeated, grinning and wagging his head, a warning not to ask for more details. "Your escort will provide you and the other two girls with your orders when you're en route." Rising, he came around the desk to shake her hand, and she stood to accept it. "Pack your gear. Your train leaves tomorrow morning at eight o'clock."

"So soon?" she asked as he showed her to the door.

"They need you immediately," he replied. "Good luck, Miss Miossec."

She thanked him and hurried on her way, stunned, relieved, and heartbroken.

Her breach of protocol had not been discovered. She was not going to be dismissed from the Signal Corps or court-martialed or sent home to her family in disgrace. She was moving closer to the front, which was what all the girls longed for. She might even be closer to Giovanni.

But her sweet, darling singers. How would she ever say goodbye to them?

16

JUNE 1918

Chaumont

GRACE

By the middle of June, the fighting in Belleau Wood appeared to have reached a vicious impasse. In the first week of the month, U.S. troops had been slaughtered by German machine guns as they had crossed waist-high wheat fields or moved uphill from one copse of trees to another, yet advance they had, and eventually they had gained a foothold in the dense woodland. Then followed a week of attacks and counterattacks in which Germans released one deadly cloud of mustard gas after another, men were mowed down by gunfire, and the once lovely, verdant trees were stripped of their foliage and shattered. As the days passed, Grace and her operators fielded calls about attacks and counterattacks, but it seemed that neither side held an advantage for long. Meanwhile, the troops' water ran low, meager food supplies grew rancid, and attempts to rescue the wounded only resulted in more casualties.

The meat grinder, as the soldiers called it, seemed untenable to Grace, so astonishingly destructive that there could not possibly be enough men and materiel left to sustain it. But it churned on. For Grace, it was one small comfort to know that her brother wasn't anywhere near it.

In late May she had received a letter from Eugene with news that Battery C, 77th Field Artillery had just arrived in Liverpool. He wrote that his regiment would soon depart for France and report to an encampment at the rear for additional combat training. Eugene was not permitted to mention any specific locations in France by name, but after a bit of sleuthing, Grace learned that the 77th was training at Camp de Souge on the Atlantic coast west of Bordeaux, more than seven hundred kilometers southwest of Chaumont, even farther from the front than most Services of Supply bases. Although she knew his respite from danger would last only until his company was deployed to the front, Grace was immeasurably thankful for it. *She* wanted to be as close to the front as possible regardless of the danger, but that didn't mean she wanted her younger brother there.

As summer came to Chaumont, and drenching rains and muddy streets alternated with days of such glorious beauty that it took her breath away, Grace and her operators consistently earned accolades from their superior officers. One day, Lieutenant Riser fairly burst with pride as he showed Grace a Signal Corps report about their achievements, a stellar review that Captain Wessen back in New York had shared with the press. "It would be impossible to brigade a troop without these girls," the captain had declared. "They are astounding everyone Over There by the efficiency of their work." The Signal Corps girls could handle three hundred calls per hour, the article noted, and they connected approximately five calls in the time it took a man to complete one. As the chief signal officer had reported to Congress, local connections had increased threefold since the women arrived, and toll calls had quintupled. Despite all the challenges they faced working in a war zone, the Signal Corps operators actually achieved faster connection times than their counterparts in larger cities back in the United States did. It was an astonishing record, one that Grace told her operators they should be proud of, for they all had played a crucial role in it.

But that same pride made Grace all the more apprehensive and dismayed when she was informed that a charge of insubordination had been filed against one of her most skilled operators, who now faced the possibility of court-martial.

Grace had contended with disciplinary issues with Louise LeBreton before, some of them rather serious. The first had occurred soon after the eleven girls from the First Group had come to Chaumont. Grace recalled that it had been a particularly busy day, and as Louise explained afterward, she had been working as usual when a red light on her switchboard indicated that someone was on General Pershing's line. Every jack was in use, but since protocol granted the general priority over all other callers, Louise yanked someone else's plug, took General Pershing's call, and said, "Number, please?"

A deep, authoritative voice asked, "What time is it, operator?"

Flustered, expecting a much more important request, Louise stammered, "I-I beg your pardon, sir?"

"Operator, this is General Pershing," the man said, patient but firm. "What time is it, please?"

Louise glanced at the clock above the door. "It is twenty minutes past nine, sir."

The general thanked her and hung up. Exuberant, Louise turned to the other girls and shouted, "General Pershing just asked me for the time!"

The other operators barely had time to glance her way, but a few of them smiled indulgently and nodded. Grace muffled a sigh. The operators were required to behave in an orderly, disciplined, and quiet manner at the switchboard at all times. Interrupting her colleagues' work by giddily shouting across the room as if she were at a baseball game was an obvious breach, one Grace was obliged to address. "Miss LeBreton, would you come with me, please?" she asked.

The younger woman's eyes widened. She nodded, removed her headset, and meekly followed Grace from the room. Outside in the hallway, where the other girls could not overhear, Grace reprimanded Louise for disrupting the office with her shout, and for spreading false rumors about General Pershing's whereabouts. "The general is not in camp this week," Grace reminded her. "I don't know what compelled you to say otherwise, but it must not happen again."

"The caller said he was the general," Louise protested.

"Miss LeBreton, please," said Grace, exasperated. "You will be confined to quarters for thirty days. Do not leave the premises except to work your scheduled shifts."

Louise pouted, but she nodded, eyes downcast, and when Grace gestured to the door, she returned to her station and carried on.

Later that afternoon, when Grace reported the incident to Lieutenant Riser, he winced and shook his head. "You made the right decision," he said, "but she probably wasn't lying. General Pershing did briefly return to Chaumont today, and he's been known to call the switchboard to ask the time."

"I'm glad to know Miss LeBreton told the truth," said Grace. "I only wish she hadn't done it quite so loudly."

"She shouldn't have revealed anything about the call at all, at any volume," the lieutenant pointed out.

Grace knew he was right, but she reduced Louise's sentence to one week and hoped she would learn from her mistake.

Then there were Louise's indiscreet letters. Not long after the incident with General Pershing, Grace was summoned to the mail department, where an indignant censor showed her a letter Louise had written to her family back home. In it, Louise had used French words and phrases to hint at her location. "That is a blatant violation of military security protocol," the censor reminded Grace indignantly as he tore up the letter.

The switchboards were so busy that day that Grace waited for the end of Louise's shift to take her aside. "If your letter had fallen into the wrong hands, the Germans could have discovered the location of First Army Headquarters," she reproved her. "You know better. Don't do it again."

"I thought it was perfectly innocent," Louise protested. "It was just a little letter to my mother and sisters."

Incredulous, Grace patiently explained why such "perfectly innocent" hints were potentially disastrous, and when Louise assured her that she understood and that it would never happen again, Grace issued a reprimand instead of confining her to quarters.

Grace regretted her leniency a few weeks later when the head censor again summoned her to his office to report "another flagrant breach of security from the pen of Miss LeBreton," as he put it, brandishing another letter. Rumors that the Signal Corps might open a new office in Langres, a town south of Neufchâteau, had been drifting around Chaumont for several days. Louise had written to her sister Raymonde in Tours to tell her about the possibility, and to suggest that they both request a transfer there so they could finally be reunited.

As every soldier knew, in their letters, they were never permitted to be more specific about their location than to say they were "somewhere in France." This time Louise had gone beyond what Grace was authorized to handle on her own. She thanked the outraged censor for notifying her, and with a heavy heart, she reported the matter to Lieutenant Riser.

"This is Miss LeBreton's second violation of censorship rules," the lieutenant said grimly as he studied the letter. "And her third offense in total, if I recall correctly."

"You do, sir," said Grace.

"We can't let this pass." He heaved a sigh and shook his head. "You are to inform her that she has her choice of company punishment or trial by court-martial. If she decides to accept company punishment, she won't be required to stand trial."

"Understood, sir."

Once dismissed, Grace went immediately from the lieutenant's office to Louise's room back at the house on Rue Brûle. Louise was lying on her bed weeping when Grace entered, but she sat up, accepted the handkerchief Grace offered, and struggled to control her sobs as Grace sternly told her what her two options were, and what the consequences might be.

"I prefer to take company punishment," Louise replied in a quavering voice, chin trembling, tears streaming down her face.

"I'll inform Lieutenant Riser," said Grace, relieved. A court-martial would have disgraced Louise and reflected badly upon the entire group of Signal Corps women, giving weight to the argument that women did not belong in the army. "You're confined to quarters for thirty days. Do not set foot outside this house, not even to go into the garden. Your shifts will be assigned to other operators."

As Grace departed, she knew from Louise's stricken expression that banishment from the switchboard was the worst punishment of all.

As the days passed, Louise's dutiful, chastened behavior around quarters strongly suggested that she had finally learned her lesson. With little else to do, she humbly asked Mrs. Ivey if she could help around the house, scrubbing floors and washing dishes and changing the linens, however she could be most useful. After consulting Grace, the hostess consented, and every morning she presented Louise with a list of chores for the day. After a week, Mrs. Ivey confided to Grace that she had never expected such a pretty little thing to work so hard and so uncomplainingly, and yet the dishes were spotless and the floors practically shone with cleanliness. Grace too was so impressed that she ended Louise's confinement early, calling it time off for good behavior. Louise thanked her profusely and promised to follow the rules to the letter from that day forward.

Grace had believed her, which made the new, even more serious charge especially troubling—but this time, after Louise explained what had happened, Grace believed the young operator had done everything exactly right.

With the addition of new operators from Group Three in May, the switchboards were covered so well that Grace spent almost all of her time supervising the other girls—managing schedules, solving problems, taking over difficult calls when required—rather than connecting lines at a station of her own. One evening, the switchboards were lit up continuously as the operators fielded a frenzied rush of calls, a result, they knew, of a new offensive the Germans had launched along the Marne. Grace was assisting another operator when a call came through Louise's station nearby, so Grace heard Louise's half of the conversation, and learned the rest afterward.

A bulb lit up, and Louise quickly inserted the jack. "Number, please."

A gruff voice barked, "Connect me with General Pershing's advance headquarters immediately."

"Yes, sir," Louise replied. "May I have the code, please?"

"You know very well where it's located, operator," the man snapped.

She did, of course, but the location of particular officers, armies, corps, artillery, and divisions was strictly confidential. According to protocol, if a caller requested a location without providing the proper code, the operator was required to reply that she had never heard of such a place.

"We are not given that information, sir," Louise replied, as she was obliged to do. "May I have the code, please?"

"This is ridiculous," he fumed. "What is your name, operator?"

"I am not permitted to give you my name, sir. I am Operator Twenty-Two."

"This is urgent! Don't you realize we are at war? Connect me at once!"

"I'm sorry, sir, but I—"

"Let me speak to a man!"

"I can connect you with my chief operator," Louise said, glancing up at Grace, who had joined her at her station when she realized the call had taken a bad turn. "But she is also a woman, sir."

Grace reached out to take the headset, but at that moment, Louise held still, listening carefully. "Sir?" she repeated. "Are you still there, sir?" After a moment, she shook her head, sighed, and unplugged the cable. "He disconnected," she told Grace, with a little shrug and a frown. She summarized the entire call, her description dovetailing perfectly with what Grace had overheard.

"Maybe he'll try again after he remembers the code," Grace said.

"Or maybe I thwarted a notorious German spy," Louise said lightly, quickly reacting as another bulb lit up on her switchboard. "Number, please?"

Grace lingered until she was sure Louise was connecting a new caller and not the irascible fellow who had given her such trouble. Then she patted Louise's shoulder encouragingly and moved on to the next task.

The next morning, she and Suzanne were heading downstairs to breakfast when Esther came running to fetch her. "Louise received a letter that has her absolutely distraught," she said, anxious. "She's begging to see you right away."

"Where is she?" said Grace, hurrying downstairs, wondering if some terrible accident had befallen Raymonde, more than four hundred kilometers to the west in Tours.

"In the parlor. Kathleen is with her."

Grace found them seated on the sofa near the window, Louise choking back tears and pressing a handkerchief to her mouth, Kathleen holding her hand, stroking her shoulder, and murmuring soothingly. "What happened?" Grace asked.

"*This* happened," said Louise in a strangled voice, holding out a folded piece of paper.

Quickly Grace took it, skimmed it, and inhaled sharply. "This can't be right." Louise had been summoned to appear before the chief signal officer at two o'clock that afternoon to answer to a charge of insubordination. "Insubordination, because of that angry caller yesterday? He was the one at fault."

"That's what I told her," said Kathleen, indignant. "Louise handled him exactly how the handbook says we must if a caller doesn't know the code. She never raised her voice at him or pulled the plug, not even when he was yelling at her and demanding to speak to a man."

"I didn't do anything wrong this time," Louise said plaintively. "I can't believe I'm in trouble for *following* the rules. But what good is my word against a colonel's? What am I going to do?"

Grace thought quickly. "You're going to report to the chief signal officer as ordered and tell your side of the story. I'll go with you," she added when Louise's lower lip began to quiver. "I can verify your side of the conversation. Everything will be fine."

"Do you really think so?" asked Louise, dabbing at her eyes.

"I do," said Grace, with more certainty than she felt. "This is just a peevish officer throwing his weight around because he couldn't intimidate you into breaking the rules for him. We'll get it sorted out."

Louise inhaled deeply, shakily, but she nodded.

Word swiftly spread to the other operators, who had finished breakfast and were gathering in the foyer to prepare for their daily march to the caserne. Grace was pleased to see that Louise was entirely dry-eyed and composed as she took her place in the double line. They set out a few minutes ahead of schedule, their deportment perhaps a bit prouder than usual, their steps crisper, as if by an unspoken agreement to present themselves to the encampment at their very best in solidarity with Louise. She was one of their own, and although she had made some errors in judgment in the past, they would not abandon her when she stood unjustly accused. If one temperamental officer could condemn Louise to a court-martial simply for obeying protocol, it could happen to any of them.

About a mile from headquarters, Grace spotted a distinctive vehicle approaching from the opposite direction, and as it drew closer, she recognized General Pershing's dark green Locomobile Model 48, a powerful, elegant Sportif touring car reserved for his personal use. The top was down, a chauffeur was at the wheel, and as the car approached, without exchanging a word or awaiting a signal, the operators saluted the general, crisply and in unison. The general promptly saluted back.

"That's a good sign," Suzanne remarked, just loud enough for Grace to hear.

Grace wished she could believe it. It could not be true literally, for General Pershing surely knew nothing about Louise's upcoming hearing and was not trying to signal his support. As for the chance encounter's value as an omen of good fortune, Grace preferred to find hope in things that were real, such as the fact that the truth was on Louise's side, and duty required the chief signal officer to rule accordingly, despite her accuser's higher rank.

Although the switchboards were very busy that morning, the hours seemed to drag by. Shortly before two o'clock, Grace escorted an outwardly serene Louise to the office of the chief signal officer. When the officer asked her to tell him what had happened, Louise did so, simply and straightforwardly, her voice clear, her chin lifted, her posture straight and graceful, her hands clasped behind her back as if she were a schoolgirl at recitation confident that her answers were correct.

As soon as she finished, the chief signal officer asked Grace if she had anything to add. "Only that Miss LeBreton's description of her end of the call is precisely what I heard," Grace said. "I'm confident that her account of the colonel's half is equally accurate."

"Very well, then," said the chief signal officer. "Miss LeBreton, I hereby dismiss the charge against you."

Louise gasped and pressed her hand to her heart. "Thank you, sir."

"You were absolutely right and you have nothing to fear," he said kindly. "Continue to be a staunch defender of protocol and everything will be fine. Return to your station where we need you. Dismissed."

Louise fairly glowed as they returned downstairs to the telephone room. "Thank goodness it's over," she said fervently. "Did you hear? He said I was absolutely right."

Grace suppressed a smile. "I heard."

"He called me a staunch defender of protocol."

"Well, to be fair, he doesn't know you very well."

"Miss Banker!" Louise protested.

Grace laughed; she couldn't help it. After a moment, Louise allowed a small smile, then she laughed too.

Lieutenant Riser had asked Grace to keep him informed about the hearing, so that evening after her shift, Grace met him in his office and told him what had occurred. As she was leaving, one of General Pershing's aides stopped her in the hallway and introduced himself. "The general was tickled to death when you and your operators saluted him so perfectly this morning," he said. "He told me, 'Those girls are regular soldiers.'"

"Indeed we are, sir," Grace replied, smiling.

"He may take a more active interest in you girls after this."

"We're here in France because of his specific request to the War Department, and we already participate in general reviews," she said. "I don't know how he could show more interest in us than that. We don't expect special treatment."

In reply, the aide smiled mysteriously, tapped the side of his nose, and sauntered off.

Grace wondered what he could have meant by that, but she soon dismissed it as an offhand remark, well intended but soon forgotten.

But the aide's words came back to her one evening two weeks later when, just as the operators were sitting down to supper, a messenger brought her a note from the general's office. Grace stared at the page, stunned. "General Pershing is coming to inspect our quarters this evening."

All the girls within earshot gasped and exclaimed. A visit from the general was a great honor, but he might already be on his way, and they had almost no time to prepare. Someone sensible hurried off to alert Mrs. Ivey, while everyone else hurried through the meal, helped clear away the dishes, and tidied up the dining room. Then they raced upstairs to put their rooms in order, freshen up, and change into clean uniforms.

Grace and Mrs. Ivey took their places in the foyer while the operators lined up in the parlor, everything ready for inspection with only seconds to spare. Grace heard the Locomobile Model 48 approaching before she glimpsed it through a gap in the curtains, slowing to a halt in front of the house. Inhaling deeply to steady her nerves, Grace opened the door and went outside to meet General Pershing as he came up the front walk. Instead she paused on the doorstep, brought up short by the sight of the general amid an entourage of six other officers, including the aide she had met outside Lieutenant Riser's office days before.

Quickly she composed herself and saluted. "Good evening, General," she greeted him. Until then she had only seen him from a distance, and he was both taller and more handsome than she had expected, with piercing blue eyes, a square jaw, a powerful build, and only a trace of silver in his close-cropped sandy hair. "I'm Grace Banker, chief operator. Welcome to the Rue Brûle operators' residence."

"Good evening, Miss Banker," the general replied, returning her salute. "Thank you for allowing me to disturb you on such short notice."

"Not at all, sir. It's an honor."

"You'll see I brought company," he said, his eyes crinkling with amusement as he inclined his head to indicate his companions. "When they heard I intended to inspect the women's billet, their curiosity got the better of them, and they insisted on coming along."

"You're all welcome," said Grace, smiling around at the officers and aides. "Please come this way."

She led them inside to the foyer and introduced the general to Mrs. Ivey, who blushed, starstruck, as she shook his hand and stammered out a welcome. Next Grace showed the general to the parlor, where the operators stood at attention in their crisp, fresh uniforms, their eyes bright with pride and excitement. Grace introduced the general to each girl in turn as he went down the line; he spoke briefly with each one, asking where she was from, perhaps, or how she liked France, or what she thought of the telephone equipment at Chaumont, or some other thoughtful inquiry. When he had met every operator, he turned to Grace. "I'm very impressed with your troops, Miss Banker," he remarked. "Now, why don't you give me the grand tour of the residence, so I can see how the AEF has been treating you ladies?"

Grace promptly complied, and with the six other officers trailing behind, she led the general up to the third floor and worked their way down, showing them the room she shared with Suzanne—they had put it in perfect military order, assuming he would want to see an example—and then another on the second floor, equally tidy, so he would know theirs wasn't an exception. Returning to the first floor, she led him through the library and the parlor, where he noted the piano and asked if anyone of the operators played. When Grace replied that a few of them did, he nodded and said that his late wife had played, but she had rarely had an instrument available at the various officers' quarters his family had called home.

"I understand there's a popular tune about you telephone operators making the rounds," he added. "I heard some of the boys singing it as they passed by my window when I was inspecting another encampment. I believe it refers to you as 'Switchboard Soldiers.'"

"It's a title we're proud to bear," said Grace. "I haven't heard the song, although I have heard *of* it. I hope it's complimentary."

The general smiled. "From the little I could make out, it was very much so."

They continued down the hall past the entrance to the kitchen. "That is the kitchen," Grace said in passing, gesturing to it but not pausing, relieved that the door was closed. She could only imagine the mess concealed within, considering how frantically the operators had cleared the dining room and had haphazardly piled the dirty dishes on the kitchen counters before racing off to prepare for the inspection.

To her dismay, General Pershing halted in front of the door. "Aren't we going in?"

"I didn't think it would interest you, sir," she said.

"Oh, I always want to see the kitchen," he replied. "As they say, an army marches on its stomach."

Grace nodded and managed a smile. "Of course, sir." She opened the door and led the general and his entourage inside—and muffled a gasp. Clad in spotless aprons and toques, the French cook and her two assistants stood proudly at attention amid a scene of perfect culinary order. Every pot and pan and plate and dish had been washed and put away, the floor swept, the counters wiped, the sinks and taps scrubbed until they shone.

General Pershing strolled the room, opening a cupboard here, inspecting a pantry there, nodding thoughtfully, satisfied. Finally, he addressed the chef, who straightened proudly, awaiting his judgment. "My compliments on the tidiness of your domain," he said. "I don't believe I've ever seen a more immaculate working kitchen."

The chef's cheeks flushed pink. "*Merci, mon général*," she replied, inclining her head in both deference and dignity.

"I'm very impressed," the general remarked to Grace as they returned to the hallway. "These accommodations are among the very best in Chaumont."

"We're very pleased with our quarters," Grace assured him. "In fact, sometimes we say this hardly qualifies as soldiering, since we are almost *too* comfortable. I imagine your encampment along the Mexican border was nothing like this."

"You imagine correctly," he said, smiling at the suggestion that she had followed his career. "It sounds as if you're eager for tougher challenges."

"We're ready and willing to serve wherever you need us, sir," she said.

He nodded, looking pleased and satisfied—and if she dared hope so, perhaps even impressed.

His inspection complete, General Pershing returned to the parlor to bid the operators goodbye. "Keep up the excellent work, ladies," he said. "This army could not function without you."

They murmured their thanks, deferential, but profoundly flattered and barely able to contain their delight. Grace escorted the general and his entourage to the door, where she thanked them for the visit and invited the general to return whenever he wished. The officers left, and Grace shut the door behind them. She listened as the touring car's engine started up and then faded as the automobile departed; only then did she close her eyes, lean back against the door, and heave a sigh of relief. They had survived their first inspection with flying colors, without a word of rebuke.

From the parlor, the operators' murmurs swelled into loud conversation punctuated by bursts of laughter, so Grace quickly composed herself and joined them. Waving them to silence, she praised them for the excellent review, all the more impressive because they had pulled it off with almost no advance warning. "I couldn't be prouder," she said, looking around at their broad smiles and shining eyes.

"Why do you suppose he came to inspect our residence?" Suzanne asked her later that night as they prepared for bed. "He couldn't possibly tour every billet."

"We aren't just any band of soldiers," Grace reminded her. "We're the first women to serve in the United States Army, and I'm sure there are politicians and others back home still arguing that we shouldn't be here. It's little wonder he wants to make sure we're being treated with respect, and with every consideration made for our safety and comfort."

"I sure can't complain about comfort," Suzanne replied, sinking back onto her feather pillow with a sigh.

Grace laughed and climbed into her own very comfortable bed.

She knew that General Pershing's concern for the telephone operators' well-being could simply reflect his keen understanding of the essential services they performed. Their status as the first women in the army, a test case that would no doubt be carefully scrutinized by the War Department, Congress, and the public alike, surely heightened his interest. After all, the Signal Corps had recruited women at his request, overruling many detractors. The women's success or failure would reflect upon his judgment, raising him in public esteem or thoroughly discrediting him.

But Grace wondered if his concern ran deeper than that.

The previous fall, after she had submitted her application but before she had received the telegram inviting her to an interview, she had studied up on General John Joseph "Black Jack" Pershing, curious about the man who would defy convention and break down barriers for women in his determination to recruit the very best personnel for a crucial job. She learned that when he was an instructor at West Point, hostile cadets who resented his strict and unyielding nature had bestowed his nickname upon him as a pejorative reference to one of his earliest postings, the command of a troop of the 10th Cavalry, one of the original Buffalo Soldier regiments. Like most nicknames, it caught on although he himself disliked and never used it. "Black Jack" was actually a modified version of the original moniker, which had included a racial slur.

Grace had known that General Pershing was a widower, but she had been shocked to learn how very tragic his loss had been. Three years before, while he was commanding troops in El Paso, a terrible fire had engulfed the officers' quarters at the Presidio in San Francisco where his family resided. His wife and three young daughters had been killed. Only his son, Francis, five years old, had survived.

Perhaps General Pershing saw the daughters he had lost in the young women under his command, the young women whose skills he needed so urgently that he had summoned them across an ocean to a country at war, where he could not possibly guarantee their safety.

17

JULY 1918

Paris

VALERIE

At the end of June, nearly a month of ferocious, bloody fighting in Belleau Wood concluded when the U.S. Marines finally cleared the forest of German troops. But although the costly victory ninety kilometers to the east was a tremendous relief, whenever the Signal Corps girls were away from the switchboards and their superior officers could not overhear, they agreed that the situation in Paris was worsening day by day. Although the bombardments were not as maddeningly, punctually relentless as they had been in late May and early June, they remained disruptive and frightening. And while the Allied forces were valiantly fighting off the German advance, rumors on the street warned that the defenders would soon be overwhelmed and the invasion of Paris was imminent. More worrisome yet, official reports often echoed the rumors, albeit in less alarmist terms.

Yet whenever Valerie strolled through the city, enjoying the simple pleasures of summer sunshine and fresh air, she observed that although all the hairdressers, storekeepers, and café proprietors were certain that the Germans would come marching down the Champs-Élysées any day now, they were not preparing to evacuate.

"My father started this shop fifty years ago," a bookstore owner told her, bemused by her question. Valerie had stopped in to buy a book for herself and a few postcards to send home to her mother and Hilde, and she could not resist inquiring about his plans. "I've worked here since I was a schoolboy. My wife and I raised our children in the apartment upstairs. What would become of this place if we fled? What would my customers do? And where would we go?" He puffed out a breath and shook his head as he counted out her change. "I don't want the Boche here, but if they do come, at least the long guns will stop shelling us."

"Well, I don't believe the Germans will take Paris," said Valerie, gathering up her purchases, "but if they do, I hope you overcharge them."

"I intend to," he growled so fiercely that Valerie almost felt sorry for the Germans, but not really.

On July 3, Inez called her operators together after their shift and solemnly told them that the chief signal corps officer had ordered them to prepare to leave Paris on twenty-four hours' notice. As they murmured in protest, she waved them to silence. "It's not just us," she said sharply. "This order includes every American stationed in Paris, men and women alike. It isn't optional. Dismissed."

Valerie's heart plummeted as the group dispersed, and she and Millicent and Drusilla exchanged looks of dismay. The threat of invasion was clearly more perilous than they had realized.

Although Valerie and her friends had intended to stroll the Champs-Élysées in hopes of finding a good meal at a previously undiscovered restaurant, none of them was in the mood for a night on the town anymore. Instead they walked back to the hotel, their spirits low, speculating about when they might receive the order to evacuate, where they would be reassigned, if they would be split up, whether the Signal Corps intended to destroy the switchboards before they fled rather than allow them to fall into enemy hands, and whether losing Paris meant that defeat was inevitable.

Valerie had kept her gaze downturned as they walked, her posture mirroring her mood, but a fluttering motion in the corner of her eye caught her attention. Straightening, she saw a woman hanging red, white, and blue bunting around the front window of her boutique. A gentleman at the milliner's shop next door was similarly adorning his front door and windows.

"It's good to see that the Parisians haven't lost their patriotic spirit," Valerie remarked, admiring the scene. "Good for them, decorating for an invasion, thumbing their noses at the invaders."

"Actually, I think this red, white, and blue is for us," said Drusilla, nudging Valerie with her elbow, inclining her head to indicate a bank across the street. Four Star-Spangled Banners hung from four brass staffs equidistantly spaced along the length of the building just above the second story.

"How thoughtful of them," exclaimed Millicent as she glanced up and down the street. Valerie marveled to see how many businesses and homes were indeed adorned with the colors that the Tricolor and the Stars and Stripes shared, in honor of Independence Day. She knew that a parade and other festivities were planned—conceding to their pleas, Inez had scheduled longer, staggered lunch breaks for July Fourth so the operators could take turns watching the parade as it passed headquarters—but Valerie had not expected the citizens of Paris to embrace the American holiday.

She walked the rest of the way back to quarters with her head held high and a smile on her lips. How could the Americans evacuate Paris after such a warm gesture of friendship and solidarity from their French allies?

The next morning, when Valerie and her colleagues returned to the Élysées Palace Hotel to report for duty, they were astonished and delighted to find an abundance of red, white, and blue decorations everywhere they looked. The American flag hung from masts and windows in every direction, and even taxicabs and delivery carts were adorned with smaller versions. Schools, banks, and other businesses were closed in observance of the holiday, and despite the ominous presence of the German army lurking not forty miles east of Paris, everyone seemed to be in a festive mood. The Signal Corps girls in their distinctive uniforms attracted even more notice than usual, and they received many good wishes, handshakes, and even a few gifts of flowers along the way to headquarters.

The telephone operators would miss most of the day's festivities; the war did not pause for Independence Day, and the switchboards were as busy as ever. Still, it pleased Valerie to think how furious and offended the Germans must be to know that the French and the Americans were celebrating together, and that even many British officers, who had good reason to consider the Fourth of July a day of ignominy, were joining in the fun. The first ceremony of the day, or so the morning papers had reported, was an early mass at the American Hospital at Neuilly, where several famous singers would perform the national anthems of the United States and France. Afterward, a delegation from the Sons of the American Revolution would place wreaths of roses at the tomb of Lafayette in the Picpus Cemetery, at the statue of Lafayette in the courtyard of the Louvre, and at the statue of George Washington in the Place d'Iéna. Then, at half past nine o'clock, French president Poincaré would lead the ceremony dedicating the former Avenue du Trocadéro as Avenue du Président-Wilson. At a plaza there, after speeches and music and much fanfare, the grand parade would commence. Thousands of French and American soldiers would march down Avenue du Président-Wilson to Avenue Montaigne and on to the Champs-Élysées, past the Élysées Palace Hotel and onward to the Strasbourg monument in the Place de la Concorde.

None of the operators on duty could watch the entire procession, but by staggering their lunch breaks, they could each enjoy part of it. As soon as Valerie's turn began, she and Drusilla raced upstairs to the fifth floor and went outside to the balcony, which offered marvelous views of the pageant below. Columns of American doughboys marched past accompanied by the lively music of a marching band, then several companies of French marines, an airplane gleaming in the sun, more soldiers, another band, and then, much to their surprise, dozens of uniformed Red Cross nurses walking in four long columns behind an honor guard, one nurse carrying flowers and three bearing the flags of the United States, France, and the Red Cross.

"Will you look at that?" Drusilla exclaimed, planting her hands on her hips. "Why were *they* invited to march in the parade and not us?"

"General Pershing can't do without us for so many hours at the busiest time of the day," Valerie said. It was the least insulting reason that came to mind.

"Oh, and their suffering patients can do without them?" retorted Drusilla, jerking her thumb in the nurses' direction. "How many of them *are* there? Did they empty out all the hospitals in Paris?"

"Don't spoil the day with jealousy," Valerie begged. The skies were cloudy, but the breeze was pleasant, the sidewalks were packed with revelers, and the Champs-Élysées was filled with color and music. The festive atmosphere offered a welcome respite from the pervasive dread that had cost Valerie too much precious sleep in recent days. "Let the nurses enjoy the applause and the attention. They've earned it."

"We've earned it too."

"We didn't join the Signal Corps for applause," Valerie reminded her. "Look at it this way: If we were *in* the parade, we couldn't be up here *enjoying* the parade."

Drusilla eyed her, incredulous, but then she laughed, shook her head, and returned her attention to the spectacle below. "I suppose that's true enough."

A few minutes before they were due back at the switchboards, Drusilla spoke again. "Are you going to do as Mrs. Crittenden said, and pack your bags in case we have to evacuate?"

"I certainly am not," Valerie replied. "I think it would be a waste of time. In a few days, we'd just have to unpack again. I'm absolutely certain the Germans aren't going to chase us out of Paris."

"How can you be so sure?"

Valerie shrugged and shook her head. "I don't know how to explain it. I just can't believe the Germans will ever break through the Allied defenses and make it to Paris. With so many American boys over here now, the tide just *has* to turn in favor of the Allies eventually, and I'm sure it's going to be soon."

"I suppose I feel that way, too," Drusilla admitted, laughing a little.

"Call it ignorance, call it typical American cockiness, but seeing our boys marching through the streets, looking so brave and fine and strong—well, how could I ever doubt them? I don't want to believe we'll ever have to evacuate Paris either."

It was time to return to the switchboards. They left the balcony, and as they descended the stairs, they heard other girls laughing and chatting as they hurried up for their turn as spectators.

"Maybe it's superstitious," Valerie acknowledged after she and Drusilla passed their comrades, "but I refuse to pack as a sign of faith in all the boys who are out there right now defending the city. I'm fully aware that this optimism may backfire and I'll end up fleeing Paris with only the clothes on my back, so follow my example at your own risk."

"Imprudent, but steadfast. I like it," Drusilla praised in an undertone as they entered the telephone room, nodded respectfully to Inez, and took their seats.

As the week passed, Valerie's newfound confidence that Paris would remained free lingered, undiminished by reports of enemy troops regrouping along the Marne. Ten days later, her faith in the Allied forces soared when all of Paris—all of France, indeed, all allied nations around the world—celebrated Bastille Day with speeches, celebrations, and a glorious procession that made the city's Independence Day parade seem like a modest warm-up for the main event.

President Wilson had cabled greetings and good wishes to President Poincaré on behalf of the people of the United States in honor of the occasion, and his remarks were reprinted in all of the Paris newspapers. "America greets France on this day of stirring memories with a heart full of warm friendship and of devotion to the great cause in which the two peoples are now so happily united," the American president had begun. Valerie would have chosen a different adverb than "happily"—"resolutely," perhaps—but it wasn't her message.

"July 14, like our own July 4, has taken on a new significance, not only for France, but for the world," Wilson continued. "As France celebrated our Fourth of July, so do we celebrate her Fourteenth, keenly conscious of a comradeship of arms and of purpose of which we are deeply proud." He concluded by noting that the French flag would fly from the staff above the White House that day, and that the people of the United States would honor it, as they did "the noble enterprise of peace and justice" that united them.

Pershing had sent a more succinct and, in Valerie's opinion, more eloquent message to Premier Clemenceau. "On this day, the 14th of July, which so well symbolizes France's will and determination," the general had written, "I desire to renew to you an expression of my admiration for the splendid courage of your people and the gallantry of its soldiers. We of the American Expeditionary Force find in France's courage the sources of constant inspiration and encouragement."

Other world leaders had sent similar messages, which made for an uplifting and inspirational read at breakfast. Valerie imagined the kaiser feeling terribly left out, seething in jealousy as his enemy was so resoundingly lauded. It was his own fault. If he wanted international friendship, he shouldn't antagonize his neighbors.

But accolades and congratulations from around the globe were only the heralds of a splendid day. Although a fine rain fell, Parisians turned out by the thousands for the grand parade, packing the sidewalks along the Avenue du Bois de Boulogne, climbing atop statuary and wagons for a better view of the soldiers, cavalry, and bands that marched for review before President Poincaré, Premier Clemenceau, General Guillaumat, and numerous French dignitaries, Allied generals, and ambassadors from around the world. French troops were joined in the procession by soldiers, sailors, and marines from the United States, Belgium, Great Britain, Greece, Italy, Poland, Serbia, and Czechoslovakia. Scotsmen in kilts marched proudly, led by pealing bagpipers. Graceful, powerful warhorses carried cavalry officers in perfect formation. Each nation's section was framed by *poilus* in faded and battle-worn horizon blue. Many of the troops had come directly from the battlefield, and the cheers and applause that greeted them at every step were often punctuated by muffled sobs. Halfway along the Avenue du Bois de Boulogne, the procession turned onto the Avenue Malakoff and proceeded by the Faubourg St. Honoré and the Boulevard Haussmann to the Madeleine and the Place de la Concorde. Spectators showered the soldiers in fragrant blossoms, casting them as generously upon the foreign soldiers as their own French troops, until in many places the carpet of flowers lay inches deep.

It was a magnificent display, and Valerie and Millicent considered themselves fortunate to catch the latter part of it, since Inez had needed some convincing before she would permit them to arrange split shifts with two other girls so that all four were able to see half of the parade. The festive mood endured even after the last soldiers marched past, the stirring music of brass bands faded, and the crowds began to disperse. The rain had tapered off at last, and shafts of golden sunshine streamed through the parting clouds, bathing Paris in light until the raindrops glittered like scattered diamonds.

Valerie and Millicent were in too fine a mood to return to quarters, so they decided to visit one of their favorite cafés, where on their off-duty hours they often drank weak coffee and enjoyed tiny pastries, pretending not to notice the effects of rationing, and struck up conversations with other customers, usually Allied soldiers on leave or French civilians. This time they arrived only to find the café packed with other parade spectators, but eventually they claimed two chairs at a shared table and placed their orders. Valerie became engrossed in conversation about rational functions with a French mathematician, a wounded veteran who wore a leather strap across his face to conceal the loss of his nose. Millicent amused herself flirting with one French officer after another, but eventually a Scotsman so charmed her that she agreed to go for a walk with him, promising Valerie she would return soon. She had been gone perhaps a half hour when she came racing back to the table.

"Valerie," she exclaimed, breathless, "I just saw your brother!"

"Henri?" Valerie said, bewildered. "Here? I don't think so. As far as I know, he's still in Tours." If he had ever been there; she wasn't entirely sure. About a month ago, Drusilla had taken a cryptic call with a message for an operator named Valerie, no last name, to inform her that her brother was safe and sound in Tours. Valerie was the only Signal Corps operator by that name in Paris, so Drusilla had passed the message along to her. But when Valerie tried to return the call a few days later, she was told that Operator Four was not available. When she tried again the next day, the girl who answered said that they no longer had an Operator Four. What was Valerie to do then? She wanted to believe her brother was safe at the Services of Supply base, and she was not supposed to use military lines for personal calls, so she did not inquire further.

"I'm sure it was your brother." Millicent gestured impatiently for Valerie to follow her. "Come on! We can still catch up to him."

Dubious, Valerie nevertheless rose from her chair. "You've never met Henri. How would you recognize him?"

Millicent rolled her eyes. "You've shown me his photo at least a hundred times since we left Chicago. I know it was him. He was carrying a motion picture camera!"

"Well, why didn't you say so?" Valerie exclaimed. Offering her apologies to the mathematician, she quickly followed Millicent as her friend darted down the sidewalk, catching up to her when she paused at the corner before crossing the street.

They hurried down the block, weaving their way through the crowd. Suddenly Millicent halted in front of another café, one popular with American doughboys on leave. "He was right here," Millicent said, gesturing in frustration to an outdoor table where a gray-haired gentleman carrying a small white dog was just being seated. "There were three Signal Corps soldiers at this table, and your brother was one of them. I swear it."

"I believe you," said Valerie, tucking her arm through her friend's. "Cheer up. He couldn't have gone far. Unless he's on his way to the train station as we speak, we may still be able to track him down."

They hurried back to their quarters, where they divided up the directory listings and began calling hotels to inquire for Henri DeSmedt. On Valerie's fifth attempt, the concierge informed her that Henri DeSmedt was a registered guest there, but no one was answering the ring in his room. Valerie left a message with her number so Henri could return her call. "*C'est très urgent,*" she told the concierge.

"*Tout est urgent, mademoiselle*," he replied, and hung up. His nonchalance didn't inspire confidence, but she paced around the room, willing the phone to ring. After twenty minutes, she sank down on the bed, discouraged, but then she popped back up again. There was nothing preventing her from going over to her brother's hotel and waiting in the lobby for him to return.

She had just put on her hat when the telephone rang.

She snatched up the receiver. "Hello?"

"Valerie? Is it really you?"

"Henri," Valerie exclaimed, laughing, tears filling her eyes. "Yes, it's me. It's so good to hear your voice."

"And yours! I had no idea you were in Paris." Henri's voice sounded deeper than she remembered, more mature, but still wonderfully familiar. "Everywhere I go, whenever I see Signal Corps telephone girls, I always ask about you. I've met several girls who admit to knowing you, but no one would tell me where you are."

"Well, of course," said Valerie wryly, thinking of the kindhearted girl who nevertheless had called with a tip from Tours. "Regulations, security. You know how it is."

"I do know."

They laughed together.

"I'm leaving Paris first thing tomorrow morning," Henri said. "How about if I meet you outside your quarters in fifteen minutes?"

"Make it ten," said Valerie, and her brother laughed and agreed.

She was pacing on the sidewalk when her brother ran around the corner and caught her up in a hug that lifted her feet off the ground. "Henri," she cried, tears in her eyes, laughing. "I can't believe it's you." She almost meant it literally. His blue eyes and thick blond curls were the same, but he had grown at least an inch in the year they had been apart, his slender arms and chest had filled out, and when he wasn't spinning her around on a Parisian sidewalk, he carried himself with a new maturity.

Grinning, he set her down and held her out at arm's length. "Look at you," he said admiringly. "That looks like a real uniform."

So much for maturity. She swatted him on the shoulder. "It *is* a real uniform, little brother, and I'm a real soldier. But Henri, tell me, what are you doing here?"

"In Paris?"

"In France! How did you get here before me? What happened to aerial photography school?"

"My orders were changed at the last minute. The Signal Corps needed another motion picture camera operator to complete a unit that was sailing immediately, and they picked me. I boarded a ship within an hour of receiving my orders." His brow furrowed. "I guess you didn't get my letter."

She shook her head. "I assumed you were in Rochester until a YMCA hostess in Southampton told me you had already passed through on your way to France. She knew you by your alias, 'Hollywood Hank.'"

Henri threw back his head and laughed. "Oh, no. Could you just pretend you never heard about that?"

She pretended to consider it. "Sorry, I don't think I can. So that's how you beat me to France. How long have you been in Paris? I thought you were in Tours."

His smile broadened. "So you did get my message."

"In a manner of speaking. It was all very clandestine and cryptic." She slipped her arm through his and they began strolling down the street; by habit, Valerie chose the route she walked every day to work. "Were you in Tours long?"

"Only a week, to film operations at Services of Supply. Before that I was in Bordeaux. I move around a lot—"

"I suppose that's your excuse for not writing?"

He playfully elbowed her. "I do write. When I can. As I was trying to say, I travel around a lot with a photography unit, sometimes attached to a specific division, other times deployed to cover a specific event. Right now, I'm in Paris to cover the Bastille Day celebrations."

"And tomorrow?" Valerie asked, already feeling a pang of loss.

"We move on to Chaumont, I think. I'll get my orders in the morning."

They fell silent for a moment as they turned onto Rue la Boétie. Then, prompted by Valerie's questions, Henri told her more about his work, how his role was to document different aspects of the war, sometimes to preserve a historical record, other times to gather information for military analysis. On some occasions, he suspected he was filming scenes that would be edited into a movie for audiences back home, either to build morale, or to persuade folks to purchase more Liberty Loans, or to convince the American people that their sons and brothers and sweethearts were fighting for a noble cause.

Eventually Henri declared that he was tired of talking about himself and it was her turn. She told him what she could about her work without divulging any classified information, which was actually quite a lot, especially when she added in the humorous bits about the soldiers being absolutely flabbergasted to hear a woman's voice on the line, and the exciting, terrifying moments when the women refused to abandon their posts even as German shells exploded all around them.

To her delight, Henri seemed thoroughly impressed. "You really are a soldier," he remarked, slipping an arm around her shoulders and hugging her to his side. "My big sister, a switchboard soldier." When she laughed lightly, he said, "What? Don't you like that nickname?"

"No, quite the opposite. I like it very much. It's certainly better than 'hello girls,' or that dreadful title some hack writer used in *Stars and Stripes* last month."

"And what title is that?"

"I can't repeat it. It's too awful."

"You have to. It's only fair. You know about 'Hollywood Hank.'"

Valerie sighed, exasperated. "He called us 'Telephonettes.'"

"What?" Henri stopped short and clasped a hand to his brow, laughing and groaning at the same time. "You're right. That's truly awful."

"I know." Valerie tugged on his arm to get him moving again. "I hope it doesn't catch on."

They walked along, sharing amusing stories about their work, confiding their worries and fears, and reminiscing about home and family and days gone by. Night had fallen, and it was dangerously close to curfew by the time their stroll led them back to Valerie's quarters. They stood on the sidewalk, drawing out their goodbyes, not knowing when they might meet again.

"Listen, Valerie," said Henri. "When the war is over, you should go back to USC and finish your degree."

"Henri, we've been through this. Our family can't afford to send us both."

"Our family won't need to. When I get home, I'm going into the motion picture business. With the training and experience I've gotten Over Here, I know I can find a job."

"But Henri—"

"Not another word. It's decided." He tugged on the brim of her hat playfully, but then his smile faded. "One more thing." He took an envelope from his jacket pocket, thick enough to hold several sheets of folded paper, and placed it in her hands. "If I don't make it—"

"Don't say things like that," Valerie protested. "You're going to be fine. You're just touring the country taking movies of parades and things. I'm the one under the constant threat of bombardment and invasion."

"If I don't make it," he began again, patient, "I've written letters for you, Mama, and Hilde. Don't read yours unless—well, you know. Will you please make sure Hilde and Mama get theirs?"

"I won't need to," she grumbled, slipping the envelope into her pocket, where it felt like a lead weight. "You're going to make it home with lots of thrilling stories and not a scratch on you. If either of us should be writing 'just in case' letters, I should."

He regarded her seriously. "Maybe you should, Valerie."

She heaved a sigh and tossed her head. "Don't be ridiculous," she scoffed, thinking of the letters she had written in early June at the height of the bombardment, already safely tucked away in her footlocker. "It's not like we're in the trenches."

"No," he said, hesitant. "Not yet, anyway."

She felt a chill, as if he knew something he wasn't telling her, but when she searched his eyes, she couldn't see any deception in them. He was only speculating about a possibility, she decided. Neither of them knew where the AEF might ask them to report for duty next.

It was time to part. They embraced, made each other promise to write soon and often, and said goodbye.

With one last kiss on the cheek, Henri smiled, turned away, and strode off down the street. Valerie lingered on the sidewalk watching after him, heart aching, until he vanished into the blackout.

18

JULY 1918

Neufchâteau

MARIE

Of all the tasks the Signal Corps had required Marie to perform since she had enlisted, saying farewell to the children's choir, especially to Gisèle, was the most heartbreaking. Marie had been given so little advance notice of her transfer that there was no time to properly prepare the children, so she asked Sister Agnès to help her break the news gently. Marie paced in the chapel where she had spent so many happy hours directing the choir during rehearsals and Sunday morning masses, trying to conjure up the right words. The few phrases she managed to string together fled her thoughts the moment Sister Agnès and another nun led the children into the chapel and quietly instructed them to be seated. Gisèle and some of her choristers entered smiling, assuming something fun and musical was about to happen, but one glance at Marie's stricken face and their smiles faded.

Marie realized then that nothing she could say would make this parting any easier to bear. So she simply told them the truth, clearly and simply: She had been transferred, which meant that she would be leaving in the morning, and she did not know whether she would return. Many of the girls wept openly, and some of the boys looked as if they wanted to, but scowled instead and balled their hands into fists.

"I've loved being your teacher," Marie told them, fighting back her own tears. "I hope you all continue to sing and to enjoy music throughout your lives."

With a sob, Gisèle bolted from her seat and ran to embrace her. A moment later, Marie was surrounded by a crowd of children, all trying to hug her at once, some declaring that they would miss her forever, others begging her not to go. It was heartrending, but she forced a smile and hugged them back and promised to visit if she could.

Marie's only consolation was that Martina had agreed to take over the children's choir and music lessons. Martina was a gifted singer and pianist, the daughter of a celebrated Belgian clarinetist and conductor who had come to the United States as the Belgian consul for Wisconsin and had accepted a professor's chair at a conservatory in Green Bay. In addition to her musical expertise, Martina was also very kind and patient, so Marie could take comfort in knowing that the children would benefit from her gentle affection as well as her tutelage.

Back in the convent dormitory, while Marie packed up her gear, friends came by her cot to kiss her on both cheeks and wish her *bon voyage*. Some of them comically lamented about being left behind while she moved closer to the front, closer to the excitement and danger and adventure they all craved. Marie laughed and teased them right back to hide the ache in her heart.

She left the convent early the next morning, an hour before the shift change, but a few friends arranged to see her off at the train station before they reported to the switchboards. A Signal Corps lieutenant met her on the platform, helped her aboard, and introduced her to two other telephone operators who were being transferred from a different Services of Supply base farther to the west. The whistle sounded, the train chugged out of the station, and about fifteen minutes later, the lieutenant gave each operator an envelope with her orders. Marie discovered that she had been assigned to Neufchâteau, in the Vosges *département*. Roughly sixty kilometers northeast of Chaumont, the Neufchâteau office was the closest telephone exchange to the front lines.

Months ago Marie would have been thrilled to receive that very assignment, but now she accepted it with numb resignation.

The journey was long and arduous, and just as when she had traveled from Paris to Tours, their train frequently was required to pull over onto a station's sidetrack in order to make way for a train on a more urgent mission. They arrived in Paris by midafternoon, but they stayed only long enough to change trains. Even as Marie and the other two operators hurried to keep up with the lieutenant's long strides as they moved from one platform to another, Marie glanced at the people she passed, hoping to see a familiar face, but she recognized no beloved relatives, no long-lost friends. So many people milled about the station that she thought she surely must know someone in the crowd, but perhaps she glanced in the wrong direction just as their paths crossed and had missed them. Perhaps loved ones were searching the crowd as she was, hoping, always hoping—but they would have no reason to let their gaze linger on the woman in the U.S. Signal Corps uniform, and so an improbable meeting was rendered impossible.

Marie and her companions reached their connecting train with time to spare, so while the lieutenant saw to their gear, the operators purchased *ficelles* and cheese from a vendor and hurried aboard just as the final whistle sounded. Marie watched the passing scenery as she ate her lunch, and chatted a bit with her companions, one a French Canadian girl from Montreal, the other an American born in Michigan to French immigrant parents. Although they did not discuss their orders, Marie assumed they were all headed to Neufchâteau, so she was surprised when the train stopped at Chaumont and all three of her companions rose, gathered their belongings, and began to disembark.

"You'll be all right on your own, won't you?" the lieutenant asked, studying her. "My orders are to report to headquarters here, but I could find someone else to escort you the rest of the way."

Marie assured him she would be perfectly fine. What could an escort do for her, she wondered as the lieutenant headed down the aisle to the exit, that she could not do for herself for the last, brief leg of the journey? She had spent much of her childhood in Lorraine, and the closer she came to the familiar landscape of her youth, the more at home she felt. The German guns were quiet for the moment, and another officer was meeting her in Neufchâteau, so an escort would have been quite superfluous—unless that escort was Giovanni, in which case she would wish the journey was a hundred kilometers longer.

She must write to Giovanni as soon as possible to tell him about her transfer, although she was forbidden to tell him where she would be posted. The censor would flag her letter if she tried. She must let him know that she had left Tours before he tried to ring her there again. What would he think if he asked for her and was told that Operator Four was gone? Or what if her number had been given to her replacement, and the new girl reported the strange call to her supervisor? Marie did not know what the consequences would be if Giovanni were caught using military lines for a personal call, and yet she could not regret, even for a moment, that he had risked it.

She smiled to herself, remembering the sound of Giovanni's voice in her ear over the wire. How wonderfully unexpected his call had been. Suddenly a wave of loneliness and longing swept over her, and she missed him with such unexpected intensity that she felt as if all the air had been squeezed from her lungs. Taking a deep, tremulous breath, she turned toward the window, pressing a hand to her lips where he had kissed her, gazing out at the twilight landscape but seeing none of it. The strength of her feelings for this man made no sense. As many hours as she had devoted to thinking and wondering and dreaming about Giovanni, in truth, she hardly knew him. He might be unkind. He might be boring. She did not know, she *could* not know, and she should not presume that she did.

And yet when she realized that he would be unable to call her again, since she could not mention her new location in a letter, her heart plummeted. He would not know where to search for her, unless he called every Signal Corps telephone exchange in France and asked for Cherubino on the chance that she would pick up.

She smiled at how easy it was to imagine him doing exactly that.

It was late by the time the train finally halted in Neufchâteau, the blackout so complete that from her window she could barely see the station on the other side of the platform. Descending from the train with her gear, she shivered as the cool breeze touched her face, a jolt to her senses after the still, stifling air of the train. Setting down her bag and footlocker, glancing around the platform for her escort, she turned her gaze to the night sky, brilliantly awash in starlight undimmed by light from the farms and towns below. Even so far out into the countryside, on what ought to be a tranquil summer night, the villagers must conceal the warmth of their lamps and hearths behind blackout curtains or put their entire community in danger.

She realized the other passengers had mostly dispersed and she was standing quite alone when the conductor leaned out of the train to peer at her quizzically. "Are you all right, miss?"

"Yes, I'm fine, thank you. I'm—" She glanced around at the empty platform, pondering her options. Her orders had not mentioned where she would be staying, so if her escort failed to appear, she would have a hard time finding her quarters. "I'm being met," she called back to the conductor, nodding to assure him all was well. He did not look convinced.

Suddenly she heard swift footsteps approaching, and she turned to see a lanky young lieutenant running toward her. "Miss DeSmedt?"

"Here," she replied, holding up her hand, an entirely unnecessary gesture since he hardly needed to pick her out of a crowd.

Even in the dim light, she could see that his cheeks were flushed from embarrassment. "I'm sorry I'm late," he said, hefting her bag and footlocker. "I hope you weren't waiting long."

"Not at all," she assured him. "I was just enjoying the quiet evening."

"We all enjoy those, when we can get them." He inclined his head toward the end of the platform, barely visible despite the faint glow of fluorescent paint. "Right this way."

She followed him down a small but precarious staircase and around to the front of the building, where a Winton Six was parked at the curb. While the lieutenant stowed her gear, Marie looked off to the distance, where intermittent flashes of light briefly illuminated rolling, forested hills. When she heard a low rumble, she asked, "Do you suppose that storm will blow this way or move on?"

"I hope it doesn't come any closer, miss," the lieutenant replied, shutting the trunk and opening the passenger door for her. "That's German artillery."

She felt a chill. "Of course," she said faintly. She seated herself in the car, and the lieutenant closed her door for her and took the driver's seat. "Are you often bombed here?"

"Often enough," he said. "I take it you didn't see much action at your previous post?"

"Nothing like that," she admitted, unable to tear her gaze away from the distant lights.

"You'll get used to it," he said. "The Germans are only about twenty kilometers off, though, so you shouldn't ever let your guard down. When you hear an air raid siren, never assume it's just a drill. Take cover immediately. Have you had gas mask training?"

"Not yet."

"Your supervisor has probably already scheduled you for it, but if not, make sure you get it done. The other girls can tell you who to ask."

"Thanks for the advice."

They drove along for a while in silence, broken from time to time when the lieutenant pointed out certain important buildings she ought to know, but they were almost entirely obscured by the blackout and she was fairly confident she would not recognize them by daylight. Weariness steadily overcame her, and she was about to rest her head against the seatback and try to doze when the automobile slowed and came to a stop before a two-story stucco residence with a steep hipped roof and dormers.

Carrying her gear, the lieutenant led the way up the cobblestone path to the front door, which opened as they approached. "Come in, come in," a woman said in American-accented English, beckoning, silhouetted by the dim light from within. "I'm Miss Macarthur, and you must be Miss Miossec. My, oh my, what a long, exhausting day you must have had!"

Marie allowed herself to be fussed over while Miss Macarthur ushered her into a narrow foyer with a stone floor, plaster walls, and a small
alcove where a brass kerosene lamp burned. The lieutenant brought in
her gear, looked around the foyer, and craned his neck to see past the
hostess down the hallway, where the sound of quiet voices and muffled
laughter came, as well as the aromas of ratatouille and rosemary bread.
"I guess I'll be going," he said, turning his gaze back to Marie. "If you
need anything while you're here, I'm at your service."

"Thank you, Lieutenant," she said, smiling. "I'm sure I'll be fine."

"Thank you," he said, taking a step back toward the door and nearly
stumbling over her footlocker. "See you around."

He left hastily, shutting the door behind him.

"Goodness," said Miss Macarthur, eyebrows rising. "He certainly is
smitten. 'At your service,' indeed."

"He was just being kind," said Marie. "He didn't even tell me how to
find him if I did need him."

"Oh, I'm sure he'll find you." Miss Macarthur grasped the handle of
her bag. "If you can manage the footlocker, I'll show you to your room.
Unless you'd like a bit of supper first?"

Marie was too exhausted to eat. "No, just a bath and bed."

"This way, then."

Miss Macarthur led her down the narrow hall, past a doorway on
the left through which Marie glimpsed a few girls reading, chatting,
writing letters, and playing chess by lamplight, the blackout curtains
firmly in place. Farther ahead, just past a staircase on the right, was a
juncture with another hallway, but Miss Macarthur trooped upstairs,
and Marie followed.

"The kitchen, dining room, and lounge are on the ground floor,"
Miss Macarthur said, huffing with exertion as they climbed the stairs.
"Laundry's out back, if you prefer to do your own, but most of the girls
trust their things to two laundresses from the village who come weekly.
Widowed sisters, very reasonable rates." At the top of the stairs, she
paused to catch her breath, then gestured down one long hallway to the
right, and the short extension to the left. "Two bathrooms, one at each

end, and with four girls to a room, the unwritten rule is that you keep your visits as quick as you can, especially at peak hours." Miss Macarthur led her halfway down the longer hall and set down her bag in front of a door that hung slightly ajar, lamplight spilling from the narrow crack around it.

"You'll be in here." Miss Macarthur knocked twice on the door. "Ladies? Your new bunkmate has arrived."

Marie heard the creaking of bedsprings, and moments later the door swung open, revealing a familiar, round, bespectacled face, a stout figure clad in a nightgown and robe. "Marie!" Berthe exclaimed, opening the door wider and stepping forward to kiss her on both cheeks. "I can't believe it! When they said we were getting a new girl, I thought they meant a *new* new girl, not an old friend from Hobo House!"

"Berthe Hunt," Marie said, delighted. "I'm so happy to see you. I assumed I was going to be among strangers."

"Who's a stranger?" asked another pajama-clad girl, stepping into view behind Berthe. She looked to be around twenty years old, with fine light brown bobbed hair, brown eyes, and an impish grin. "Oh, hello. You must be the new girl. Come on in. Make yourself at home."

"We can take it from here, Miss Macarthur," said Berthe, lifting Marie's footlocker while the younger girl took the bag. They brought her into the room, which was deeper than it was wide, with rough walls of dark horizontal wooden slats and a dormer window at the far end. Beneath the window was a desk, upon which rested an alarm clock and a kerosene lamp, nearly identical to the one in the foyer. Two beds were placed end to end along both sides, and the walls above three of them were adorned with photographs, pictures from magazines, and a poster of Joan of Arc. The bed to Marie's immediate right was neatly made up, but the walls were bare, which told her it was as yet unclaimed. Sure enough, her bunkmates stowed her gear beneath it.

Berthe quickly made introductions. The younger girl was Adele Hoppock, from Seattle; she had come to Neufchâteau directly from Le Havre when the Third Group arrived in France in May. "Was my sister with you in Tours?" she asked, hopeful. "Her name's Eleanor. She left

New York with the Fourth Group at the end of June."

Marie shook her head. "I'm sorry, no," she said, removing her shoes and sinking down onto her bed. The mattress was thinner than those in the convent, the pillow flatter, the blanket rougher, but it would do. "No one from the Fourth Group had been posted to our Services of Supply base yet."

"They might still be at sea," Berthe mused, "or in Southampton."

"Well, they won't post Eleanor here, that's for sure," said Adele glumly. "They always split up sisters."

Marie's third bunkmate, they told her, was Alice from Chicago, also from the Third Group. At the moment she was downstairs in the lounge, playing chess with a partner if she had been able to coax someone into a game, playing against herself if she had not. "She's fun to play against if you like a challenge," said Adele, "but if she asks you if you want to make it a little more interesting—"

"Decline," Berthe interrupted. "Unless you enjoy losing your money."

"Thanks for the warning." Marie thought fondly of Valerie, whom she had not seen since Hoboken. She too loved a competitive game of chess. "Berthe," she asked tentatively. "You haven't mentioned your husband. Is there any news?"

"I haven't heard from Reuben since the end of March." Berthe bit her lips together, forcing a tight smile and a shrug. "The men can't send letters when they're at sea, of course, so I wasn't really expecting anything. I trust he'll post a letter or two when his ship finally comes into harbor."

"Sometimes no news is good news," Adele reminded her.

"That's what I keep telling myself. I haven't heard anything about any attacks on the *Moccasin*, so I must assume that Reuben is safe, wherever he is." Berthe removed her glasses, cleaned them with her handkerchief, and returned them to the bridge of her nose. "We knew when we parted that we wouldn't be able to correspond regularly, so we're each keeping a diary. After the war, we'll exchange them, and we'll learn what the other experienced."

"We never heard you say that," said Adele, stretching out on her bed and folding her arms beneath her head. It was strictly against regulations to keep a diary, due to the potential for a serious security breach if it fell into enemy hands. Marie was surprised to hear that someone as dutiful and principled as Berthe would break the rules, but then again, Grace Banker was equally scrupulous, and Marie had seen her writing in a cloth-covered notebook when she thought herself unobserved. As long as a diary was a record of one's personal experiences and impressions rather than a catalog of military secrets, Marie couldn't see the harm.

Heartened by her bunkmates' friendly welcome, Marie went to the bathroom to wash and to brush her teeth, and returned to find her three bunkmates already in bed. In whispers she introduced herself to Alice, who offered her a cheerful if drowsy welcome. After changing into her pajamas, Marie hung up her uniform on the pegs near the foot of her bed and stole quietly across the room to dowse the lamp. Before she could, Berthe, whose bed was nearest, propped herself up on one elbow and reached for the switch. "I'll get it," she whispered. "You get into bed first, so you don't trip in the dark."

Marie thanked her and climbed into her bed, but as darkness filled the room, she remembered an important question. "Berthe? What time does our shift begin in the morning?"

"We run three shifts of eight operators each," said Berthe through a yawn. "You're our twenty-fourth. You're probably on the day shift with us, from eight o'clock until four, since we've been one operator short."

"You must be on day shift," Adele chimed in sleepily. "Girls from different shifts are never assigned to the same rooms, or we'd be waking each other up all the time."

Marie was surprised that as a newcomer, she had been given the best shift. "I'm relieved I wasn't assigned to nights," she confessed, settling back against her pillow. "I imagine that's the least popular."

"Not necessarily," said Berthe, her voice fading. "Some girls prefer to be at the switchboards when the air raids come rather than being jolted awake by the siren. We've had long stretches when the girls on the night shift are better rested than anyone."

Marie inhaled deeply, unsettled, yet her exhaustion was so complete that not even the fear of German bombs could keep her awake. A moment later she sank into sleep, the faults she had found with her bed earlier completely forgotten.

The next morning as Marie and her bunkmates prepared for the day, Adele cheerfully told her that their residence had no modern conveniences but did employ an excellent cook, so they ate well. Both claims proved true after Marie hurried through a sponge bath, slipped into a clean uniform, and enjoyed a breakfast of flaky croissants with honey, fresh raspberries, and real coffee with cream.

The abundance struck Marie as incongruous with the haggard conditions of the refugees from eastern France who had fled to Tours. "Where did all of this come from?" she marveled as she spread honey on a croissant.

"The raspberries grow wild, although every garden in the village seems to boast a raspberry patch," said Berthe. "The cream and butter are purchased from local farms."

"Everything else comes from Uncle Sam," said Adele, raising her coffee cup to her nose, closing her eyes, and inhaling deeply, savoring the aroma.

Marie hoped that meant the local farmers were eating well too, but it was hard to imagine how they managed to grow crops unspoiled by Germans bombs. She also hoped the armies did not buy up all the local produce, leaving nothing for the villagers.

The telephone office was about a mile away down a rustic country road from their residence in Neufchâteau to the Division Headquarters the AEF had constructed south of the village. The morning was still cool and misty as Marie, her bunkmates, and the other four day shift girls set out on foot, but the bright sunshine promised summery warmth by midday.

"Don't let this fine weather fool you," Alice warned. "It rains here, a lot, and when it does, this road is a quagmire."

As they walked along, Adele and Berthe told Marie about her new posting, with occasional interjections from the others. Since late 1917, the AEF compound had served as a training facility for infantry and engineers, and included barracks, offices, hospitals, YMCA huts, and other essential buildings. Some of the infantry training took place in the hills beyond Fréville, about ten kilometers southwest of Neufchâteau, but the engineers had also constructed a network of training trenches in the countryside near the base, including a system of fire, cover, and support trenches large enough for an entire battalion to practice attack and defensive maneuvers.

"Naturally, all of this activity fascinates the Germans," said Berthe. "It's a rare day when they don't have observation planes in the skies above us."

"We're a favorite target of their long guns and bombs too," said Adele. "Our soldiers don't dare go about in large formations, and we've all learned to evacuate buildings quickly so we don't get trapped in a collapse."

"Stay close to us until you get the hang of it," Berthe advised. "We'll look out for you."

When they reached the AEF base, Marie discovered a veritable city of large wooden structures on concrete foundations, all efficiency and function with no regard for aesthetics, incongruously planted in the lovely French countryside. On the dirt roads between them, hundreds of officers, soldiers, nurses, and civilian employees bustled about on urgent business, making way for automobiles, trucks, and horse-drawn delivery wagons. The Signal Corps building, discernible at a distance by the profusion of telegraph and telephone wires emanating from it, was near the administrative heart of the base, adjacent to Division Headquarters. Marie's companions showed her inside to the telephone office, a large room on the first floor, where a quick glance revealed two vintage camp boards and a two-position magneto local board, of French manufacture circa 1880, from the look of it. The entire system looked alarmingly worse for wear, but based upon the swift, steady, controlled motions of the night shift operators and the low hum of their voices, everything seemed to be in perfect order.

Berthe presented her to Elsie Hunter, the chief operator and a fellow member of the First Group. Elsie welcomed Marie cordially and invited her to walk the aisles and observe the night shift girls before taking her station, "Just in case there are any significant differences between our equipment and Tours," she explained.

"There are, but I trained on this model in Chicago," Marie assured her.

"This one has a few quirks. If a bomb goes off close enough to shake the walls and windows, active calls will drop and it can be all but impossible to connect with anyone new." Elsie shook her head, exasperated. "That's if you can even hear the callers over the sounds of the explosions. And oh, when those bombs drop, the pressure wave goes right through you. You'll find out."

Marie laughed weakly. "Not today, I hope."

"You and me both." Elsie glanced at her watch. "Speaking of attacks, you should report for gas mask training after your shift. Do you know where the chemical department is?"

"We'll show her the way," said Adele. "We'll get her safely back to quarters afterward too."

Elsie nodded her approval and left to assist another operator. Marie had a few minutes to familiarize herself with the switchboard before it was time to relieve the night shift. From the moment she took her station and put on her headset, the calls came in at such a fast, relentless pace that she had little time to dread gas mask training or to wonder why she might need an escort afterward. A few days earlier, the German army had launched an offensive to expand their salient at the Marne and encircle Reims, thrusting across the river into the mixed French and American units deployed there. In response, numerous U.S. Army divisions had joined the effort to force the Germans back from the Marne to the Vesle, weakening the salient and eliminating the threat to Paris.

The switchboard fairly sizzled with activity. The operators could barely keep up with the pace of calls—calls conveying military orders, news of advances and withdrawals, requests to evacuate wounded men—and there never seemed to be enough cords or jacks to handle the volume. Marie was exhausted when an operator from the afternoon shift relieved her hours later, but she suspected that the worst task of the day still awaited her.

"Gas mask training isn't pleasant," Berthe admitted as she and Adele showed Marie to the chemical department, a mostly concrete building on the edge of the compound. "Just follow the instructions and you'll be fine."

"We'll be waiting for you right here," Adele called after her as Marie steeled herself and went inside.

Signs directed her to a small room where two nurses and at least ten men from a variety of AEF departments waited, scattered in pairs or trios among the rows of folding chairs. Adele sat near the other women, close enough to be friendly but not to intrude, and waited while a few other men hurried in. Last of all, a grim-faced sergeant entered followed by two privates, each carrying a pile of khaki cloth haversacks. Marie had noticed the other telephone operators carrying identical bags, but she had not asked what they were. Now she knew.

"This is your gas mask," the sergeant declared as the soldiers began distributing them to the trainees. "Carry it with you at all times. If you use it properly, it could save your life."

The privates, who had each kept a haversack for themselves, returned to the front of the room and flanked the sergeant, facing the trainees. "Watch carefully," the sergeant barked, then went through the instructions for using the gas masks while his assistants demonstrated. Then the sergeant ordered the trainees to stand and to follow along as he walked them through the procedure.

"Carry the haversack on your left side with the sling on your right shoulder and the flap next to your torso," he ordered.

Marie quickly obeyed, glancing from her haversack to the nearest assistant and back to be sure she was doing it properly.

"Use the buckle on the left side to adjust the length. Do not, I repeat, do not hook any gear through the buckle. It is not meant to carry equipment." The sergeant eyed them, frowned, and continued when everyone was ready. "For alert position, raise the haversack onto your chest and engage the fastener, adjusting for the correct height with the buckle on the right side. *Right* side," he repeated for the benefit of an engineer in the front row. "Now take the cord from the knapsack, pass it through the right-hand ring on the bottom of the haversack, around your body, and tie it securely to the ring on the left side."

Marie quickly imitated the assistants. All around her, other trainees followed or fumbled through the instructions with varying degrees of success. "It's easier than a corset," one of the nurses whispered to her companion. Marie hid a smile.

"At this point, yank the flap open, but keep it folded against your body to keep out the damp," the sergeant continued. "Or the rain, or the snow, or the mud, as the case may be." He looked around the room. "Try to keep up," he said sharply to a pair of Signal Corps linemen. "All right. Now, when the alarm sounds, remove the mask from the haversack. Use both hands, your thumbs pointing upward under the elastic. Push your chin far into the mask, and pull the elastic over your head as far as possible."

Marie obeyed, wincing at the strangely acidic smell of the rubberized cloth. The assistants' motions were more difficult to observe through the mask's glass eyepieces, but she managed.

"Next, shove the rubber mouthpiece into your mouth, placing your lips over the rubber flange, and grip the mouthpiece with your teeth."

Marie struggled to comply, carefully easing the mouthpiece in rather than shoving it. It seemed much too large and she feared she might gag. She willed her heart to stop racing as the sergeant described how to adjust the nose clip to seal the nostrils by pinching the circular wire from the outside of the mask.

"If you must speak," the sergeant said, "first, breathe in deeply. Leave the nose clips in place, remove the mouthpiece, say what you have to say, and replace the mouthpiece immediately. Again, do not touch the nose clips."

Marie resolved never to attempt to speak during a gas attack. Hand gestures would have to suffice.

"That's all there is to it," the sergeant said, planting his hands on his hips and surveying the room. "Let's try it again, this time at a pace that won't get you killed."

He led them through the procedure again and again while his assistants demonstrated, each time at a faster pace. "This must become second nature to you," he said, pacing the aisles, correcting one trainee, nodding approval to another. Finally, when he was satisfied, he told them to keep their masks on and follow him down the hallway, where he paused before a closed door, solid, without windows. "Gas canisters have been deployed in this room," he told them. "You are to go inside, and when you hear me pound on the door, remove your masks. Keep them off until I pound on the door a second time, and then put on your masks."

Marie's heart thudded. Removing her mouthpiece, she asked, "Is there mustard gas inside, Sergeant?"

He regarded her for a moment with something that might have been sympathy. "No, miss. Not mustard gas. The Germans have several deadly gases at their disposal. This is one of the least harmful, and we're using a weak concentrate. We don't want to injure you. We just want you to understand why the masks are so necessary."

Marie nodded and replaced her mouthpiece, checking with her hands to make sure every part of the mask was in place. The sergeant gave the trainees one last appraising look, then donned his own gas mask, opened the door, waved them in quickly, and slammed the door shut behind them.

Marie struggled to keep her breaths slow and even, but her heart pounded and she wanted to bolt from the room. It was difficult to breathe through the mask, and she tasted and smelled rubber, but although the air was faintly, ominously cloudy, it did not burn her skin.

Two loud thuds sounded on the door.

Everyone held still for a moment, but then one officer began removing his gas mask, and everyone else quickly followed suit. As soon as the air struck Marie's face, she smelled something acrid and began to cough and sneeze. Tears streamed from her eyes as if she were weeping, mucus from her nose. It was horrible, uncontrollable, but even when she squeezed her eyes shut the tears flowed.

Two more dull thuds. Hands shaking, Marie struggled to put her mask on again, but even after she had everything in place, her eyes stung and throat burned. The gas must have contaminated the inside of the mask the moment she removed it. Was it doing her any good at all now?

Just then she heard a loud mechanical buzzing overhead, and as she glanced around for the source, she saw that the cloudy air was clearing, enough that she could see two large ventilation fans whirring at the opposite end of the room. Eventually the door opened, and the sergeant stood before them. "You can exit now," he told them, gesturing. "Wait to remove your masks until you're in the hallway."

Marie followed instructions, pulling off her mask, leaning against the wall, gasping and wiping her eyes. Though her vision was blurred, she could see that the other trainees were similarly disoriented. If this was one of the least harmful gases, she shuddered to imagine what the troops at the front endured in a real attack, what Giovanni might endure.

Soon thereafter, the sergeant led them back into the other room. There, while his assistants demonstrated, he told them how to clean the masks after use. Marie's symptoms had begun to dissipate by the time she finished.

"What you experienced today is negligible compared to what you would endure in an actual gas attack," the sergeant told them. "Some of the kaiser's poisons blister and burn the skin. Imagine what they would do to your lungs. Your haversack should never be beyond arm's reach, whether you're posted to the front lines or an office."

The trainees nodded solemnly. The sergeant asked for questions, but no one had any, so the training session ended. Marie made her way outside, where she found Berthe and Adele waiting. Berthe gave her a handkerchief soaked in cool water, and Marie carefully bathed her eyes, easing the sting.

"How was it?" asked Adele.

"It was pretty terrible, actually," said Marie, managing a wan smile.

Her vision was still blurry, and tears still leaked from her eyes. Anyone who saw her would think she had suffered a devastating loss.

"Let's get her home," Berthe said to Adele. To Marie she added, "Lean on us if you need to."

A wave of gratitude swept over her. "Thank you," she said, clearing her throat. "I will."

She did not know if she would ever call Neufchâteau home as Berthe had, even only as a convenient name for their quarters, but kind and thoughtful friends could make this unfamiliar, hazardous place seem a little less harrowing.

They were within sight of their residence when the air raid siren began to wail.

Adele seized Marie's hand. "Come on," she urged, breaking into a trot. "We'll show you to the bomb shelter."

Berthe took Marie's other hand, and they ran.

19

JULY–AUGUST 1918

Chaumont and Ligny-en-Barrois

GRACE

On July 20, the German commander ordered a retreat, and in the days that followed, the German armies were forced back to the positions from where they had launched the Spring Offensive months before. At the end of July, after weeks of brutal fighting, the Allied counteroffensive led by Supreme Allied Commander Ferdinand Foch finally drove the Germans out of the Marne region.

From the end of July into August, the Allies continued to hammer away at the German defensive line, assaults that resulted in massive casualties for little gain. By August 6, the Allied counterattack stalled when the Central Powers renewed their offensives. Even so, the front had been moved eastward roughly forty-five kilometers, restricting the enemy behind a line running along the Aisne and Vesle Rivers. As significant as the strategic gains in territory were, Grace thought that the surge in morale might eventually prove to be equally important. The Allied victory in the Second Battle of the Marne decisively ended a streak of German victories, and Grace dared to hope that the tide of the war had turned at last.

Now it seemed that the attention of the AEF had shifted to Amiens and certain regions along the Somme, but what General Pershing's intentions were, Grace could only guess. Yet at Chaumont, the war seemed to pause for a single day, when President Poincaré came to town to award General Pershing the Grand Cross of the Legion of Honor, the highest and most distinguished decoration France could bestow.

The telephone lines hummed the day before the ceremony as the arrangements were made for the French president's visit. General Pershing was away from headquarters, but he would return by train early the next morning in time to meet President Poincaré when he arrived at nine o'clock. From the station, the general would escort the president to the caserne and present him to his chief officers, after which they would travel together to the parade grounds where the decoration ceremony would take place.

When final plans for the ceremony were announced, the Signal Corps operators were thrilled to learn that they would be included among the troops presented for review.

At nine o'clock in the morning of August 6, Grace and her comrades stood in formation on the parade grounds among the other units and battalions, their uniforms perfect in every detail. Despite the early hour, the day promised to be the hottest of the summer thus far, with clear skies and sunshine streaming down upon the Allied military representatives and the French troops, who had formed an orderly square around the perimeter. A trumpet fanfare heralded the arrival of the dignitaries, but as far as Grace could tell, everyone remained at attention, eyes forward and backs straight, resisting the temptation to crane their necks and look. Soon the famed dark green Locomobile Model 48 pulled up to the quadrangle, and General Pershing and President Poincaré disembarked, the general splendid in his uniform, the president elegant in a dark suit and hat. Accompanied by their aides, the two leaders separated and headed in opposing directions, and as an American military band played "La Marseillaise," the general and the president entered the square formation from opposite sides and strode with great dignity and purpose to meet in the center.

President Poincaré addressed the assembly first, in heavily accented

English, declaring himself delighted to have the honor to present the *Grand-croix de la Légion d'honneur* to the organizer and leader of France's valiant ally. He said he was especially pleased to seize the opportunity to thank General Pershing and the brave army under his command for the gallant work accomplished on the battlefield in recent weeks. Then, rising up on tiptoe, the five-foot-four president lifted the wide red ribbon over the six-foot-tall general's head, placed the medal precisely on the center of his chest, and kissed him soundly on both cheeks. At the last moment, General Pershing had stooped slightly to make the traditional kiss easier for the shorter man to bestow, but the flush rising in his cheeks revealed that he had not expected the very French gesture.

The general recovered his composure in time to make a few brief remarks of his own, thanking the president for the honor, which he valued as a mark of friendship and respect from France for the entire U.S. Army. Then, as the military band struck up a stirring march, General Pershing and President Poincaré reviewed the troops. Grace hardly noticed the hot sun pouring down, nor the strain on her muscles from standing at attention, so thrilled and honored was she to be a part of the historic moment. The Republic of France could offer no greater military distinction than the Grand Cross of the Legion of Honor, and it had been bestowed upon General Pershing not only as a symbol of the nation's great esteem for the man, but also for the country that had chosen him to lead its armies.

As soon as the ceremony was over, General Pershing, President Poincaré, and their aides departed in the general's car to escort the president and his entourage to the train station. The troops were dismissed, and whether the telephone operators hurried off to the switchboards, returned to the house on Rue Brûle, or strolled into Chaumont, all left glowing from pride and a sense of accomplishment for their role in General Pershing's success.

Grace's spirits were still buoyed from the grand event the next afternoon when she attended a meeting in Lieutenant Riser's office to discuss the imminent arrival of several new operators from Group Four. The other officers clearly shared her feelings, for after their business was concluded, they lingered to chat about the ceremony and how well the Signal Corps had acquitted itself at the review.

"Miss Banker, could you stay behind for a moment?" Lieutenant Riser asked when the group finally dispersed.

"Of course," she said, and after the other officers filed out of the room, she seated herself in one of the two chairs in front of his desk. "What can I do for you, Lieutenant?"

He began to speak, hesitated, then leaned forward to rest his elbows on his desk. "I wondered if you might be free for dinner Saturday evening."

For a moment Grace could only look at him, struggling to conceal her dismay. She and the lieutenant had become quite good chums during the months they had worked together, but she considered him a friend and colleague, nothing less but nothing more. She wanted the lieutenant to respect her as a fellow soldier, not to court her.

Her thoughts flew to Mack. Although he had been absent from Chaumont many weeks, whenever he returned to headquarters they saw each other, and were seen together, every day of his visits. Lieutenant Riser must have observed them often at dinners, parties, dances, and strolls around Chaumont. While it was true that they were careful to keep their kisses quick, discreet, and regrettably rare, surely Lieutenant Riser must realize that Grace preferred Mack.

Unless—perhaps the lieutenant knew something about Mack's preferences that Grace did not.

Grace and Mack had not spoken since early July, when he had stopped by the operators' house to tell her goodbye before he departed on an important mission. Although he could not reveal where he was going, as details came through the wires about Allied troop movements in northern France within days of his departure, Grace surmised that he had most likely gone south of the Somme near the village of Hamel, where several companies of American troops had been attached to Australian divisions for a joint operation, with additional support from British tank divisions. For more than a year, a German salient around the village had exposed Allied troops to unchecked enemy fire, and the

Australian commander had intended to retake the village, eliminate the salient, and strengthen the Allied defense line.

Grace had suspected that Mack was involved with this mission, but she had known nothing for certain. Unfortunately, she connected so few calls to the region that she overheard almost nothing about the battle once it had begun, and she knew better than to ask any of her superior officers, who would tell her nothing and might admonish her for prying into classified military matters beyond her purview. She understood the necessity for absolute secrecy, and she would never intentionally provoke a leak that might endanger the troops. Even so, she wished she knew whether Mack was indeed at Hamel, for uncertainty made her imagine the worst.

Perhaps Lieutenant Riser believed Grace had lost interest in Mack since he had been away so long. "Saturday," she said carefully, pretending to mull it over. "I'm not sure whether I'm free."

"Let me try that again," said the lieutenant, chagrined. "I've invited Miss Langelier to dinner at the Hôtel de France on Saturday. She has accepted, but we agreed that it would be appropriate for us to have a chaperone. We both believe that as her supervisor, and as someone who is excellent company, you would be ideal."

"I see." Grace smiled and heaved a sigh of relief. "In that case, I'd be delighted to join you and Miss Langelier for dinner."

"Very good. Thank you." Lieutenant Riser grinned, and then began to chuckle. "But if it were just me—"

"No," said Grace, laughing too. "I'm sorry, but the answer would have to be no."

"Say no more," said the lieutenant, sitting back into his chair, waving her off. "I mean that sincerely. Please, say no more. My ego is bruised enough already."

"Don't be ridiculous. You don't mean that." Grace wiped at her eyes, her laughter subsiding. "But you did have me very nervous for a moment."

"I'm truly sorry," he said, abashed. "In hindsight, perhaps Miss Langelier should have been the one to ask you."

"Yes, that might have been better," Grace agreed, rising from her chair. "Until Saturday, then."

She was still smiling to herself as she left the office and headed downstairs. It had been a grueling day on the switchboard, and she was looking forward to meeting Suzanne and Esther at their favorite café for a quick bite before unwinding with a scenic walk in the cool shade of the woods.

She was a few paces away from the exit when the door opened and Mack walked in.

She stopped short at precisely the same moment he did. For the space of a heartbeat he held her gaze, stunned, and then a broad smile broke across his face. "Miss Banker," he said, striding toward her, hand outstretched. "I was hoping to find you here."

"Captain Mack," she said, a trifle breathless, shaking his hand. It was as if her reminiscences had conjured him up, for there he was, at long last, looking a bit sun-browned but otherwise fine. Better than fine—unharmed, healthy, smiling, and as handsome as she remembered. "When did you get into town?"

"About an hour ago." He still held her hand, and his eyes had not left her face since he saw her from the doorway. "I went to the house on Rue Brûle, and they told me you were still here. Listen, could we . . . go for a walk?"

"Of course," she said. Mindful of the many eyes upon them, she quickly squeezed his hand before releasing it. He held the door open for her as they left the building, and by unspoken agreement, they turned toward the old town, one of their favorite places to stroll.

"I'm afraid I won't be in Chaumont long," he said after they had walked a few moments in silence.

Grace clasped her hands behind her back. "No time for dinner, then?"

He shook his head. "My train leaves in thirty minutes."

Despite her disappointment, Grace had to laugh. "In that case, we're heading in the wrong direction." Halting, she touched his arm to bring him to a stop too. "Why don't I escort you to the station instead?"

He gazed toward the old town, regretful. "This route has better scenery, and better memories." Nevertheless, he turned, and they walked side by side toward the depot.

Grace's cheeks grew warm at the vague compliment—he had meant memories of their time together, hadn't he?—but she kept her gaze on the road ahead. "Can you tell me where you're going?"

From the corner of her eye, she saw him frown ruefully and shake his head. "I'd like to, but you know I can't."

"Never mind," she said airily. "I don't need your help. I'll just note the direction your train takes and figure it out on my own." She threw him a smile to show him she was only teasing, but it quickly faded. "I wish I knew that you were on your way someplace quiet and calm."

"I wish I could tell you that was so."

She nodded, a catch in her throat. That was the only hint he would give her, but it was enough for her to know he was heading for the front.

"I wish we had more time," he murmured, as if thinking aloud. Suddenly he halted. "Miss Banker—Grace, I hope you know how much I've enjoyed our time together, and how much I've come to care about you."

For a moment she couldn't speak. "I feel the same," she managed to say. "I hope next time you pass through Chaumont, we'll have time for a proper conversation over a good meal."

"I'd like that very much, but while I'm gone—" He reached into his breast pocket and withdrew a small, flat case about the size of his palm, dark brown leather with brass fastenings. "I was wondering if you could keep this safe for me."

He held it out to her, and she gingerly accepted it. She lifted the lid to discover a medal, a bronze cross about two inches in height and slightly narrower in width, with an eagle in the center above a scroll that read, "For Valor." The service ribbon had a wide blue stripe in the center flanked on both sides by one narrow white stripe and one red.

"Mack," Grace gasped, "you earned the Distinguished Service Cross!" She had seen illustrations of the new medal President Wilson had established at General Pershing's request, but she had never seen one in person. It was the U.S. Army's second highest military decoration, bestowed to recognize extraordinary heroism and meritorious service to the government of the United States. "How—what—"

"I can't tell you why I received this honor," he said apologetically. "Not yet. After the war, yes, but not now."

She nodded, overwhelmed, and felt frightened for him after the fact. She was certain now that he had been at the Battle of Hamel, and had clearly risked his life there. "I look forward to hearing the whole story," she said, voice trembling, "after the war."

She closed the case, but when she tried to return it, he shook his head and closed her hands around it. "I'd like you to wear it."

"Wear it?" she echoed, stunned. "I couldn't possibly. I have no right. Whatever you did to earn this—"

"Then at least keep it safe for me." His voice was low and compelling, and yet it carried a note of humor. "It's likely to get lost or damaged where I'm going, and I don't think President Wilson would issue me a replacement."

Grace choked out a laugh. "Well, I'll keep it safe for you, since you put it that way, but only until you can take proper care of it."

"Agreed." He smiled warmly. "That'll do for now."

She smiled back, but suddenly holding his gaze became unbearable, and she looked away, the need to tuck the leather case safely into her pocket offering the perfect excuse. Then inspiration struck. "Here," she said, removing her Signal Corps pin from her lapel and holding it out to him. "Please accept this with my compliments."

He took the pin, brow furrowing slightly, and then grinned. "Is this collateral for the medal?"

She spread her hands and shrugged. "I don't have any paper to write out a receipt."

"All right, then." He fastened the pin to his shirt over his heart, where his uniform coat would conceal it. "It's a fair trade."

"A temporary exchange," she reminded him. "When you return"—he must return, he *must*—"we will each reclaim what is ours."

He nodded solemnly. "I'll willingly agree to that."

She felt heat rising in her cheeks again, and she wondered if he had heard more than she had intended to say. "Take good care of that pin," she said, keeping her voice steady. "I want it returned to me unharmed."

"I promised I'll do my best."

He reached for her hand, just as a train whistle blew. "That's my ride," he said, glancing over his shoulder.

"Oh dear." She wished they could have just a few moments alone for one wonderful, lingering kiss. "Now you'll have to run."

He took her hand, hesitated, and for a moment she thought he might pull her closer. Instead he squeezed her hand once and released it. "I'll make it," he said, taking two steps backward before breaking into a trot. "Take care of yourself, Miss Banker."

"You too, Captain Mack," she called after him as he broke into a run. She watched until he disappeared around the corner, her hand resting on the outside of her pocket that held his medal. Then she drew in a deep breath and went to join her friends at the café.

"You've been quiet this evening," Suzanne remarked later that night back at the residence as they prepared for bed. "Something on your mind?"

"Yes, actually." Grace withdrew the case from her pocket, lifted the lid, and showed her friend the medal inside. "It's a heavier weight than it seems."

"My goodness." Suzanne bent closer to examine it. "Congratulations, Grace. I've always said you're the best chief operator in the Signal Corps. It's about time General Pershing honored you."

"It's not mine, silly," said Grace, giving her a playful swat on the arm. "It's Captain Mack's."

"Oh?" Suzanne straightened, eyebrows rising. "He gave this to you?"

Grace nodded. "For safekeeping, he said, earlier today, when he passed through Chaumont. I had no time to think it over, and now he's gone, so I can't return it."

"Do you *want* to return it?"

"I don't know." Grace turned the case toward herself and contemplated the medal. Everyone knew its significance as a military honor, but what did it mean as a token when given from the man who earned it to a girl he admired? "He asked me to wear it. That would be completely inappropriate, of course, but I did promise to keep it safe for him."

Suzanne frowned quizzically. "So . . . what do you suppose this means?"

"I have no idea."

"Well, there's the obvious," Suzanne mused. "He loves you, and this is a symbol of the understanding between you."

"But we don't have an understanding, as far as I know, and he's never told me he loves me."

"Have you ever told him that you love him?"

"Of course not." A lady never confessed her feelings for a gentleman until he first expressed his own and made his intentions clear. In fact, it was prudent for a lady never to let herself feel too much for a gentleman until she was certain of his affections. What was certain about Captain Mack? His intentions were opaque, and saying that he enjoyed spending time with her and cared about her were hardly declarations of love. "I don't know if I *do* love him." Grace sighed, frustrated. "It would be so much easier if only I knew how *he* felt."

"Why do you suppose he hasn't told you?"

"I don't know. Maybe he doesn't feel anything for me."

"Obviously he feels *something*," said Suzanne, gesturing toward the medal. "If all he wanted was someone to look after this while he was traveling, he could have asked Lieutenant Riser. Do you want my advice?"

"Yes, please."

"When Captain Mack returns to Chaumont, tell him how you feel."

"I couldn't possibly," said Grace, aghast. "Not without knowing his intentions. I could never be that brazen."

"Not if you were back in New Jersey, sure, but maybe that's not how it's done in Australia. Maybe Australian men wait for the lady to show clear interest in a man before he burdens her with unwelcome attention."

Suzanne was her best friend in the Signal Corps, but Grace had never confided in her about the stolen kisses and brief embraces shared on those rare occasions when she and Mack were entirely alone. Grace was on the verge of confessing the whole truth, but at the last moment, she remembered that she was Suzanne's superior officer, and it was unfair to burden her with such a secret. "I'm sure he knows I'm interested," she said instead, hoping her friend would not ask her to elaborate.

But how interested was she? Not enough to risk losing her operators' respect—and possibly even her position in the Signal Corps—by openly carrying on a romance with a handsome Australian officer. And how interested was he? Mack might think of her as nothing more than a wartime dalliance, a bit of harmless fun and flirtation to stave off loneliness and the fear of death. If she expressed deeper feelings, she might repulse him and humiliate herself.

"He has to show his hand first," she said firmly.

"You don't have to decide anything tonight," said Suzanne with a sigh, climbing into bed. "Maybe the best thing to do is not think about it at all. Just wait and see what Captain Mack does when he returns."

Grace agreed that might be for the best. She doused the lamp, and as she lay down, plumping her pillow and trying to get comfortable, she could not bring herself to voice aloud another possible explanation for Mack's reticence on this one subject, when Australians were famously friendly and open.

Perhaps he was fond of her, very fond, but he had a girl back home.

That dreadful possibility seemed even more plausible on Saturday evening when she chaperoned Lieutenant Riser and Miss Rose Langelier on their dinner date and observed the spark between them, evident in every smile and laugh and lingering glance. The lieutenant was a perfect gentleman, yet it was obvious he was smitten with the pretty, charming operator. Lieutenant Riser was transparent. Why was Captain Mack so inscrutable? Perhaps his work in military intelligence had trained him too well to hide his feelings. Or perhaps he was deliberately suppressing them—permitting himself to enjoy Grace's companionship, approaching but never crossing the line, knowing his heart was committed elsewhere.

Grace muffled a sigh and forced a smile as Rose laughed at a small, self-deprecating joke Lieutenant Riser told. She was thinking about this entirely too much. Even if Captain Mack had no prior attachments, and he returned to Chaumont, took her by the hand, and declared his everlasting adoration, what could she actually do about it? Captain Wessen and Mr. Estabrook had made it perfectly clear that chief operators must set an example of utmost discretion and restraint for the operators under their command. Inez Crittenden insisted that it would be inappropriate for a chief operator to engage in courtship of any kind, to allow frivolous romance to distract her from her duties. Grace was inclined to agree with them. As the first women in the U.S. Army, the Signal Corps operators must be above reproach, their leaders most of all. So many skeptical eyes were observing them, waiting to see if General Pershing's daring wartime experiment would succeed or fail. For the moment, public opinion was on the operators' side, thanks to their exemplary performance, but a scandal could ruin everything, not only for the young women in uniform now, but for their daughters and granddaughters in generations yet to come.

Suzanne meant well, but Grace dared not encourage Captain Mack to declare feelings he either did not have or was reluctant to confess. There was simply too much at stake, not only for herself but for countless other women. If he did tell her he cared for her, she would not reject him, but they would have to proceed slowly and with discretion.

But none of that would matter if she was nothing more to him than a wartime fling.

As the warm August days passed, Grace had much to occupy her thoughts and keep her from brooding over the captain. The first distraction was the sheer volume of work the operators faced every day. General Pershing had convinced Marshal Foch to approve a daring plan to reclaim territory in Lorraine that the Germans had occupied since 1914. From what Grace overheard on the lines, attention seemed focused on a German salient near Saint-Mihiel, a town on the banks of the Meuse River in northeast France.

The second distraction was a curiosity, perhaps related to the first, perhaps not. Several times a week, sometimes on the streets of Chaumont, more often in the halls of the caserne, Grace would cross paths with Colonel Parker Hitt, General Pershing's signal officer. Invariably, he would fall into step beside her and strike up a conversation full of nonchalant queries that struck her as non sequiturs—who were her five best operators? Which of her girls were especially good with code station work? Were any of them particularly hardy or athletic, able to withstand hardships better than others? Since Colonel Hitt was her superior officer and his questions did not involve military secrets, Grace answered them readily, but she suspected that their chance meetings were not by chance at all, and that something was up.

The third was too devastating to be called a distraction.

It came in a telegram on August 17, and if Grace had not been so preoccupied with her duties she might have paused to consider how strange it was that Lieutenant Riser had summoned her to his office to read a telegram instead of having a messenger bring it to her, and why she had received a telegram at all instead of a letter. Then she opened it, and as the words sank in and her throat constricted and her head grew light, it was all too clear why the lieutenant had not wanted her to be alone when she read the terse, devastating lines.

Her father had died, a month ago to the day at their family home in Passaic, New Jersey.

The terrible news struck her with almost physical force, knocking the wind out of her, rendering her numb with grief. Lieutenant Riser expressed his condolences and explained why the news had taken so long to reach her, but Grace hardly heard him. "Has my brother been informed?" she heard herself ask distantly. The lieutenant did not know, but he promised to look into it. Grace had not received a letter from her brother in weeks, but the last she had heard, the 77th Field Artillery was at Fismes, about twenty-five kilometers west by northwest of Reims. At that moment, staggered by loss, she feared for her brother's life more than ever before.

The lieutenant urged her to take a few days off. She spent one day resting at the house on Rue Brûle before she realized that there was nothing she could do to help her father, but if she did her job well, she might yet be able to help Eugene. She returned to work, grateful for the relentless pace that made it impossible for her to succumb to grief, grateful for the dear friends who lent her their strength and did not make her talk about her loss when she found it unbearable to do so.

Work gave her purpose and solace, but even as she focused on her duties, she was aware in the periphery of rumors drifting through Chaumont that General Pershing intended to move his command center closer to the front. A week after she received the devastating telegram, Colonel Hitt again just happened to run into her as she was leaving Lieutenant Riser's office. "Miss Banker," he said, lowering his voice, "have you heard that General Pershing might establish a new headquarters closer to the front?"

"I haven't heard a thing," said Grace, feigning surprise. "I should be asking you. You're in a much better position to know."

He put his hands in his pockets and leaned forward to peer into her eyes. "You haven't heard even the slightest rumor?"

"Rumors?" Grace furrowed her brow. "Who listens to rumors? They contradict each other and they're almost always wrong."

The colonel nodded thoughtfully, wished her a good day, and sauntered off. Grace watched him go, her curiosity piqued. Yes, something was definitely up.

The next morning, as Grace stood outside the telephone room reviewing notes from the night shift while her operators prepared to take over at the switchboard, a Signal Corps major she knew slightly from staff meetings took her aside. "I'm in a bit of a bind, Miss Banker, and I was hoping you could assist me."

"Certainly, if I can."

"A fifth group of telephone operators arrived in France last week. Most of them were deployed to Services of Supply, but I can request that some be transferred here if we need them." He rubbed at his jaw. "The problem is, I'm not sure how many we need."

"I see." Grace hugged her clipboard to her chest. "I would need to check the duty rosters, but off the top of my head—"

"The current duty rosters won't help, unfortunately." He lowered his voice and glanced over his shoulder. "I've heard that a few of you girls have been reassigned to the new headquarters Pershing is setting up closer to the front. It would help me considerably if I knew how many of you are going and when."

Grace regarded him, feigning puzzlement. "What new headquarters? The only switchboard closer to the front that I know of is at Neufchâteau."

"No, no, no." He shook his head, impatient. "Not Neufchâteau. The new place."

"I'm sorry, but I have no idea what you're talking about."

"Oh, come on." He smiled, turning on the charm. "You girls hear everything."

"Not me, I'm afraid, and certainly not about this." She offered an apologetic shrug. "But if you could request six additional operators from Group Five, I think that would be ideal."

"I'll see what I can do," he said, and left her. Grace muffled a sigh and finished reading the report just in time for her operators to relieve the night shift. If that curious conversation had been a test, she hoped she had passed.

Scarcely fifteen minutes into the day shift, Colonel Hitt entered the telephone room and asked Grace to join him for a moment. She quickly murmured instructions to one of the supervisors and followed him to a secluded corner of the caserne foyer.

"General Pershing is moving First Army Headquarters closer to the front, and he'll need a telephone exchange," he said quietly. "You and your two best operators will depart in one hour. We'll pick up three more operators at Neufchâteau on the way."

"My two best operators are Suzanne Prevot and Esther Fresnel," Grace told him, her voice steady though her heart was pounding.

"I'll inform Lieutenant Riser," the colonel said. "You go tell your operators, and then get packed up, quick as you can. Take only the essentials, no more than what you can carry in one small bag. The car will meet you at your residence in an hour."

"Understood, sir," Grace said, and swiftly returned to the telephone room.

Grace spared a few minutes for goodbyes before she, Suzanne, and Esther hurried back to the residence. Breathless, they packed their essentials in haste, entrusting their footlockers containing most of their belongings to Mrs. Ivey, who promised to look after them as long as necessary. Then they raced from the house to find a large touring automobile waiting at the curb, a driver at the wheel. They stowed their bags, climbed aboard, and barely had time to shut the doors before the vehicle sped away.

"Are you allowed to tell us where we're going?" Grace asked the driver as they left Chaumont behind.

"Ligny-en-Barrois," he replied, tossing her a grin over his shoulder. "It's a small town about thirty-five kilometers southwest of Saint-Mihiel. Should take us about four hours to get there, with one stop on the way to pick up three more girls."

For more than an hour they drove northeast through the French countryside to Neufchâteau. When the car halted outside a two-story stucco residence, Grace and her companions got out to stretch their legs while they waited for the other girls to join them. Five minutes ahead of schedule, the front door burst open and Berthe Hunt, Marie Miossec, and another girl Grace did not recognize hurried out carrying a single bag each. After they flung their luggage in the trunk and scrambled aboard, Berthe introduced the third girl as Helen Hill from New Haven, Connecticut, who had sailed with the Fourth Group.

As the car rambled northwest, the Chaumont girls had plenty of time to get acquainted with Helen and to renew their friendships with Berthe and Marie, whom they had not seen since the First Group had been divided up in Paris. Even with Helen and Marie up front, it was a tight squeeze in the back, and every jolt and sharp turn crushed them against one another. They slowed whenever they passed civilians trudging along in the opposite direction, pushing carts piled high with suitcases, bedding, and children; more rarely, a wizened nag wearily pulled a hay-strewn wagon filled with refugees clutching cloth-wrapped bundles.

More often, the automobile came upon Allied troops marching in the same direction. At the sound of the engine, the soldiers would move aside off the road, their weary faces brightening when they glanced up and spotted a car full of young women passing. Recognizing their Signal Corps uniforms, the sun-browned, dusty boys cheered and waved their helmets in salutation. The telephone girls merrily cheered them right back, applauding and waving. Suzanne and Helen blew kisses.

It was midday by the time they reached Ligny-en-Barrois, a village nestled in a valley encircled by hills, along the same Canal de la Marne au Rhin that flowed past Chaumont. The driver left them at the telephone office, a former residence on the village's main street. "Don't get too comfortable," he advised with a grin before he gunned the engine and drove off.

"Why do you suppose he said that?" Esther asked. "Because we won't be here long, or because it would be a futile effort?"

"He was probably just trying to be clever," said Helen as they all turned to look up at the weathered façade of their new workplace. Sandbags piled high around the outside walls warned ominously of past or anticipated bombings. Inside, Grace and her companions discovered a large, bare room, with a few dilapidated switchboards. Behind them, rolls of wire and kegs of nails were piled haphazardly, suggesting the equipment had been installed only recently. A large packing box nearby seemed to serve as both a makeshift chair and desk.

Several Signal Battalion boys sat at the switchboard, but at the sound of the girls entering, they tore off their headsets and bounded to their feet, eager to meet them. Distracted by the flashing lights and dangling jacks of the unattended switchboard, Grace barely caught any of their names, but she did learn that there were no other operators in the village. Now that the more qualified girls had arrived, the Signal Battalion boys would begin working the evening shift, but even between the two groups they did not have enough personnel to provide twenty-four-hour service, and would only be required to do so in emergencies.

The boys showed them around the exchange, which took no time at all since it was entirely contained within that single room, and the girls had all trained on similar systems in New York. One important difference was something the Signal Battalion boys called "operation lines"—certain wires, recently installed and gleamingly new, which were to be used only to handle calls related to the upcoming offensive. Then, while the boys went off to get a hot meal and some sleep, Grace and her operators took over, leaving their bags piled up against the wall, grateful for the sack lunches their YWCA hostesses had packed for them, since the switchboard was too busy and their numbers too few to allow for breaks.

When the Signal Battalion boys relieved them later that evening, their chief operator, a corporal, offered to escort the six girls to the mess hall for supper, and then on to their quarters. Famished, they readily agreed, so he led them off down the block, offering a cheerful narration along the way. Often he had to raise his voice to nearly a shout, for the narrow cobblestone streets were packed with troops marching and heavy trucks rumbling by, loaded down with supplies and artillery. After a simple but filling meal of rabbit stew and coarse bread, he escorted them to their YWCA hostel, or at least to the sign hanging above the alley that he promised would take them from the main street to the hostel's entrance.

Grace led the way down the dark, narrow passageway to a small paved courtyard open to the sky, dark blue with twilight. As the six women looked around appraisingly, wondering which of the several doors was the main entrance, a woman in her thirties, her dark hair cut in a wavy bob, bustled out through one and greeted them pleasantly in American-accented English and French. Beckoning them to follow, she led them to the far side of the courtyard, where two well-worn stairways climbed in opposite directions along the wall, one to two rooms over a shop, and the other two rooms over a barn used for drying herbs and for storage. Berthe and Grace would each have a room to themselves, and the other girls would pair up. Grace was the last to be shown to her room, which was in the rear over the barn. She hid her surprise when the hostess proudly showed her a large canopy bed with heavy maroon draping, over which hung a cross of dried flowers at least a foot high. Like the sword of Damocles, Grace thought as she left her bag at the foot of the battered wardrobe and returned the hostess's cheerful good night.

Alone, she shut the door and sized up her accommodations, which smelled faintly of laundry starch and bleach and floor wax, promising signs of cleanliness. A pitcher of water sat next to a basin on a low, broad bureau. Two windows on the far wall probably looked out over the street rather than the courtyard, but she resisted the temptation to pull back the blackout curtains and peek.

Exhausted, she made ready for bed, knowing she would have to rise before dawn the next morning. She climbed beneath the covers, which were old but scrupulously clean, and lay down to discover that the pillow was plump and full of down, but the mattress was strangely lumpy and prickly, as if it were stuffed with straw, and some sort of horizontal rod or beam pressed uncomfortably into her spine. She shifted her weight, rolled onto her side, curled her knees up to her chest, but no matter what she tried, the rigid bar still poked her in one place or another.

Grace rolled onto her back again, closed her eyes, and reminded herself that she would not notice the discomfort after she fell asleep. Remembering the driver's parting words, she had to laugh. She wished she could tell him that he needn't worry. She would have no trouble heeding his advice not to get too comfortable.

20

SEPTEMBER 1918

Paris

VALERIE

Although the Allied victories along the Marne had relieved Paris of the threat of imminent invasion, occasional air raids still interrupted their sleep and sent Valerie and her bunkmates scrambling downstairs in the darkness to the cellar or the courtyard *abri*, listening for the drone of aircraft or the pounding of long guns, bracing themselves for the direct hit upon their hotel that mercifully never came. Valerie wondered if their attackers were aware that about 280 kilometers due east, General Pershing was preparing for a massive offensive around Saint-Mihiel with the intent to break through the German lines and capture Metz, a fortified city on the Moselle River.

When Valerie heard that General Pershing would command 110,000 French troops in addition to the American Expeditionary Forces in the attack, she thought she had misunderstood. She was neither a military strategist nor a psychologist, but it seemed very unlike Supreme Allied Commander Foch to agree to such a plan. Despite the AEF's successes at Belleau Wood, Hamel, and the Marne, the other Allied commanders remained skeptical of the capability of the U.S. First Army to fight as an independent force, preferring instead to embed the American troops with French and British divisions. Their misgivings made this particular mission an even more unlikely assignment. French battalions had made numerous attempts to drive the Germans out of Saint-Mihiel and had failed every time; one disastrous offensive in 1915 had ended in a stalemate and had cost the French 125,000 dead and wounded. Valerie knew she heard only fragments of the various military plans and none of the strategy behind them, but an American-led assault on Saint-Mihiel seemed so improbable that she concluded either the entire thing was a feint meant to distract the Germans while other Allied forces prepared to strike elsewhere, or General Pershing had argued extraordinarily well and had convinced Commander Foch to let him make the daring attempt. The former, as contrived and complicated as it was, seemed far more likely than the latter.

If Valerie had bet on it, she would have lost. Early in the morning of September 12, American troops went over the top at General Pershing's command. The drive to take Saint-Mihiel and Metz was on.

For three days the battle raged. In their initial assault, the Americans had unwittingly surprised the Germans while they were in retreat, their troops unprepared and their artillery out of place, and so the Allies met with greater success than they had expected. All too soon, though, their progress stalled as transport vehicles became mired in the muddy roads and artillery and food supplies had to be abandoned. German machine gunners fired down upon American troops from the cover of the forests, killing more than 4,500 and seriously wounding 2,500. The numbers were horrifying enough when Valerie heard them over the phone lines. She did not dare imagine what it would be like closer to the scene of the slaughter.

Despite the terrible losses, the battle was declared an Allied victory, an essential test of General Pershing's leadership that he had passed with flying colors. The Allies took 15,000 German soldiers prisoner and liberated more than two hundred square miles of French territory that the Germans had occupied since the early months of the war.

In the days that followed, the Paris newspapers were filled with stories and photographs of French citizens, trapped behind enemy lines for four long, terrible years, emerging from their ruined homes to embrace their Allied liberators. Church bells rang; impromptu parades filled the bomb-cratered streets; the red, white, and blue Tricolor flew from every staff, window, and balcony, the colors reflected in men's ties, women's hatbands, and girls' hair ribbons.

Perhaps in retaliation, perhaps from spite, on September 16, the Germans hammered Paris with the worst air raid of the war. Valerie and her friends huddled in the cellar of their hotel, joking to conceal their terror, determined to remain stalwart soldiers to the end, if that night proved to be their end. At daybreak, they washed, fixed their hair, put on clean uniforms, and walked to the Élysées Palace Hotel, passing Parisians on their way to work, shopkeepers opening their doors, matrons getting an early start on the day's errands. As beleaguered as they all felt, no one spoke of evacuating the city anymore, at least not in Valerie's hearing.

Later that day, when Valerie returned from her lunch break, she found Inez Crittenden waiting for her outside the exchange, a stack of binders and folders in her arms. "The officer in charge of training Signal Corps men to operate the magneto switchboards at the front has been hospitalized with influenza," she said. "I've been told to appoint a replacement, and I've chosen you."

"Me?" said Valerie, taken aback. Without warning, Inez thrust the binders and folders at her, and Valerie had to take them or they would have fallen to the floor. "Why me? I don't have any teaching experience."

"Neither do any of the other operators here, but you've done an excellent job training the new girls since you were made a supervisor. You also have the air of authority and the backbone necessary to keep a classroom full of men in line."

Valerie was pleased by the compliment, but that didn't mean she wanted to prove she deserved it. "You know who would be great at this job?" she said, wincing as the corner of a binder jabbed the tender flesh beneath her arm. "Grace Banker. She was an instructor with AT&T before she joined the Signal Corps. Oh, even better—Berthe Hunt. She used to teach middle school. This would be practically the same thing."

"The job is yours, Miss DeSmedt," said Inez. "Both Miss Banker and Mrs. Hunt are absolutely essential in their current posts at the front. Even if I did request transfers, their commanding officers would never agree."

"It was worth a try," Valerie muttered.

Inez raised her eyebrows in a mild rebuke and gestured to the burden in Valerie's arms. "Those are your teaching materials, including the course curriculum. Your students already have their workbooks. Your predecessor distributed them on the first day of class, which was only yesterday. Isn't it fortunate that you're taking over at the beginning of the course rather than halfway through?"

"Yes, lucky me," said Valerie. "Back up a minute. You're saying that my predecessor, who is currently in the hospital with influenza, was in that classroom yesterday with those same students?"

"I've been assured that the room has been thoroughly scrubbed and aired."

"And the students? Have they been thoroughly scrubbed and aired too?"

"Wear a mask, if you're concerned. I would in your place." Inez gave her a look that fell between beseeching and exasperated. "Please don't make this more difficult than it has to be. These men need to learn and someone must teach them. Do you want them to go to the front not knowing how to place a call?"

Of course not. "Fine, but I reserve the right to expel any man who coughs or sneezes."

"Do that, and you'll have half the class feigning illness." Inez pressed the back of her hand to her forehead and closed her eyes for a moment, sighing. "I should warn you, I've heard that some men resent being assigned to telephone duty, just as some dislike being posted to Services of Supply."

"Little wonder," said Valerie. "You can't spend decades dismissing a job as women's work and then act surprised when men don't want to do it. Do they understand that they'll be on the battlefield dodging bullets and bombs like every other infantryman?"

"Perhaps you should emphasize that. Flutter your eyelashes, gush about how big and strong and brave they are."

Valerie snorted. "No, thanks. Not my style. Maybe I should tell them how much we girls would love to take their places in the trenches just as we have at all the other exchanges in France."

"What a fine idea. Shame them into learning."

"I told you I wasn't right for this job."

"Nevertheless, it's yours. The class begins at two o'clock—"

"Two o'clock *today*?"

"Yes, today. I suggest you spend the interim reviewing your course materials."

"What about the rest of my shift?"

"I'll take care of that. You have enough to worry about."

Valerie laughed feebly, almost dropping a binder. "Isn't that the truth."

"Two o'clock," Inez said emphatically. "Second-floor conference room."

Valerie grumbled assent and staggered off with her burden.

Upstairs, she found the conference room already arranged as a proper classroom, with a desk, chair, and wheeled blackboard up front, rows of tables and chairs in the center, and magneto switchboards arranged in the back. Heaving a sigh, she seated herself at the desk and began reviewing the lesson plans, complete with illustrations. The good news was that the material was almost identical to the instruction books she had used in her own training. The bad news, the thoroughly alarming news, was that whoever had designed this curriculum had crammed a two-week training program into three days.

"That's insane," Valerie said aloud just as her first student entered the room. He stopped short, glanced over his shoulder as if to see what she was referring to, then nodded hello and took a seat in the front row.

Valerie was too exasperated to be nervous as the rest of the men filed in. All of them did a double take when they saw her standing in their teacher's place. Some quickly composed themselves and greeted her politely, while others grinned appreciatively as they looked her over from head to toe. A few scowled, nudged their companions, muttered inaudibly, and flopped into chairs in the back row, so unsoldierly that for a moment she could have imagined herself back in high school in Los Angeles.

At precisely two o'clock, Valerie closed the door and began class. "Good afternoon," she said, her voice firm and clear. "I am Supervising Operator DeSmedt. As you may be aware, your previous instructor has stepped down for medical reasons, so I will be filling in for him. You have a lot to learn and very little time to master it, so let's get started. Please take out your workbooks and turn to page four."

Most of the soldiers promptly obeyed, but a sergeant in a back-row seat stretched out his legs, folded his arms over his chest, and said, "Miss Teacher, if I'm going to be a telephone operator, where are my skirts?" He pressed the tip of his left forefinger into his left cheek, plucked his trousers between his right thumb and forefinger at the thigh, and mimed a little curtsey. His buddies guffawed, and some of the other men smirked. A few, including the first soldier to arrive, looked uneasy.

"Not my department, Sergeant," said Valerie smoothly. "Check with your quartermaster if you need a replacement uniform. Any other questions before we begin?"

The first soldier raised his hand.

"Yes, Private?" Valerie prompted.

"When do we get our pigeons?"

For a moment Valerie could only blink at him. "I beg your pardon?"

"When do we get our pigeons?" His expression was hopeful, his vowels midwestern flat. "My bunkmate got his two days ago."

Pigeons? Suddenly Valerie understood. "Oh. You must mean the Signal Corps homing pigeons. I gather your bunkmate is in the Army Pigeon Service?"

"Yeah, that's right, miss. He grew up on a farm, like me, and now he's tending pigeons. His favorite is a pretty bluish one named Lola."

Someone in the back snickered, but Valerie ignored him. "I'm sorry, soldier. We don't work with pigeons here, only switchboards, cables, and jacks." When his face fell, she quickly added, "But you can name your magneto board if you like."

He brightened. "I can?"

"Well, sure. Why not? Pilots name their airplanes, don't they?" She shifted her line of sight to take in the entire classroom. "Make no mistake, what you will do at the front with your switchboards will be as essential as anything those pilots do in the skies. How do you think they get their orders? How do you think they report to the commanders at other bases what they've observed from above or how a bombing run went?" She waited for an answer, and when none came, she supplied it. "By telephone."

The private shot his hand into the air. "And by pigeon."

"Yes, and also with the able assistance of those brave, daring, remarkable homing pigeons." She inhaled deeply. At least most of the men were paying attention now. "Look. Any soldier can carry a gun, but the success of a mission or the safety of your entire division might depend on your unit's switchboard and the skill of the man operating it." She fixed her gaze on each of them in turn. "I've connected thousands and thousands of those calls since I've been Over Here, and believe me, I know what I'm talking about."

The sergeant leaned across the aisle to mutter something to a buddy, who chuckled and gave him a shove.

"Did you have something you wanted to contribute to the discussion, Sergeant?" Valerie asked, putting her most honeyed smile into her voice.

He shrugged. "Not much. Only that I don't think you know what you're talking about at all."

A frisson of avid interest passed through the men—surprise, annoyance, anticipation, gleeful malice. Valerie knew then that if she did not gain control of the situation immediately, that would be it. They would learn nothing from her.

"You've been in the Signal Corps, what, Sergeant, five minutes?" she queried, allowing a note of lofty skepticism into her voice. "I've been here for months, so I'm more experienced and I outrank you. Why don't you just *taisez-vous, s'il-vous-plaît*, listen, and try to learn something?"

At his confused look, she added, "That was French for 'Be quiet, please.' Memorize that one. I suspect you'll be hearing it a lot."

The other men grinned and smothered laughter, glancing over their shoulders at the red-faced sergeant and then back at Valerie, new respect in their eyes.

But the sergeant was not finished. "I am not going to report to any woman," he thundered, slamming his fists on the table.

She regarded him in calm silence for a moment. "In that case, you aren't going to learn what you need to know in order to run that switchboard, and men are going to die because of your incompetence. Maybe you," she said, fixing her gaze on the buddy to his left, who lowered his gaze, chagrined. "Maybe you," she said to the buddy on the right, who looked faintly ill. "Definitely not you," she said, smiling approval upon the private in the front row, who blushed. "I can tell you're going to be a quick study." Taking up her book, she passed a pointed gaze around the classroom. "If any of the rest of you want to join this brave private in helping General Pershing win this war, please turn to page four."

Every man did, except for the sergeant, who scowled and glowered and never touched his workbook, but at least he kept his *bouche* closed.

For four hours, with a ten-minute break halfway through, Valerie taught the men how the old-fashioned magneto boards functioned, what the various parts were, how to place a call, how to receive one, and everything else they would need to know. The sergeant did not return after the break, but everyone else did, and they diligently practiced on the switchboards as Valerie walked them through the operations. By the time class ended and she dismissed the men, she was thoroughly exhausted. Still, she was also relieved that she had survived her first day as a real teacher, satisfied with how much of the lesson plan they had been able to cover, and mildly impressed with how quickly the men had picked things up. Perhaps her little speech had motivated them.

She had almost finished tidying up the classroom when one of her superior officers appeared in the doorway. "How did it go?" Captain Pederson asked.

"Fine," she said, feigning regret, "except that every single one of my students declared that they would much rather have you as their instructor. I told them I'd see what I could do."

He barked a laugh. "I'm sure every one of them would prefer to have a pretty young woman like you at the front of the classroom rather than spending the day looking at my ugly mug."

"You might think so," said Valerie wearily, "but you'd be wrong."

She told him about the sergeant, and with each phrase, the captain's expression grew more incredulous. "He left at the break and never returned?"

"Yes, sir. I'm afraid so."

"This isn't some civilian job where he can quit anytime he likes. His CO ordered him to report for this training. He doesn't get a choice. This is the army!"

Valerie sighed and leaned back against the desk. "He'd probably be a willing pupil for a different instructor."

"He doesn't get to choose his instructor either." Captain Pederson frowned and shook his head. "He'll be back in class tomorrow morning, you can be sure of that."

Valerie wasn't sure she wanted him back. "And if he refuses to participate?"

"Put him on K.P."

Valerie paused. As a supervisor, she had been required to discipline her operators only very rarely, and she never meted out more than a stern lecture or a written reprimand in the offender's file. Kitchen patrol was considered the lowest form of punishment. "Can I do that?"

"Of course. Why not? Telephone operators are accorded the status of officers, isn't that so?"

"That's what we've been told, but the title of 'operator' is rather ambiguous. I've never been entirely sure of my rank."

"Well, I assure you that as an officer of any stripe, you outrank a sergeant. If your troublemaker doesn't do his duty, put him on K.P. If he tries to argue the point, tell him to come to my office. I'd be delighted to review military regulations with him."

Dubious, Valerie agreed to do as the captain advised, but secretly she hoped the sergeant would be reassigned to a less distasteful task than accepting instruction from a woman—cleaning out the pigeon coops, perhaps.

The next day, Valerie worked at the telephone exchange in the morning and reported to the classroom in the afternoon. The sergeant was the last student to arrive, swaggering and wearing a disgruntled scowl. He flopped into his seat, folded his arms across his barrel chest, and eyed her contemptuously as she began class by reviewing the previous day's lesson. Afterward, when she asked the students to open their books, the sergeant's remained closed on the table before him, while he glared up at her defiantly.

"Sergeant, do you need help finding the page?" she inquired.

"I don't need your help, and I don't need your lesson," he retorted. "I told you yesterday, I won't answer to a woman."

"Keep it up, and I'll find someone else for you to answer to whom you'll like even less," she said evenly. "Last chance, Sergeant. Open your book and follow along. If you apply yourself, you'll catch up to the rest of the class in no time."

He muttered something under his breath to his buddy, who looked at him askance and did not reply.

"Very well, Sergeant," said Valerie briskly. "Report to the mess hall. You're on K.P."

He gaped up at her. "What?"

"You're on K.P. Go." She inclined her head toward the exit. "That way. Now."

"You—you can't put me on K.P.," he spluttered. "You're just a girl!"

"Oh, I'm not just any girl. I'm your instructor, and I outrank you." Valerie strode to the door, opened it, and made a graceful sweeping gesture to show him the way out. "If you're confused on this point, Captain Pederson kindly volunteered to refresh your memory about certain military regulations you've apparently forgotten."

"But—but—" Red-faced, he pushed back his chair but did not rise. "You can't—"

"Look at it this way. You didn't want to be here anyway, right? Now you can learn how to peel potatoes swiftly and efficiently, and best of all, you'll have a male instructor." She smiled, steely. "Good day, Sergeant."

Fuming, he bolted from his chair, treated Valerie to a blistering tirade of all the profanities in his vocabulary, and stormed out of the room, slamming the door behind him.

"Well, then," said Valerie brightly, clasping her hands together and smiling upon her remaining students, "shall we continue?"

The rest of class, that day and the next, went perfectly smoothly. Valerie would have preferred an extra week to train the men until every task they would ever need to perform on the magneto switchboards became second nature, but that was not to be. Upon the completion of the course, she sent off her students fairly confident that they would acquit themselves well, but before the second course began, she convinced her superiors to extend the training sessions from four hours a day to eight, with a break for lunch. Practice made perfect, she explained, and the more time the men had on the switchboards in class, the better they would perform under fire at the front.

The second course went much better than the first, thanks to the additional hours, her newfound experience, and the absence of belligerent sergeants. By the time the third session began, she felt entirely comfortable in front of the classroom and proud of her accomplishments there, although she did miss the excitement and energy of the telephone exchange and the girls' camaraderie.

On the first day of her fourth course, she was astonished to see the formerly disgruntled sergeant walk into the classroom. He took a seat in the middle of the room, set his workbook and pencil on the table, and looked up to await her instruction, chastened and attentive. She did not know what to expect, but she decided to pretend that he was a new student beginning class on the same fresh page as any other. Much to her surprise, he became one of her best pupils.

By the end of August, her predecessor had been discharged from the hospital, and although he had not fully recovered his strength, he was reinstated as instructor. Valerie knew Inez had been pestering their superiors to return her to the telephone exchange. Her stint as instructor had never meant to be permanent, and the exchange had been getting by one supervisor short too long already.

On her first day back at the switchboard, Valerie learned why Inez had so persistently requested her reinstatement. Due to General Pershing's offensive at Saint-Mihiel, call volumes had soared while the number of telephone operators had remained the same, pushing each of them to the limit of her endurance. Worse yet, the arrival of additional operators they urgently needed and had been expecting for weeks had been delayed indefinitely.

"What about Group Six?" Valerie asked when Inez warned her that there was no relief in sight. "I thought their ship reached Southampton a week ago."

"She did," Inez said, lowering her voice and glancing over her shoulder to make sure she was not overheard. "The *Olympic* docked, but no one was allowed to disembark. They had an influenza outbreak aboard."

Valerie felt a chill. "How bad was it?"

"I can't get official numbers, but rumor has it that hundreds of soldiers fell sick during the crossing." Inez's eyes were dark with apprehension. "This influenza, it's changed somehow. It's different from what we experienced on the *Carmania*. Robust young men can seem perfectly healthy in the morning and be dead by nightfall. It's like something out of a nightmare. Their lungs fill with a bloody froth that spills from their mouth and nostrils, and they drown in their own fluids. When the victims are near death, their flesh turns blue or purple due to the lack of oxygen."

Shocked, Valerie pressed a hand to her chest and felt her heart thudding. "That's—that's simply horrifying. If the disease reaches Paris—"

"Not if, I'm afraid. When."

Valerie took a deep, steadying breath. "*When* it reaches Paris, we'll have to take precautions to avoid anyone who is sick. We'll have to wear masks again, just as we did aboard ship."

To her surprise, Inez looked dubious—Inez, who had ordered the Second Group to sew piles of masks until no more fabric could be found to make them, who had railed against mask slackers until many of her operators had come close to mutiny. "I don't know if our commanding officers will permit that, at least not when we're at the switchboard. Our speech has to be easily understood over the lines."

"So we'll speak up and enunciate. A muffled telephone operator is better than none." And none could be all that remained if one of the operators caught the disease, given how closely the girls lived and worked together. The virus could sweep through an exchange or a hostel, cutting them down like wheat before a scythe. "What about Group Six? Were there any fatalities?"

"None that I know of," said Inez. "But of the thirty-five operators in their group, fifteen were left behind in quarantine in Southampton, too sick to cross the Channel. None of the twenty who reached Le Havre have been assigned to Paris."

Only a few minutes before, Valerie had been exasperated to learn that no new operators would be joining their exchange anytime soon. Now she felt guiltily relieved that no one from the ill-fated *Olympic* would be working alongside her and her friends. She knew her wariness was illogical and misplaced; those twenty girls were surely perfectly healthy, or they would have been detained in Southampton with the others. It was far more likely that a traveling merchant or a soldier on leave would bring the dreaded disease to Paris. Perhaps it was already there.

How long did they have, Valerie wondered, before their tenuous security crumbled?

21

SEPTEMBER 1918

Ligny-en-Barrois and Souilly

MARIE

As General Pershing prepared to attack the German forces holding Saint-Mihiel, troops poured into Ligny-en-Barrois on foot and in trucks until the town fairly overflowed with soldiers and tent encampments filled the open fields surrounding it. A private railway car stationed at the edge of the forest served as General Pershing's quarters. Throughout the long, exhausting days, Marie and her five comrades swiftly connected him to his officers and his Allied counterparts, their hands flying over the switchboards, their voices clear, assured, and purposeful. Signal Corps engineers tested the general's lines several times a day to be sure they would not fail in a critical moment. Nothing could be left to chance.

The vast majority of the calls that passed through the exchange related to battlefield communications, and as preparations for the drive accelerated, engineers installed a new dedicated switchboard, with plugs painted white and a large letter A labeling each jack connecting to the artillery unit. Grace assigned Berthe to work the station, and although she readily accepted the assignment, later that evening as they walked back to quarters, she confided to Marie that she was nervous. "Don't tell anyone I said so," she murmured pensively, "but the responsibility is almost too much for one person."

"I wish I could help share the burden," Marie replied, taking Berthe's hand as they walked along and giving it a reassuring squeeze. "Try not to worry. Miss Banker is confident that you're up to the task, and so am I. Think of how proud Reuben will be when you tell him."

That cheered her up. Berthe smiled her thanks and squeezed Marie's hand twice before letting go.

On their brief lunch breaks, Marie and her friends would collect their rations from the same barrels the soldiers did—hard loaves of bread, a smear of fruity jam, a small slab of meat, a handful of prunes, and coffee. If the weather was fair, they would climb one of the hills encircling the town and take turns peering through binoculars toward Saint-Mihiel, fifteen miles distant, where flashes of light signified Allied cannons firing on German fortifications. Mostly, though, it rained, day after day of downpours, leaving the cobblestones slick underfoot, turning the country roads into thick rivulets of mud. On such gloomy days the operators would spend their breaks at the window or outside on a stone terrace running the length of the building, shielded from the deluge by deep, sturdy eaves overhead. Whenever soldiers would march past—the happy, smiling, exuberant boys they had met on the ocean crossing long since transformed into worn, sun-browned, hardened men—the girls would wave, cheer, applaud, and shout greetings and encouragement. At the sound of their voices, the men's heads would turn their way, smiles lighting up their dirty, sweat-streaked faces, their expressions shifting from astonishment to delight when they realized the women wore the uniforms of the U.S. Signal Corps.

Marie knew the launch of the attack was imminent when their commanding officer ordered the operators to undergo pistol training. For a week, after their shifts they reported to a ridge some distance from the village and practiced loading, aiming, and firing their weapons until the fading light of dusk made it too difficult to see the targets. Marie and Helen turned out to be crack shots, with Grace nearly so. They carried their gas mask haversacks and steel trench helmets everywhere, hanging them from the backs of the chairs when they were working the switch-boards. They braced themselves for an aerial assault, like the one they heard had recently demolished a portion of the Signal Corps barracks in Neufchâteau, injuring no one, fortunately. Whenever German bombers soared over Ligny, American antiaircraft guns chased them away, but Marie suspected the kaiser's pilots would become more aggressive after the assault on Saint-Mihiel began.

Every day more troops marched past the telephone exchange on their way to the staging grounds, line after line of them, for hours on end. Marie was watching the procession from the window on her lunch break when Colonel Hitt unexpectedly stopped by to announce a staffing change. "The Signal Battalion boys have always taken the overnight shifts," he said, "but we're expecting a surge in calls with the upcoming offensive. Frankly, I'm concerned they aren't up to it."

Colonel Hitt paused, giving Marie and Berthe time to exchange a guarded look. If the boys didn't take the shift, the women were the only alternative, so unless more telephone operators were transferring to Ligny from other exchanges—

"Beginning today, you six are on twenty-four-hour duty—eight hours on, eight hours off, in a system of offset shifts that will keep four operators at the switchboard at all times," the colonel said. "I understand that this arrangement is less than ideal, but it is crucial."

"We understand, sir," said Grace.

"Yes, sir," Marie said, as the other girls chimed in the same, hiding any dismay they may have felt. Marie knew the new schedule would become only more grueling as their fatigue accumulated over time, but she was determined to keep up the pace, without any diminishment in accuracy or efficiency. She refused to be the broken cog that made the entire engine grind to a halt.

Just when she thought she could not bear the tension of preparations a moment longer, the order came. Before dawn on the morning of September 12, the U.S. Army attacked the German lines around Saint-Mihiel.

From the moment the assault began, calls passed through the

exchange in an unceasing torrent, each one more essential and urgent than the last. Marie and her comrades worked at a relentless, breakneck pace, heartened by reports that the Allied forces were advancing and the Germans were in retreat. On and on it went, eight hours at the switchboard, a hasty meal, a careful slog through the muddy streets to quarters, a quick wash, a few hours' sleep, waking to the alarm clock, a wash, a clean uniform, a quick breakfast, and back to the exchange. Marie lost track of the days as one shift blended into another, until, just when she thought she had reached the limits of her endurance, word came down the wires that the Germans had been routed. Relieved and exultant, the operators celebrated the wonderful news at the switchboard: The battle was ended, and General Pershing's victory was well in hand. It had come at a terrible cost, but after four long years of war and occupation, Saint-Mihiel was liberated at last.

In the aftermath of the battle, the relentless pace of the telephone exchange eased enough to allow the Signal Battalion boys to return to the night shift, and the girls resumed their previous routine. Grateful for the respite, they caught up on their sleep, did their laundry, wrote letters home, and tended to all the little tasks they had neglected during the offensive. Grace had an unexpected visitor, a very handsome Australian captain, but to Marie, the chief officer seemed more flustered than happy to see him. They went out walking together after work one day, and when Grace returned to quarters later that evening, her cheeks were flushed but her smiles seemed strained. When the girls teased her for details about her twilight stroll, she said only that she was glad the rain had ceased so the roads were less of a quagmire, but Captain Mack had warned that clearer skies increased the likelihood of German air raids. "When the moon comes out from behind the clouds," she said, "the German bombers can more easily see their targets below."

"That's what you talked about, after weeks apart?" Suzanne exclaimed, incredulous. "Air raids and muddy roads?"

"That's not *all* we talked about," said Grace, not meeting anyone's gaze as she helped herself to the tin of biscuits on the table. "Honestly, I was so astonished to see him I hardly remember a word of our conversation. He must have been a real Sherlock Holmes to find us."

"He wasn't looking for us," said Esther, amused. "He was looking for you."

Grace shrugged modestly and nibbled on the biscuit. Marie studied her, curious. She couldn't believe that levelheaded Grace had forgotten most of her conversation with the handsome captain, but her claim preempted any teasing demands to tell all that her friends otherwise might have made. If only Giovanni were an intelligence officer, Marie thought wistfully, with the resources and freedom of movement Captain Mack apparently enjoyed. How wonderful it would be to answer a knock on the door and find Giovanni standing on the threshold, smiling, his arms open to embrace her. But a visit was too much to hope for. She would be content with a second phone call, just to hear his voice again and know he was safe.

Later that night, they all remembered Captain Mack's prediction about clear skies when the air raid siren wailed, jolting them awake and sending them racing for shelter. Yet despite the interruption, they slept better than they had while on twenty-four-hour duty, and Marie woke feeling almost refreshed, curious to see what the day would bring. The people of Saint-Mihiel had barely begun celebrating their liberation when rumors arose in Ligny-en-Barrois about what General Pershing would do next. Some of the Signal Battalion boys believed they would all be on the move again soon, as the general would surely want to relocate his headquarters to follow the retreating front. That seemed plausible to Marie, but if their commanding officers had given Grace any advance warning, she had not passed along even the slightest hint. For the moment, Marie was content to wait and see. They still had their duties to perform, and their morale soared despite their fatigue, for they knew their hard work had made General Pershing's victory possible.

Colonel Hitt was so impressed with the operators' performance under extremely challenging circumstances that he had begun joining them for meals in the mess, querying them about their work, the challenges they faced, and what adjustments to equipment or procedures might make their jobs easier. He listened respectfully to their tactful suggestions, and whenever the conversation turned toward their telephone work in their civilian lives or their families back home, he seemed genuinely interested in what they had to say. For Marie, it was a rare occasion when she felt as if a man regarded her as a colleague, albeit a subordinate, a fellow soldier rather than a simple "hello girl."

On the second sunny day after the battle concluded, Marie was walking along the main road through Ligny-en-Barrois with Berthe and Helen when they saw Colonel Hitt and General Pershing on the other side of the street. The officers had spotted the operators at the same time, and after the women offered a crisp salute, the two men exchanged a few words and began crossing the busy street to join them.

"What should we do?" said Berthe from the corner of her mouth as the officers worked their way through the passing troops and trucks.

"We wait and see what they want," Marie murmured back. "They obviously want to speak to us. It would be rude, not to mention insubordinate, to pretend we didn't see them coming."

Instinctively, the girls made tiny, surreptitious adjustments to their uniforms to be sure they were in perfect order. Marie found herself standing taller and straighter as the general approached, and by the time the officers reached them, she and her companions were standing at attention with as much military bearing as if they were troops on review.

"General, allow me to introduce three of the Signal Corps's most accomplished telephone operators," Colonel Hitt said, gesturing to each of them in turn. "Miss Miossec, Miss Hill, and Mrs. Hunt. Ladies, I'm honored to introduce you to the commander of the AEF, General Pershing."

"Congratulations on your exemplary work during the last offensive," said the general, nodding approvingly as he shook each operator's hand. "We couldn't have achieved this victory without you."

Marie thanked him respectfully along with her friends, pleased and proud. Of course his army could not have won without the telephone operators, who had connected every call conveying every command and report, but it was very good of him to acknowledge it.

"Your outstanding performance is even more impressive given the circumstances," the general remarked, glancing to Colonel Hitt to see if he concurred, prompting the colonel to smile proudly and nod. "I've been a soldier a very long time, so I feel quite at home in all this, but not everyone enjoys roughing it." General Pershing gave their surroundings an appraising glance, offered a rueful shake of the head for the mud-choked streets, and turned back to Marie and her companions. "Are you happy to be so near the front?"

"There's no place we'd rather be, General," declared Helen.

"We only wish to be nearer, sir," said Marie, and Berthe nodded.

The general studied them for a long moment thoughtfully before turning to Colonel Hitt. "Well, Colonel," he said, "take them where they want to go."

The men wished the women good afternoon and continued on their way. "What do you suppose the general meant?" Marie wondered aloud as she and her starstruck companions resumed their walk.

"It was probably just an offhand remark," said Helen, shrugging.

Berthe shook her head. "I think it means that the rumors are true, and he's going to move his headquarters closer to the front again. If he does, it sounds like he intends to take us with him."

Marie was inclined to agree with Berthe, and the prospect both thrilled and worried her.

The next morning, Colonel Hitt was waiting at the exchange when Marie and her comrades reported for duty, and even before he spoke, Marie knew he would confirm their suspicions and their hopes. General Pershing was preparing to move his headquarters about twenty miles north to the town of Souilly, the last inhabited village before the Argonne Forest, where the First Army would launch a massive Allied offensive in the rugged, wooded terrain. The six Ligny telephone operators would establish an exchange in the new headquarters, and a seventh—Adele Hoppock, Marie's and Bertha's bunkmate from Neufchâteau—would join them there.

On September 20, while other officers and soldiers boarded trains and trucks for the journey north, Marie and her comrades were whisked off in a touring car as swiftly as the rough, damaged roads would allow. To Marie, the urgency to get the operators in place was an ominous sign that the start of the offensive was only days away, perhaps merely hours.

As they traveled through Bar-le-Duc and began passing battered, bullet-ridden signs for Verdun, conversation in the car fell silent as Marie and her companions took in the scenes of devastation and destruction amid the wasted landscape. Farmers' fields lay fallow and burned, their houses and barns in ruins. Shattered trees stripped of leaves and bark raised bare, broken limbs to the overcast skies. Bomb craters in the road forced the driver to slow and ease the touring car onto the shoulder or into adjacent drainage ditches before creeping carefully forward to level ground. Marie knew they were near Souilly when she glimpsed ammunition dumps shrouded in mounds of dirt some distance from the road. Soon thereafter, their vehicle was forced to slow at the trailing end of a convoy of trucks and artillery that seemed to stretch ahead of them for miles.

Eventually they reached Souilly, where they discovered that the First Army had established its headquarters not in sturdy stone buildings within the village as in Chaumont and Ligny, but in the old Armée Adrienne barracks on the outskirts of town, long abandoned until now, and for good reason. The flimsy structures were little more than wooden sheds set upon a thickly muddy plain, dilapidated relics of 1916 when the French had held the fortress of Verdun against ferocious German attacks.

The operators had been dispatched from Ligny with such haste that Marie had assumed they would be among the first to arrive at the new headquarters, but to her surprise, the encampment was already teeming with troops, nurses, and civilian personnel. One of the larger buildings had been converted into a hospital, and orderlies were already carrying sick and wounded men inside. A sign over the front door to a smaller structure identified it as a YMCA hut, while the one next door belonged to the YWCA. Marie touched Berthe's arm and inclined her head toward the window. "How did they get here before us?" she asked, amazed. "They aren't even in the army." A dark-haired woman standing in the doorway of the YWCA building saw them watching, smiled brightly, and waved. Helen and Berthe waved back.

Their driver left them in front of one long wooden building in a row of barracks, Number Eight, where he unloaded their bags, pointed them to the correct entrance, and sped off on another assignment. Inside, Marie and her companions found themselves in a large rectangular room, almost entirely bare except for the two portable switchboards arranged against the long wall opposite the entrance and the four chairs set before them. A small woodstove would provide heat, but perhaps not enough of it. A closed door stood at the center of each of the two shorter walls, to the left and the right.

"Let's leave our gear here and see what we have to work with," said Grace, setting down her bag in the middle of the room and eyeing the switchboards speculatively as she approached. Adding their bags to the pile, Marie and the others joined her, noting the model and condition of the equipment. When they slipped on the headsets to test the lines, they heard only dead air at some stations, while others connected to G3, the U.S. Army's Operations Section. They had just calculated that each operator would be responsible for fifty lines when a Signal Corps officer entered through an interior door. Visibly surprised to see them there so soon, he introduced himself as Captain Keller and assured them that the entire exchange would be fully operational within the hour. "In the meantime, you could settle into your quarters," he said, indicating the door on the far end of the room, "or get something to eat at the Signal Corps officers' mess." He gestured with his thumb over his shoulder to the door through which he had entered.

Her companions' expressions told Marie that she was not the only one surprised to learn that they would be sleeping, eating, and working in the same building. "Thank you, sir," said Grace, replying for them all. "We'll drop off our things and have a quick bite, but we'll be ready to get to work the moment you say the word."

They gathered their bags and followed Grace into the adjoining room, which was about half the size of the telephone office and even more sparsely appointed. Ten cots were arranged in two perfectly even rows of five in the center of the room, but there was no bedding, nor any other furniture. Layers of old newspapers and maps lined the boards between the framing posts, improvised insulation that Marie imagined did very little to keep out the cold. Faint water stains on the ceiling betrayed a history of leaks. Four translucent windows on the two walls perpendicular to the door allowed light to filter in from outside, but when Marie went to open one to let in some fresh air, she discovered that instead of glass, the frames held oiled paper. The windows could be pushed out on a hinge and propped open, like those in a chicken coop, and a heavy, opaque black cloth was wrapped around a roller attached to the wall above each, ready to be unfurled and pinned into place during blackout hours.

Suzanne set her bag at the end of one of the cots, planted her hands on her hips, and turned around in place, inspecting their new domain. "Well," she remarked, "at least there isn't much to dust."

"And without bureaus," Grace noted, smiling, "we won't have to waste time unpacking."

"I wish we had a few pegs on the walls, though," said Helen. "I'd like to hang up my spare uniform."

"We could probably contrive something," said Marie. "A few nails hammered into those framing posts should do it." She didn't say so aloud, but she was more concerned about the thinness of the walls. Noise from the exchange on the other side of the interior wall was likely to disturb their sleep, and the ersatz insulation put up by previous occupants suggested that the room would become increasingly uncomfortable as autumn descended into winter.

Just then, a knock sounded on the outside door, but before any of them could respond, it swung open, and the same dark-haired woman Helen and Berthe had waved to from the automobile peered in. "Hello, ladies," she greeted them cheerfully, entering without waiting for an invitation. "Welcome to Souilly. I'm Julia Russell, a hostess at the YWCA hut just down the road. My goodness, I heard your accommodations were spartan, but I hadn't imagined this." She returned to the doorway and called to someone outside. "In here, girls!"

At her summons, three women in the belted khaki coats and long skirts of the YWCA entered carrying bundles, which they distributed to the operators. "This is just to get you started," Julia said, as Marie and her friends gratefully accepted the gifts. "Each contains a blanket, a towel, an oilcloth, a pair of wool socks, and a nightcap. If there's anything else you need right away, please come by the hut and let us know. Often we can requisition things from our organization faster than the army quartermasters can from Services of Supply."

"Thank you so much," said Grace, setting her own bundle down on a cot and crossing the room to clasp Julia's hand in both of her own. "I feel more at home already."

Marie appreciated the YWCA ladies' generosity as well, but she longed for the comfort and security of the convent in Tours, with its stone walls, roaring fireplaces, and plump pillows. Just then, artillery rumbled somewhere in the distance, and the walls rattled. Restful quiet and relative safety, too, were luxuries she had left behind in Tours. Even Neufchâteau seemed charming in comparison.

After the YWCA girls departed, the operators passed through the telephone exchange, where they found a few Signal Corps engineers at the switchboards connecting wires and turning screws. "Fifteen more minutes, tops," a corporal promised cheerfully, glancing up from his work. They thanked him and continued on through to the officers' mess hall, which turned out to be a room similar in size and appearance to the exchange, but with a single long table comprised of pine planks on sawhorses running down the center of the room, with wooden benches flanking the sides. Marie thought she detected the aromas of cooking from somewhere unseen, but since it was between mealtimes, the mess was empty except for one Black soldier sweeping the floor. When Grace approached him and asked where they might find something simple to tide them over until supper, he left through another door and soon returned with a tray of bread, cheese, and apples. Famished, the girls thanked him profusely and began helping themselves, and they thanked him again when he returned moments later with a tray of cups and a pot of hot coffee.

"Least I could do for our switchboard soldiers," he said, smiling. "Like the song says, you're our brave angels on the line."

Marie and her friends exchanged smiles. "Another lyric," Esther remarked. "Eventually we'll be able to piece together the entire song."

"Do you know it well?" Marie asked the soldier, hopeful. "Honestly, it's taken on an almost mythical quality for us. We've been told that it exists, but none of us has ever actually witnessed a performance."

"I'm sorry, miss," he said, regretful, "but I only heard it the one time, when I was on leave. I don't have much of a voice, but I know the first line is, 'My switchboard soldier, brave angel on the line.' And the end goes something like, 'Switchboard soldiers, Signal Corps sweethearts, we're going to win the war together.' That's not quite it, but it's close."

Marie and her companions applauded, and the soldier grinned and gave them a joking bow.

The melody was familiar, but it sounded nothing like what the two soldiers had attempted at the YMCA in Southampton. "If you happen to hear it again, or if you remember any more, would you please let me know?" Marie asked, indicating the door to the telephone exchange. "I'll be working in there, and if I happen to be off duty, one of the other girls will give me the message."

The soldier's face fell. "I'm sorry, miss. I'm not allowed in there. Just the kitchen and this room, and only when I'm cleaning or serving."

"I see," said Marie, a spark of indignant anger kindling. She didn't need to ask why. "In that case, would you please watch for me at mealtimes?"

She was aware of the other girls' silence, the furtive looks they exchanged.

The soldier managed a tight smile. "Sure, miss," he said. "If I hear the song, I'll get word to you somehow. Good day, ladies." He inclined his head in a polite bow to all the girls and turned away, carrying the empty tray from the room.

"'Brave angel on the line,'" Esther echoed thoughtfully, breaking the silence. "I quite like that."

"Me too," said Helen, and the others agreed.

The girls were just finishing up their quick meal when Colonel Hitt entered and pulled up a bench. "I've heard a rumor that you soldiers have no furniture," he said.

"We have cots," said Berthe, shrugging. "That's more than the boys in the infantry get."

"Even so, I'll get some men from the Twenty-Seventh Engineers to construct a few useful things for you." The colonel looked around the table, his smile grim. "I don't need to tell you that the volume of calls is always heaviest preceding an offensive, as troops are getting into position and supply units are racing to equip them."

"Yes, sir," said Grace, as Marie and the others nodded. "We know what to expect and we're ready to begin anytime."

"We'll be running twelve-hour shifts around the clock," the colonel continued. "Miss Banker, you'll determine the individual assignments. Start with equal shifts of three and three, and after our seventh operator arrives, you can assign her to either days or nights, as you deem best."

"Yes, Colonel," said Grace.

Marie exchanged a look with Berthe, and she knew they shared the same thought: The colonel did not want to disparage the Signal Battalion boys, but he had not included them in the rotation, and that spoke volumes. Time and again, when experience, poise, accuracy, and efficiency mattered most, Colonel Hitt—and General Pershing—wanted the most capable operators at the switchboard, and that meant the Signal Corps women, Marie and her comrades.

In the days that followed, while the 27th Engineers constructed shelves, tables, washstands, benches, and other furnishings to make their quarters more tolerable, the women worked tirelessly at the switchboards, connecting calls at a whirlwind pace. When they were not at the switchboards, they were committing the new codes to memory; Souilly was "Widewing," and a call for "Widewing Ten" meant a call for their chief signal officer. Long guns boomed ominously in the distance, and ambulances often drove past Barracks Number Eight on the way to the evacuation hospital in the woods just beyond. Colonel Hitt made sure they learned the fastest route to the underground *abri* where they must seek shelter in the event of an air raid, and Grace had them practice evacuating their quarters in the dark. Not far from their shelter was another *abri*, even deeper underground, where a single switchboard had been installed in case of an extreme emergency. Marie hoped they would never need to use it.

Marie soon understood why Colonel Hitt insisted upon having women operators at the switchboard continuously rather than entrusting the Signal Battalion boys with the night shifts, which were usually slower and less critical. During the daylight hours, Allied military convoys concealed themselves within the cover of the forest and held position, all but invisible to any German scout planes prowling the skies above. It was at night that the army advanced, as stealthily as half a million armed men and artillery could do so, a nocturnal predator ten miles deep and thirty miles long, relentlessly stalking its prey. At night the calls came in swiftly and ceaselessly, almost every message in code, until sometimes all seventy-five cords were in use and still new connections were demanded. Sometimes Marie half expected the switchboard to sizzle and smoke from overuse.

Very early in the morning on September 25, Marie was at her station when she heard the French army unleash a heavy barrage upon the German fortifications, an opening stratagem meant to distract the enemy's attention away from the First Army's maneuvers. German guns thundered back. One bombardment followed another, back and forth, as the night sky gave way to dawn.

Around five o'clock, Marie was on the line with General Pershing arranging a connection to the Operations Section when suddenly he yelled in her ear, a piercing, wordless exclamation. "Sir?" she said, alarmed. "Are you still there, sir?"

"Yes, operator, I'm here," he said. "I didn't mean to shout at you. A shell just whizzed past my window."

Marie's heart thudded. "I'm glad all is well, sir. I'm connecting you now." When both parties were on the line, she withdrew, her hands shaking as she pulled the plug. If that errant shell had struck the general's railcar, she could not imagine what the AEF would have done without him.

The constant barrage continued throughout the morning. "It's worse than the roar of the Atlantic surf during a storm," Grace said as they crossed paths in the doorway to the officers' mess, Marie racing inside, stomach rumbling, for a quick bite of breakfast, Grace rushing back to the exchange.

When the day shift operators relieved them at eleven o'clock, Marie wearily handed over her headset and returned to quarters, grateful that it was only a few steps away. She washed and undressed, so exhausted that she barely flinched when the walls and oiled-paper window rattled with each distant explosion. She slept dreamlessly and woke in time to wash, change into a fresh uniform, and join Berthe and Helen for supper in the mess. There, other Signal Corps officers bustled in and out, wolfing down their meals and racing back to work. Desperate for fresh air, Marie and Berthe ventured outside and walked as far up a nearby hill as they dared, eager to see whatever might be visible at that distance, but deeply reluctant to make themselves easy targets. Without the binoculars, all they could make out were red and yellow flashes in the distance beneath a thick haze of smoke.

They returned to quarters as twilight descended, double-checking to make sure the blackout curtains were secured. At eleven o'clock they joined Helen in relieving the day shift, listening carefully to their updates about certain exchanges and developments. Grace Banker was already there, hard at work, as she had been when Marie had gone off duty. Marie wondered if she had slept at all.

Marie had been at her station little more than an hour when suddenly, shortly after midnight, a ferocious eruption of artillery split the air above them, as if a million cannons had fired simultaneously, the concussions of sound so intense that Marie felt as if her bones were rattling. For one terrifying moment, calls dropped up and down the switchboard, but Marie and her comrades frantically reconnected as many of them as they could. A harrowing few minutes later, the exchange was functioning normally again, as best that she could tell, the shock having apparently caused no lasting damage.

The crisis had been averted, and just in time. The Allies' vast offensive in the Argonne had begun.

22

SEPTEMBER-OCTOBER 1918

Souilly

GRACE

As distant artillery boomed and Barracks Eight trembled, Grace flew from one task to another, directing her operators, liaising with her superior officers, but most often connecting calls at a station, for they were too shorthanded for her to merely stand back and supervise. One September morning, in her first five minutes at the switchboard, Grace fielded a call from a Signal Corps officer requesting counterfire to draw off heavy shelling, another from a French operator warning her American counterparts of approaching German aircraft, and a third from the commander of an artillery division requesting the precise time down to the second in order to calibrate their shots with another unit.

All the while, amid the rush and bustle and increasing danger, Grace held in the back of her mind the unsettling certainty, confirmed in confidential meetings with Colonel Hitt and others, that the Meuse-Argonne offensive was not merely ambitious but audacious. The plan as she understood it was to clear the dense forest of all German troops, who were firmly ensconced in a chain of networked trenches reinforced with concrete, pillboxes, and machine-gun nests, behind hundreds of miles of barbed wire that in some places was several yards deep and higher than a man's head. In the next stage of the assault, the army intended to advance east across the Meuse River, expel German troops stationed on a ridge on the opposite side, and drive into the Woëvre Plain in Lorraine, which extended from the city of Luxembourg in the north to the French city of Toul in the south.

Colonel Hitt had impressed upon Grace the stark truth that the upcoming offensive would be the AEF's first sustained confrontation with battle-hardened German divisions, and although the Americans were fresh and therefore well rested, that was unlikely to be an advantage. It had been no small feat to move so many men and so much materiel from Saint-Mihiel to the Argonne in time to launch another major attack only a few days after the previous significant battle had concluded. More troubling yet, of the nine U.S. divisions that had jumped off that morning, five had never seen combat, and they were confronting seasoned German troops, tenacious fighters who knew how to exploit an inexperienced unit's weakness. Supply lines were too short, and fog and foul weather interfered with navigation in the rough, unfamiliar terrain. Grace and her operators did all they could to make communications swift and accurate, but it was the only aspect of the battle they could control. Sometimes even that was thwarted by severed lines, the loss of vital equipment to shelling, and the inability to understand a caller whose words were drowned out by the crash and roar of artillery.

Julia Russell from the YWCA came by the exchange several times a day to see to the operators' comfort, bringing them coffee, finding a cushion for a chair, reminding them to take breaks to eat, bringing them food when they could not leave their stations. Once, during an unexpected lull, Captain Keller invited Grace and Julia outside to observe the battle from a distance. Grace could spare only a few moments, but that was enough for her to grasp how truly harrowing and thrilling the spectacle was. Field cannons roared in her ears, and all along the horizon she glimpsed great flashes of light like a menacing, uncanny aurora borealis.

Even those few minutes away from the exchange felt dangerously negligent, so Grace hurried back to the telephone office and again plunged into the surging tide of work. She soon lost track of the hours, marking the time by news of one division's advance and another's assault on a crucial German entrenchment. She had just disconnected a call and had risen from her chair to work a knot out of her shoulder when she felt a hand on her arm.

"Miss Banker?" said Julia. "Are you quite all right?"

"It's nothing. I'm just a bit stiff," said Grace. "I thought you had returned to the YWCA hut to get some sleep."

"I did. I've returned." Julia studied her closely. "How long have you gone without sleep?"

"I don't know," said Grace, taken aback. "What time is it?" Wordlessly Julia pointed to the clock on the wall, which seemed curiously blurry. Grace blinked several times, squeezed her eyes shut tight, and opened them again. She was relieved when the hands came into focus, but startled by what they revealed. "I've been on duty twenty-one hours straight. That can't be right."

"No, it isn't, but not in the way you mean," said Julia. "Whatever you're working on now, finish it up, go have something to eat, and then get some sleep."

When Grace protested, the kindhearted but firm YWCA hostess insisted upon accompanying her from the exchange to the mess and then on to her quarters to make sure she complied. "You have to look after yourself," Julia urged in an undertone rather than scold her in front of the other operators. "You'll be no use to the girls under your command if you collapse from exhaustion at the switchboard."

Grace was too weary to argue with her, especially when she knew Julia was right, at least in part. Grace would have gone off duty at the end of her regular shift if she had not been needed so urgently, but there had been too much to do and not enough girls to do it. Their office's lines to the front were in continuous use, and many calls through the French exchanges ran headlong into interminable delays, which required persistent cajoling of the French operators to open up lines for them. Calls from the front to the evacuation hospitals soared in frequency with each passing hour, a worrisome portent of staggering casualties. By the time Grace returned to the exchange on the second day of the battle, it was evident that the Allies had met with fierce resistance and had not advanced as far as expected. The mood throughout Barracks Eight was grim, and it only worsened as cold, drenching rains driven by strong winds pummeled the building.

"If it's this bad here, imagine how awful it is for the boys on the front lines," Berthe said as they bolted down a quick meal at the mess before racing back to the switchboard. Grace was not surprised later that night whenever she overheard Berthe spending the rare respites between calls chatting with boys in their miserable, rain-soaked dugouts, doing her best to raise their spirits. The operators' own morale was boosted when Adele Hoppock finally arrived from Neufchâteau and immediately got to work. Grace would have gladly taken on an additional half dozen operators, but the other exchanges could not spare them.

On the second day of the battle, the First Army captured Montfaucon, strategic high ground the Germans had been using as a lookout post. Grace and the other girls had heard from their French counterparts that the French commanders, who had been absolutely certain that the position would not be taken for months, were deeply impressed by the Americans' success. The operators' hopes for an imminent victory soared, but in the days that followed, the Allied advance slowed and then stalled. More disheartening yet, General Pershing sometimes ordered his forces to draw back, never terribly far and never in a rout, but the lack of forward progress was discouraging.

One afternoon at the end of the month, the sound of raindrops hammering upon the roof diminished and sunlight faintly illuminated the oiled-paper windows. It seemed impossible to believe that Souilly had been granted a respite from the miserable weather, but when Grace's midafternoon break came, she stepped outside, blinked in the sunshine, and marveled at the clear blue sky, broken only by a few profusely puffy cumulus clouds. Inhaling deeply, savoring the fresh air, she shaded her eyes with her hand and walked out into the street, halting abruptly at the sight of a German aircraft soaring through the blue. It was so far above her that she could not hear its engines, and it seemed harmless at that distance, like a dragonfly flitting through a meadow.

Then she heard the pounding of American antiaircraft guns, saw white puffs like cotton bolls around the German plane, and went cold as shrapnel suddenly began to fall to earth.

Heart in her throat, she turned and fled back toward the barracks. One of the doors burst open and Colonel Hitt appeared, shouting, gesturing frantically, but before she could reach the foot of the stairs, a chunk of metal slammed into the ground four feet to her right. Instinctively flinging her arms up to protect her head, Grace stumbled a moment before regaining her footing, racing up the stairs and darting into the mess hall. Colonel Hitt slammed the door shut behind her.

"What were you thinking?" he thundered, rounding upon her as pieces of shrapnel continued to pummel the muddy road outside. "Where is your helmet?"

"It's—" Gasping for breath, Grace gestured toward the door to the exchange. "It's on my chair."

"You know better than to go outside without your helmet," the colonel scolded, furious. "We could have lost you."

"I'm very sorry, sir," Grace said, struggling to compose herself. "I have no excuse. It won't ever happen again."

"It damn well had better not." Inhaling deeply, Colonel Hitt fixed her with a stern glare. "You'll face an official reprimand for this, Miss Banker. You're too valuable to the army for us to permit you to squander your life so recklessly."

Grace had never been a reckless person, and though perhaps she deserved it in that moment, the rebuke stung. "I understand, sir."

He ordered her back to work, and she hurried off, duly chastened.

On the first day of October, the fighting came to an unexpected standstill along the miles-long front—unexpected to Grace and her operators, if not to General Pershing and his commanders. Not quite trusting the indefinite peace that had descended over Souilly, Grace, Suzanne, and Esther ventured out along the Voie Sacrée, the road connecting Bar-le-Duc in the south to Verdun in the north, so named earlier in the war for its essential role as the only viable route for supplying troops, armaments, and supplies to the battlefields during the Battle of Verdun. Four French soldiers passed them walking in the opposite direction and saluted them respectfully. Soon thereafter, an American cavalry officer galloped by and tipped his hat.

They had not walked far when they came upon a small wooden cross a few feet from the road, a tattered piece of cloth fluttering from its crossbar. Drawing closer, Grace and her companions discovered that the cloth had once been a French Tricolor, faded by the sun so that the red, white, and blue were barely distinguishable, and the cross was roughly engraved with the phrase "Mort 1914." As they walked on they discovered more crosses, most with hand-carved epitaphs. One marked the final resting places of three *cannoniers*. Grace felt her throat constricting in grief as she thought of the innumerable graves, marked and unmarked, scattered across the once verdant fields and forests of France and Belgium. It was impossible not to imagine her own dear brother meeting a similar end.

In the distance, Grace heard a faint rumble and hoped it was only thunder. "We should get back," she told her friends. Silent and solemn, they linked arms and retraced their steps back to headquarters.

The next morning, Colonel Hitt addressed all the operators together at shift change. "The Germans are putting up a stronger fight than expected," he told them, confirming what they had already surmised. Unlike the assault on Saint-Mihiel, when the Germans had retreated, they now seemed determined to make the Allies fight for every inch of territory, for if they did not, the Allies could march directly into Germany itself.

"Consequently, we now expect to remain here in Souilly longer than anticipated," the colonel continued. "The gear and personal belongings you left behind in Chaumont or Neufchâteau will be brought to you. You should also work with the quartermaster and the YWCA to scout out whatever additional clothing and necessary items you might need for a long, cold winter."

"Yes, sir," Grace replied stoutly, and the operators promptly echoed her. Although she was confident that her girls were up to whatever hardships lay ahead, she felt heartsick at the thought of the war dragging on so long. Every day ambulances rumbled past Barracks Eight carrying the wounded to the evacuation hospital, and every day that the struggle continued, more young men would be killed or grievously wounded. She had not heard from Eugene for months. She knew the 77th Field Artillery had taken heavy casualties in the attack on Saint-Mihiel, and that they were currently deployed to support the Third and Fifth Divisions, but whether her brother was among them or was languishing in a hospital at the rear or had been—

She inhaled deeply, steadying herself. She did not know her brother's whereabouts or condition, and she must steel herself against the worry and fear that inevitably accompanied uncertainty. Though she spent her days surrounded by the most sophisticated communications equipment in the world, she could not speak with her brother. She could not even use it to find him.

As the meeting broke up and Grace slipped on her headset and set herself to work, it occurred to her that if the operators were going to remain in Souilly indefinitely, she would have to make their quarters more comfortable. With the autumn nights growing colder, weatherproofing must be the first order of business. She hoped to get that leaky roof fixed before the first snowfall, and to fill the gaps between the siding boards with something more durable than crumpled newspaper before the nighttime temperatures dipped below freezing. Still, their quarters were luxurious compared to the rough trenches the boys slept, ate, and lived in every day in all weather, and she would understand if the repairs she wanted could not be a high priority.

As she connected her first calls of the day, Grace quickly learned that the momentary respite in the fighting had passed, and the second stage of the offensive had resumed in brutal fashion. Several companies from the 77th Division had been ordered to leave all rain gear, tents, blankets, and spare rations behind so they could advance swiftly through the rugged Argonne Forest and overwhelm the German positions before the enemy had time to react. Two other American units, including the 92nd Infantry, would support their left flank, while French troops would support them on the right.

Moving at such a swift pace, it was almost inevitable that the troops would move beyond the extent of the Signal Corps telephone lines, and until they could secure the area and Signal Corps engineers could install the necessary wires, they would rely on carrier pigeons and runners to communicate with headquarters. To Grace, who had come to think of the telephone wires as veritable lifelines, venturing so close to the enemy without that connection seemed like walking a tightrope without a net, but obviously, nothing would spoil a surprise advance more than a unit of Signal Corps engineers darting ahead of the infantry to install cables. Signal Corps units traveled with each battalion, laying wire on the move, but so much could go wrong during the precious few minutes it took to establish an exchange at the front.

Fierce fighting continued throughout the day, not only where the 77th was advancing up the Ravine d'Argonne, but elsewhere within the Argonne Forest and along the Meuse River. Grace felt a prickle of uneasiness on the back of her neck when she heard that nine companies from the 154th Infantry Brigade were advancing more swiftly than the others, but she reminded herself that the rest of the 77th was bound to catch up, and other Allied forces were alongside them, guarding their flanks.

The hours passed. Grace and her operators worked at their usual breakneck pace, assembling piecemeal reports of the progress of the 77th from the details they gleaned from the calls they connected. A few hours after nightfall, Grace was preparing a checklist for the shift change when she heard a loud gasp and a clatter. Whirling about, she found Helen, eyes wide with shock, one hand pressed to her lips, the other fumbling for a cord she had apparently dropped on the floor.

Grace hurried over, picked up the cord, and handed it to Helen. "What happened?" she asked.

"The French troops couldn't advance," Helen replied bleakly. "The Germans launched a massive counterattack and forced the French to fall back. The entire left flank of the 308th is exposed."

Grace's heart plummeted. The 308th Infantry was one of the regiments from the 77th that had advanced more swiftly than the others. "Do they know the French troops aren't with them?"

Helen shook her head. "We can't raise them. The Signal Corps engineers suspect that the Germans cut their phone lines."

Then there was no way to warn them, except to send a runner on foot. Grace took a deep breath to steady herself. "Anyone have news of the 92nd Infantry?" she asked the room.

Esther held up a hand, finished connecting a call, then turned away from the switchboard to reply. "They've stalled," she said, apprehensive. "Neither of the American units supporting the 77th's right flank were able to advance."

"What?" Suzanne exclaimed, while Helen shot Esther a look of alarm. "You mean the 308th is surrounded by Germans on three sides?"

"Stay focused, girls," said Grace, gesturing to the blinking lights on the switchboard. "We don't know the whole story, but this is how we help them, by keeping communications going."

They nodded and immediately turned back to the switchboards, their voices calm and clear as they connected headquarters to the front, the front to evacuation hospitals, call after call, fervently hoping that the orders they put through would help the imperiled men. But the reports only worsened. The commander of the 308th must have realized that they were out there alone, for they had apparently dug in to a rocky prominence, known as Hill 198 at headquarters, and had assumed a defensive posture. In the meantime, the Germans had closed in behind them, surrounding the Americans on all sides. Six companies from the 308th, one from the 307th, and two from the 306th were entirely cut off from the rest of the First Army.

Grace trusted that every effort would be made to rescue the men, but the thought of more than 550 American doughboys hunkering down in the darkness and cold in hastily dug entrenchments deeply worried her. The troops' supplies of food, water, and ammunition were surely limited since they had been ordered to leave most of their gear behind in the interest of haste. If they were not relieved soon, dehydration and hunger could prove to be as deadly as German artillery.

She knew the other girls shared her worries, but she was unprepared for Marie's reaction at shift change, when Grace always reported the most significant developments of the day and alerted the incoming operators to any matters they should pay particular attention to. When Grace mentioned the three different regiments to which the stranded companies belonged, Marie's face went white. "Which company of the Three-Oh-Seventh?" she asked in a strangled voice. "Which company?"

"Company K," Grace replied, studying her. "Company K of the Third Battalion. Are you all right?"

"Yes, of course," said Marie shakily, pressing a hand to her chest, tears in her eyes. "I'm fine. My apologies."

"Do you know someone in the Three-Oh-Seventh?"

Marie pressed her lips together and nodded. "I have a—a friend in Company B."

"What's his name?"

"Corporal Giovanni Rossini. He may have enlisted as John Rossini."

Corporal Rossini was surely more than a friend, to provoke such terror. Lowering her voice so the other girls would not overhear, Grace said, "Maybe you should take a moment to compose yourself before you relieve Esther."

"Thank you, but that won't be necessary." Indeed, some of the color had already returned to Marie's face. "I'm ready now."

Grace let her go. She knew all too well that sometimes the only remedy for grief and fear was hard work.

She turned the exchange over to the night shift—Marie, Berthe, and Adele—and went to the mess for a late supper before heading off to quarters and to bed. She prayed that the stranded troops would be rescued overnight, but when she, Suzanne, Esther, and Helen reported for duty shortly before shift change, they learned that the men were still trapped in the pocket, as it had come to be called, but curiously, the Germans had not attacked them. Something was holding them back, and it was surely not mercy or a sense of fair play. Either they thought the Americans outnumbered them, or they suspected it was an elaborate trap meant to draw their fire, or something else entirely. Grace could only speculate.

By midafternoon, the Germans had cast aside their restraints and had unleashed a ferocious assault on the pocket from all sides. With all lines of communication cut off, it was impossible to know the number and severity of the casualties, but given how the Americans were pinned down, the toll was surely staggering. Distant Allied observers reported that the German forces in the area had nearly doubled in number throughout the day and were closing in on the pocket. In the meantime, the rest of the 154th Brigade and the entire 77th Division launched a series of fierce attacks in an attempt to reach the men, but they were repelled again and again.

The next morning when Grace went to the mess for breakfast, every conversation seemed to center on the stranded troops, who apparently believed that the orders they had been given at the onset of the attack still applied, for rather than attempt a stealthy retreat under the cover of night, they stubbornly held their position. The press had got wind of the crisis, and lurid reports referring to the 308th as the "Lost Battalion" had already begun to appear in papers throughout the United States. Grace felt a surge of indignation at the nickname. The men were not lost in the sense that their location was a mystery, nor in the sense that they had been abandoned, all hope of rescue gone. At that very moment, they were fighting back against the encircling enemy, and the remaining brigades of the 307th and 308th were doggedly pushing forward against a German onslaught, determined to reach them. When Grace reported for duty, she learned that the 152nd Field Artillery Brigade planned to support the ground attacks by firing a "barrage of protection" around the pocket in order to draw German troops away.

Later that afternoon, just as Grace returned from a meeting with Colonel Hitt, Suzanne removed her headset, turned a stricken glance Grace's way, and beckoned her closer. "I just connected a call between 77th Division Headquarters and artillery," she murmured, her face ashen. "The boys in the pocket managed to get a homing pigeon out. The message begged them to call off the artillery barrage. The bombs were landing right on top of them!"

"Oh, no." Grace grasped the back of Suzanne's chair for support. "The artillery brigades must have had the wrong coordinates."

"Their own army's weapons, cutting them to bits." Suzanne's voice trembled, tears forming in her eyes as she slowly shook her head from side to side. "Can you imagine the agony?"

"Hold it together, Suzanne," Grace murmured, squeezing her shoulder comfortingly. "You put the call through. The message has been received. The assault has already been halted by now. It's over."

Suzanne pressed her lips together tightly and nodded. She inhaled deeply, patted Grace's hand where it rested on her shoulder, then put on her headset and turned back to the switchboard. They both knew it was not really over, except for the dead. For those who yet lived, especially the grievously wounded, only rescue would end their unendurable misery.

The days passed. The brigades struggling to reach the pocket made little progress. On several occasions the 50th Aero Squadron tried to airdrop supplies to the stranded men, who must have exhausted their rations by then and had no access to fresh water except for a stream along the bottom of the ravine—which was undoubtedly guarded by German snipers, waiting to pick off the Americans one by one as desperate thirst overcame their better judgment. But despite the pilots' skill and daring, dense foliage and fog in the ravine made the doughboys' exact position difficult to pinpoint. By the time the relays were called off, the squadron had lost three aircraft to German ground fire, and all of the dropped parcels had wound up in enemy hands.

During her report at shift change on the night of October 6, Grace soberly informed the girls that the Lost Battalion had endured the fiercest attack yet that day, and had apparently nearly exhausted their dwindling supply of ammunition. Nevertheless, the Americans had fought back vigorously, as they had throughout their ordeal, while the remaining brigades of the 307th and 308th continued to drive forward, putting intense pressure upon the Germans from the south and southeast. Mindful of Marie's worries, wanting to forestall a potential shock as reports came in, Grace carefully noted, "It appears that Company B of the Three-Oh-Seventh is in the lead."

"Whoever's in front, let's hope they break through the German lines and relieve those brave boys," said Adele, folding her arms over her chest. When the others agreed, Marie caught Grace's eye and nodded. Her expression was grave but her eyes were clear, so Grace knew she would be all right.

The next day, at long last, the news they had anxiously prayed for finally came in: Company B of the 307th had broken through to the Lost Battalion. The valiant men who had held their position for five torturous days had been brought food and water and respite. The wounded were being treated and evacuated, the remains of the dead buried. As the casualty reports came in, the revised numbers were staggering. Of the 554 officers and men who had entered the ravine on October 2, scarcely more than a third had been able to walk out again six days later. More than 100 men had been killed, nearly 200 had been wounded, and more than 60 were yet missing, either captured or dead, their remains unidentified.

Not included in that reckoning were the soldiers who had sacrificed their lives in the attempt to rescue the Lost Battalion.

Yet despite the sobering losses, and the criticism and blame that were already beginning to circulate, it was also a day for joy, relief, and thankfulness. Around suppertime, Grace heard the celebration beginning on the other side of the thin wooden wall that separated the exchange from the mess, and her heart rose as she connected the calls that helped the wounded get to hospitals or essential supplies to the units at the front that urgently needed them. Her work was difficult, but she knew it was absolutely essential. Her girls were wonderful, and she was immeasurably proud of them. Their superior officers respected them and made them feel valued as professionals and soldiers, from Colonel Hitt all the way up to General Pershing. As improbable as it might seem to someone taking note of her long hours, her uncomfortable quarters, the cold, the dirt, the noise, and the danger, Grace was happy. She did not want the war to last a single day longer than absolutely necessary, but she was glad and grateful to be exactly where she was, serving her country, proving herself braver and more capable than she had ever imagined as an ordinary hello girl back in New York.

The celebration was still going on a few minutes before eleven o'clock, when Marie, Berthe, and Adele entered through the door to the mess hall, smiling and laughing. The moment they closed the door behind them, they became all business, ready to get to work, though their mouths still turned up at the corners and their eyes sparkled with elation.

Grace hoped their happiness would sustain them through the night, for call volume invariably remained high in the aftermath of a battle, and the war was far from over—although that night it did seem a great deal closer to the end. As she delivered her usual report, Grace noticed Marie following along even more intently than usual, and she could easily guess what Marie wanted most to know. "There were some casualties among the rescuers, including Company B of the Three-Oh-Seventh," Grace told her. "I'm sorry, but I don't have any specific details."

"*Ne t'inquiète pas*," said Marie, sighing softly, managing a tremulous smile. "Everyone here is anxious about someone, isn't that so?"

"My philosophy is that no news is good news," said Adele, patting her reassuringly on the shoulder. "Don't worry about something until you absolutely must."

"I'll try that," said Marie wanly. And with that, the night shift relieved the day shift, and Grace, Suzanne, Berthe, and Helen went next door to join in the celebration that had been a long time coming. Several officers cheered when the women entered, provoking laughter from the others, and soon Grace felt herself caught up in the revelry as the mess hall became a haven of camaraderie and contentment that the surrounding storm of death and destruction could not breach.

And yet the needs of the women under her command could never be far from her thoughts.

Spotting Colonel Hitt talking with a few other officers at a nearby table, Grace pulled up a bench on the opposite side and sat down. "Sir, could I have a moment?" she asked during a lull in the conversation.

"Of course," he said, turning toward her, his grin vanishing as he glanced past her to the door to the exchange. "What's wrong?"

"Everything's fine at the switchboards," she quickly assured him. "This is more of a personal favor."

"Certainly." He leaned forward and rested his arms on the table. "What can I do for you?"

"One of my operators has a friend in Company B of the Three-Oh-Seventh—"

"A friend?" he broke in, eyebrows rising.

"A sweetheart, I think," Grace acknowledged. "She's worried about him, understandably so. Since she isn't family, if anything happened to him, she wouldn't be notified."

"Maybe it's better not to know," the colonel replied, brow furrowing. "Until the worst happens, you can still hope."

"That's good in theory, sir, but not in practice. The uncertainty is anguish. Constantly bracing yourself for the worst, not allowing yourself to hope too much—it's exhausting, as well as distracting."

The colonel rubbed at his jaw. "So you're saying it would help your operator perform better on the job if we could put her mind at ease."

"Simply to know either way would be helpful."

"Let me see what I can do. What's the soldier's name?"

Grace told him, and as she rose to leave, she thanked him in advance for anything he could do.

The following afternoon, Colonel Hitt stopped by the exchange and told her what he had been able to discover from his counterpart with the 307th and the Red Cross. Grace did not wait for the shift change, but hurried off to quarters, where she found Marie seated on her cot, a book balanced on her lap like a desk, writing a letter. She glanced up as Grace entered and froze, pen suspended above the page, her expression wary.

"Corporal John Rossini is not listed among the dead, wounded, or missing," Grace told her. "Nor is a Giovanni Rossini. I can't tell you precisely where he is, but we do know that much."

"That's enough," said Marie, her shoulders relaxing as if relieved of an immeasurable weight. "That's everything. *Merci*. From the bottom of my heart, thank you."

"It's the least I could do," said Grace, lingering a moment to share in Marie's relief before hurrying back to the exchange.

In the days that followed, the war churned on, and yet the rescue of the Lost Battalion infused the operators with a new hope that victory was not only possible, but perhaps only a few short months away. The winter was sure to be arduous, and setbacks along the way were inevitable, but they dared hope that spring would bring sunshine, warmth, and peace.

One morning between breakfast and the start of her shift, Grace was walking back to Barracks Eight after leaving some letters home at the post office when a truck passed her and halted right in front of the exchange. "Hello, Miss Banker," Major Bruce Wedgewood called cheerfully, climbing down from the front passenger seat. "You're just in time for a special delivery for the switchboard soldiers!"

Curious, Grace hurried to catch up. "A new switchboard?" she called back.

"Something even better," the major promised as he and the driver opened the back of the truck.

Grace craned her neck to watch as they climbed inside and removed a tarpaulin from a large, rectangular object. She glimpsed polished wood, a bench— "A piano," she exclaimed. "Where on earth did you find a piano?"

"Some boys from the Seventy-Seventh liberated it from a particularly ostentatious German fortification," he said, beaming. "One of their officers remembered that you girls had a piano in your residence in Chaumont, and he thought you might enjoy having one here."

"Yes, please," Grace exclaimed. "A German brought a piano to the front?"

"Why not?" Major Wedgewood replied sardonically as he and the driver began maneuvering the piano to the edge of the truck bed. "They've been entrenched there since the war began, and they never imagined they'd be dislodged." He gestured to a few passing soldiers who had stopped to watch. "Hey, boys, care to give us a hand?"

They hurried over, and with some effort and much wisecracking, the six men managed to unload the piano out of the truck and onto a flat sheet of wood to keep it from sinking into the mud. Drawn by the commotion, several Signal Corps officers emerged from the mess hall to watch, and Esther and Suzanne appeared in the doorway to their quarters. "Is that ours?" Esther gasped, spotting Grace as she directed the moving crew.

"It is if we have room for it," Grace said cheerfully, hefting the bench and resting it on her hip. "Otherwise we can squeeze it into the mess."

"We'll make room," Suzanne declared, flinging the doors open wide. She and Esther disappeared for a moment, and by the time Grace had guided the six men and the piano over the threshold, she discovered that her friends had cleared out the driest corner of the room, where they usually stacked their footlockers.

"This shall be our parlor," Esther proclaimed, with a grand sweep of her arm.

The men carefully maneuvered the piano in place, Grace set the bench before it, and Helen and Suzanne briskly wiped it down with clean cloths. One of the soldiers sat down and began banging out a ragtime tune, which the small audience greeted with applause and cheers of delight. Almost immediately the door to the exchange swung open, and Marie and Adele appeared in the doorway, gaping in astonishment.

"Where did that come from?" Adele asked.

"Marie plays piano!" Beaming, Suzanne gestured for her to hurry over, while the soldier grinned and made room. "Come on, Marie, give it a whirl!"

"Well, I—" Marie glanced over her shoulder to the switchboards.

"Go on," they all heard Berthe call from the other room. "I can handle this for a few minutes."

Marie's gaze met Grace's, and Grace hesitated only a moment before giving a good-natured shrug and waving her on. Marie sat gracefully down upon the bench, ran her hands up and down the keys, and glanced up smiling. "It could use a good tuning, but it's a fine instrument."

"Play something," Suzanne urged. "Sing for us, like you did in Southampton."

"Yes, please," implored Esther, and a chorus of teasing demands arose.

Laughing, Marie shook her head and waved her hands to silence them. "I'll play," she said, "but let's all sing together."

"One song for now," Grace added. "We can't leave Berthe alone at the switchboard for long."

"I'm fine," Berthe shouted from the other room, and they all burst out laughing.

Marie played a few chords, thinking. "This is in honor of the generous German patron who provided this lovely gift of music," she said ironically. "May the kaiser hear us and cower in fear as he awaits his inevitable defeat."

With that, she began to play "La Marseillaise." The operators, Major Wedgewood, and several of the soldiers joined in, raising their voices, holding their heads high, singing as if the proud, bold words would reach the battlefields, heartening their allies and making all enemies of democracy tremble.

23

OCTOBER 1918

Paris

VALERIE

No one would ever accuse Valerie of taking herself too seriously. She understood the power of a lighthearted remark to defuse a tense situation. She didn't mind being the subject of a good-natured joke, and she rather enjoyed fond nicknames if they were kindly meant. Nevertheless, when Signal Corps girls at telephone offices throughout France began admitting to one another how much the sobriquet "hello girls" had come to annoy them, she understood exactly what they meant.

For one, the name had been used to refer to female switchboard operators ever since telephone exchanges were invented. It was a generic diminutive that in no way conveyed the Signal Corps women's status as soldiers in the U.S. Army. For another, it was precisely that—a diminutive, and too cute by half. Although "hello girls" had never been the Signal Corps operators' official title, the nickname had been appearing more and more frequently in official communications. Some operators didn't mind, but most worried that if the irksome habit wasn't curtailed soon, the army as well as the general public would forget that they had ever been known by the more distinguished title of Signal Corps telephone operators.

American infantry soldiers were sometimes fondly referred to as "doughboys," but that name never appeared in official documents or insignia as if it were their rank and title. Sailors were never called "boat boys," nor were engineers referred to as "construction boys." Still, it wasn't the word "girls" that bothered the operators; indeed, the phrase they most often used to describe themselves was "Signal Corps girls," which conveyed the dignity of their unit as well as a sense of camaraderie and friendliness. Like many of her buddies, Valerie had once accepted the term "hello girls" as an endearment, but she had grown up since joining the army, and as an adult, she wanted to be appreciated more for her professional acumen than for her charm. "Hello girls" as an official designation seemed less of a way to express affection than to put her in her place, a condescending pat on the head when she wanted a salute or a firm handshake.

Thus, when one of the chief operators in Chaumont proposed submitting a formal protest to the War Department to request that they cease perpetuating the nickname "hello girls" before it became adopted as their official title—the inevitable outcome of so much repetition—Valerie eagerly signed on. The War Work Council of the YWCA took up their cause, and several high-ranking officers in the Signal Corps expressed their support for a more respectful designation for the switchboard soldiers who had contributed so much to the war effort.

Valerie was in the telephone room at the Élysées Palace Hotel guiding a new operator through a long-distance connection when Inez rushed in, brandishing a telegram overhead. "The War Department has granted our request," she declared, triumphant. "We are now officially known as the Women's Telephone Unit of the American Signal Corps!"

"Hurrah!" Valerie cried, and her cheer was echoed up and down the switchboard, much to the confusion and amusement of callers from Bordeaux to Souilly.

But later that day, Valerie was astonished to learn that as hard as Inez had fought for the telephone operators to receive the more respectful title they deserved, she herself would not use it much longer.

The operators were walking back to quarters after a grueling shift when Inez caught Valerie by the arm and gestured for her to hang back for a moment. Valerie complied, and after the other girls had moved out of earshot, Inez said quietly, "I wanted you to be the first to know, and I'll get right to the point. I'm leaving the Signal Corps."

"What?" Valerie exclaimed. Drusilla glanced over her shoulder to see what was wrong, but Valerie motioned for her to continue on without them. Whirling upon Inez, she said, "You can't be serious."

"I am serious." Inez laughed shortly. "When am I not serious?"

Fair point. "How can you go home before the war is won? With so many down for the count with influenza, you're needed here more than ever."

"I'm not going home," Inez replied, smiling as she shook her head. "I'm not even leaving Paris. I'm just transferring to the Office of the U.S. Committee on Public Information."

Valerie stared at her, uncomprehending. "You're leaving the Women's Telephone Unit to work in propaganda?"

"Public relations," Inez corrected her, suddenly defensive. "Is it so hard to believe that another bureau would want me?"

"Of course not—"

"Believe it or not, many of our superior officers believe that I've done an excellent job running the Paris exchange. This isn't like the *Carmania*. In Paris, I'm appreciated. I've received a commendation for my efficiency. The director of the Paris branch of the CPI personally recruited me and petitioned General Russel to release me from the Signal Corps so I could accept. The general had to get official permission from the secretary of war to—"

"Yes, yes, you're very much in demand." Then something gave Valerie pause. "What do you mean, Paris isn't like the *Carmania*?"

"Oh, come on. Don't pretend you don't know." Inez folded her arms and glared. "Some of the operators complained about me to the commanding officer on board because they thought my orders were too strict. He wrote to the commanding general of the Seventy-Seventh Division to say that it would be in the best interest of the service to reassign me because of my so-called lack of tact managing other women."

"I didn't know that."

"Everyone knew."

"*I* didn't," Valerie said emphatically. "And I'm probably not the only one, so you might want to stop spreading that story around. No one else is."

Inez studied her for a moment, suspicious, but then she sighed. "Fine. You didn't know. The girls haven't been gossiping about it behind my back for months."

"They haven't been," Valerie insisted. "Is this why you're leaving the Signal Corps? Because in that case—"

"It's not the only reason," said Inez, the brittle edge leaving her voice. "I'm flattered that the CPI recruited me so vigorously, and I'm excited for a new challenge. I'll be doing important, fascinating work."

"You're already doing important, fascinating work," Valerie grumbled, though she knew it was futile to try to change Inez's mind. "How much longer will you be with us?"

Inez resumed walking, so Valerie fell in step beside her. "I start on Monday."

"Monday? So soon?"

"All of our superiors have known for weeks." Her defensive tone returned. "I'm not leaving anyone in the lurch. Which brings me to something else. I want you to know that I recommended you to replace me as chief operator, but they chose Nellie Snow instead."

"Well, obviously. She has seniority."

"Yes, but you'd be better at the job. Also, I like you more."

"Thank you," said Valerie, taken aback. "I don't know what to say."

"It's not that I *don't* like *her*, but—" Inez shrugged. "You've always been more cooperative and amenable."

Valerie raised her eyebrows but said nothing. She'd received worse compliments. "The girls are going to be sorry to see you go." When Inez laughed shortly and tossed her head, Valerie added, "No, I mean it. They will. You have to let me throw you a farewell party."

"No one will come."

"They will if we have it at La Buvette de Simone."

Inez threw her a skeptical sidelong look. "You could get us in at Simone's? Is she a friend of yours or something?"

"I know a guy in the band. A trombone player named Guillaume. He's got a bit of a crush."

"You and your admirers." Inez heaved a sigh. "Fine. If it's at Simone's, I'm in."

"Why so glum?" protested Valerie, laughing. "It's a party in your honor, not a funeral. It'll be fun."

"It'll probably be interrupted by an air raid."

"Then we'll move the party down to the wine cellar." Valerie linked her arm through Inez's, a gesture the prickly chief operator usually resisted, and propelled her along more briskly so they could catch up to the others. "Can you imagine a better place to spend a bombardment?"

Back at quarters, Valerie quickly spread the word among the girls to keep their Saturday evening free, her invitation to the party doubling as an announcement of Inez's departure. She secured a reservation at Simone's after Guillaume pulled some strings in exchange for the promise of a dance, and Inez called in one last favor with their commanding officer to have some Signal Battalion boys fill in for the women so that all could attend the party.

As Valerie had promised, it was great fun. The music was brilliant, the dancing wild, the food and drink the best wartime provisions could offer. The girls pooled their resources and presented Inez with gifts of flowers, wine, and homemade fudge, and throughout the evening, everyone found a moment to kiss her on both cheeks, wish her well, and tell her sincerely that she would be missed. At times Inez looked somewhat startled to discover that she had been rather well liked after all.

Soldiers and Frenchmen had been admiring the merry group of girls all evening, and the party was in full swing when a group of officers approached and asked to buy them all a round of drinks to thank them for their service. Valerie graciously accepted on her friends' behalf, and she was helping pass the bottles of wine when she noticed two of the officers speaking with the band.

"Something's up," she told Inez, nudging her and inclining her head toward the stage.

"I am not making a speech," Inez warned flatly.

But that was not what the officers had in mind. The song concluded, and as the audience clapped and cheered, a captain came to the front of the stage. "Ladies and gentlemen," he began, "you've no doubt noticed that we have a particularly remarkable group of soldiers in our midst. You've probably also heard the new song about them that's become all the rage. It was composed by a fellow in the Ninety-Second—"

"The Seventy-Seventh!" a deep voice bellowed from the crowd.

Everyone burst out laughing, and the captain good-naturedly gestured for them to settle down. "Well, whatever insignia he wears, he's a proud American soldier who wanted to pay tribute to the lovely ladies without whom no one Over Here would be able to tell anyone where to go or what to do when they got there." Another ripple of laughter followed. "So, tonight, in honor of the girls of the United States Signal Corps, we give you—well, I don't know what it's called, actually."

"'Switchboard Soldiers,'" the same deep voice called.

More laughter. "'Switchboard Soldiers,'" the captain repeated. "Feel free to sing along if you know the words."

As the band struck up a merry tune in a march rhythm, Valerie and her friends exchanged glances of delight and amusement. They stood proudly, smiling, as the captain sang their praises in a rather fine tenor.

My switchboard soldier,
Brave angel on the line,
Whenever I hear your voice
Oh, my heart feels fine.
When you ask me, "Number, please,"
It makes my heart feel so fine.

When artillery shells light up the night,
Falling with the rain,

You call in the rescue,
Time and time again.

Our switchboard soldiers
Loyal, valiant, and true,
On the line to save the day
For the red, white, and blue,
When you say, "Allô, j'écoute."
We vow to win the war for you.
Switchboard soldiers, Signal Corps sweethearts,
We shall win the war with you!

The room erupted in cheers and applause. Valerie's cheeks ached from smiling so broadly, and she cheered as lustily as the rest. As the band resumed their set, the captain descended from the stage, joined his buddies, and then all came over to introduce themselves to the Signal Corps girls.

"Aren't you going to miss this?" Valerie teased Inez. "The fame, the glory, the handsome officers composing odes in our honor?"

"That might happen in the CPI too," countered Inez, smiling, but she did look a bit wistful.

Just then, the captain asked Valerie to dance, and she gladly accepted. Afterward, she queried him about the song, but although he obviously wanted very much to impress her with his knowledge, he admitted that he knew only what he had shared from the stage. Valerie hoped eventually to learn more. She had definitely never heard those lyrics before, but the melody was somehow familiar. Had she heard it before, but in a different key, or rhythm, or tempo? Was it a traditional folk tune adapted to modern tastes? Marie would probably know, but Valerie lacked her formal music training. If the song was as popular as the captain claimed, and as the response of the crowd affirmed, perhaps she would hear it again someday. Or perhaps the composer would be written up in *Stars and Stripes*, with all due credit given and mysteries revealed.

At the end of the evening, Inez thanked Valerie for giving her such a lovely send-off. "I'm not leaving Paris," Inez reminded her. "Perhaps we could meet for lunch sometime, and you can needle me about all the fun I'm missing."

"And you can tell me about all the devious strategies you're using to sell the war to the American public," Valerie teased.

Rather than leave it to chance, they made a date for the following week. Still, while Valerie was pleased that they would remain in touch, she knew it wouldn't be the same as sharing a workplace and living quarters.

On Monday, the telephone exchange did feel different without Inez there, as if everyone had taken a deep breath, exhaled, and relaxed, as if they were no longer bracing themselves to be reprimanded for the slightest mistake. The quality of work didn't seem to suffer without Inez's palpable scrutiny; if anything, the girls seemed more cheerful and energetic than since they had first arrived in Paris. Perhaps, Valerie thought, Inez had been wise to change careers.

But even that revelation did not make up for the hard truth that they were shorthanded, and Inez's absence hurt them. The girls from Group Six had finally been released from quarantine and been posted to Signal Corps exchanges throughout France, but the shadow of the pandemic loomed over everything. Thousands had fallen sick in Paris, although precise numbers were impossible to know since the newspapers rarely reported them. Valerie had heard from her counterparts in Le Havre, Saint-Nazaire, and Bordeaux that troopships carrying American soldiers to France deposited hundreds of afflicted soldiers in the port cities, where they packed barracks, hospitals, and YMCA huts, sometimes languishing on pallets of blankets on the floor because all the beds were taken. She had heard rumors of shocking fatality rates aboard the troop transports, and from the sound of it, the toll in the camps, both in France and back home, was not much better. Whenever one of Valerie's operators complained to her of a fever or chills, she took no chances but separated her from her bunkmates and confined her to quarters until she felt better, or until a visiting nurse recommended she be admitted to the hospital. Only one of the girls had been taken to the hospital, and she was going on her second week in the sick ward. Valerie took what precautions she could, but sometimes she felt that except for the doctors and nurses she spoke to, she was the only one who perceived the threat steadily growing all around them.

When she tried to discuss her apprehensions with her friends, they told her not to worry. Some who had crossed the ocean with her in Group Two blamed Inez, saying that she had blown everything out of proportion with her insistence upon masks and frequent hand-washing, and she had planted phobias in Valerie's mind. Drusilla believed that they weren't reading about the influenza in the papers or hearing about it from their superior officers because the illness wasn't that serious, especially compared to the other hazards of war. Valerie was extremely skeptical of this theory. She didn't expect the army to be forthcoming, since with the military everything was so terribly hush-hush all the time, but the press was another matter. They wanted to sell papers, and in her opinion they always tended more toward exaggeration than understatement. The fact that they said so little rather than raising the alarm was deeply troubling.

In the second week of October, she mentioned her concerns to Captain Pederson, who had always struck her as an honest, rational man. "I don't understand the lack of urgency," she said. "Soldiers are dying by the thousands. Sometimes it seems that the troop transports are more dangerous for a soldier than the front lines. Why isn't anyone in the army talking about this?"

"They *are* talking about it," he told her in an undertone, glancing around for eavesdroppers. "They're just not talking to *you*, or to the press. We don't want to start a panic."

"Why not?" she demanded in a whisper, pushing her luck. "Shouldn't we get the word out?"

"Our medical officers and nurses are getting the word," he assured her. "It's a noble instinct to want to warn people of a possible threat, but you have to consider the broader implications. We can't let the Germans believe that our military readiness has been hindered in any way by widespread disease. If they suspect our troops are ill or weak, they'll strike us with such force that it could reverse all the gains we've made over the past few months."

Valerie paused. "I suppose that's a valid concern."

"Rest assured, Miss DeSmedt, if a soldier reports symptoms, we believe him, and he receives whatever care we can give him. Our only pretense is for the Germans. If they sense an advantage and become emboldened, it could prolong the war, and that would result in even greater loss of life over time."

Valerie thanked him for speaking with her and returned to work, both better informed and more uneasy than before.

Yet even as the influenza became increasingly menacing, she found reasons for hope in the news from the front lines, where it seemed that the momentum of the war had shifted in favor of the Allies at last. The German forces appeared to be weakening, and on October 12, the German chancellor accepted President Woodrow Wilson's Fourteen Points as a foundation for negotiating peace. Later that same day, Valerie learned that Berthe Hunt in Souilly had been the first Signal Corps girl to hear the good news, for she had connected the crucial call from G2 to General Pershing's office. Berthe and the other operators at First Army Headquarters quickly spread the word to the other Signal Corps exchanges, sending hope and jubilation along the wires. For the Germans even to acknowledge that they would consider a negotiated truce was an astonishing admission that they were no longer certain of victory. Apparently they did not want to fight to the last man after all. It was ironic, Valerie thought, that the Allies too did not wish for the total destruction of their enemy. If the German government was destroyed utterly, there would be no one with whom to discuss the terms of their surrender, and chaos would follow.

But the operators' hope that the end of the war was imminent was short-lived, for soon thereafter, Supreme Allied Commander Ferdinand Foch declared that the Allies would accept nothing short of unconditional surrender. And yet Valerie and her comrades sensed that the tide of the war had shifted in an irrevocable way, even though the Allies and the Germans continued to launch fierce artillery assaults against each other in the days that followed. Again and again, rumors that the Germans had surrendered rose up and were swiftly dispelled. German long guns hurled destruction down upon the small towns along the front, including Ligny-en-Barrois, as if their commanders were stabbing blindly in the dark in hopes of striking First Army Headquarters. Thus far, Souilly had been spared, suggesting that the Germans did not know where General Pershing was. The Signal Corps's insistence upon absolute secrecy had helped to protect the general thus far, but all that could be undone in one devastating moment if a German gunner choosing towns at random from a map had a very lucky day.

As the autumn days grew colder, and the lovely chestnut trees in Paris faded from green to burnished gold, word came down the telephone lines that the British had liberated Ostend, Belgium, on the North Sea.

Valerie's heart soared, and tears sprang to her eyes. How she wished she could be with her mother and sister and brother at that moment, embracing them, celebrating the joyful news that the German occupiers were being expelled from their homeland!

Surely this was only the beginning. The kaiser's grip on her beloved Belgium was weakening, and the Germans must know it. Surely the Allies would drive them out soon, back within the confines of their own borders where they belonged, and Belgium and France would be free.

24

OCTOBER 1918

Souilly

MARIE

In mid-October, Berthe took Marie aside and quietly told her that four of the Signal Corps officers and operators, including Grace, would celebrate their birthdays before the end of the month. Berthe proposed throwing a party in their honor, with a delicious feast, festive decorations, and excellent company, and she asked Marie to help her organize it. Marie was happy to oblige, especially since Berthe had already put a great deal of thought into the gala and really only needed an assistant. Marie's mouth watered just reading Berthe's ambitious menu, full of delicacies no one had savored in Souilly in years. They would now, thanks to Major Wedgewood, one of the guests of honor, who had somehow managed to obtain what they needed from Paris. Berthe had worked another miracle in tracking down a skilled chef from a nearby French airfield and hiring him to prepare the meal.

Meanwhile, Marie enlisted volunteers from the Signal Battalion to man the switchboards so all of the Signal Corps girls could attend the party. She also asked a few electricians from the 27th Engineers to string a canopy of lights above the mess hall table, into which she wove lacy green angelica flowers. On the morning of the celebration, she ventured into the countryside to gather more flowers, beautiful marguerites with yellow petals and gold centers, which she arranged into several center-pieces dispersed down the center of the long wooden table. One of the colonels lent her several red-and-white semaphore flags, a festive touch to adorn the walls.

The mess hall was charmingly transformed, but when the guests gathered around the table, the sumptuous feast outshone everything else—lobster, caviar, an assortment of cheeses, nuts, roast goose with stuffing and mushroom sauce, roasted potatoes, and fresh cauliflower, with champagne to drink and a *gâteau Basque* filled with pastry cream and raspberry jam.

"I can't believe my eyes," Grace exclaimed, astonished, from her seat at one end of the table as the dishes were placed before them. "It's truly *magnifique*."

The celebration lasted long into the night, full of laughter, camara-derie, and gratitude for the astonishingly marvelous feast. To Marie it felt as if they were not only celebrating their friends' birthdays, but an anticipated end to the war, an Allied victory, a hard-won peace after years of strife. It all seemed within sight now, if not quite within reach.

A few days later, on Grace's actual birthday, her operators presented her with gifts, tokens of their affection and respect. Marie offered her a lovely bouquet of autumn chrysanthemums and sang a medley of her favorite songs. Berthe gave her a basket of fresh fruit, Grace's favorite treat, something they had all taken for granted back home but was dif-ficult to find at the front. Esther and Suzanne presented the chief oper-ator with a gift that evoked blushes from some and uproarious laughter from all: a lacy French brassiere, flirty and feminine, a distinct contrast to their austere, dignified uniforms and a wistful reminder of the pretty frocks they had left behind back home. "I wish French lingerie couturi-ers had designed our bloomers," Grace said, evoking a chorus of agree-ment and laughter from the other girls.

The operators had surprised Grace with their thoughtful gifts, but the next morning, she had an even bigger surprise for them: Ma-jor General Hunter Liggett, to whom General Pershing had delegated leadership of the First Army so that he could focus on his duties as commander in chief, intended to move headquarters again, keeping up with the AEF as it swiftly advanced. "We seven will accompany them to the new headquarters," Grace announced. "Five operators from Chaumont, Langres, and Neufchâteau will replace us here. They're due to arrive tomorrow, and we'll help them get oriented before we depart."

"Where are we going?" asked Adele.

Grace shrugged and shook her head. "I don't know."

"And if you did, you couldn't tell me."

"Exactly," their chief operator replied, smiling. "I assume they'll let us know when we're en route." In the meantime, she added, their commanding officers had issued two pages of new codes, so when the operators weren't on duty or sleeping, they needed to study, to commit the new phrases to memory as quickly as possible. A new offensive was in the works, and they must be prepared.

Later that morning, Colonel Hitt surprised them all with news that with winter approaching, the Signal Corps had decided to make much-needed improvements to the telephone exchange and to the operators' quarters. The existing switchboards were transferred to the barracks next door, new lines were installed, the electrical connections were rerouted, and additional switchboards were taken over from the French. Marie and her comrades worked amid an earsplitting cacophony of hammering and sawing and pounding as the modifications went on all around them. Back in Barracks Eight, their quarters were being expanded into the former telephone office to give the operators more space. "Just in time for us to move somewhere else," Adele noted in an undertone between calls, and Marie had to laugh.

On October 28, the day after the five replacement operators arrived, word came down the wires that Austria had surrendered. Overjoyed, the operators cheered and embraced, and even after they quickly returned to work, they could hear echoes of other celebrations from Barracks Eight and in the streets outside. The disappointing news that soon followed— Germany had not yet given up the fight—did little to diminish their spirits. Without their staunchest ally by their side, surely the Germans too would soon capitulate.

Two days later, after finishing their shift, Marie, Adele, and Esther had lunch together at the mess and then went for a stroll to enjoy the rare sunny day. The wind blew cool and steady, scattering fallen leaves down the muddy streets, and the forest beyond the encampment was awash in vibrant autumn hues. They climbed a nearby hill to take in the view, discussing how to best prepare the new operators who were replacing them, and speculating about where they would be posted next and when they might depart. On the way back to their quarters, they glimpsed Signal Corps officers passing in and out of Barracks Eight on various errands. One officer stood out for his stillness as he leaned against one of the posts of the stairs to the mess, arms folded, looking around expectantly.

"Well, look who it is," said Esther, nudging Adele. "Lieutenant Mills."

"Isn't it curious how often errands bring him from Ligny-en-Barrois to Souilly?" mused Marie.

"Stop it," murmured Adele from the corner of her mouth as a blush rose in her cheeks. Just then, Lieutenant Mills saw them, smiled broadly, and began walking their way.

"You have to play chaperone, Marie, because I have work to do," said Esther, grinning. Hurrying on her way, she waved to Lieutenant Mills in passing. "Hello, Lieutenant! Back so soon?"

"Yes," he replied agreeably, waving back. "Errands. You know how it is."

"Yes, I *do* know," Esther called back, laughing, as she disappeared through the doorway of the new telephone exchange.

Lieutenant Mills watched her go, puzzled, but his smile broadened as he approached Adele. "Hello, Miss Hoppock," he said, his gaze fixed on hers. After a moment he remembered to add, "And Miss Miossec."

"Hello, Lieutenant," Adele replied brightly.

Marie echoed her, but for the most part she kept out of the

conversation, knowing that the pair really only had eyes and ears for each other. She was wondering if she dared slip away to quarters and get some sleep before her next shift when she caught the scent of something burning. A moment later, she spied a plume of black smoke rising from the building next to Barracks Eight—the offices of G2, Army Intelligence.

Alarmed, she clutched Adele's arm and gestured. "I think G2 is on fire!"

Adele looked over and gasped; Lieutenant Mills turned about, saw the smoke, and started running toward it. "Stay back!" he called to them over his shoulder.

For a moment they were too shocked to do anything but obey, but then Marie saw Colonel Hitt burst out of the Barracks Eight mess and sprint toward the fire. A moment later, Grace and Suzanne emerged from the new exchange next door. "Fire!" Suzanne shouted, cupping her hands around her mouth. "Fire!" When Grace and Suzanne began hurrying toward the burning building, Marie did too.

Alarms began to peal. Officers and soldiers raced out of G2 hauling cartons of documents as flames began to flicker through the roof. Marie's heart plummeted as she took in the flimsy wooden walls scorching black from within before her eyes, the oil-paper windows, the tarpaper roof—it was a tinderbox, impossible to save, and yet soldiers were trying, shouting orders, forming a bucket brigade, dumping water onto the flames. Thick plumes of smoke and flame rose into the sky, and the winds carried glowing embers aloft, where they whirled and drifted and settled lightly down upon the adjacent rooftops. One caught on fire, and then another.

Marie caught up to Grace and Suzanne, who had halted several yards from the engulfed G2 building, looking about frantically for some way they could help. Adele soon joined them. "Look," she shouted, seizing Grace's arm and pointing. "Barracks Eight is on fire!"

Marie turned, and her heart plummeted at the sight of red tongues of flame dancing along the wall facing G2.

"Save whatever you can," Major Wedgewood shouted as he ran past them into their quarters.

Immediately the operators raced after him, knowing they had only moments to salvage what they could. Assisted by other soldiers who had come running from all directions, they grabbed whatever was in reach, carried it from the smoldering building, deposited the rescued belongings in the street upwind of the flames, and hurried back inside for more. On her second trip, Marie gasped as if struck. "The piano!" she called out to anyone who might hear, darting around the cots to the nook they called the parlor. "The piano!" she shouted, grabbing one side and shoving the heavy instrument toward the doorway with all her might. It barely budged. "Please, someone help me!"

She planted her feet and pushed again, coughing as tendrils of smoke encircled her. "The piano!" she screamed again, tears of frustration filling her eyes. "Help, please!"

Suddenly two burly soldiers appeared beside her. "We've got it, miss," one of them shouted over the roar of the flames. "Get out while you can!"

Coughing, eyes streaming, she hesitated, watching as they shoved the piano closer toward the door. A third soldier joined them, and together the three men lifted the piano and began hauling it toward the exit. Glancing wildly about, Marie spotted the piano bench, snatched it up in her arms, and followed after the men as quickly as she could.

Outside, she made her way across the street, coughing and clearing her throat. Suddenly Grace and Adele were with her, one taking the bench, the other supporting her as she stumbled along. They halted at the barracks facing their own, watching, heartsick and dismayed, as smoke and flames rose from the place they had called home. Scattered around them were the blankets Julia Russell had given them when they had first arrived, bundled around random belongings snatched from the conflagration. Uniforms, blouses, shoes, hairbrushes, papers, photographs, and other possessions were strewn upon their mattresses, now soaking in the mud.

Suddenly, like an exploding shell, Barracks Eight went up in flames, entirely engulfed.

"We all got out just in time," said Suzanne, her voice strangled. "Everyone got out, right?"

They all nodded, wordless, trembling, hoping it was true.

"Thank goodness the exchange was transferred to the other building," Grace said, pausing to clear her throat. "That was a stroke of luck."

"Maybe not," said Adele, apprehensive, gesturing. "Look!"

Churning clouds of smoke from the burning buildings were flowing in through the open windows of the new telephone office. Glowing embers spattered the roof. As one, the operators began shouting and waving to the soldiers in the bucket brigade, who looked where they were pointing, recognized the danger, and immediately redirected their efforts to saving the exchange.

"Has anyone seen Berthe, Helen, and the others?" Grace asked sharply, scanning the crowds.

"They're still inside," Marie realized, horrified. "They'd never leave the switchboards." She wouldn't have, either, if she had been on duty. The operators would never voluntarily cut off contact with embattled regiments on the front lines. They all knew that every call connected could mean a soldier's life saved, every call neglected a company lost.

Driven by the shocking image of her friends at the switchboard encircled by flames, Marie ran toward the bucket brigade and joined the line passing empty buckets back to the pump. Soon Grace, Suzanne, and Adele lined up beside her. Men were shouting, smoke clouds rising, water soaking their skirts and shoes as they passed the buckets from hand to hand. Marie's gaze darted from the bucket line to the front doors, where she watched in vain for the operators to emerge, to the rooftop where two officers—red-faced and sweating from the heat, coughing, their clothing streaked with soot—overturned buckets of water upon the smoldering tarpaper and wood. Marie imagined water leaking through the cracks and spilling upon the switchboards below. The exchange must be saved. The generals intended to launch a new offensive the next day, and without functioning telephones, they would be unable to issue orders to artillery crews or to the infantry pushing their way through the dense, rugged forest.

The smoke grew thicker. Coughing, eyes watering, Marie paused long enough to tie her handkerchief around her nose and mouth before continuing to pass buckets back to the pumps. The intense heat of the fire seemed to sear her face and hands. Her heart thudded as she imagined her friends at their stations, calmly connecting calls as smoke filled the room and burning embers fell all around them. They had to get out before the building collapsed, before they succumbed to choking smoke. "Grace," she shouted over the roar of the flames, reaching for the chief operator's shoulder. "Grace, we have to—"

She broke off when she realized that Grace's gaze was fixed on the back door of the new exchange. Colonel Hitt was sprinting inside, and moments later, the telephone operators ran out, the colonel following close behind, waving them on. Marie saw him issue orders to a team of engineers, who entered the building and returned soon thereafter hauling the switchboards, the wires severed but otherwise apparently intact. The engineers set the switchboards in the nearby field and formed a second bucket brigade.

Marie watched to make sure Berthe and the others were safe, then glanced worriedly to the switchboards, wires dangling, lights extinguished, buzzers silenced. On her left, Adele caught Marie's eye and shook her head, grim. For the first time since the AEF had come to France, First Army Headquarters was completely out of contact with the troops at the front, the commanders at other bases, and all their allies.

With swift military precision, the soldiers soon extinguished the fires. Incredibly, the new exchange building was saved, but seven other structures, including Barracks Eight, were burned to cinders.

Signal Corps linemen promptly brought the switchboards back indoors and began reinstalling the equipment and repairing the cut lines. Meanwhile, the telephone operators wandered through the piles of salvage searching for their belongings. Miraculously, Marie found her footlocker and its contents—letters from home, family photos, her spare uniform, a few music scores—entirely unscathed, but her bag and all the clothing she stored in it had been reduced to ash. But she would not mourn anything she had lost. The piano had been saved. Everything else could be replaced.

Berthe found an assortment of her belongings in a bag, including her illicit diary, a small bundle of letters from her husband, and three eggs she had bought from a local farm the previous day to bake a cake. "Not a crack in them," she marveled, holding one up to the sunlight. Grace discovered her own footlocker nearby, but her toothbrush was in a shoe several yards away next to her prayer book, which she found in a frying pan on top of a piece of steak.

Everyone found at least a few relics, but most of their belongings had been destroyed along with their quarters. The operators were reassigned to another building, but it was only partially finished, so while they searched the ruins for anything else that might be salvaged, the 27th Engineers swiftly placed floorboards in their new barracks and took care of other essential repairs, enough to make the building habitable by nightfall. Julia Russell and her YWCA volunteers organized new cots, blankets, pillows, and towels for the operators with astonishing speed, and Julia vowed to replace their other necessary items within a day or two. Artillery invited the women to share their mess hall, but Logistics had asked first, and Grace had already accepted. When Logistics offered to find room for the piano, an officer from Artillery retorted, "They can't have the girls and the piano too!" Most of the other operators found that hilariously amusing, but Marie spent a few tense minutes observing the debate until Major Wedgewood pointed out that the piano had been delivered to the switchboard soldiers at the specific request of the troops who had liberated it, and it should accompany the women wherever they resided in Souilly.

An hour after the operators had reluctantly evacuated—or been forcibly removed by Colonel Hitt, as some of the girls told it—the telephone exchange was partially restored. The day shift operators hurried back to their stations to connect whatever calls they could while the repairs continued around them.

Reluctantly concluding that combing the ruins of Barracks Eight was unlikely to yield anything else worth saving, Marie, Adele, and Esther decamped to the Logistics building, where they washed up, tidied their hair, and went to the mess hall for a late lunch. The G4 officers welcomed them warmly. So many of them individually joked about how jealous the Signal Corps men were to have lost the women's company that Marie suspected there was as much truth as humor in the remarks.

While they were eating, a G4 lieutenant came by their table, welcomed them to Logistics, and expressed his sympathy for the loss of their belongings and quarters. "We figured out how the fire started, if you want to know whom to blame," he added wryly.

"Yes, do tell," said Adele, folding her arms and leaning forward to rest them on the table. "I want to start plotting my revenge."

The lieutenant winced and shook his head. "I don't think the army will allow that." He went on to explain that a German POW laboring in the Army Intelligence building had overturned a stove in an attempt at sabotage. He would be punished for the destruction of property and the minor injuries his actions had caused, but fortunately, no one had been killed. Marie could not imagine why anyone had considered it a good idea to assign a German prisoner to work in the Army Intelligence offices, of all places, but she had been in the service long enough to know when to keep her opinions to herself.

By that time, Marie and her fellow night shift operators were thoroughly exhausted. They made their way to their new quarters, where they found Julia Russell and her crew arranging the new cots and bedding, while engineers patched gaps between the wallboards and hammered together rudimentary furniture, as they had done when the operators had first arrived in Souilly. Through an open door, which in Barracks Eight would have led to the telephone exchange, Marie glimpsed the piano, looking none the worse for its ordeal. As she crossed the room, she noticed grass poking up between the floorboards, but some of the YWCA ladies were putting down carpets, worn and faded but clean, adding a touch of color to the plain room while keeping out the worst of the chill. Or so Marie hoped they would. The onset of winter, only weeks away, would be the real test.

Taking in her friends' haggard faces, the weary slump of their shoulders as they chose cots and sank heavily down upon them, Marie asked the engineers and the YWCA volunteers, kindly but firmly, to continue their work another time, after the operators had slept. A bit embarrassed that they had not thought of it themselves, they apologized and hurried off. Marie and Adele drew the blackout curtains while their bunkmates undressed, pulled on their pajamas, and climbed into bed, some stuffing their ears with cotton wadding before pulling the covers up to their chins. Soon Marie too was in her new cot beneath a fresh new blanket, sinking into sleep.

When she woke, hours later, she smelled faint traces of smoke. Sitting up, she discovered that someone had left her belongings in a neat pile at the foot of her cot. Placed carefully on top were two envelopes.

Marie tossed back the covers and rose swiftly from bed. "It's good that the mail was delivered after the fire rather than before, isn't it?" said Adele, stretched out on her back on the next cot over, reading a letter. "All of this news from home could have gone up in smoke."

"One stroke of good luck is better than none," Marie agreed, taking up her letters and settling back upon her cot. Tears of happiness sprang into her eyes when she saw her mother's familiar handwriting on the first envelope, knowing that it would soon transport her back home to her family, if only in spirit, and if only for a few minutes. The handwriting on the second, thicker envelope was unfamiliar, and for a brief moment her heart leapt, hoping that perhaps she had heard from Giovanni at long last, but then she noticed that it had been sent from Tours. Curious, she opened that envelope first and laughed aloud with delight upon finding a letter from Sister Agnès, letters and drawings from the children, and a photograph of herself with the choir. How sweet and dignified the children seemed as they gazed at the camera— except for Gisèle, who had been caught in the act of exchanging a smile with the girl beside her, whose hand she clasped.

Laying out the photograph and the drawings on the cot before her,

Marie pressed her hand to her lips as she studied them, smiling, blinking back tears. She had forgotten that the Signal Corps photographer—Valerie's brother—had taken the picture. He had promised to send prints to the convent, and she was immeasurably grateful that he had kept his word. How kind of Sister Agnès to send a print to her! The good, compassionate nun must have known how much it would lift Marie's spirits to have this memento of the children's performance, and to see in their words and drawings that they were safe and thriving.

On a day when so many cherished possessions and memories of home had been lost, the photograph and the love, kindness, and friendship it represented was a true and welcome gift.

25

OCTOBER–NOVEMBER 1918

Souilly

GRACE

For an entire day and night after the fire, Grace and her operators were subjected to a steady barrage of complaints from operators at other bases, who chastised them for negligently allowing their exchange to fall silent for an entire hour. Suppressing her frustration, Grace tried to no avail to placate the new chief operator at Chaumont, who upbraided her relentlessly, reminding her of her responsibilities, describing in great detail how much the Souilly operators had inconvenienced everyone else, and scolding her with vivid hypotheticals of all the terrible consequences the troops might have suffered while Grace and her girls were ignoring their switchboards.

Grace endured the reprimands stoically, assuring her less experienced counterpart that it would never happen again. She wished she could silence the barrage by explaining why the Souilly exchange had fallen out of contact so abruptly, but she couldn't. Their superior officers had forbidden Grace and her operators to tell anyone about the fire, for if word spread and the Germans picked up the threads of the story, they might weave them together and realize that First Army Headquarters must be at Souilly. That was a risk they dared not take, so they endured the undeserved criticism without defending themselves.

"After the war, when the truth comes out, we will be vindicated," Grace assured her operators. "Those who berate us now will be lining up to apologize in the future."

"That's certainly something to look forward to," Suzanne remarked dryly, folding her arms.

"To be fair, the girls at the rear don't understand how difficult conditions are here at the front, or the challenges that confront us," said Marie. "I didn't, before I was transferred to Neufchâteau. They go about their days in peace. We live in the midst of war. Still, wouldn't each of us prefer to be here at the front, despite the hardships, than at the rear in comfort?"

Grace and the other operators nodded and murmured assent, although the hardships were many. They had heeded just in time Colonel Hitt's warnings to prepare for a long, hard winter. Even before the fire had forced them to decamp to more ramshackle barracks, they never went hungry, but cleanliness, warmth, and comfort often eluded them. Mud and dirt were everywhere, tracked in from the roads to their quarters, the exchange, and the mess hall no matter how diligently they wiped and scraped their shoes. Despite the frequent downpours, there were often shortages of fresh, clean water. Baths were but a fond memory, although a clever engineer had rigged up a shower in an old shed. When Grace's turn to use it finally came, she shivered in the thin trickle of water as she washed herself from head to toe, and emerged feeling pleased and refreshed, only to become dirty again as she dried herself with a towel. In the operators' quarters, ice formed overnight in the pails they used as washbasins, making sponge baths and teeth brushing an exercise in fortitude. Chapped skin was as common as clean clothes were rare. The operators wore their white blouses several days in a row, and after that, if they could not find enough time or sufficient clean water to do laundry, they turned their shirts inside out and wore them a few days more.

Two weeks earlier, Grace had narrowly avoided serious injury to her feet when she had collapsed into bed after a grueling shift, thoroughly exhausted, and slept soundly through the night, only to discover upon waking that the roof had leaked above the foot of her cot, soaking her blanket. It had nearly frozen solid around her feet, which were so numb she could not feel them. Throwing off the blanket, she had been horrified to discover that her feet were white and swollen. Heart pounding, she vigorously rubbed life back into them, her fears easing only after they began to ache painfully. She could not fit her bloated feet into her shoes, so for days she shuffled about in a pair of large boots lent to her by the quartermaster. If the overnight temperatures had dipped any lower, the medic had said, she might have suffered frostbite. "Be more careful, miss," he had scolded her.

She had already moved her cot away from the leak. What more could she do?

"I understand that the operators at the rear can't even imagine what we endure here, but knowing that they all believe we failed in our duties—" Adele shook her head, frowning. "It's unbearable."

"We've all borne worse," Grace reminded them. "Let's just hope the worst is behind us."

They all could agree to that.

Two days after the fire, as light snowflakes swirled in the skies above Souilly, Grace was walking back to the exchange after a meeting in the relocated Army Intelligence offices when she heard a man call her name. Turning carefully to avoid twisting an ankle on the ruts in the frozen mud, she felt a frisson of surprise and relief at the sight of Captain Mack making his way toward her, a scarf wound about his neck, his hands thrust into the pockets of his woolen overcoat. "Good morning, Miss Banker," he called, smiling.

"Why, if it isn't my favorite wandering Australian," she replied. "What brings you back to our humble village?"

"I heard about the fire," he said, halting before her. His smile was warm, but his face had grown lean and haggard, and his eyes were ringed with exhaustion. "I wanted to see for myself that you were all right."

"I'm fine, as you can see," she replied, warming to his words, but concerned about his obvious fatigue. "Barracks Eight was a total loss, but the exchange and all the switchboards were saved."

"That's fortunate."

"Rest assured, your Distinguished Service Cross is safe and undamaged."

His brow furrowed. He raised his hands as if he intended to place them on her shoulders and draw her closer, but at the last moment he caught himself and let them fall to his sides. "I hope you didn't risk your life to save it."

"Not at all," she said, which was mostly true. "But Miss Miossec did risk her life to save the piano."

He cocked an eyebrow. "Now, that's a risk worth taking."

She laughed and agreed, studying his expression as he turned in place, noting the changes the fire had wrought. "Do you want to see our new quarters?" she asked tentatively. "We've gone with an understated, minimalist theme with our décor this time. It's really quite impressive."

He smiled, too tired to laugh. "Lead on."

She peeked inside first to make sure none of the girls were indisposed, then invited him in. He greeted the other operators, who were relaxing on their cots, reading and writing letters, playing cards, or simply chatting with friends. Taking a loaf of bread and a pot of jam from the stash in her footlocker, Grace led Mack into the adjoining room, which some of the girls referred to as the parlor and others as the conservatory, due to the piano. She quickly made him a jam sandwich, which he devoured hungrily while she prepared a second.

"I hear rumors that headquarters will be moving soon," he said, after thanking her for the food and patting his stomach in satisfaction.

"I hear rumors too," she said lightly, shrugging.

"I also heard that I missed a magnificent feast in honor of your birthday."

Grace smiled. "That rumor I can confirm, although I was only one of four guests of honor. I would have invited you, but I didn't know where to send the invitation."

"That's my fault," he said ruefully. He reached into his deep coat pocket, brought out a parcel wrapped in brown paper tied neatly with string, and presented it to her. "A belated happy birthday, Miss Banker."

Struck speechless, she unwrapped the parcel and discovered a beautiful handbag, black satin embroidered and beaded in a graceful, swirling pattern of red, white, and blue. "How exquisite," she breathed.

"I found it in Domrémy-la-Pucelle, and thought of you."

"The birthplace of Joan of Arc." She traced the pattern with a fingertip. "And how perfect—the colors of the United States and France."

"And Australia," he protested, feigning injury. "Don't leave us out of it."

"Never," she said, smiling. "Thank you very much."

"You're very welcome. I'm only sorry I missed your real birthday."

"Don't be," she said. "I'm not. That was before the fire. This lovely gift might have been lost along with everything else."

"Then I'll be grateful for the delay, even though it kept me from you." His eyes met hers and held them. "We've all seen too much loss."

She felt heat rising in her cheeks and tore her gaze away. "You did miss a wonderful feast, though," she said, making a show of admiring the beadwork, though that just provided an excuse not to stare into the captain's eyes. "Bread and jam can't compare."

"I don't know about that. That jam was quite excellent." Following her example, he traced the pattern of beads and embroidery with a fingertip, his hands broad, strong, and capable. "Red, white, and blue."

"The United States and France."

"And Australia," he said firmly, smiling, interlacing his fingers through hers. "It's a marvelous country, full of wonders and endless potential. Have you ever considered visiting it?"

"I can't say that I ever have," she replied, fighting to keep her voice steady. "It's a long way from New Jersey."

"Worth the journey, though?"

"Perhaps. If it's as wondrous as you say."

"It is. And the people are friendly too. You'd like them, especially my sisters and my mother. They'd make you feel right at home."

Grace's heart thumped. What was he trying to say? "I imagine you miss your homeland very much."

"I do. I never thought I would quite so much." He released her hand and sat back in his chair, sighing, his gaze suddenly far away. "After the war, I believe I'll request a transfer back to Melbourne. If I don't get it, I might retire from the service."

"Melbourne," Grace echoed, nodding, heart sinking. Of course he would want to return to his own country. Didn't she want to do the same? A few of the operators from small midwestern towns mused dreamily about remaining in Paris after the war, but almost everyone else spoke longingly of the homes, families, and friends they had left behind and yearned to see again.

Mack had given her a beautiful birthday gift, he regretted being kept away from her, but he would not come right out and tell her why he missed her when they were apart. She was fond of him—very fond—but she was tired of wondering how he truly felt about her. She could not confess her feelings before he declared his, but maybe he had nothing substantial to declare. And if he intended to return to Australia, while she wanted to go home to the United States—

Perhaps he had recognized this inevitable quandary long ago, and that was why he had held back.

She reminded herself that she enjoyed his company, and that he was visibly exhausted and needed a respite, not more conflict. So she asked him if he wanted another jelly sandwich, and she asked him to tell her more about Australia. Before long, other operators and officers arrived, for the conservatory had become a popular gathering place for the displaced former occupants of Barracks Eight. Some joined Grace and Mack in conversation, and others gathered around the piano while a Signal Corps lineman played ragtime tunes. An hour passed, as Grace discovered when she checked her watch, and she eventually told Mack that she had to report to the telephone exchange. "Shall we meet for dinner?" she asked, rising. "Logistics invited us to share their mess. I'm sure they won't object if I bring a guest."

He shook his head, regretful. "I have meetings until late. Breakfast?"

"Breakfast," Grace replied, smiling. "Seven o'clock at G4?"

"It's a deal." He held out his hand, and she laughed as she shook it. He held on longer than he needed to, longer than was prudent in a room full of watchful friends and colleagues. She was the one who had to pull away, apologetically, and hurry off to work.

The switchboard was active all afternoon, fielding calls related to the battles ongoing at Valenciennes and the Sambre, so Grace was too busy to brood. The next morning after a good night's sleep, she felt more serene about the whole bewildering situation, more accepting of Captain Mack's reticence. He cared about her, that much she knew. Eventually he would tell her so, or he wouldn't. In the meantime, she would enjoy his company, and have no expectations for the future. As she had told herself so many months ago, she had joined the Signal Corps to serve her country and to defeat the kaiser, not to find a husband. All that mattered now was winning the war and looking after her operators. She suspected Mack would be the first to agree.

At breakfast, Mack seemed much more relaxed, smiling and joking as he had when they had first met in Chaumont. It was a wonder what a good night's rest, a clean uniform, and a decent meal could do. Grace enjoyed herself quite a lot, now that she had let go of her expectations for the future of their relationship. Nothing was certain this close to the front, not victory, not the roof over one's head, not another day of life. She would enjoy the time they had together now, and not dwell upon tomorrow.

They parted with a handshake, a wish for good luck, and hopes to see each other again soon.

Later that evening, after supper, Grace returned to their new quarters just as Berthe was distributing the day's mail. "Here's one for you, chief," she said, holding out an envelope to Grace as she passed.

Grace skimmed the envelope and cried out in delight when she recognized the handwriting. "It's from my brother!"

"Thank heavens," said Suzanne, glancing up from her cot, where she was reading a letter of her own. "It's been weeks. When did he send it? Where is he?"

"Give me a minute," said Grace, laughing as she made her way to her own cot, between Suzanne's and Esther's. Tugging off her shoes, she sat down and carefully opened the envelope. *Dear Grace*, the letter began. *First, the good news: I'm alive and the medics expect me to make a full recovery.*

She must have gasped aloud, because Suzanne darted to her side. "Grace? What is it?"

"Eugene—" she murmured, clutching the letter, heart pounding. "He's been—injured, I—I think."

She read on. *The bad news*, he continued, *is that my unit was gassed in the recent offensive. Despite my mask, I inhaled more than my share, and my lungs are giving me a bit of trouble. More good news: My eyes are perfectly fine. Some of my buddies were not so fortunate.*

"He was gassed," she told her friends, who had gathered around her, their faces stricken. She read on. "He's at Tours, recovering in a convalescent hospital. He says it's comfortable and the nurses are providing him with excellent care." She let out a small, shaky laugh and glanced up at Marie. "He says a children's choir recently treated them to a delightful concert of French folk tunes."

"I've seen that hospital," Marie said, her expression solemn and sympathetic. "It's in a beautiful fifteenth-century chateau in the countryside. It's a safe, restful place to recuperate, and the nurses seemed very competent and caring."

"I'm sure Eugene is in very good hands," said Suzanne, taking a seat beside Grace and putting an arm around her shoulders. "Look. This is his handwriting, right?" Grace nodded. "If he's strong enough to write letters on his own rather than dictating to a nurse, he must be on the mend, don't you think?"

Grace nodded again and shrugged, acknowledging the point.

"My sister Eleanor is at Tours," said Adele, rising from her cot. "I'll call her right now and ask her to check in on Eugene as soon as she can, to cheer him up and to see that he has everything he needs."

"The lines are for—"

"Military matters only, yes, I know," Adele tossed over her shoulder. "Our chief operator's morale is a military matter."

"Hear, hear," declared Suzanne.

When the other girls assented, Grace let it go. "Make sure he's telling me the truth about his condition," she called to Adele. It would be just like Eugene to put on a brave face rather than worry the family.

The family. Her heart plummeted. Had he written to their family? She imagined their widowed mother clutching a letter, weeping, their anxious sisters concealing their own worry in an effort to comfort her. And their father was gone, and Grace was thousands of miles away.

Two days later, Grace was patiently assisting one of the new girls through a complicated long-distance relay when Adele waved her over, beaming. "Eleanor just returned from visiting Eugene," she reported. "She says he's in excellent spirits, he's breathing well, and he's able to walk around the garden unassisted. She also mentioned that he's quite good-looking and has a droll sense of humor she found thoroughly charming."

"That's Eugene all right," said Grace, smiling, tears of relief springing into her eyes. She hoped with all her heart that he would remain at Tours long enough to fully recover, slowly and steadily, rather than being rushed back to the front. He wouldn't like it, no doubt, but she would consider it a blessing if he remained at Tours through the end of the war.

A few days later, on November 8, Colonel Hitt summoned Grace to his office to receive her new orders, the advance with First Army Headquarters they had been expecting since late October. "Next week, you'll proceed with five operators and establish a new exchange at Dun-sur-Meuse," he told her. "Mrs. Hunt will remain here as chief operator, but otherwise you should choose the five operators you consider best suited for challenging conditions."

"Yes, sir," she replied. Dun-sur-Meuse, a village about fifty kilometers north of Souilly, was where, only three days before, the 5th Division had stormed across open fields under heavy fire and crossed the Meuse River. "I assume we should plan to travel light?"

"Yes. One bag apiece, only the essentials." The colonel winced.

"From what I've heard, our new headquarters will make this place seem like a resort on the Riviera."

"I'll put together a team," Grace said.

She hoped the rumors about conditions at their new base were exaggerated, but she suspected they were not, considering how long the region had suffered under German occupation. And with the German army becoming increasingly more desperate as they were driven back behind the Hindenburg Line and the 5th Division prepared to cross the Meuse, the new posting was sure to be the operators' most difficult and dangerous yet.

Grace realized, too late, that she should have returned Captain Mack's Distinguished Service Cross to him, and not only because she had never felt deserving of the honor. After First Army Headquarters relocated, the medal might be safer in his care than her own.

26

NOVEMBER 1918

Paris and Souilly

VALERIE, MARIE, AND GRACE

For weeks, intelligence reports Valerie had sent through the Paris telephone exchange had described a Germany roiling with unrest. Citizens and laborers protested in the streets over food and water shortages. Influenza swept through the cities. In Bavaria, a political faction in Munich had forced King Louis III to abdicate and had declared themselves a separate Bavarian republic. In early November, sailors of the *Hochseeflotte* had mutinied in Kiel rather than obey orders to sail out into the English Channel for a final battle with the Royal Navy. Only yesterday, rumors had swept through Paris that Kaiser Wilhelm II had abdicated after being informed by his military leaders that they had no confidence in him. Later that day, the rumors were confirmed by reports that two prominent political leaders had each declared themselves in charge of the provisional government. While the two factions argued in the Reichstag over an agreement that would haul their floundering nation back from the brink of collapse, their followers marched and fought one another in the streets.

Just that morning, the phone lines at the Élysées Palace Hotel had hummed with a stunning new report: The former emperor had departed

Germany by train and crossed the border into the Netherlands, which had remained neutral throughout the war. The news had been so startling, the implications so hopeful and thrilling, that Valerie had not left for her lunch break on time. When she finally pried herself away, she nearly broke into a run down the Champs-Élysées rather than be late for her weekly lunch date with Inez.

When Valerie arrived at Jambon et Deux Oeufs, she expected to find her former coworker seated inside, already perusing a menu. At the sight of Valerie scurrying in late, she would no doubt glance up, arch her eyebrows, and tap her wristwatch sardonically, as she had done numerous times before. But to Valerie's surprise, Inez was nowhere to be found. As if the morning had not been full of enough surprises, carefree Valerie had arrived right on time and fastidious Inez was late. Valerie requested a table for two, wondering at her friend's delay. Perhaps the Committee on Public Information was scrambling to create posters and press releases to accommodate the stunning recent developments, and Inez, caught up in her work, had lost track of time.

Valerie waited, but after fifteen minutes passed and Inez still had not appeared, she ordered a bowl of onion soup, bread, and ersatz coffee, keeping one eye on the door as she ate. Inez prided herself on her punctuality. Something very interesting indeed must have come up at her new workplace for her to fail to keep an appointment. Valerie expected her to rush in at any moment, chagrined, but Inez still had not appeared by the time she finished her meal.

Valerie paid the tab and was about to return to work early when curiosity prompted her to turn instead in the direction of Inez's new office. Although the skies were overcast and a stiff wind blew dried leaves down the boulevard, the anticipation she glimpsed in the faces of other pedestrians felt as fresh as springtime. Nearly everyone now believed that an Allied victory was certain, inevitable, only a matter of time. Wounded veterans making their careful way down the sidewalks and citizens wearing cloth masks as they went about their errands hinted at past loss and future danger, but hope too seemed to drift on the air all around them, compelling them to hold on just a bit longer. Peace would come, heralding, for many, long-awaited reunions with absent loved ones and the return to homes they had fled in fear.

Mindful of the time, Valerie hurried to the CPI office building, which was marked with a discreet sign by the front entrance. Climbing the stairs to the second floor, she approached the receptionist's desk, introduced herself as a friend of Mrs. Crittenden, and asked to speak with her. "We were supposed to meet for lunch," she said, smiling. "It's very unlike her to forget a date, so I thought I'd come down here to embarrass her properly, in person."

"My apologies, miss," the receptionist replied, dismayed. "I thought we had contacted everyone on Mrs. Crittenden's calendar. She's been out all week due to illness." Her voice dropped to a whisper. "Spanish flu."

Valerie felt a chill. "You're certain."

The woman nodded.

"Where is she?"

"At home, I believe."

Valerie pressed her lips together, nodded goodbye, and hurried off. Apparently none of Inez's new coworkers had thought to check in on her. If she had remained with the Signal Corps, the other operators would have cared for her faithfully, as they had for the other operators who had fallen ill. Instead, it seemed that Inez was suffering alone.

Fortunately, the flat Inez had taken after moving out of the telephone operators' hostel was only two blocks from the CPI offices, and Valerie knew the shortest route. The doorman, a disabled veteran, waved her right in, so she raced up the stairs and pounded on her friend's door. "Inez?" she called. When no one answered, Valerie pounded again and raised her voice to a shout. "Inez? Answer if you can."

No reply. Valerie tested the doorknob. Locked.

"*Mademoiselle n'est pas chez elle,*" a young voice behind her piped up.

Turning, Valerie discovered a girl of about thirteen years peering out from the flat across the hall. "Do you know where she is?" Valerie inquired in French. "She's a dear friend of mine, and I'm concerned."

"I heard the men say they would take her to the American Hospital."

Valerie had to think for a moment. "Did they mean the one at Lycée Pasteur?"

The girl made a face, uncertain. "I think so. Is there another?"

Valerie thanked her and dashed off again, down the stairs and outside. A quick glance to the left and right, a search of her memory, a glimpse of a streetcar approaching, a decision. She boarded the streetcar as soon as it slowed; impatient, she silently willed the driver to speed up, and jumped off a block before her stop, convinced she could run faster.

She was out of breath by the time she entered the Lycée Pasteur and found the entrance to the influenza ward, or at least what had originally been the entrance; the ward had expanded into so many adjacent departments that she could not find the beginning or the end. As she searched down one corridor and then another, the true extent of the epidemic that the scene revealed appalled her, but she should not have been surprised. Nearly two thousand Parisians had died each week in October, or so she had overheard at the exchange. She should have known that the hospitals would be overwhelmed.

At last she stumbled upon what appeared to be a registration desk. A soldier was seated behind it in a wheelchair, his nose and mouth covered by a white cloth mask. At the sound of her footfalls, he looked up, shook his head, and held up both hands with his palms facing her, a warning not to approach any closer. "Mademoiselle, you're not permitted on this floor without a mask," he said. "This is a quarantine ward. Only medical personnel can enter."

"I'm here to see a friend," she said, taking the mask she carried everywhere from her pocket and putting it on, silently berating herself for neglecting to do so earlier.

His eyes above his mask were incredulous. "No visitors allowed."

"Then I'm here to see my sister. Mrs. Inez Crittenden. She's an American."

He cocked his head, skeptical. "No family is allowed either. I'm sorry, but I have to ask you to leave."

"Could you at least tell me how Mrs. Crittenden is doing?" Valerie implored. "Is she even here? What's her prognosis? Is there anything she needs, anything I could bring to her? If I can't see her, can she talk on the telephone?" She took a deep, shaky breath. "Please. She doesn't have any family Over Here. Please tell me whatever you can."

He hesitated. "Since you're her *sister*," he said, emphasizing the word, "I can list you as her next of kin, and you'll be permitted to call and inquire about her status. But I can't promise you'll be able to speak to anyone. Every bed is full, and every phone call with a concerned family member means time away from patients."

"I understand," Valerie replied. "Thank you."

He passed her a form and a pencil. Valerie provided Inez's full name, her address in Paris, and then her own name and address, and the telephone numbers for her quarters and the exchange, including her operator number. The soldier promised that someone would call when they had information to share, but he warned that it might not be soon.

By the time Valerie returned to the Signal Corps headquarters, she was nearly half an hour late, but no one seemed to notice. The switchboard was fairly sizzling with activity, with calls coming in from First Army Headquarters, port cities, Services of Supply, French exchanges, and seemingly everywhere else in France, as everyone from Marshal Foch to General Pershing and all the way down revised plans in response to the kaiser's abdication and the power struggle within the German provisional government. Valerie waited, anxious and impatient, for news from the hospital. When no word came, she was tempted to call them, but she refrained, reluctant to annoy the hospital staff and make them less willing to help her. She pushed her worries aside and threw herself into her work in a vain attempt to make the time pass more quickly.

After her shift, she went straight back to quarters, hoping someone from the hospital had left a message there, aggrieved to discover that no one had. She had supper at the hostel with a few of the other girls, who responded with alarm and sympathy when she told them Inez was ill. They had nearly finished eating when the YWCA hostess approached the table and told Valerie that the American Hospital had rung for her. Valerie nearly knocked over her chair in her haste to get to the telephone.

Inez Crittenden was a patient in the influenza ward, a nurse confirmed. She was in serious condition, and everything that could be done for her was being done. She was not lucid enough to speak on the phone, but if she regained consciousness, she would be told that Valerie had visited. If her condition changed significantly for better or worse, the staff would contact Valerie again.

"Mademoiselle, if I may be frank—" The nurse hesitated. "The only thing you can do now is pray."

Dismayed, Valerie thanked her and ended the call.

Rumors that the war was nearly over had circulated through Souilly for days, but it was not until the second week of November that Marie overheard credible references to an imminent armistice based upon President Wilson's Fourteen Points, which included among its stringent requirements the right for the Allies to occupy Germany. As the girls began to whisper among themselves, hardly daring to believe that peace might be at hand, Colonel Hitt came to the exchange to address all of the operators at shift change. "I should not need to remind you that any messages you might overhear regarding arrangements for the armistice are strictly confidential," he said, sweeping a stern look over them all. "Any leaks will result in immediate dismissal."

Marie exchanged a look with Berthe, eyebrows raised. Berthe muffled a sigh and gazed upward, a restrained version of rolling her eyes. They all liked and respected the colonel, but surely by now they had proven themselves a hundred times over. He ought to know better than to question their loyalty and discretion.

Traffic on the switchboards remained heavy throughout the day as the front lines moved closer to the German border, Allied commanders shifted their troops, and arrangements to transfer First Army

Headquarters to Dun-sur-Meuse proceeded. Marie had just returned to her station after a hasty, late supper when, at eight o'clock, an Artillery lieutenant entered the switchboard office and spoke briefly to Berthe.

He had no sooner departed than Berthe called the operators to order. "It's my great honor and delight to announce that the armistice is officially at hand," she declared, a broad smile lighting up her face. "All fighting will stop in fifteen hours, at precisely eleven o'clock tomorrow morning."

Marie cried out with joy, and as her comrades tore off their headsets and bolted from their chairs to embrace one another, cheering and exclaiming with delight and relief, she bowed her head and crossed her hands over her heart, murmuring a silent prayer of thankfulness. Then she too rose and joined the celebration, kissing her friends on both cheeks, clasping their hands, congratulating one another, laughing and crying.

Berthe soon clapped her hands for their attention. "We are still on duty," she reminded them. "The war isn't over yet, and swift, accurate communications are as crucial as ever."

Smiling and wiping away tears of joy, the operators hurried back to their stations, threw on their headsets, and adjusted the mouthpieces. Soon thereafter, they heard soldiers in the roads outside the exchange shouting and cheering as word of the forthcoming armistice spread.

About an hour later, the door burst open, and as if blown in on a gust of cold wintry air, a group of French communications operators swept into the barracks, singing, laughing, dancing. "*La guerre est finie!*" one sergeant proclaimed joyfully as his companions darted through the room, trying to kiss the operators on both cheeks as they continued to connect calls and translate messages.

"I am so happy, I could jump up and hit the ceiling!" a corporal cried out in heavily accented English.

"That's lovely, thank you," said Berthe, nodding, smiling, her arms widespread as she attempted to steer the jubilant soldiers to the exit. Eventually she got rid of them, and the operators, smiling and shaking their heads, were able to continue their work undisturbed.

Late into the night, Marie listened to the distant rumble of artillery barrages as she and her comrades connected the last calls of the war.

. . .

When Grace reported for duty early on the morning of November 11, the first thing Colonel Hitt told her was that her orders to move to Dun-sur-Meuse had been countermanded. That decision more than any rumor, more than the celebrations outside her barracks window, told her that the war was truly nearing its end.

Marshal Ferdinand Foch had signed the Armistice of Compiègne at 5:45 a.m., the colonel told her, officially ending the hostilities on land, at sea, and in the air between the Allies and Germany, the last remaining of their Central Powers adversaries. While the agreement marked a victory for the Allies, it did not require Germany to formally surrender. Many of the officers Grace spoke to had grave misgivings about that, while others assured her that it would bring an end to the bloodshed and prevent Germany from ever again taking up arms and plunging the world into war.

"The Armistice will go into effect at eleven o'clock this morning," the colonel added. "Keep your head down until then."

"You too," she replied solemnly. They were so close to surviving the war. What a wretched tragedy it would be to perish in the last few hours of the conflict!

Leaving Colonel Hitt's office, Grace reported for duty at the telephone exchange, where she found herself repeatedly glancing at the clock, counting down the minutes until the war ended. In the distance, she still heard the boom and rumble of artillery, so utterly senseless at that point that she could only shake her head in frustration and bemusement. She imagined telegraph units attached to companies at the front, poised by their receivers, awaiting the signal that the Great War was finally over. Only then would it be official. Only then would the soldiers lay down their arms while their leaders began the hard work of building a lasting peace.

Suddenly, a few minutes before eleven o'clock, the door to the exchange burst open and a captain from the Signal Corps telegraph office burst in, his eyes wild with panic. "Our lines are down," he gasped.

"We can't telegraph the news across the front! I have to get the official announcement out before eleven o'clock!"

"Here, Captain," Grace said, handing him her own headset and guiding him to a station. He pulled the headset on, adjusted the mouthpiece, and then, while she swiftly connected him to one exchange after another, he shouted his message to anyone who answered. Her hands flew over the switchboard; the captain's voice grew hoarse. The battleground was so vast, the stations so great in number, that it was impossible to reach everyone simultaneously. At one point, the sounds of celebration outside compelled her to glance up at the clock. Her heart sank when she saw that it was five minutes past eleven, for although the war was over, not everyone knew it. Soldiers were still fighting and still dying, as they would until the captain's message was received everywhere along the front.

Eventually, finally, the captain finished. He removed the headset, wiped his brow with the back of his hand, returned the headset to Grace, and thanked her gruffly. "I hope it was soon enough," he said wearily, rising from the chair. "I hope no men died because of this delay."

He trudged off, and when the door closed behind him, Grace sank into the chair he had vacated, drained.

"Why didn't they trust us with this task in the first place?" said Adele, agitated. "If each of us had been given the authority to deliver the signal, we could have divided up the calls and spread the word in a fraction of the time."

"That's the wrong question," said Marie, an edge to her voice. "We ought to ask why General Pershing didn't order his commanders to suspend all attacks and offensives during the final hours of the war. He knew the Armistice was imminent. He could have ordered all combat to end at midnight, or even at dawn. How many thousands of men died this morning because he allowed the fighting to go on until the last minute?"

Grace had no answer for either of her operators.

At last, the war was over. After enduring unfathomable hardships and worry for so many long months, it did not seem possible that the end to the conflict could have come so simply and quietly, and yet it had.

At the eleventh hour of the eleventh day of the eleventh month, the Great War had finally ended.

By noon, the celebrations outside the Élysées Palace Hotel had escalated into a wild, jubilant *fête* as tens of thousands of Parisians and Allied soldiers spilled into the streets, cheering, laughing, waving the flags of France and her faithful allies, setting off firecrackers. A group of French soldiers wandered past the windows of the telephone exchange, arms slung over one another's shoulders, singing "La Marseillaise" at the top of their lungs. When they peered in the windows and spotted the telephone operators toiling at the switchboards, they grinned, whistled, and gestured and pleaded urgently for the girls to come join them in merrymaking.

"Not so fast," Valerie warned, smiling, as a few of her girls began to rise from their seats. "We're still on duty. The calls still must go through. Trust me, the party will still be going on after your shift."

From the sound of it, the party might continue for the rest of the month—and she couldn't be happier.

As soon as their shift ended, Valerie held a quick conference with the supervisor relieving her, then met Drusilla in the foyer, and together they dashed outside to join the party. "The whole city has gone mad with joy," Drusilla exclaimed, laughing, over the din of cheers and shouts and song.

Valerie could not think of a more apt description of the scene. Every shop and residence up and down the boulevard had again unfurled their red, white, and blue bunting from every window and balcony, and the French Tricolor and the Stars and Stripes flew from staffs and poles affixed to buildings and from the outstretched hands of exultant citizens. Impromptu bands paraded down the Champs-Élysées, where vehicles drove slowly along, sounding their horns with earsplitting delight. Boys and girls marched together in their school uniforms, banging tin pans with sticks and making as much noise as they could. French soldiers were kissing every woman they saw, and in their distinctive uniforms, Valerie and Drusilla inspired particularly enthusiastic affection and gratitude. "Americans fought with us, so Americans should be kissed, if they are agreeable," one handsome *capitaine* declared as he swept Valerie into his arms.

It was very sound logic as far as Valerie was concerned. "Oh, I'm agreeable," she assured him, and kissed him back.

It had been announced earlier that day that at half past four o'clock, every bell in France would ring out to rejoice in the liberation of their country and the Allies' hard-won victory. When the bells began to peal from every clock tower and cathedral, a surge of emotion swept through the crowd, shouts and cheers mingling with tears of joy and cries of sorrow. The war was over. The people of France and Belgium could reclaim their lives, their homes, their homelands. The living would remember the dead and honor their sacrifices.

So much loss, Valerie thought, her elation fading. So much senseless death. So many young lives snuffed out. So many innocent victims rendered homeless and destitute. Could they ever truly come back from such loss? She had to believe it was possible. Perhaps this would prove to be, as the writer H. G. Wells had argued four years before, the War to End All Wars. One could only hope.

As the afternoon waned but the revelry continued as boisterously as ever, Valerie and Drusilla made their way back to quarters, famished, hoarse, laughing, and lightheaded from the frenzy. They had barely crossed the threshold when the YWCA hostess hurried over to Valerie, held her by the shoulders, and regarded her with earnest sympathy.

"The American Hospital called for you, my dear," she said. "I'm afraid it's terrible news. Would you join me in the parlor?"

Valerie's thoughts flew to Henri, and for a moment she felt as if she were reeling, as if the bottom had dropped out of her life. Wordlessly, she nodded and let herself be led away. Drusilla followed after, and they sat together on the sofa clutching hands as their hostess gently told them that Inez had passed away that morning from influenza, even as the streets outside her window had filled with rejoicing Parisians and Allies.

"Was she aware that the war was over?" Valerie heard herself ask. "When she passed, did she know that the Allies had won?"

The hostess shrugged, helpless. "I'm sorry. I don't know."

"I'm sure she knew," Drusilla said tremulously, squeezing Valerie's hand. "Mrs. Crittenden was always two steps ahead of everyone, wasn't she?"

Yes, she was. She had been.

Valerie took a deep, shaky breath as her tears began to fall. She hoped Inez had known. Inez had given her life for the Allied victory, and she deserved to know that her sacrifice had not been in vain.

Military order still reigned in Souilly, yet soldiers paraded through the streets, shouting and singing and waving flags. Ordinarily stoic officers grinned and shook hands and pounded one another on the back. Marie glimpsed some of the Logistics officers sharing cognac and cigars with Army Intelligence, their squabble over the piano and the company of the Signal Corps girls forgotten. The work of the First Army Headquarters went on, but a tremendous emotional burden had been lifted. The occupiers had been driven out. Peace was at hand. Marie heard some dark grumbling about exacting retribution and reparations from their conquered enemies, but only as an undercurrent to the great, sweeping rush of triumph and thanksgiving that filled the encampment.

Eleven hours after the Armistice began, the original seven Souilly telephone operators turned the exchange over to the five newcomers and hurried back to their barracks with only minutes to spare before the Signal Corps and Logistics officers arrived for a victory party in the conservatory. Berthe stoked the woodstove with enough logs to drive the cold from the room despite the bitterly cold winds gusting outside.

Marie and the others arranged chairs and cleared space for a dance floor, as the guests began to arrive. Everyone brought food to share, until their makeshift table was packed with delicacies saved for a special occasion. Urged on by her friends, Marie played the piano and sang her complete repertoire of wartime favorites. Everyone joined in merrily on the rousing marches, but she performed solo the more melancholy, wistful songs about missing loved ones far away.

Eventually she rose and bowed, good-naturedly declining their calls for an encore. "I have to rest my voice," she demurred, shaking her head and smiling. "Someone else should take a turn."

Immediately a lieutenant from Logistics settled down on the bench, interlaced his fingers and flexed them with comic exaggeration, and began playing "Mary Had a Little Lamb" with one finger. Everyone burst into laughter, and when he grinned mischievously and segued into a flawless rendition of Chopin's Opus 64 No. 1, they laughed even louder from surprise.

After the lieutenant played a few more classical pieces, four Signal Battalion boys took over. One seated himself at the piano while the others briefly conferred in low voices, grinning and nodding. Before long one of the quartet, a second lieutenant, stepped forward. "My buddies and I heard a great new tune when we were on leave in Paris last month," he said, searching the crowd, his face lighting up when he spotted Marie, Berthe, and Adele in one group, and then Grace, Helen, Esther, and Suzanne in another. "It's a tribute to some of the best soldiers Over Here—certainly the prettiest soldiers anywhere—without whom we would not be celebrating this victory tonight. Although our Signal Corps girls deserve much better than our humble efforts—"

Some of their buddies in the audience guffawed, and one called out, "That's for sure!"

The second lieutenant waved off the friendly hecklers, grinning. "Fine, we all agree they deserve better than us. Nevertheless, we dedicate this performance to them, our switchboard soldiers." He nodded to the accompanist, who began to play a brisk, cheerful march in

A-flat major. The opening bars sounded familiar, but Marie was not sure why.

The second lieutenant and his two buddies began to sing:

> *My switchboard soldier,*
> *Brave angel on the line,*
> *Whenever I hear your voice*
> *Oh, my heart feels fine.*
> *When you ask me, "Number, please,"*
> *It makes my heart feel so fine.*

With each measure, the melody emerged into something new and yet wonderfully familiar. It was Mozart, but not as he had composed it. "'Voi che sapete,'" Marie murmured, joy and astonishment rising up from her heart to fill her head in a dizzying rush. It had been transposed to a lower key, it had been reworked as a march—or perhaps a rollicking drinking song—and the lyrics were entirely new, but the melody was unmistakably Cherubino's aria from *The Marriage of Figaro*, the song she had performed aboard the *20th Century Limited*, the song that had drawn Giovanni to the railcar door to listen.

She laughed aloud and pressed her hands to her heart, tears springing into her eyes. Giovanni must have composed the song. Who else would have paired that melody with those lyrics? Only Giovanni—and although it paid tribute to every Signal Corps girl, she knew he had meant it especially for her.

He had sent his song out into the world, hoping it would find its way to her, and at long last, it had. She wished with all her heart that she could tell him so.

Within twenty-four hours of the Armistice, American troops were already returning to Souilly from the front. Grace watched them as they marched past the barracks and the exchange, smiling broadly, waving to the girls, their joy and relief evident despite the dirt and fatigue on their faces. Line after line of them, the victors, the survivors. Grace had never witnessed such happiness.

She had little time to observe the triumphant soldiers, for the switchboards were as busy as ever. Divisions still needed to receive orders and supplies. Instead of coordinating attacks, the generals needed plans for the occupation of Germany. The relocation of First Army Headquarters to Dun-sur-Meuse had been canceled, but Grace suspected they would not remain in Souilly indefinitely. Already the French were withdrawing units from the encampment and deploying them elsewhere. The French communications officers with whom Grace and her girls had worked so closely over the past few months had already come by the exchange to bid them farewell. There were smiles and tears, and one officer, Sergeant Alexandre, shook each operator's hand and solemnly wished her *bonne chance* and *bon voyage*. Afterward, he removed his cap, placed it over his heart, and said, "*Au revoir, mesdemoiselles.*" Then he replaced his cap, turned sharply, and departed. Grace was certain she would never see him again.

Bon voyage, he had wished them, and yet Grace had no idea where she and her operators would go next or when. Some of the girls had already began to muse aloud about returning to the United States, but they had enlisted for the duration, and it was evident that their services were still needed—and would be for months to come, Grace suspected.

She too missed home, much more than she had expected to, since she had become accustomed to military life. Eugene's injuries at the front had made her keenly aware that life was fragile and fleeting, and she could not take even a single day with her beloved family for granted. Her father's sudden death had driven that point home. How could she imagine moving halfway across the world to Australia to be with Mack, never to see her mother and siblings again? He had not proposed—not yet, but his last letter hinted that he might upon their next meeting—but if he did, when he did, she would have to refuse him. The thought of it pained her, and perhaps in the years to come she would regret letting him go, but she was as sure as she could be that she would regret leaving her family more.

She supposed it was just as well that they had proceeded so cautiously rather than allowing passion to sweep them away. Perhaps they had always known that it was not meant to be, and they had both deliberately held back, unwilling to risk the inevitable heartbreak.

Later that day, a messenger brought a letter to the exchange from Brigadier General Edgar Russel, chief signal officer of the AEF. During a momentary lull, Grace read it aloud. "To the Members of the Telephone Operating Unit Signal Corps, AEF," she began. "Number one: On the occasion of the going into effect of the armistice with the enemy, I desire to avail myself of the opportunity to express to you the satisfaction with which I and the officers associated with me have observed the quality of your work in these past months and to congratulate you on the large part you have had in our glorious victory."

"Three cheers for us," Suzanne cried out. The other girls laughed and applauded.

"Number two," Grace continued, holding the page up dramatically. "The bringing of women telephone operators to France for service with the American Expeditionary Forces had no precedent, and for this reason the experiment was watched with unusual interest. It pleases me a great deal to say that by your ability, efficiency, devotions to duty and the irreproachable and businesslike conduct of your affairs, personal and official, you have not only justified the action taken in assembling you but have set a standard of excellence which could hardly be improved upon and which has been responsible in no small measure for the success of our system of local and long-distance telephone communication."

"Why, that's very kind of him to say," said Helen, pleased. The others beamed with pride, nodding and murmuring agreement.

"Why shouldn't he say so?" said Adele. "Every word of it is true."

"He not only said it, he put it in writing," said Suzanne. "Would this be a good time to ask for a raise?"

"Number three," Grace read aloud, raising her voice a bit to be heard over the banter. "While this is a fitting occasion to express appreciation of your work in the trying period just ended, it will no doubt be some time before the telephone business over our system shows any signs of decreasing. It is not questioned that the brilliant reputation your unit has established for itself will be maintained to the end and that you will continue individually and collectively to maintain the high standard of service you have already set." Grace lowered the paper and smiled at her operators. "Signed, E. Russel, Brigadier-General, C.S.O."

"Wait," said Suzanne sharply. "What was that part about the telephone business not decreasing for some time?"

"He's merely acknowledging what we've already observed," said Marie. "The soldiers may lay down their arms, but our work continues."

A few of the girls nodded.

"I believe," said Berthe tentatively, "he's also warning us not to expect to return home anytime soon."

Grace watched carefully as her girls absorbed this.

"Well, that's fine with me," said Adele airily. "I wasn't ready to go back to Seattle anyway."

"You just don't want to leave Lieutenant Mills behind," teased Esther.

Blushing, Adele gave her a playful swat.

Marie looked around the room, her expression calm and determined. "I signed up for the duration," she said. "I'll stay as long as the Signal Corps needs me."

Most of the other girls nodded solemnly, but Suzanne laughed. "You don't have a choice," she teased. "We're in the army. This isn't the YWCA or the Red Cross. You can't just show up for the party and go home when you've had your fill of fun. We have to stay and clean up afterward too."

The other girls groaned and booed, laughing, but Grace could not miss the pride shining in their eyes. "I'm glad you're all planning to stick to your posts," she said wryly. "That said, I think you've all earned a little time off. I can't promise anything, but I'll put in requests for leave for all of us."

The girls cheered and applauded again.

Grace tucked the general's letter into her pocket and urged the girls back to the switchboards. They had worked tirelessly for months, long, grueling shifts and almost no days off. If anyone deserved a holiday, her operators did. General Russel would surely agree.

It was truly wonderful to know that their hard work was appreciated. They had not only helped the Allies to win the war, but they had proven that women belonged in the U.S. Army, that they were as capable as any man of serving their country with distinction and honor.

They were the first, Grace knew, but their success meant that they would not be the last.

Two days after the Armistice, two days after Inez's death, Valerie and Drusilla went to their former chief operator's flat and packed up her personal effects. She had acquired few possessions since coming Over Here, and her pride in military order and efficiency was evident in the precisely folded clothing in the bureau drawers, the crisply pressed uniforms hanging in the wardrobe.

Valerie was folding the uniforms and stacking them carefully on the bed when Drusilla gasped and called her over to the bureau. After removing a layer of scarves and gloves, Drusilla had discovered several bundles of letters, neatly separated by author and tied with white grosgrain ribbon. According to the return addresses, the two thickest bundles were from Emily Murphy and Blanche Teale, whom Valerie knew to be Inez's mother and elder sister, respectively. One of the thinnest bundles, all letters sent through the military post, was from Nathaniel Crittenden.

"Inez was in touch with her ex-husband," said Valerie, astonished. "She never said a word."

"And he's Over Here," said Drusilla, tugging on one end of the ribbon. "I wonder if they ever saw each other on leave."

Valerie snatched the bundle of letters from Drusilla's hands. "Don't even think about it. We can't read these. They're private."

"What harm could it do?" Drusilla protested. "Inez is gone."

"Nathaniel may very well still be alive," Valerie pointed out. "Either way, whatever passed between them is none of our business."

"Aren't you the least bit curious?"

Of course Valerie was, and as Drusilla wheedled and begged, she felt her resolve weakening. Eventually she agreed that they could examine the outside of each envelope, but not the letters within. That was enough to deduce that Nathaniel was with Company C of the 165th, and he had been in France at least as long as Inez had. Apparently he had been wounded in late July, after which he had been transferred to a base hospital to Paris. Whether Inez had visited him there, and whether they had reconciled or planned to reunite after the war, Valerie would never know. It pained her to think that although she was surely Inez's closest friend in France, Inez had not confided in her.

Soberly, Valerie and Drusilla packed Inez's personal effects, including the ribbon-tied bundles of letters, into a single carton, which the Signal Corps had agreed to send to her mother in Oakland. Valerie had enclosed a letter explaining how Inez had died, and in much greater detail, how honorably she had served as a chief operator for the Women's Telephone Unit. Valerie had no doubt that Inez's skill and devotion to duty had saved lives, not only those of the operators under her command, but of countless Allied soldiers.

Although Inez had ended her career with the CPI, Valerie insisted, and her superior officers agreed, that she must be honored as one of their own. With Captain Pederson's help, Valerie arranged for Inez to be interred in the U.S. military cemetery on Boulevard Washington in Suresnes. Her metal coffin bore the inscription, "Died in the service of her country at Paris France November Eleventh, 1918."

On her grave marker, her rank was noted as "Chief Operator."

Valerie could think of no greater tribute than for Inez to be remembered always as a true switchboard soldier.

27

NOVEMBER 1918–JUNE 1919

Paris and Koblenz

MARIE

After the Armistice, operations gradually subsided at Souilly as various departments were transferred elsewhere, but it was not until late November that Marie and her fellow operators were relocated to the First Army Rest Camp at Bar-sur-Aube, about 125 kilometers southwest. Within hours of their arrival, before they even had time to unpack, their long-awaited and fervently hoped-for leave was granted. Marie decided to join Grace, Suzanne, and a few of the other girls on a holiday in Nice, but Berthe had other plans. Her husband's ship had docked in Brest, and they planned to meet at her uncle's home in Paris and spend two blissful weeks together.

"*Bon voyage*," Marie told her when they parted, kissing her on both cheeks. She had never seen Berthe so happy; she fairly glowed with joy and anticipation. How lucky she and Reuben were to have met and to have fallen in love, to have survived the war and to soon be reunited. If only Marie knew where Giovanni was, not even the Riviera could tempt her from his side. But she did not even know if he was alive. He could be anywhere in France or Belgium or Germany, or lost to her forever.

She had his letters, his song, and hope. She must believe that he yet lived, and that somehow they would find each other again.

In Nice, Marie and her companions luxuriated in two glorious days of strolling on the beaches of the Baie des Anges, dining, sightseeing. Then Grace received an urgent telegram.

"Our leave has been canceled," she announced, rueful. "We're to report immediately to Paris. The War Department needs us to operate the exchange for the peace conference at Versailles."

They all regretted leaving Nice so soon, but peace between nations was a noble purpose, one they were honored to serve. "Duty before fun," Esther said for them all as they returned to their rooms to pack.

In Paris, Marie and her companions reported to the headquarters for the American Commission to Negotiate Peace at the Hôtel de Crillon, one of two mansions on the Place de la Concorde the U.S. government had leased for the American peace commissioners and others serving with the delegation, including their clerks, military and naval attachés, and several of the civilian officials' wives. When the operators learned that they too would be quartered in the luxurious hotel, they were so astounded that at first they thought it was a mistake. "Don't tell them," Suzanne pleaded as Grace set off to inquire. "It's not nice to embarrass people by pointing out their errors."

To their delight, Grace returned with uniformed staff who took charge of their gear and escorted them upstairs to their suites. After the bellman left, Marie lingered in the doorway and took in the elegantly decorated room, a catch in her throat. The thought of clean linens, soft beds, delicious food, hot water, regular baths, and peaceful nights uninterrupted by shelling so overwhelmed her that she had to sit down on the edge of the bed to compose herself.

"I heard that when President Wilson arrives next week, he'll be staying somewhere else," remarked Esther, stretching out on her back on the other bed. "Can you imagine how marvelous a president's hotel must be, if they put telephone girls here?"

"I can't imagine anything finer than this," said Marie, closing her eyes and sinking back against her pillow. "But why shouldn't Signal

Corps operators have quarters as comfortable as a president's? I think we've done as much to win the war as President Wilson has."

She expected Esther to agree with her, but instead her bunkmate tossed a pillow at her. "That's our commander in chief you're talking about."

"*Merci.* I wanted another pillow. Don't think you're getting this back." Smiling, Marie hugged it to her chest. "I thought you disliked Wilson. You cheered when you heard that Alice Paul burned him in effigy in front of the White House."

"I like him a lot better ever since he started demanding that Congress pass the suffrage amendment." Bedsprings creaked as Esther climbed out of bed. "He praised women for our exemplary performance in the war, and he said, 'The least tribute we can pay them is to make them the equals of men in political rights.'"

"He said that?"

"He did."

"Hmm." Marie opened her eyes and sat up too, knowing that if she didn't, she would soon fall asleep in the extraordinarily comfortable bed. "You do know that German women have had the right to vote for years?"

Esther took Marie's hands and pulled her to her feet. "All the more reason we American women should have the vote. If we're going to fight for democracy abroad, we should certainly practice it at home."

I am a Frenchwoman, not an American, Marie almost reminded her, but she said nothing. Over the past year, such distinctions had blurred among the telephone operators as they had worked shoulder to shoulder in exceptionally difficult conditions. It seemed rather absurd to bring it up now.

When the operators returned downstairs to report to duty, Marie was surprised to discover that the famed luxurious Grill Room had been transformed into a telephone exchange, with eight state-of-the-art switchboards lining the walls, concealing much of the birdseye maple paneling and the large, ornately framed mirrors and velvet hangings. After a brief conference with their new commanding officer, the operators were assigned to shifts. Marie, Helen, Suzanne, and Esther were put to work immediately along with four girls who had also been transferred to Paris from other bases. Their chief operator was Merle Egan of Helena, Montana, who had sailed to France with Group Five.

Two days after Marie and her companions arrived in Paris, Berthe joined them, glowing from her happy reunion with her husband. She worked with the same diligence and skill as ever—they all did—but as the December days passed and preparations for the peace conference intensified, Berthe confided to Marie that she had requested a transfer to Brest, where her husband's ship remained in port. "Reuben is free to come and go as he pleases, and to choose his own quarters," she said. "If I could be posted there, we could finally live together again."

Berthe also confessed that she found the work of the peace conference dull after the excitement of their duties at First Army Headquarters. "This is just plain hello girl work, finding hotel rooms for stranded officers, arranging their dinner reservations in the evening," she griped, frustrated. "I enlisted to serve as a soldier in the United States Army. This is so— It seems so dull and inconsequential after the important work we used to do."

"This work is important in its own way," Marie consoled her, but she had misgivings of her own. She missed her old Signal Corps family, which had broken up after the Armistice. Colonel Hitt and the other Signal Corps officers had been transferred to other posts, and the eighty-four telephone operators who had been summoned to Paris from bases throughout France had been dispersed among several exchanges within the city. Even Grace had been reassigned as chief operator of a new exchange at the mansion of Prince Joachim Murat on the Rue de Monceau, which the prince and princess had graciously invited the French government to offer to President Wilson as his residence during the conference. Like Berthe—like many of the girls, Marie supposed— she too missed the camaraderie of Souilly and the certainty that her work was essential and meaningful. A part of her missed the excitement and even the danger. But whenever she felt dispirited, she reminded herself what had often been said at Services of Supply in Tours: Even if one's own task seemed insignificant, it was essential to the success of the mission, and thus deserved respect.

And when she thought of the last group of Signal Corps telephone operators, who had already boarded a ship in New York Harbor and had been preparing to sail for France when the Armistice came, canceling their deployment, she remembered how fortunate she was to have been permitted to serve at all.

The operators' work schedule was certainly less grueling at the peace conference than it had been at First Army Headquarters, so Marie had ample off-duty hours to spend sightseeing with friends or reuniting with long-lost French friends and relations. In late December, just before Christmas, she was granted leave to visit the convent in Tours. She rejoiced to see Sister Agnès and the other kindhearted nuns again, and to embrace the children—yet she was astonished to find that their numbers had dwindled by more than half.

At first she feared that they had succumbed to influenza or been killed by German bombs, but Sister Agnès assured her all was well. The photograph that Valerie's brother had taken of Marie and the children's choir had appeared in many French newspapers, and soon thereafter, the story had been taken up by *Stars and Stripes* and the British press. Desperate parents who had been separated from their children in Lorraine had recognized their own sons and daughters or their children's friends in the photograph, and they had rushed to the convent to take custody of them. Marie had missed Gisèle's reunion with her mother by two days, but she felt no disappointment for herself, only joy that Gisèle's family had found her at last.

Before returning to Paris, Marie rode out to the convalescent hospital at the chateau outside Tours to visit Grace's brother, knowing Grace would welcome news about his progress. To her surprise, a nurse informed her that Eugene had been discharged a fortnight ago. Marie supposed he had been assigned to one of the first ships that had begun transporting wounded men back to the United States after the Armistice rendered the ocean crossing safe again. Grace undoubtedly already knew, but since they were no longer working at the same exchange, Marie would not have heard. Still, the trip was not wasted. The chateau was beautiful, even in winter, and she distributed the gifts of chocolates, pastries, and magazines she had brought for Eugene to other soldiers, who seemed grateful for them.

Marie spent her last two days of leave visiting with her comrades from her stint at Services of Supply and was not surprised to find them as busy as ever. The Army of Occupation required shipments of supplies and materiel; the hospitals were filled to capacity with the injured, disabled, and sick; and nearly two million soldiers and officers needed to be repatriated to the United States—and none of that could be accomplished without efficient telephone service. "I think we Signal Corps girls may be here until the very end," Cordelia told her.

Marie was inclined to agree. "Save me a berth on the last ship to New York," she said, and they both laughed ruefully. Although thousands of doughboys were already heading home, the 223 women telephone operators in France were still on active duty. She knew of a few, like Berthe, who had requested transfers to other bases, and several others who had asked to be discharged and returned to the United States, but all of those requests had been denied. Marie was willing to remain in France indefinitely, for it was her native country, but her parents wrote to her often to ask when she planned to come home, by which they meant Cincinnati. Their imploring letters made her miss them all the more, but she had sworn an oath to serve for the duration, and she intended to keep it.

On Christmas Day, the YWCA hosted a grand party for the operators, including a feast that rivaled the one Marie and Berthe had organized two months before in Souilly. The AEF presented each Signal Corps operator with a lovely gift, a hardcover memento book bound with lavender cording. Adorned with glossy photographs of General Pershing and General Russel, the books contained snapshots of other officers and, best of all, dozens of letters expressing the officers' deep and sincere appreciation for the Signal Corps girls' "skillful performance of the essential communications work that contributed in no small measure to the victory," as one grateful officer had written.

Marie knew she would cherish her book always.

The reminder of the Signal Corps girls' accomplishments made Marie unexpectedly nostalgic for her time at First Army Headquarters, where every call had been absolutely critical and she had reported for duty every day certain that her work mattered. Thus at the end of December when the AEF asked for volunteers to go into Germany and operate the exchange for the Army of Occupation, she promptly stepped forward.

On New Year's Day, she reported to the train station with her gear, her desire to serve rejuvenated. She was the only volunteer from the Hôtel de Crillon, so it was not until she saw the other women gathered on the platform that she discovered who else would be joining her in Germany—Grace, Valerie, Millicent, and several other girls whom she had never met.

First, she greeted Grace, kissing her on both cheeks. "I knew you would volunteer for this duty," she said. "Prince Murat's mansion must have seemed terribly dull compared to Ligny-en-Barrois and Souilly, even with President Wilson in residence."

"I wouldn't say dull," Grace replied diplomatically. "We connected calls for the president, after all, and now that all the theaters and restaurants are open and the blackout is over, what better place to spend my off-duty hours than in the City of Light?"

Marie regarded her knowingly. "And yet you volunteered to go to Germany."

"Yes," Grace conceded, smiling. "I did."

Next, Marie kissed Valerie's cheeks. "Months ago, I met your very handsome and charming younger brother in Tours," she said, "and I have a story to share that will make you very proud of him."

Valerie's eyebrows rose. "I'm already excessively proud of him. What more could he have done?"

As they boarded the train, Marie told Valerie about the photo of the choir and the children who had been reunited with their families because of it. As the train chugged away from the station, Valerie laughed aloud from delight. "I didn't think I could be any prouder of Henri than I already was," she declared, "but Marie, you've made it so."

From Paris, the train carried them more than three hundred kilometers east, past picturesque towns that Marie found achingly reminiscent of her childhood and on through vast stretches of landscape devastated by war. In Metz, a town that had mingled French and German traits even before the war, Marie and her companions changed trains and headed north into Luxembourg, then northeast into Germany. Many hours and more than six hundred kilometers since they had departed Paris, they arrived in Koblenz, a city on the Rhine that inexplicably reminded Marie of Cincinnati. The station was clean and modern, and when their escort drove them to their quarters, they noted streets bustling with traffic and shoppers strolling along the sidewalks, perusing the goods attractively arranged in shop windows.

Suddenly Marie felt a spark of indignation kindle in her chest. Looking around, one could almost believe the country had never gone to war. When she thought of the devastation and ruin the Central Powers had inflicted upon the villages of France and Belgium, she wanted to race back to the peace conference, storm into the room where the dignitaries were negotiating a lasting peace, pound her fist on the table, and demand reparations in full. The defeated aggressors could not restore the lives they had taken, but they could, and they must, reduce the suffering of the survivors.

Her expression must have betrayed her anger, for Valerie was studying her, curious and concerned. Marie arranged her features into a mask of serenity and willed her pulse to stop racing. One prosperous street in a single town did not mean the country was not also suffering, she reminded herself, nor was Koblenz entirely unchanged by the war. As they drove on, the presence of the Army of Occupation became more evident, with soldiers from the United States, Great Britain, and France marching here and standing guard there. American and Allied flags were displayed on numerous buildings, and she could not ignore the unsettling absence of German men of military age.

"Look, Grace," Valerie suddenly exclaimed, indicating a group of soldiers entering a pub. "Their insignia. Wasn't that the Seventy-Seventh Field Artillery?"

Grace quickly craned her neck to look, but she was too late. "I couldn't see," she said. "Eugene wouldn't be with them in any case. He's convalescing at a hospital in Tours."

"No he isn't," said Marie, surprised. "I went to visit him when I was on leave, and a nurse told me he had been discharged."

"How thoughtful of you," said Grace, but then her brow furrowed. "Wait. He's been discharged?"

"That's what I was told. I assumed he'd been sent back to the United States."

Grace shook her head. "He would have written to tell me so. We were planning to meet and see Paris together before either of us went home."

"This is the place," their escort broke in, slowing the automobile. "Your new home away from home."

The auto halted at the curb in front of a stone residence with a half-timbered second story and a modest garden encircled by bare-limbed trees. Snow had been cleared from the front walk leading to the covered entryway, where an American soldier paced, hands tucked into his pockets, collar pulled up to his chin. As he caught sight of the Signal Corps girls through the windows, his face brightened.

"Eugene?" Grace exclaimed, scrambling out of the vehicle. She ran toward him, he met her halfway, and they embraced, laughing.

Soon, after the joyful tears subsided and introductions were made all around, Eugene explained that after he had received his medical clearance, he had returned to the 77th Field Artillery, 4th Division, which had been attached to the Army of Occupation. The previous day, one of Eugene's superior officers, knowing that he had a sister in the Women's Telephone Unit, had mentioned that a group of Signal Corps operators was scheduled to arrive the next morning. Eugene had recalled that the YWCA often managed the operators' quarters, and a few questions to the right people had led him to their new residence. "I didn't know for sure that you would be one of the operators," Eugene told his sister, grinning, "but it seemed like the sort of thing you would volunteer for."

Grace laughed and flung her arms around him again.

While Grace visited with her brother, Marie and the other operators settled in to their rooms, taking Grace's gear along to the room she would share with Suzanne. Eugene joined them for supper at the hostel and entertained them with amusing stories of his buddies and his own misadventures as a green artillery corporal. He said nothing of the horrors he had witnessed at the front, or of the gas attack that had nearly killed him, and the girls knew better than to ask. Some of those stories might come out later, Marie thought, perhaps when he and Grace were alone, safe on the other side of the Atlantic.

In the weeks that followed, Grace saw her brother quite often, for their duties, while more engrossing than at the peace conference, were far less strenuous than they had been before the Armistice. The women ran the exchange in two shifts during the day, and Signal Battalion men took over for the relatively tranquil nights. As for the Signal Corps officers and even soldiers like Eugene, their schedules too seemed almost relaxed, for the military. The officers and operators were all housed in the same fashionable residential area of Koblenz, in fine, modern houses that had evidently once belonged to quite well-to-do families. What had become of the former occupants, Marie did not know, but she assumed they had fled east as the front lines had moved closer to the German border, just as many French citizens had once fled west ahead of the invading German army.

Marie had expected to have more contact with the citizens of Koblenz, but the operators' work and their off-duty social activities kept them almost entirely within the American enclave around their residence. Marie rarely saw Germans on the streets on her twice-daily walk between her quarters and the telephone exchange, but occasionally she and a friend or two ventured deeper into the town to shop or to dine, and they might have a curt, perfunctory conversation with a German proprietor as they purchased a souvenir or paid a tab. Although Marie never faced overt hostility, the shopkeepers and waiters she met accepted her money grudgingly, their resentment for the occupiers so tangible she imagined it radiating from them like shimmering air above a hot pavement in summer.

As spring came to Germany, she thought of Giovanni often and wondered where he might be. She wrote to him in care of his brigade and company with dwindling hopes of receiving a reply. In late April, she learned that the 307th Infantry had sailed from Brest for New York aboard the USS *America*, and her heart broke a little. She knew she ought to feel only joy and relief that he was homeward bound, but she had hoped so desperately to see him before he left France, and she was bewildered and hurt that he had not tried to see her before he sailed, or at least to call or write. She could think of only two reasons for his silence: His feelings for her had changed utterly, or, the unthinkable, he had perished in the Argonne Forest in the attempt to rescue the Lost Battalion. She would rather believe that he lived, but it was impossible to imagine that he no longer loved her.

By that time, hundreds of thousands of doughboys had returned to the United States. Many telephone operators, not only in Koblenz but throughout France, had requested discharges so they too could return home and resume their prewar lives. Marie had heard that Louise LeBreton had asked to be released so she would arrive in California in time to enroll in the summer session at Berkeley and complete her education. Berthe Hunt was already there; she had departed from Brest on March 15 and presumably had already reunited with her husband, who had sailed for the United States on February 3. The need for bilingual operators was diminishing day by day, and with her parents' pleas for her to come home increasing in urgency, and her last, foolish hope of an unexpected reunion with Giovanni somewhere in France extinguished, Marie decided to apply for a discharge.

The day after she submitted her paperwork, she received word that she had been awarded a special commendation signed by General

Pershing himself. The ornate decoration read, "Awarded for service at First Army Headquarters at Ligny-en-Barrois during the St. Mihiel drive, August 1918, and at Souilly during the Meuse-Argonne campaign, September–November 1918."

She was one of thirty Signal Corps operators recognized in such fashion, but soon thereafter, Grace Banker learned that she would receive the highest honor of all: the Distinguished Service Medal.

On May 22, at a full military review, General Hunter Liggett, commander of the First Army, pinned the gold-and-enamel medal to Grace's uniform while her loyal operators and her beloved brother looked on proudly. The ceremony, which took place at the Schlossgarten on a beautiful spring day beneath cloudless skies, was captured as a motion picture by a Signal Corps photography unit. After the presentation, as the telephone operators gathered around Grace to congratulate her, kiss her cheeks, and admire her medal, one of the photographers ran over and swooped Valerie up in a hug. She shrieked, he laughed, and when his cap tumbled off to reveal thick blond curls, Marie recognized him as Valerie's brother.

"Hollywood Hank," Valerie cried after he set her down again, and flung her arms around him.

When the excitement of the siblings' reunion subsided, Marie asked Grace to read her citation aloud. At first she modestly demurred, but when all of the operators as well as Eugene and Henri insisted, she complied. "For exceptionally meritorious and distinguished services," Grace read. "She served with exceptional ability as Chief Operator in the Signal Corps Exchange at General Headquarters, American Expeditionary Forces, and later in a similar capacity at First Army Headquarters. By untiring devotion to her exacting duties under trying conditions she did much to assure the success of the telephone service during the operations of the First Army against the Saint-Mihiel salient and the operations to the north of Verdun."

"Three cheers for Grace!" Valerie proclaimed.

"Hurrah!" Marie cried in unison with her friends. "Hurrah! Hurrah!"

Grace's cheeks flushed pink with embarrassment. "Whatever glory may come with this medal," she said, looking around at them all, "I believe it belongs in large measure to the small but very loyal and devoted group of Signal Corps girls who have served with me." She smiled around at them all, shaking her head in admiration. "You're all just so dandy, faithful, and ever ready, and I'm so very proud of you!"

They all laughed and applauded, and Marie felt her heart glow with affection and pride. For a moment she regretted applying for a discharge, but then, seeing Grace with her brother and Valerie with hers, she missed her younger sisters so painfully that she had to blink away tears.

The next day, she and Valerie were returning to their quarters after seeing Henri off at the train station when they spotted Grace standing in their residence's covered entryway with a man in the uniform of the Australian Imperial Force. "That's Captain Mack," Marie murmured, seizing Valerie's arm and bringing them both to a stop.

"Who?"

"Grace's friend, or her sweetheart. None of us were ever quite sure." Reluctant to interrupt what appeared to be a difficult conversation, Marie and Valerie remained at a discreet distance, out of earshot and watching from the corner of an eye. Only after Grace and the captain shook hands and the captain strode off alone did they approach the residence. Grace stood in the entryway lost in thought, her arms wrapped around herself as if to ward off a chill, but her downcast expression quickly shifted into a strained smile when she glanced up at the sound of their footfalls on the stone path.

"Wasn't that Captain Mack?" Marie asked casually, inclining her head toward the officer, who was soon lost from sight amid other pedestrians.

"Yes—yes, it was," said Grace, her eyes shining with unshed tears. "He heard about my award and came to congratulate me. He had entrusted his Distinguished Service Cross to me for safekeeping while he traveled to and from the front, but now that the war is over—" She shrugged and managed a tremulous smile. "It's just as safe in his foot-locker as in mine, and he'll be taking it home to Melbourne soon."

Marie regarded her sympathetically and touched her shoulder, a ges-ture of consolation for whatever sorrow or disappointment Grace would not admit aloud. She was grieving the loss of love, yes, but in her eyes Marie detected relief and acceptance beneath the sorrow. Grace's heart was bruised, but not shattered. She would find love again one day.

"You don't need his medal," said Valerie, waving a hand dismissively. "You've earned one of your own."

Grace's smile deepened. "Thanks, girls." Reaching into her pocket, she withdrew a small, shiny object and fastened it to her collar. When she let her hands fall to her sides, Marie saw that it was her Signal Corps pin. Until then, Marie had not noticed it was missing. "Anyone inter-ested in a coffee before we report for duty?"

Marie and Valerie exchanged a quick glance. "Absolutely," said Ma-rie, smiling and linking her arm through Grace's. "I know the perfect place."

They set off together, arm in arm.

Two weeks later, Marie received word that her request to be dis-charged from the army had been approved. Her ship would sail in three days. She and Esther, who had also been granted a discharge, would travel together via train more than eleven hundred kilometers through Paris to Brest.

They had to pack in such haste that their friends had no time to throw them a farewell party; there was barely enough time to exchange home addresses, embrace one another, and kiss cheeks. Before Marie could truly grasp that she was leaving, she and Esther were bidding their comrades one final farewell and boarding the train.

Marie and Esther settled in for a long journey, chatting, reading, and watching the scenery as they swiftly sped from Germany, through Luxembourg, and back into Marie's beloved France. She hoped to re-turn in better times, perhaps as soon as two years, after the pandemic subsided, God willing, and the country recovered from the ravages of war. In letters Marie had exchanged with her mother since the Armistice, they had revived their once abandoned plan to tour Europe so Marie could audition for opera companies. The idea of traveling with her mother was very appealing, but she was no longer as sure as she once had been that opera was her future. She would always adore classical music, and her conservatory training would serve her well whatever she chose, but she had found such joy and satisfaction in singing popular tunes for the operators, the officers, and the doughboys that the thought of composing her own songs and exploring innovative new styles intrigued her.

Her parents might need some convincing, but they had granted her permission to serve in the Signal Corps during the Great War. After that, giving her their blessing to change musical genres would be easy. And if the opportunity to lead a children's choir ever came along, she would happily accept.

Many hours passed before they reached the outskirts of Paris. Twilight was descending, and from a distance they could see the lights of the city glowing in the distance. When the train pulled into the station, Marie and Esther rose and stretched, straightened their uniforms and gathered their gear, descended from the train and checked the schedule for their connection. The platform was bustling with soldiers in uniform, civilians, and families with children.

"Twenty minutes," Esther said, nudging Marie, her gaze fixed on the display board on the wall above.

"We'll make it," Marie replied, lifting her chin to indicate the correct direction. She led the way from the crowded platform into the station, and out another door where the westward lines departed. The strap of her bag pressed uncomfortably into her shoulder, so she paused, set down her footlocker, and adjusted the bag's weight. As she did, she glimpsed an American soldier supporting his weight on a cane, his gear slung over his shoulder, as he made his way, limping, toward the doors Marie and Esther had just passed through.

For a moment she could not breathe. She had glimpsed him only from a distance and from the back, but his resemblance to Giovanni was so striking that she stood rooted in place, staring after him as he disappeared through the doorway.

"Marie?" Esther asked. "Is everything all right?"

"Yes, it's only that—" Marie shook her head and picked up her gear. "Nothing. It's nothing."

"Are you sure?"

"Yes, let's go."

They continued on toward their platform, when Marie suddenly halted. "I'm sorry. You go on ahead. I have to know for sure." She turned and headed back across the station house.

"Marie?" Esther called after her, alarmed. "You'll miss the train. That means you'll miss the ship home!"

"I'll be right back," Marie called over her shoulder, quickening her pace. "Don't wait. Save me a seat on the train."

She did not glance back to see if Esther complied, but broke into a swift walk, as fast as she could go encumbered with her gear. On the other side of the doors, a train whistle pealed.

Pulse quickening, she passed through the doors and stepped onto the platform just as the conductor called a final warning. As steam billowed and the locomotive slowly lurched forward, she glanced frantically up and down the length of the platform as passengers leapt aboard. One of the last was the dark-haired soldier, balancing himself on the cane and hurling his duffel bag into the railcar ahead of him.

"Giovanni," she shouted as another passenger held out a hand to him. He seized it and hauled himself aboard. "Giovanni! John!"

She dropped her gear and broke into a run, but the crowd blocked her way. Frantic, she wove her way through and pushed forward, but the train had begun to pull away. She could not remember which car the soldier had entered, but it had surely passed her already. Heart sinking, she continued to search for him through the windows, but although the train was still moving slowly enough for her to see the soldiers within, Giovanni was not among them. Grief and anger and frustration welled up in her chest as the last railcars chugged by. The soldier she saw probably wasn't even Giovanni, she told herself, closing her eyes against tears.

How foolish she had been, to pursue a memory. Now she had almost certainly missed her train to Brest.

"Cherubino!"

Her eyes flew open. Heart pounding, she whirled around and discovered a dark-haired soldier standing at the far end of the platform, duffel bag at his feet, the train receding into the distance behind him.

"Giovanni," she murmured.

He smiled and held out his hand. A sob broke from her throat as she ran toward him.

Then she was in his arms, and he was kissing her, and in his embrace she dared to imagine they had seen the last of war.

After Armistice Day, the women of the U.S. Army Signal Corps were among the last to depart Europe, for they were needed to handle calls and translations throughout the peace conference. Months after the Treaty of Versailles was signed, they managed telephone communications for the Army of Occupation and the repatriation of nearly two million officers, soldiers, and civilian employees. In the two years that the women served, they connected more than twenty-six million calls and contributed immeasurably to the Allied victory in the Great War.

Upon their return to the United States, the switchboard soldiers, proud of their service and eager to resume their peacetime lives, applied for veterans' benefits and sought to join veterans' groups. When asked to produce their discharge papers, the women contacted the War Department, only to be informed that they were not veterans. Although they had worn uniforms and military insignia, had saluted superior officers, had served in combat settings, and had not been free to resign their jobs at will as civilians could, the government insisted that they had never been more than paid civilian employees serving under contract.

All of the women had sworn military oaths to serve their country as members of the U.S. Army Signal Corps, some of them multiple times as they moved through the application process or were promoted during the war. Not one of them had signed an employment contract.

Shocked and heartbroken, the women realized that the nation they had served with such distinction now denied that they had ever been soldiers. They did not qualify to receive honorable discharges. They were not eligible for medical benefits, medals, or bonuses. They could not march in Memorial Day parades or join their local chapters of the VFW. They could not call themselves veterans. Before Inez Crittenden sailed for France, she had purchased war risk insurance, a transaction witnessed by a second lieutenant in the Signal Corps. In May 1919, a family member applied to collect on the policy, but a claims officer for the U.S. Treasury decreed that Crittenden had never actually been a member of the military, rendering the policy null and void.

Appalled by these injustices, officials at AT&T petitioned the War Department on the telephone operators' behalf. For years, many of the Signal Corps officers who had served with the women, including General George Squier, Major Robert B. Owens, Major Roy Coles, Captain Ernest Wessen, and Major Stephen Walmsley, lobbied the U.S. Army, the American Legion, the War Department, and Congress in a determined effort to get the telephone operators the status, recognition, and benefits they deserved. Their efforts were in vain. As one congressman confided to Captain Wessen, "There is no doubt in the world but that your telephone operators were combatants, and should have been bona-fide members of the military establishment, but if we provide for this tiny group at this time we shall be forced to reopen the cases of thousands of other applicants."

In the years that followed, some of the members of the Women's Telephone Unit, led by the indomitable Merle Egan Anderson, undertook a new mission to acquire from Congress recognition of their status as veterans. Finally, in 1977, more than sixty years after the end of World War I, President Jimmy Carter signed a bill awarding the women of the U.S. Army Signal Corps honorable discharges and World War I Victory Medals, officially recognizing them as military veterans. By that time, only fifty of the Signal Corps telephone operators remained alive to celebrate this last victory, including Cordelia Dupuis, Merle Egan, Esther Fresnel, and Louise LeBreton.

Sadly, Distinguished Service Medal recipient Grace Banker was not among them. She had continued to serve with the Signal Corps until the last group of telephone operators departed from Brest aboard the USS *Mobile* on August 24, 1919. The 1920 U.S. Federal Census indicates that Grace lived at home with her parents and two sisters, and that she was employed as a secretary with the YWCA, but telephone directories for Passaic, New Jersey, from 1919 through 1923 all list her occupation as telephone operator. On March 4, 1922, Grace married Eugene Hiram Paddock, a civil engineer from New York City, with whom she would have four children. She died on December 17, 1960, after a long battle with cancer.

Marie Miossec and Valerie DeSmedt are fictional characters whose imagined lives are inspired by numerous Signal Corps telephone operators' experiences. Although Grace Banker did mention a Captain Mack in her wartime diary, she never revealed his full name, and his identity could not be determined conclusively. Thus the Captain Mack who appears in this novel is almost entirely fictionalized.

Like the millions of men who served in the War to End All Wars, the women of the U.S. Army Signal Corps answered their country's call to duty, served with honor, and played an essential role in achieving the Allied victory. Their perseverance, courage, and dedication helped convince a skeptical president, Congress, and public that women too deserved the right to vote. Having bravely accepted the responsibilities of citizenship, including the willingness to sacrifice their lives in defense of democracy, they had proven themselves beyond all doubt well deserving of a citizen's fundamental rights.

In serving their country, the valiant switchboard soldiers of the Women's Telephone Unit broke down barriers and cleared the way for generations of women who would follow after, not only in the military, but in all aspects of public and professional life.

ACKNOWLEDGMENTS

I am grateful beyond measure to everyone at William Morrow and Massie McQuilkin who contributed to *Switchboard Soldiers*, especially Maria Massie, Rachel Kahan, Ariana Sinclair, Emily Fisher, Kaitie Leary, Laura Cherkas, and Elsie Lyons. I'm very fortunate to have had an amazing team working on behalf of this novel and all my work through the years.

Geraldine Neidenbach, Heather Neidenbach, and Marty Chiaverini were my first readers, and their comments and questions about early drafts of this novel proved invaluable. My brother, Nic Neidenbach, came to the rescue whenever technology failed me. My son Michael Chiaverini composed the original song "Switchboard Soldiers," credited to Giovanni in the novel. My dear friend and fellow quilter Valerie Langue kindly helped me with French translations. Many thanks to you all.

Switchboard Soldiers is a work of fiction inspired by history. The sources I found most useful for this book include:

Bell Telephone News, vols. 7–9 (August 1917–July 1919).

Cobbs, Elizabeth. *The Hello Girls: America's First Women Soldiers.* Cambridge, MA: Harvard University Press, 2017.

Dumenil, Lynn. *The Second Line of Defense: American Women and World War I.* Chapel Hill: University of North Carolina Press, 2017.

Gavin, Lettie. *American Women in World War I: They Also Served.* Niwot: University Press of Colorado, 1997.

Lavine, Abraham Lincoln. *Circuits of Victory.* Garden City, NY: Doubleday, Page & Company, 1921.

Lipartito, Kenneth. "When Women Were Switches: Technology, Work, and Gender in the Telephone Industry, 1890–1920." *American Historical Review* 99, no. 4 (October 1994): 1074–111.

Martin, Millicent. "My Great Adventure." *The Green Book Magazine* 22, no. 4 (October 1919): 30–34, 102–4.

Pacific Telephone Magazine, vols. 11–12 (July 1917–June 1919).

Raines, Rebecca Robbins. *Getting the Message Through: A Branch History of the U.S. Army Signal Corps.* Washington, DC: Center of Military History, United States Army, 2011.

United States Congress, Senate Committee on Veterans' Affairs, Subcommittee on Health and Readjustment. *Physician and Dentist Special Pay and Other Pay Amendments: Hearing Before the Subcommittee on Health and Readjustment of the Committee on Veterans' Affairs, United States Senate, Ninety-Fifth Congress, First Session, on S. 1775 and Related Bills, July 1, 1977.* Washington, DC: U.S. Government Printing Office, 1977.

I consulted several excellent online resources while researching and writing *Switchboard Soldiers*, including the archives of digitized historic newspapers at Newspapers.com (www.newspapers.com); the Library of

Congress website (www.loc.gov); and census records, directories, and other historical records at Ancestry (ancestry.com).

As ever and most of all, I thank my husband, Marty, and my sons, Nick and Michael, for their enduring love, steadfast support, and constant encouragement. *Switchboard Soldiers* was my second novel written during the pandemic, and I could not have done it without you. Thank you for Bear Patrol, the music and comedy performances, the inside jokes, the perfect cups of tea, the fresh-baked bread, the homemade pasta and pizza, the movie nights, and the endless supply of hugs and laughter. I'm grateful beyond measure for the courage, optimism, resilience, and humor you've shown in these difficult times, and I will always love you.

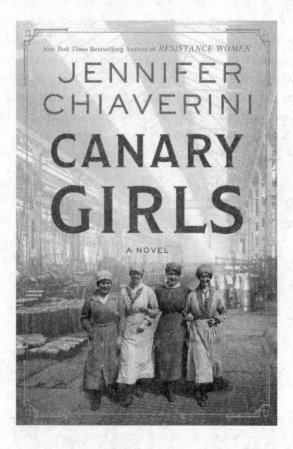

Read More by
JENNIFER CHIAVERINI

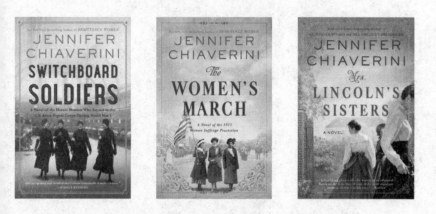

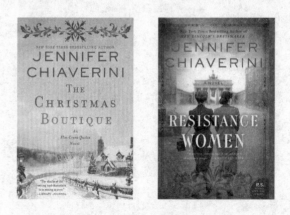